Fiona Collins grew up in an Essex village and after stints in Hong Kong and London returned to the Essex countryside where she lives with her husband and three children. She has a degree in Film and Literature and has had many former careers including TV presenting in Hong Kong, traffic and weather presenter for BBC local radio and film/TV extra. Her first novel, *You, Me and the Movies*, is also published by Corgi.

You can find her on Twitter @FionaJaneBooks.

Also by Fiona Collins

YOU, ME AND THE MOVIES

and published by Corgi

SUMMER IN THE CITY

Fiona Collins

CORGI BOOKS

TRANSWORLD PUBLISHERS
Penguin Random House, One Embassy Gardens,
8 Viaduct Gardens, London SW11 7BW
www.penguin.co.uk

Transworld is part of the Penguin Random House group of companies
whose addresses can be found at global.penguinrandomhouse.com

First published in Great Britain in 2021 by Corgi,
an imprint of Transworld Publishers

A CIP catalogue record for this book
is available from the British Library.

ISBN
9780552176378

Typeset in 11.5/13pt Garamond MT by Jouve (UK), Milton Keynes
Printed and bound in Great Britain by Clays Ltd, Elcograf S.p.A.

The authorized representative in the EEA is Penguin Random House Ireland,
Morrison Chambers, 32 Nassau Street, Dublin D02 YH68.

Penguin Random House is committed to a sustainable future
for our business, our readers and our planet. This book is made from
Forest Stewardship Council® certified paper.

To my lovely Dad

Chapter 1

Summer 2018

'Did you see it?'

A woman in the recognizable navy and red polyester uniform of a London Underground worker is staring at me. She is so close to my face I can see myself reflected in her tortoiseshell glasses. I look slightly confused; she looks concerned. I press my overheated body against warm, pale green tiles, away from her searching eyes.

I'm leaning against the wall inside Warren Street station. A busker is in full flow at the bottom of the escalator to my right, strumming on a guitar and murdering 'Streets of London'. My sister Angela used to love that song but it never had me convinced – it's a lovely thought, it really is, but I doubt someone's troubles can really be erased by traipsing the capital's streets, hand in hand with some earnest do-gooder, gawping at the homeless . . . Anyway, this bloke's really going for it; people are chucking coins and the odd note into his guitar case – perhaps they're hoping if they give him enough, he'll call it quits, pack up his guitar and go. I know if my dad were here, he'd happily sacrifice another sense to not have to listen to it.

'Have you just come from Platform One, Northbound?' asks the London Underground worker with the tortoiseshell glasses. 'Are you OK? Do you need to sit down?'

It's really hot. We're a couple of weeks into a God-knows-how-long London heatwave. I came over a little peculiar further down the tunnel and am catching my breath before I tackle the escalator and the crowds again, but I don't think I need to sit down. I'm not *that* old, am I? I know I'm not far off fifty, but does she think I'm about to keel over?

I look at her and she looks at me. Her face is kind. *My* face, in her glasses, and under its thick layer of foundation, is a bumpy and sweaty moonscape.

'No, thank you,' I say, in the clipped tones of a woman in a 1950s public service announcement. 'I'm perfectly all right.'

I've been to the dentist. Only an unavoidable appointment gets me out of the flat these days. Sometimes, it's taking Dad two doors down to the eye clinic on Adelaide Road for one of his check-ups, when they nod at him and say, 'Yes, Mr Alberta, you're still blind', and we go home again. Sometimes it's for me – smear test, eye test (just to make sure *I'm* not going blind, too – joke!) – general things, to keep me tip-top. I'm Dad's only carer. Well, I'm not really a *carer* at all; I'm more of a silent companion – but I don't want to go under. Sometimes I go and see someone to ask if new technologies mean my birthmark can be lasered off me, at last, but the answer is always 'no'. Not in my case. After they've told me, 'Sorry, you're staying ugly for ever', sometimes I pop into the dress agency next door to the clinic and flick through – and sometimes buy – other people's beautiful cast-offs, but I never wear them.

I don't like my dentist. When he stuck that needle into my gum to numb me for my filling, he tutted at me for wriggling in the chair and I had an overwhelming urge to bite his thumb. Before that, I'd attempted to make small talk with him, but he wasn't interested. Gruff bastard. As he did the filling, I lay back in the Smurf-coloured dentist chair and concentrated on a row of thank-you cards on the windowsill and the fly flitting lazily between them. The dental nurse sipped from a 'Get ready for a great smile' mug and leant forward to make one of the cards into a ramp for a crossing plump ladybird, then plopped her unceremoniously out of the open window.

After my own escape, I walked to the tube with my lips like sausages, extended three feet from my face. The tube was stifling and I successfully avoided the eye of every single person wedged like sweating anchovies – brackish and intermittently hairy – in the carriage. An old lady dropped a book on the floor, from her seat, and I bent forward, from mine, to give it back to her. She smiled at me and I smiled back, then I quickly looked down again. I don't like to be on any sort of radar, even if her smile was friendly and her eyes gentle.

When I got off at Warren Street to change for the Northern Line, there was suddenly a fleet of us, hot and sticky, going nowhere on the lower concourse.

'What on earth's going on?'

'Bloody hell!'

'It's too *hot* for this!'

There was a problem. Platform One, Northbound to Edgware, was inaccessible. I found myself in a wedged funnel of people all wanting to turn left on to the platform but unable to budge. We were not happy. We swore a bit under our breaths; we scratched at the back of our necks; we sighed theatrically and competitively. As we desperately tried not to touch each other's body parts, we were distracted by a bright red balloon with 'Happy 30th' printed on it, its string tied into a small bow at the end, which bounced and bobbed above our heads. I decided it belonged to some pretty young thing; that right after someone told her *just* how pretty she was, she giggled and lost her grip on it before rushing off to an early rush-hour drink in some swanky bar, where she would be admired and fussed over.

'Sorry.' A man jostled against me. His hand accidentally landed on my right shoulder, just above my breast. *Me too*, I wanted to say, as a joke, but I could see he was terrified, and that joke has already been played on me too many times. (*Yeah, Me Too . . .*) Instead, I said, 'It's OK,' and he smiled sheepishly at me and moved away through the stiffened crowd. He didn't get very far. The balloon bobbed and mocked overhead.

It was *my* birthday last week. My forty-eighth; one toe in the grave . . . It was a small affair: a few close friends, some finger sandwiches and a three-tiered hand-piped chocolate cake sliced to much delight, as Stevie Wonder sang 'Happy Birthday' to me from a pub's stereo . . . No, not really, it was just Dad and me, eating some shop-bought Battenberg in front of *Countdown*, although I'd splashed out on a bottle of Shloer. We know how to live it up, Dad and I. They could probably hear the whooping all the way down at Dingwalls.

I decided to head the other way, for the exit. I'd walk to Euston and pick up the Northern Line there. I walked quickly; I was feeling a bit claustrophobic. Sweat was beginning to drip off me; I knew my mask was melting and I would be exposed. I also wanted to get home for *A Place in the Sun*. People were queuing to get on the escalator. The busker at the bottom was earnestly singing 'Streets of London', his fretting at the guitar vibrating through the heavy air. There *was* no air. My lips still felt weird. I stopped and leant against a tiled wall. Tried to take a deep breath of airless atmosphere. Then the transport worker came up to me.

'People react in different ways, you know?' she says.

She sounds Welsh. She's soft-spoken and has really nice blue eyes, behind her lenses. 'It's hard to predict, you know?'

No, I don't know, I'm afraid, as I have no idea what she's talking about. Her glasses have a smear on one of the lenses; I have the urge to take the hem of my over-sized T-shirt and wipe it clean for her.

'Here, take this. Call the number on the back if you want to speak to someone.' She hands me a card and I take it. *TFL Counselling Service*, it says. It's yellow and red, with a London number underneath.

'You get two or three free sessions. I think it could really help you, if you, you know, needed help. Someone to talk to.'

'Thanks.' I look back at her; her blue eyes are warm, sympathetic.

'And can I take your name and number please? I think they have enough witnesses, but just in case?'

Now I *really* don't know what she's talking about. Has the heat gone to my head? Am I hallucinating? I mutter a fake name and an even faker mobile number. I thank her again, adding a couple of 'sorrys' for incomprehensible measure, and head for the escalator. The busker stares at me as I walk past. He's wearing a T-shirt that says, 'Difficult Roads Often Lead to Beautiful Destinations'. I'm trying to focus on something other than the strange encounter I've just had, so I stare back at him until he looks away. Inspirational *quotes*. I'm not sold on them. In fact, they make me snappy. In my eyes, things don't happen for a reason, they just happen. I don't like lemons and I don't want to make lemonade. I won't dance like nobody's watching. And I won't live, laugh, love, in that or any other order. In fact, you know people have those giant letters in their houses spelling 'Live, laugh, love'?

I've just put a display on the windowsill at home that says, 'Live, laugh, bollocks'. I know any day soon Dad will suss it when he's dusting, but until then . . .

I don't find the *world* that inspirational, I'm afraid. And everyone is *not* beautiful in their own way – another one trotted out on Instagram, I should imagine, over a photo of a very beautiful person gazing out over a glassy lake.

I should know that better than anyone.

A disembodied voice comes over the Tannoy – crackly and empathetic as a disembodied London Underground voice can be – apologizing for the closure of Platform One, and the suspension of the Northern Line '. . . due to a person on the tracks'.

Ah, I get it. The transport woman. The card. Was that what I was supposed to have seen? A jumper? Someone throwing themselves under a London tube on a Wednesday afternoon? Oh God, how horrible. I'm glad I didn't see what that tube worker thought I had. I'm sorry I was a case of mistaken identity and wasted time and – self-centredly – that I looked so terrible she thought I needed help. I feel sad. I let a long sigh escape me at the thought of wasted life. And I put the card in my canvas shopper and I stand still on the right-hand lane of the escalator as it slowly carries me to the noise and light of the city above.

Chapter 2

'Good afternoon.'

People always look at me oddly when I walk up to the brown double doors halfway along the Haverstock Hill flank of Chalk Farm tube station, place a key in the rusting lock and step inside. Well, a little more oddly than usual, anyway, and if Dad's with me then it's quite the party.

'Afternoon.'

The man who has wished me 'Good afternoon' is wearing a panama hat and a headache-inducing paisley shirt. He's stopped on the pavement beside me, a little too close. He hasn't seen me put my key in the lock yet: I can't find the sodding thing in my bag – its contents are one huge, shifting mass; a haystack for many needles. He *has* seen me knock on one of the doors, but Dad never comes down if somebody knocks, going conveniently deaf as well as blind on such occasions.

'What's in there, then?' the man asks.

I have my back turned so the late-afternoon sunlight can bucket into my enormous bag and aid the search for my key. 'My purse, a box of Tampax and Estée Lauder's Double Wear foundation,' I retort. 'Amongst a million other things.'

'No, behind the doors,' he adds. He looks cross with me and I have no idea why.

'I live here,' I say.

He looks up at the windows. 'Unusual.'

'Yes.'

It *is* unusual, I'll give him that: Dad and I live in a flat above Chalk Farm tube station. The Palladian, as it's known, is one of a kind – the only residence to actually form part of an underground station in the whole of London.

The man looks from me to one of the arched, small-paned windows above us, then back to me again. I'm still rummaging in my useless bag.

'Seen enough?' I ask. The man just shrugs.

It's a handsome station, Chalk Farm – one of several original Victorian underground stations in the city. A curved wedge of a building under glazed oxblood tiles undimmed by time, with a rounded prow overlooking the intersection of two busy north-west London streets: Adelaide Road and Haverstock Hill. Our flat, The Palladian, a conversion done in Edwardian times, starts four semicircular Diocletian windows back on each side (I'm not sure what's behind the further two, nothing now, but I imagine they once housed dusty offices full of typewriters and men in green visors) and extends into the apex, fronted by a magnificent Palladian window – a large central arch with two rectangular side panels – which presides rather grandly over the streets below.

Found it! I unlock the doors and step inside. The man looks disappointed. Did he want me to invite him in and take him up the winding iron stairs with me? Point out to him the metallic green jangle of incomprehensible spaghetti pipes below them, the old Victorian framed poster leaning against the peeling wall to the left, which says, 'Avoid all Anxiety! Take the Two Penny Tube'? Show him to the plain white front door of The Palladian, with its absence of knocker and bell and letter box (there's a narrow letter box at the base of one of the double doors; I've shoved the two envelopes that were waiting on the mat in my bag), but with a brass handle more suited to an interior door – where I insert my second key?

8

'I'm back, Dad!' I call, as I open the door. Our small hall is bright, white and has sweet touches like Bakelite light switches and tiny alcove shelves. Our flat has intricate cornicing, deep skirting boards and a honeyed-oak parquet floor throughout. Behind its plain white door, it has charm and character and panelled doors and ceiling roses. It's pretty; in fact, this quirky Grade II listed flat is far too pretty for us two dull misfits – blind father, disfigured daughter. There should be a glamorous woman of a certain age called Gloria living here, who alternates her hours lying decorously on a faded chaise longue in a palm-print kaftan and wafting into the West End to truffle for goodies at the Harrods Food Hall.

'OK!' Dad calls from the sitting room at the front of the flat. I know exactly where he'll be: sitting in his armchair with his feet up on the footstool.

'Aren't you going to ask me how I got on?'

I slip off my flip-flops, leaving them on the front doormat – a very flat, rubber variety, so that whenever I do take Dad out, he doesn't trip and headbutt the inside of the door before he's even stepped outside. Our whole flat is blind-proof; it was done before we moved in. And the layout here is perfect for Dad. Off to the right is a door that leads to his bedroom, beyond that is the bathroom; on the left is my bedroom, then the cosy spare bedroom where we keep our clothes now, then our galley kitchen. And the tiny hall opens out into the sitting room, where the grand Palladian window proudly flares its curved nose over the street below.

'How did you get on?' Vince Alberta, former architect, current recluse, sits in his faithful chair several feet back from the window. The chair is a modern lazy boy with a steel base. Dad's feet, in Union Jack socks, rest on a Moroccan leather pouffe. He's wearing stay-press trousers and a white Fred Perry T-shirt.

My dad is not that old. He had me young, very young: he's sixty-four.

'Well, I'm all sorted,' I say, resting my hand briefly on his slight but firm upper arm. 'Apparently the tooth is saved.'

Dad looks up at me and gives me a short smile. You wouldn't, at first glance, think he is blind. One eye looks slightly narrower than the other, nothing else is remarkable; but your second glance, and definitely your third, would tell you those eyes are unseeing – that they are slightly milky-looking and without focus.

'Good,' he says. 'I'm not sure I could have put up with all the howling.'

'Well, no.'

Dad doesn't like *any* noise – really, any sounds, particularly words, especially *my* words. He returns, as ever, to his iPad with the connected Braille reader, a nifty device the size of a small keyboard that converts text to Braille, courtesy of rounded pins on its surface. He's currently reading the biography of famous architect Norman Foster – again.

'What are we having for dinner tonight?' I ask him.

'Carbonara,' he says, without looking up.

'Lovely.'

Dad cooks. He's Italian, and as well as retaining the rhythm and inflection of the accent, he has both inherited and perpetuated my grandmother's utter brilliance in the kitchen. I am a terrible cook – you could have grouted a shower with the last creamy pasta sauce I attempted, and the drop scones I made at school were literal – and a very bad tea maker, but I wash up. I have some uses.

'I've done the laundry,' adds Dad, his head still bowed over the iPad, his finger tracing the surface of the Braille reader. 'Will you be able to eat? The tooth?'

'Yes, I'll be fine.'

I walk across the parquet flooring and place my inef-fective bag on the narrow console table in front of the window.

'It's bloody hot in here,' I remark.

The Palladian window is closed again. I walk over and open it, letting in the noise and the smells of Chalk Farm. I know Dad will grumble, like he always does, but he used to love standing at this window, with it wide open, and listening to life on the street below. He used to sit by it on stormy evenings, absorbing the sound of the rain. Now he likes the window closed and the flat quiet; far from the world.

'I like it shut,' he complains.

'I know, but we need to let some air in. It resembles a fusty old garden shed in here.'

'I didn't think you'd be able to talk, after the injection,' he says.

I roll my eyes. I have to be as silent as he is blind.

'I'll just go and get changed.'

By *just go and get changed*, I mean, take off my make-up now there's no one to see my face.

I use baby wipes. It usually takes about six or seven of them to remove my thick foundation and expose my heart-shaped monstrosity. I have it down to a fine art. We only have one mirror and it's in our bathroom; it's badly lit in here, but that's OK. My birthmark is already angry-looking as I disturb it with my wiping and rubbing, my unveiling and my disclosing. I don't need to see it clearly. It's not like I don't know it's there. Yet, sometimes it still surprises me. Even after all these years. I might catch sight of it in a mocking shop window or in a bastard mirror I'm not expecting – at the clinic, say, or at Dad's doctors' sur-gery, and think, Oh, look at that. That's horrible.

A *strawberry* birthmark. How anodyne and Enid Blyton and Pollyanna that sounds. It isn't. It's raspberry red and

11

asymmetrical and bumpy and is a bugger to blend into the rest of my face with that thick, thick foundation, now deposited on baby wipes. Most days I still feel really despondent about it. *Every* day I just want to hide from the world and never come out.

That feels better, though. My face can breathe. I throw the browned baby wipes in our little pedal bin and head back to the sitting room and my bag, to open one of the letters I picked up downstairs. Oh, it's another architectural magazine, wanting to do a feature on where we live. There's a lot of interest in the only flat created inside a London tube station.

'Someone else wants to talk to us about The Palladian,' I say. 'Another magazine.'

'Oh, God.' Dad gets up from the chair and walks to the kitchen – he knows exactly how many steps it is from here to there and doesn't need his cane – where he starts clattering around. I always leave him to it; he doesn't require help in the kitchen, unless something does something it shouldn't – like a rogue lid flinging itself off a jar and on to the floor.

'Another Leslie Green fan!' I call to him.

'They all love Leslie!' he calls back.

Leslie Green was the architect who designed Chalk Farm underground station and forty-nine other tube stations, in a five-year period from the early 1900s – before he died of tuberculosis at the age of thirty-three. I know a lot about the long-admired Leslie Green. Dad knows an awful lot more. But we will turn down the inquisitive magazine person, like we always do. Dad doesn't want anyone coming into his beloved home, doesn't want to talk to anyone about anything, even the things he is most interested in. I mean, he bought this flat because of Leslie Green. But he won't engage with anyone about it now.

I put the letter in the recycling box in the hall, then go

12

and stand in the doorway of the kitchen. The room has been organized so it's easier for Dad. We have talking scales and measuring jugs. Braille labels. All spices and condiments and sauces are kept in wicker baskets, so things can't be accidentally swept on to the floor. Neither of us is the tallest – I'm tiny, actually – and everything is no more than shoulder height, to avoid droppages. And everything goes back in its place in a military system. Only twenty per cent of blind people are actually totally blind, so many visually impaired people may have items colour-coded in a kitchen – with heightened contrasts between light and dark – but my dad is one of the unlucky twenty per cent with NLP: No Light Perception. He's been blind since 17 August 1980.

'I don't need any help, Prue.'

'I know you don't.'

Dad is already getting out chopping boards and utensils. He makes delicious food for us both every night, in near silence. Once upon a time he used to cook to music: to The Kinks and The Doors and The Jam and the New Faces. He used to hum along or sing as he worked. We have a really good music system here, excellent speakers, but we don't use it any more. We also have a vintage record player in the corner of the sitting room, but the duck-egg-blue lid stays closed.

'So, go away and leave me to it. Go and catch up on all your women.'

He means the women I like reading about. Talented women, heroic women, pioneering women; women nothing like me . . . Recently I've been reading a lot about Amelia Earhart, Indira Gandhi and Dian Fossey. Most of yesterday afternoon was spent down a Catherine the Great-shaped rabbit hole. Dad likes the fact that I can occupy myself without bothering him. I don't talk to him beyond the necessary: 'What are we having for dinner tonight?', 'I'm doing the online shop; do you still like apple juice?', 'Can I help with that, Dad? No? OK.' I eat quietly, looking through Facebook on my phone in silence. I'm not really *on* Facebook – I have an account with about ten 'friends' that I never post on, but I use it to stalk abusers I knew at school and scoff at my sister. At any other point in time, I'm either watching telly or listening to music through headphones, the volume as low as I can bear it. Anything else I fear he views as some kind of attention-seeking. Obviously I *am* seeking his attention. There's nobody else bloody here.

I open the second letter: an A4 envelope. I'm not particularly intrigued; it's probably another brochure from a local estate agent with an accompanying missive trying to persuade us to sell our flat. *Oh*. Inside is a very belated 2018 calendar from Gourmet Burgers for Dogs with a Great Dane demolishing a quarter-pounder on the cover. I used to work at Gourmet Burgers for Dogs, until I resigned from packing vacuum-packed home-made burgers for dogs into cardboard boxes, at age forty-five. Actually, I resigned from all jobs at that point. The burgers simply pushed me over an edge I'd been teetering near for a while.

I flick through the calendar; September looks cute.

There is a clatter from the kitchen.

'Can I help?'

'No, I'm all right!'

I can hear Dad counting the steps to the fridge under his breath. I put the calendar back in the envelope. God knows why they keep on sending me the things – I really don't need a reminder of how my far-from-illustrious working life finally came to an end.

'Oh, bugger it!'

'Shall I come in?'

'No, no, I'm fine.'

14

I put *A Place in the Sun* on. Plug in my headphones. Watch lucky people browsing beachfront properties in Barbados. I tell myself I'm Dad's companion now, that I *need* to be here – not working – but we both know that's not true. I just haven't got the will or the confidence to put myself out there any more. Still, we're all right for money as I've always saved hard, in all my jobs, even though I now do nothing at all, and Dad has his compensation pay-out and his handful of investments – and we've no mortgage – so we're ticking over, 'like a clapped-out Ford Cortina', as he puts it.

I take off my headphones. I can hear grumble, grumble, clatter, clatter, from the kitchen; I can smell onions being sweated in olive oil and garlic; I can already taste the pancetta and the parmesan and the peppery, creamy sauce. I can also see exactly how the evening will pan out, just as it always does. Dad and I will have dinner, then retire to our chairs: me to browse the internet or watch TV or listen to not-loud-enough music; Dad to read on his Braille reader or listen to a podcast – always on architecture, a subject he has never stopped studying. The light will fade; we'll stay in our chairs. We might have a snack, a glass of beer. At around eleven, Dad will say, 'Well, I think I'll turn in, Prue', and I'll say, 'Me too, Dad', and we'll go to bed. Always the same, day after day, month after month, year after year. And that's OK. We like it like this. We wouldn't have it any other way. What other way is there, for Dad and me?

'Fifteen minutes, Prue,' says Dad.

'Righto, Dad,' I reply.

Chapter 3

'Angela called,' Dad yells from the kitchen twenty minutes later.

'Oh? What did she have to say for herself?' I try to make my voice sound bright and not at all like I've been asleep for the last quarter of an hour. It's a shameful habit I have – nodding off during daylight hours – considering I don't work or do anything all day. Dad naps a lot too. Our morning routine tends to be *BBC Breakfast* followed by *The Wright Stuff* followed by *This Morning*, then we stop for a bit of lunch – some ciabatta or pasta, a salad or some soup, depending on our mood or the season – then it's the music or the podcasts or more television and two or three small afternoon naps each. We're like a couple of bloody dormice. And if *we're* a couple of dormice, then my sister Angela is an ant, or a busy busy worker bee – always working, always socializing, always shopping or baking, always *doing* something. My little sister (she's forty-six) checks in with us from Canada every three months or so, not that she needs to; her life is on Facebook. Where she's been, how work's been, how well her perfect girls have done at school and nursery, what she had for dinner last night . . .

'I didn't answer,' Dad calls. 'I had my headphones on. She left a voicemail that she'd call back.'

'Oh, OK.'

Angela is all Photoshop filters and clinking champagne glasses and beautiful local scenery and home-made cakes and gorgeous children and new shoes. We have absolutely nothing in common.

'Maybe she'll call back after dinner.' Dad sounds about as enthusiastic as I feel.

'Maybe,' I say.

I plug back into my headphones and put on the Bonnie Raitt album, *Luck of the Draw* – an old favourite of mine, except I always avoid 'I Can't Make You Love Me', because its lyrics make me cry. I like female singer-songwriters. I like Janis Joplin and Joni Mitchell and Dolly Parton and Sheryl Crow. I like Carole King and Carly Simon. I like strong women with something to say because I am not a strong woman and I have nothing to say. I don't always agree with all their lyrics, though. 'Jolene' could have had him, for example, and good riddance . . . If he's *that* vain, it really isn't going to help that this song definitely *is* about him . . . I'm also sad for how someone like Janis Joplin lived and died, but when she rasps her way through 'Summertime', I am utterly transported.

I take my phone from my bag as I listen and have a nose on Facebook – Angela has a new bag and went to the cinema with it last night. Some idiot I knew at school has had another baby and named it after a shampoo. I go on the *Daily Mail* online, the Sidebar of Shame: their showbiz gossip. I look at their news column. Then I go on to Safari and search 'News, Warren Street tube station', and it comes up straight away: 'Incident on the line, suspected jumper':

British Transport Police were called to Warren Street underground station this afternoon. At least 10 emergency services vehicles were seen outside the station and the Northern Line was suspended for three hours. Sadly, a woman was pronounced dead at the scene.

How awful, I think. It makes me feel funny – a feeling of vertigo, almost, or that I am as lightweight as that balloon, floating to nowhere. Although I saw nothing, I was so *close* to where it happened, mere feet from where this woman lost her life. I wonder how old she was, if she had children. How bad her life was that she wanted to bring it to an end. I remember the card I was given by the well-meaning London Underground woman. Did *I* look bad? Just being me? So bad she deduced I must have seen something?

I mooch around the internet some more, gaze at lovely tropical holidays I'll never go on, then head on to Twitter, where I follow a handful of achieving, purposeful blind people, to get ideas for Dad to reject. Then I read a new article about Billie Holiday.

Dad comes out of the kitchen and plonks two steaming plates of carbonara on the little round table between our chairs.

'Here we are,' he says, like he always does. '*Buon appetito.*' He's so proud of his Italian heritage. Well, I am, too, of mine. I'm half Italian, a quarter Swedish. Dad's parents – Papa and Nonna – came to London in the early 1950s and ran a *gelato* parlour in Clerkenwell, where gangsters and organ grinders alike enjoyed their *stracciatella*; my mother's parents met in London when Nana Larry (her real name was Brigitta) had a week off from the Electrolux factory in Stockholm, came to London with a friend and met Grandpa Larry outside the Ritz, in a rainstorm. My family history – well, some of it – is the most interesting thing about me.

I go over to the table. We eat. We do not talk. I want to talk.

'Hey, Dad, did you know there's a blind architect?' I pause, brave, my fork over my steaming bowl, toying with a cube of pancetta. 'In Hawaii. He's about your age. He's semi-retired but he consults, he teaches. There was an article in the *Evening Standard* about him and I've found his profile on Twitter. He's really interesting.'

Dad sighs. '*Really?*'

'Yeah. He's called John Harrison Burrows; he consults on conference spaces and art galleries – multi-sensory, accessible to all. He's got a studio on the Big Island. He teaches architecture at the university there.' I gabble, trying to get the words out before he shuts me up.

'That's nice for him.'

'*You* could be a blind architect. Or you could teach. You probably know more about architecture than anyone in the *world*!'

'No, I couldn't.'

'Why not? You could read all about this guy and see what he does. He does TED Talks and stuff. He uses special technology.'

'I don't think so.'

'It's not *impossible*.'

Dad became blind when I was ten. He had just qualified to be an architect and was embarking on his first project.

Dad lays down his fork. 'Why don't you look up all the people who are blind and *aren't* architects?'

'Don't be silly.'

'Or those blind people who can't do anything at all.'

'*Dad.*'

The accident was such a blow after everything my father had done to turn his life around. He became a parent at sixteen; for some that would have been game over, but Dad, who left school to become a carpenter not long after I was born, got what he termed a 'fire in his belly' for architecture while working on early development of the Barbican. He took his A levels at night school and got into University College London on a scholarship. He caught the bus from our little house in Clerkenwell to Russell Square every morning. He studied every night. With Nonna and Papa doing the school runs and looking after us after school – Nonna making us *cannoli* and

Bolognese and *focaccia*, and Papa entertaining us with his sleight-of-hand magic tricks and his false tooth that he would pop out into his hand whenever he felt like it. Dad continued with the degree and he became an architect. For a while.

'No, drop it, Prue. It's utterly ridiculous.'

'OK, Dad, subject dropped.'

We eat in silence for a few seconds. I don't really have a leg to stand on anyway, I think. I'm hardly out there setting the world alight and *I'm* not even blind. I silently thank Dad for not pointing this out.

As usual, after dinner, Dad stays at the table while I clear the plates and take them to the kitchen. After I've washed up and dried up, with one of Nonna's old red gingham tea towels, and put everything away and tidied up the kitchen, which Dad has left pretty spotless anyway, Dad will be back in his chair again and I will take to mine. Sometimes I wonder what would happen if I were to sit in his chair, or he in mine? Spontaneous combustion, probably, leaving just our feet on the floor, in front of those chairs.

I return to the comfort of Bonnie Raitt and my phone. There's more news now on Warren Street. 'Breaking News', they call it, which is so ubiquitous a phrase now it carries a degree of anticipation not always rewarded, but it doesn't say much more.

British Transport Police say the woman, who has not yet been named, was in her twenties and worked in the entertainment industry.

So young, I think, and what was she, an actress, a TV presenter? Why on earth would she jump under a train? I feel so sad for her that I have to come off my phone. I'll watch a film. I look across at Dad, in his chair. Will he watch with me? He sometimes does. I note that he needs a shave, but I know he'll do it in the morning. He is fastidious; always clean-shaven, and what hair he has left is kept neat monthly by the mobile barber who comes. Standards never slip when it comes to my father. Although he can't witness his own appearance, he never forgets others can, even if it's just me. It may be the Italian in him.

I find *The Talented Mr Ripley* on Amazon and start watching it on my own as Dad says he doesn't fancy it. It's hardly a *cheery movie*, but I love it, and I enjoy gazing at everyone's gorgeous outfits. Dad has his headphones on and is listening to an audiobook. Now and again he'll laugh, a sound only elicited by the voices of strangers. The light fades. We have a snack, a glass of beer.

'Well, I think I'll turn in, Prue,' says Dad, at just gone eleven.

'Me too, Dad,' I reply.

He rises from his chair and I rise from mine. I wait while he uses the bathroom then I go and brush my teeth and wash my face and gently dab Savlon on my left cheek. I know it won't do anything. I know when I look in the mirror in the morning my birthmark will still be there, loud and proud, but hey, sometimes people are really, relentlessly stupid.

I get into bed, place my phone on the floor to charge, and lie there with the lamp on for a few minutes. I can hear Dad bumbling round his bedroom: opening and closing drawers, getting into bed with a creak of his bedframe and setting his morning alarm on the iPad, like he always does – with the help of Siri – despite there being nothing to get up for. After I hear Dad turn his light off, I turn off mine.

21

Chapter 4

My sister often forgets the time difference and calls us in the middle of the night.

'Prue?'

'Ug?'

'It's Angela.'

Angela has a Canadian inflection to her voice now. It's super-annoying. I prefer it when people who run away keep their original accents.

'It's two in the morning,' I say, leaning over and noting the time on my mobile phone.

'Sorry.'

I know she is not sorry. She's the kind of person who does what she feels like, when she feels like it.

'I forgot. Never mind, I know you don't sleep well.' Well, that's true, but there's no need to hold it against me . . . or disturb my sleepless hours. She always was a disturber. She would dance in front of the television if I was watching it, knowing I hate to miss anything. Sometimes it was ballet, sometimes a jazzy freestyle; sometimes it was just *hopping,* and always with a mischievous look on her face as I screeched and pelted KitKat wrappers at her. I'm one of those people who rewinds snatches of dialogue they've misheard, who has to look again at something in a drama they think might be a clue. And I *hated* having *Worzel Gummidge* danced in front of.

'How are you? How's Dad?'

'He's fine. Still blind, you know . . .'

'There's no need to be like that!'

We have this same exchange every time she calls. Neither of us can help ourselves.

'How are you?' I ask flatly. I know how she is. She's happy. She's the only one out of the three of us who has managed it.

'Great, thanks. I need to ask you a favour,' she says chirpily. 'Not now, of course, when you get up.'

'What is it?'

She was always one for favours, our Angela. Or Angela Pangela, as I sometimes called her. She had a way of asking them, when we were kids, that made it seem like she'd give you the earth in return; for lending her your best cardigan – the one with the robin on it – or bringing her a glass of orange squash ('Strong, with two straws, please') as she lolled on her bed in her candy-pink bedroom with a book about ponies, or for fibbing to Dad on her behalf about where she was last night (telling him she was round at Paula Dawson's doing homework and not out with Mark Sinclair, the baddest boy at school, doing an underage pub crawl round Camden). She never gave the earth. She'd just say 'thanks' in a breezy voice and move on to her next thing.

'Been up to anything recently?'

'It's two o'clock in the morning, Angela! What's the favour?'

'So? You don't have to get up in the morning. Or do you have a job again now?'

I sigh. 'No, I don't have a job.'

'Thought not.' Ah, the eternal air of superiority. She's pretty, she's got a career, she's *married*.

Angela was always moving on. I knew she would run away. As she approached the end of her teens you could see the waves of *restlessness* just rolling off her like static electricity. She plotted her escape for a year. She hung around the local community college, attended a pottery class, but mostly she lurked in the café so she could chat up wealthy foreign students who'd come to learn English; she hoped that one of them would take her *away from all this*. The poor sap she eventually ensnared was actually the pottery teacher – thirty-one-year-old Warren Defaille from Nova Scotia, who was returning to Canada at the end of the summer term. She went with him.

I adjust the phone slightly away from my ear: Angela's voice is loud.

'Have you left the flat recently?'

'No,' I say. I'm not telling her about the dentist and the 'jumper' and the card. I never tell her anything.

'Dad should see people,' she says, after a giant tut (I don't bother to pick her up on her terrible choice of words). 'It's no good for either of you, being stuck in that flat. You really should make a change, reconfigure your lives.'

When did my little sister become so humourlessly superior? I wonder. It hadn't always been this way. At one time we had fun. At one time I was her *protector*. Now I refuse to stroke her inflated ego and her younger-sister-made-good superiority. To indulge her transatlantic tripe.

'So, what's the favour, Angela?' I repeat. 'Is it, you know, the one about looking after our father for ever so that you don't have to?'

Angela sighs back at me. 'Oh, Prue. *Really?* That self-pitying baloney again? You've said yourself he doesn't need looking after. No, the favour is, *actually*, dig up a photo for me and send me a shot of it? Please. I told Warren about that picture of us on the beach in Old Leigh – you know, up from Southend – when I fell in that rock pool and got a crab on the end of my nose?' She laughs her flute-y laugh; the one that really irritates me.

'Yeah, I know the one,' I say. And I had a massive birthmark on my face – permanently – I think. Nobody

24

even used suncream in those days, so it would shine out like a Belisha beacon from the coast. Ships used to launch themselves at it. 'All right, I'll look for it. Is there anything else?' I add. I'm beginning to get a headache and I want to go back to sleep.

'No, there's nothing else. Hey, you haven't heard from Cherry Lau, have you?'

'Cherry Lau?' There was a blast from the past. 'No, why?'

'She found me on Facebook. She sent me a message.'

'Oh?'

'Yeah, she's in corporate entertaining or something now, in Shanghai.'

'Shanghai!' Cherry Lau used to live next door to us, above her parents' takeaway place. She was round at ours all the time, when she wasn't working there. And when she was, I was over there. For a while.

'Yeah, she looks ever so glam. Expat husband. Two children, like me. Doing ever so well for herself.'

Like me, I think she's going to repeat, but she doesn't. Angela's eventual escape was rather glamorous, too. She went long haul, flying by British Airways to Halifax Stanfield International Airport, Nova Scotia, with Warren the pottery teacher, when she was nineteen. She ended up getting a job in air traffic control at that very airport; she was one of the top people, until she had the girls – Clara when she was forty-one and Amelie when she was forty-three – via IVF. A whole life was waiting for her in Nova Scotia. Dad and I didn't even know she was *on* that British Airways flight – we thought she'd gone on a girls' weekend to Camber Sands. But she did it. She escaped Dad and me – the burden of the blind father and the ugly sister – to take off into the love story of the century.

Bloody bon voyage, Angela!

'Did Cherry ask after me?' I say.

'No.'

I am not surprised. I did the dirty, eventually, on Cherry, the 'funny little Chinese girl' – as she was horribly christened at school – who lived next door and temporarily became my best friend, until I fucked things up.

'You don't ever speak to her?'

'No.' *I don't speak to anyone*, I think, *no one at all. And I don't particularly want to speak to you, either, Angela. Not even every three months.*

'Right, I guess I'll have to call back again,' she says. 'To speak to Dad . . . Do it as soon as you wake up, can you? The photo? I don't mind what time it is here.'

No. 'Yes, OK.'

We used to sit and chat for hours, me and Angela. Usually on her bed, while I painted her nails and she scolded me for not doing it right. We'd laugh, too. Laugh so hard at ridiculous things until one of us fell off the bed and dragged the other with her on to the pink fluffy rug with all the gum and hairclips and jelly sweets embedded in it, and we'd lie there looking at the cracks in the ceiling and giggling at other ridiculous things until Angela got bored and would get up.

'Can I leave you with something?'

'If you have to. What is it?'

'Be the change you wish to see in the world. Gandhi said that.' *Unbelievable.*

'Bye, Angela.'

I put the phone down, unprop the pillows and let the sheet fall loosely over me. My fanlight window is open and I can hear a police siren competing with a car alarm competing with Mr Alkazi's alarm at the newsagent's, which goes off between midnight and three every night. Outside the window there's a shout for 'Janine!' and the barking of a disgruntled dog. The sheet is light and cool, but I suddenly feel draped in dark, dank dread, a shroud

26

of it wrapping round me. Angela, my fun, flighty sister, has escaped. Cherry Lau is now popular and successful, sipping mysterious cocktails in mysterious bars in Shanghai. And I am tethered here with no friends, no one to tell my dark secrets or the dull truth of my life to, and how it is slipping away, day by day, nothing to nothing.

I live with my father but I am as alone as a woman who has leapt to her death under a tube train. I had dreams once, dreams of happiness and fulfilment, long since gone. I had hoped for love, at some point, but that is now a stale joke; a joke first played on me years ago when I loved a man who couldn't love me back. I am as blind as my father is to the world. I lie in my bed night after night, watching as shadows and slices of light slide across my bedroom window: whites, reds, yellows, greens; the blue of a police car. My view never changing. Never evolving.

I shift my head so it's on the coolest part of the pillow and go back to sleep.

The next morning, before Dad stirs, I take the Transport for London card from my purse and sit at the console table by the Palladian window. Outside in the world, real people are already busy.

'Hello,' I say into my phone, feeling nervous. 'I'm phoning up about the free counselling session.'

I know, I know – it's damn cheeky of me. I didn't see the jumper. I saw nothing, except the crowded entrance to a platform and a horrendous busker. I have not been affected in any way, except giving her life some thought, and wondering about mine. I am taking advantage.

'Which incident?' says a voice that could be announcing the next train to Edgware.

Which incident . . . ? My entire life? 'Er . . . the jumper on the tube. Northern Line. Warren Street. Yesterday. Wednesday.'

27

'In the afternoon?'

'Yes, in the afternoon.' How many jumpers did they *have*?

'OK. Hold on one moment, please.' There is a muffling and a shuffling, something that sounds like a cup of coffee being stirred with a plastic spoon and a folder being dropped on the floor. 'Next Monday, ten a.m. until eleven a.m.; 34 Princelet Street, E1. Press the buzzer for Room B. Do you need a pen?'

I almost say, *Look forget it, I don't want to come after all*, but I don't. 'I say, 'No, I can remember that. Thank you.'

'Good luck,' says the voice, and the call ends. Very British, that *good luck*, it covers a multitude of future scenarios – although sometimes it sounds like a trap.

Chapter 5

It's Monday. Days usually roll around like monoliths for Dad and I. Dull and indistinguishable. For some, it's 'Another day, another dollar'; for us, it's 'Another day, another day . . .', but today I'm already at my second destination. My first, *Loved Before*, the dress agency next to the laser clinic in Muswell Hill, was quiet early this morning. I go there now and again – and not just when I've been to an appointment next door. I don't frequent high-street clothes shops. They have gorgeous, unblemished girls slinking out of cubicles with smug looks on their faces; bored and beautiful women manning the cubicles. Too many mirrors. I like charity shops and this rather wonderful boutique, a haven of blush-pink walls and chandeliers and a polished dark-wood floor, where the only mirror is in the gorgeously lit changing room and I never feel intimidated.

'Hi, Prue.'

Maya, the owner, appeared from behind the swishy pale gold curtain of the back room with a mountain of delicious-looking things over one arm. I like Maya. We've chatted a few times.

'Hello, Maya.'

'One of my favourite contributors brought in lots of *amazing* items this morning,' she said, walking over to me, a vision in a tangerine slip dress and bejewelled sandals. I was fingering the hem of a gorgeous lace shift dress I'd never have the guts to wear in a million years . . . 'This woman's *always* travelling,' she explained. 'She just came back from Belize. I reckon she never wears the same out-fit twice.'

Loved Before sells second-hand party wear and beautiful work wear, nothing else, and strictly no tat. Everything acquired by the shop is what Maya calls 'lovely quality' and has been previously owned by women who live glamorous, useful lives. Women with stories to tell. That's how I see these women, anyway. I imagine women glittering at cock-tail parties, stepping on to giant yachts with a glass of champagne in their hand, dancing barefoot on the beach on tropical nights and storming it in the boardroom in stern, sexy navy and the highest of heels, as shards of the shattered glass ceiling fall around them. Women who are literally going places. Places I would never go.

'I'm here for a jacket,' I told her. I feel a jacket will set off my usual T-shirt-and-leggings combo and make me feel a little more together for my counselling session. Or at least not such a fucking fraud. I love clothes – I've loved them since I was a little girl and I looked through Nonna's giant mail order 'club' catalogues, marvelling at how the models could be transformed from one thing to the other just by what they wore: twinkling party-goer, tousled beach babe, efficient office girl – but I am not brave enough to wear the ones that really make my heart sing. The beautiful ones. Because *I* am not beautiful. I am not brave enough to go *anywhere*, either. And the stories I have to tell would not inspire or delight a soul.

'Lots came in at the weekend. Let me show you,' Maya said, directing me away from the beautiful dresses I can never resist looking at to Workwear, where I was ready to choose a workaday plain black office jacket, but Maya persuaded me into a smart grey hip-length blazer with white stripes, which, she said, complements my skin tone and honey-coloured hair. It's chic, and I feel it provides me with just the right protective barrier I need.

It's making me very hot, though. I'm currently wearing it sitting opposite a TFL counsellor, somewhere inside a red-brick building in Spitalfields, and I have the sleeves pushed up like Simon Le Bon in the 'Reflex' video.

Verity Holmes, BACP registered, accredited counsellor, is wearing possibly the prettiest pair of shoes I've ever seen. They are velvet T-bar, blocked-heeled sandals – in floral and polka-dot print – with burgundy bows along the T-bar and the heels wrapped in a kind of floral silk. They are amazing. She's also wearing a full cotton skirt, white with London buses on it, which I know to be Cath Kidston, and a purple T-shirt topped with a pendulous necklace of wooden beads. She looks about thirty-five. She has nice curly auburn hair. I have my leggings and long T-shirt and flip-flops on, like I do every day in the summer, but I've painted my nails for this occasion, and I have the *jacket*.

I've got Verity Holmes's name written on a piece of paper on my lap. She gave it to me when I came in. I'm worried I should have given her something with *my* name on, but surely she already knows it. She tucks two sprigs of spiralled hair behind each ear; she crosses and uncrosses her legs, displaying those beautiful shoes. She's kindly pretending she hasn't noticed the birthmark, but I know she's clocked it. I've barely given it one coat today, so Verity knows what she's dealing with. The hope is I won't feel such a fraud if she can see I'm already a flawed person. That I have *issues*.

I look around me. The room is less glamorous than Verity. The walls are wood-chipped beige, the carpet a sticky caramel. There's an incongruous, slightly lopsided Betty Boop poster on one wall, one of those anodyne faded paintings of a bowl of fruit on another. A fly, over at the window, lazily trails its way up the dirty pane, fizzes a bit, then scoots down again. I randomly muse on whether Verity in her lovely shoes is going to stick any whale music on. Is that what counsellors do? Or is she going to make me hold a pink crystal in my hand for the duration?

The fly buzzes in an attention-seeking fashion. I idly wonder if it's the same fly that was at the dentist's. Is it *following* me?

Finally, she speaks. 'Good morning, I'm Verity Holmes.'

I sit back on this too-soft sofa that smells faintly of tea tree oil and gone-off cinnamon. 'Hi, I'm Prue. Prudence. Prudence Alberta.' I'm trying to sound perky but my voice has gone a bit husky, like I'm on sixty a day. I clear my throat. I'm nervous. I feel as though I'm in a job interview, a terror I haven't visited for a while. Having to pretend I'm something I'm not ... In the case of job interviews: a hard-working 'people person' who sees the cashier position in the local bookies as a long-term career progression. Today: the authentic witness to a tragic suicide. Could I conceivably stand up and say, 'Sorry, I can't do this!' like they do in films? Grab my bag from the sofa and flee, leaving Verity with a startled look on her face? I don't have the courage to do that. It takes less courage to stay and pretend I have seen some poor woman take her own life by jumping in front of a train.

'So, Prudence, how are you? How are you feeling? You saw something tragic on the underground last Wednesday? Or you saw the aftermath?'

Oh, she's straight to it. Her romantic shoes belie her desire to get things cracking. I thought she might start with my school days, or something. I was ready with the story about the paper bag and the Tippex ...

'Er, yeah. I saw it. Both.'

In my small defence, I *have* thought about her a lot. The jumper, Philippa. She's been named. She was called Philippa Helens and she was twenty-nine years old and

32

from High Barnet. There was a photo of her online this morning: long blonde hair, brown eyes, really pretty. She looked *happy* in the photo. She looked like a proper, well-put-together person who'd *got this*. Not someone who felt the opposite. I wish I hadn't seen her picture, really, but in a strange way it does make me feel slightly more qualified to talk about her. I've had that photo on my mind since five o'clock this morning.

Verity's eyes are fixed on my face. I can feel my birthmark beginning to itch, to pulsate. 'And how did you feel about that?'

I've implied I saw everything: a figure leaping on to the tracks, a body struck, a horrific after-scene. When do I tell her I only saw three hundred heads and a balloon?

'Well . . . I was disturbed.'

'Disturbed?'

'Wouldn't anyone be?'

'Well, you tell me, Prue. If you can. Tell me how you feel.'

What's another word for 'disturbed'?

'Are you angry with her in any way?'

'Angry? Why would I feel angry with her?'

'For disrupting your journey, for making you an involuntary witness, for causing you and many other people to feel sad and shaken and, well' – she smiles at me sympathetically – '*bad*.'

Well, yes, I do feel bad, I think. I feel bad for the many other people who really *were* witnesses and may need help but haven't asked for it, while I sit here on this smelly sofa under false pretences. But I am not *angry*.

'I feel sorry for her,' I say.

Poor Philippa. Her face swims before me again: smiling, happy, those deep brown eyes that were supposed to see the world for many years to come. A photo that will now be consigned to a box of others by her grieving family – *that was our Philippa*. Or placed lovingly in an album, sealed for ever behind a polythene sleeve. Damn, I haven't done the photo for Angela yet, I realize. I'll do it tonight, if I remember. I'm not in any rush. And I'll crop me out of it.

'I feel sorry for the woman who jumped,' I repeat. Now this is the truth . . . 'Philippa. I've been thinking about her and I feel sorry for her.'

Verity nods. She makes some notes on a little notepad on her lap. Is she writing 'lunatic' . . . 'terrible birth-mark' . . . ? I don't know when she'll ever refer to these notes. I mean, I won't be coming back.

'Any flashbacks, nightmares?'

Not about that. 'No.'

Verity nods again. She uncrosses her legs and places both shoes neatly on the carpet. She pouts slightly. I decide to give her something. 'I'm having preoccupa-tions, though. Intrusive thoughts.' Well, I am, aren't I? I'm looking for updates about Philippa on the news all the time.

'Are they impacting on your day-to-day life? What do you do for a living?'

'I work from home,' I lie. God, I want to take off this lovely jacket.

'So you have remote colleagues?'

All my colleagues in all my jobs were pretty remote, I think, because I kept them that way. 'No, I kind of work on my own.'

'And what's your home situation? Are you married?'

I look down at my ringless left hand, where she is also looking. 'No.'

'Children?'

'No.'

Do I tell her I've not exactly been a success when it comes to relationships? That I lost my virginity in a

34

student bedsit when I was seventeen (I was never a student but my first terrible lover was – a very drunk boy who kept his plimsolls on)? That my love life stalled at that point and never got going again? That two particular encounters in my life have meant relationships are not something I go looking for?

'I live with my blind father and we don't get out much any more,' I blurt out instead.

'Did you used to?'

'What?' I'm already regretting saying it.

'Get out much.'

'Yes, we did. Well, obviously *I* did, when I was working. I started . . . er . . . working from home three years ago.'

'What is it exactly that you do? I haven't missed that, have I?' She frowns, consulting her notes.

Oh, sod it, I think. I've only got the hour. 'I don't work,' I say. 'Not any more. I used to.' I take a deep breath and I launch. 'I left school at sixteen and drifted for a few years in dead-end, go-nowhere jobs, then, somehow, one of those cards in the Job Centre landed me the role of catering assistant at the North London Conference Centre, in Highbury, when I was twenty-one. I enjoyed it. I did well there. Badging, Bookings, then management . . . I worked at the conference centre for twenty years, until I was made redundant, then I returned to those dead-end jobs again – bars and bookies and pound shops and taxi offices and dog-burger companies . . .' I give a wry smile. I enjoy Verity's look of surprise at 'dog burger'. 'And for the past three years I've done nothing at all. Which is how I like it. My father doesn't do anything either, although back in the day he used to have a life, despite being blind . . . a good life, really.' I pause. Verity is interested, I can tell. I can see she's fighting not to raise her eyebrows. 'Until we lost the guide dogs.'

'Oh?' says Verity Holmes, leaning forward. She looks

really interested. Is the crystal about to come out? 'Tell me more about that.'

I take another deep breath and I tell her. We had such a gorgeous series of dogs: Sunny and Milly and Folly. Sweet, loving and clever, each of them, in turn. Life-savers, literally. They kept Dad afloat and because we had the dogs, we were happy in our little unit, in the life we had never expected. Dad adjusted amazingly. He cooked the tea, made sure my sister and I got up and dressed for school, that our faces were clean and our uniforms ironed, supervised homework, took us for days out and, most importantly – for us and for him – continued to take us and pick us up from school. Things were fine for a long time, at home, right up until I was twenty.

'But Dad got severe asthma when he was thirty-six, a pet allergy, and there could be no more guide dogs,' I say. 'I mean, how unlucky was that? It was *awful*. He just went in on himself, like there was no point to anything any more. He just switched off.'

She nods solemnly, but her eyes are lit up. 'Do you talk? Talk to each other? Air your feelings? While you're in the flat?'

'No, not really. Less and less, actually, over the years. We don't really talk at all these days.' And what I've just said in this room is the most I've spoken in *decades*.

'What about your mother?'

'She doesn't feature.'

'Feature? Has she passed?'

Passed? Passed where? Passed 'Go' without collecting her £200? 'No. She's just not in my life.' I want Verity to move on.

'And do you have friends around you?'

'I don't really have any friends.'

'Oh, I'm sorry.'

'It's OK,' I say.

'Do you miss having someone to talk to?'

'Yes.' I could have made friends at my various jobs, but I let any contenders drift away from me like minnows in a stream, while I have stayed stuck in the mud, weeds wrapped round me, *safe*. I stayed surface-level friendly only with Sally and Justine and Paula and Yvette. I batted away invitations from Jeanette and Diane and Stevie. Colleagues, acquaintances; people I have never let get too close to me . . .

'Is that why you're here?' she asks kindly.

There's a pause, then a rattle at the door. It opens and a sheepish face is there, framed by a giant dehydrated umbrella plant in the poky hall.

'Sorry, wrong room,' says a man with a doughy face. 'I was looking for Martin?'

He scans the room, his eyes lighting on me and staying there too long.

'*I'm* not Martin,' I proffer.

'Up the corridor,' says Verity, with a pretty, business-like smile. She turns her smile back to me. It is full of compassion, which makes me feel uneasy.

'Is that why you're here? To talk to someone?'

'To talk to someone about my trauma,' I add lamely.

'You didn't really see anyone jump, or the aftermath, did you?' she asks softly.

'No, I didn't.'

'You came here just to talk to someone, didn't you?'

'Yes, I did.'

She looks at me for a few seconds. I reach behind me to my bag. As I've been sitting, a packet of Extra Strong Mints and a tube of concealer have rolled out. I stuff them back in.

'I'll go,' I say, my back still to her. When I turn around, she suddenly stamps the heel of one of her pretty shoes down on the carpet.

'Spider,' she says.

'Oh,' I reply. *Why do people always save the ladybirds and never the spiders?*

'Please don't go yet,' she says. 'Can I ask you something else? I hope I'm not being indelicate, and please say if you think it isn't pertinent but, your birthmark, is it something that adversely affects you?'

Hold the crystal, people, I don't like where this is going! 'What about it?' I am suddenly curt, dismissive. Actually, I've already dismissed myself from this session, haven't I? There should be no more questions now. I am out of here. I stand up, pick up my bag and I walk to the door.

'Do you shy away from life because of it, Prue?'

I turn in the doorway, blushing furiously. 'Yes, of course I shy away because of it! I hardly go skipping through life like a bloody unicorn!' She is kind, but I am angry, although not at her. 'I've had it for a *really* long time, I'm more than used to it, but there's no getting away from it, is there? I have a monstrous great birthmark on my face and although I cover it in thick make-up, sometimes it makes me want to hide away for ever and never see another living soul ever again. How about that?'

She ignores my tantrum and nods sagely. 'So, your father's blindness and your low self-esteem have become tremendous barriers you can't see past?'

'Well, *he* can't see past them . . .' I retort.

'You don't go out and you don't even communicate now, so much so that you have fabricated witnessing something you haven't in order to receive an hour's free counselling? In order just to talk to someone?'

Her tone is so gentle that I mumble, 'Sorry. Sorry,' like an overgrown schoolgirl.

'Look,' she says, leaning back in her chair, 'I'm going to dish out some advice. You and your father sound like

38

you're stuck in a horrendous rut. If he can't see, why don't you become his eyes?'

'Become his eyes . . .' I repeat dully.

'Take him out and about. You live in one of the most exciting capitals in the world,' she adds. *That explains the skirt*, I think. 'Did he used to enjoy London?'

'Yes, he did,' I say. 'He was supposed to design some of it. He was an architect, before he went blind.'

'That's a real shame. And did *you* enjoy London?'

Enjoy was a bit of a stretch; it's not like it's chocolate cake. 'I suppose so,' I respond. *No. Not really.*

'Find out where he'd like to go and do some day trips together. Force yourself to go out, be your father's eyes.'

'Day trips?' My father is blind and I am probably the grumpiest woman in London. I can't really see us going on *day trips*.

'Yes, day trips. And talk to each other.' She smiles at me again, in a way I feel she means to wrap this up. Well, I'm ready. I'm in the doorway. 'I wish you all the best, Prue.'

'Thank you,' I mumble.

'Goodbye, Prudence.'

I take one last look at her beautiful shoes.

'OK, thank you, Verity. Thank you very much. Goodbye.'

Chapter 6

Three sets of stairs and an infuriatingly hard-to-open door later and I have never been so relieved to breathe the air of a London street into my lungs, in all its exhaust-fumed glory. I flee up it (unwise to run in flip-flops, but needs must), a very guilty fugitive, the new jacket flopping over one arm like a limp fish. That was horrendous. Verity was kind, but I have been exposed as a charlatan of the highest order. And 'day trips'! Dad won't want to go on any day trips! He barely talks to me; he's hardly going to want to go strolling round London, bumping into things and making polite conversation with me about the weather while I ping poisonous looks at all the people staring at us . . .

The jacket falls off my arm and on to the pavement and I retrieve it and put it in my bag. I really don't think my father wants me to become his eyes. I don't think he would appreciate my surly, moody vision of the world. And I'm not sure I can take on the responsibility of guiding him around, either. Not on proper outings. We're safer in The Palladian, surely? I don't think it would do either of us any good to be let loose on the streets of London, an unwieldy double act. None of my forays into the world have *ever* been successful, after all.

I skitter up the road, rushing towards home. Thank you for your advice, Verity, I think, but there can be no day trips. I didn't see anything, remember? So absolutely nothing needs to change.

*

'This is new, you going out all the time.'

Dad is in his chair when I get home, the window shut on the muffled sounds of buses rumbling past. He is cooking something for lunch – macaroni cheese with extra garlic, it smells like.

'Hardly *all the time*, Dad.' I go to the kitchen for a drink of water. Glug it down in one go. 'I've been out twice in a week, that's all.'

'That's a lot, for you.' I told him I was going for a wander to the charity shops. I told him I fancied some fresh air. I currently feel as fresh as a daisy that's been trampled on by a muddy welly. 'What's the weather like out there?'

'Glorious. Boiling.'

He nods and reaches for his headphones. He doesn't want to talk further, which is probably for the best. I won't end up telling him I've just been bare-faced lying to a TFL-endorsed counsellor who then rumbled me, or that I pretended I'd seen someone commit suicide so I could go and chat to a complete stranger.

I plonk down in my chair, slip off my flip-flops. I take out my phone and my own headphones – I need music; I need solace. It's time for a bit of Janis: 'Me and Bobby McGee'. I sit back and allow the force of that woman's voice to wash over me. That's better. Janis was also bullied at school, you know – called a pig and had pennies thrown at her. At the University of Texas she was once declared 'Ugliest Man on Campus'. She moved to San Francisco to escape, and I used to think I'd go there, one day, to check out her house. We have a lot in common, me and Janis – apart from all the talent, of course. And the drugs.

After a while I check the news. I search for more on Philippa and there's a small update. Oh, she wasn't an actress or something glamorous – she worked as a crew member at Ultra Laser in Enfield, one of those places where kids run around in the dark firing neon beams at

41

each other from plastic guns. This is quite different to what I imagined. My vision of her needs adjusting. I wonder if she got depressed working in the blackness all the time. If she got tired of putting on a smiley, energetic front for all those kids. Maybe she came out of there, after each shift, blinking into the light and wondering if this was all there was . . . I feel even sadder for her. She was so young. Janis Joplin died in her twenties, too – a member of the tragic '27 Club' of Cobain, Winehouse, Morrison and the like. In her case, a heroin overdose. I realize I have lived almost twenty years longer than all of them, and I have absolutely nothing to show for it.

Dad is tapping me on the shoulder. 'It'll be twenty minutes,' he says, above my low-level Joplin. 'I'm just toasting the cheese on the top.' He can't see the dish he's created, but he always knows the exact moment it'll be ready. Picture-perfect food he will never see.

Picture perfect . . . I remember the photo for Angela. I'll do it now, before lunch. I don't want her phoning up again in the middle of the night.

The photo album is on the top shelf of the tall cupboard to the right of the sitting room, under Dad's ancient *A–Z*. It has a terrible pattern on the cover: a sort of Pollock-esque 1980s mess in purple and black swirls – like a bad nightclub – and the 90s was about the last time anyone opened it. Dad and I don't do photographs, for obvious reasons.

'What are you up to?' asks Dad. He 'oofs' down in his chair, stretches his legs out to the footstool and plonks his feet on top.

'Getting the old photo album down. Angela wants a picture from it. She rang last week – in the early hours, one night.'

'Ah, right,' says Dad. 'The photo album. Is she going to phone back?'

'I expect so, as she missed you. You know you could always phone *her*,' I add. Like many men, including those who make a million phone calls a day for work, Dad has an aversion to instigating family calls – and *I'm* not bloody phoning her. It's twelve years since Angela last came to London and we've only seen her three times in total since she absconded. She flew over for Papa's funeral in 1998, two nights only, and for Nonna's, arriving on Millennium Eve, because the flights were cheaper, and returning three days later, then she and Warren came in 2006 for two weeks in the summer – they stayed at the Travelodge in Marylebone and spent most of their time at the Tower of London and Madame fucking Tussauds. But even when I do spend time with my sister, we end up rowing over stupid things, like sisters who don't like each other very much do.

'She'll phone back. Bring the photo album over here,' Dad says, slapping his knee. I'm surprised. He never asks for it. 'I used to know the first ten or fifteen pages of it by heart.'

'Really?' I ask. 'You want it?'

'Yes. You can start going out all the time . . . I can ask for the photo album.'

I come and perch on Dad's footstool and place the album on his knees. He peels open the front cover and traces his hand over the first page and the photos clamped into place under their plastic sheet. I watch as his fingers navigate one of those satisfying bubbles.

'You and Angela as babies,' Dad says, lowering his face as though he can see the photographs, and yes, here we are, sitting on blankets in the tiny garden of our first childhood home, in Clerkenwell, toothlessly grinning from highchairs, sleeping in carry cots . . . Angela looks cute; I wince at the sight of me and that thing on my face. I hope Dad *doesn't* know these photos off by heart. I hope, somehow, he has forgotten the blighted baby, that he doesn't see the birthmark when he thinks of me. But how could he not? How could he ever imagine a 'me' without it being there?

I keep on turning. Here's Dad with his foot on a spade in the tiny garden, triumphantly holding a turnip aloft. All three of us laughing under a crocheted blanket with Nana Larry in her front room; Dad pushing me in a wheelbarrow down some random hill; Angela and I in Southend, standing in front of a scary moving waxwork where a cowering man looks like he's permanently going to get his head chopped off – huge lemon Rossi ice creams covering half our faces.

'Is that one with us in Southend still in here, the one with the giant ice creams?' Dad asks.

'Yes, it's still here.'

'Which one?' asks Dad.

I take his forefinger and trace it over the photo. 'I remember it,' he says. 'I remember the taste of that lemon ice cream.'

I carry on turning the pages. There's Angela and I, in red and grey uniform, on Angela's first day at school – she's grinning and looking all cheeky; I am perfecting a grimace and look pissed off. Angela dressed as the Tin Man from *The Wizard of Oz* for a Halloween disco. Me, coming down the road on my bike, chubby in knee-high socks and a *Wombles* T-shirt.

'Which ones are you on now?'

'Photos of Angela and me, a bit older. Do you remember her as the Tin Man?'

'If she only had a heart,' says Dad, and it's a joke but kind of true all the same. I like this, I think, us talking about these photos. It's surprising, but I like it.

I shift the position of the album a little and a Polaroid falls to the floor, which I pick up. It's one I had slid between the long-unopened pages a few years ago, when

44

it hurt too much to keep coming across it in my bedside drawer. It's one that makes my heart give a hitch now. It's a Polaroid picture of the man I once had to stop myself from loving. A friend of mine. *Kemp*. His nickname, a reference to brothers Martin and Gary from Spandau Ballet. His heart, something I could never hope to secure . . . as we were only ever friends. I went to school with him, many years ago. I've cried over him, to that particular Bonnie Raitt song. It's a good photo, this one I took of him, despite him being an actual photographer, by profession, and me just being a general numpty. It's out on the dark street outside our pub, the one we used to go to. He is laughing and handsome. He is wearing a green woolly scarf I gave him. I look at the photo for far too long then slip it back into the pages of the album.

Here's the photo Angela wanted. Yes, she does have a crab on her nose but I'm pretty certain she put it there herself, for effect. I'm standing next to her and squinting into the camera. I peel back the plastic film and dislodge the photo from its sticky background.

'This is the photo Angela asked for,' I say. 'Me and her when we were crabbing.'

'I don't really remember that one too well. Remind me?'

'Angela has a crab on the end of her nose.'

'A crab, yes.' He looks like he is concentrating. 'A crab on the end of her nose.'

I put it to one side, to take a shot of it for Angela. There are some teenage photos now – ones that Dad took, on our instruction. We are often off-centre, with parts of us chopped off, and a blind man taking photos certainly gave passers-by something to talk about. There's Angela on roller-skates on the pavement outside The Palladian, dressed in neon, a laughing smile on her face; me, standing in the hall before a trip to a terrible nightclub, in a black minidress and trowelled-on make-up. Weren't they always terrible? Standing in sticky-floored bars, nodding to music while sipping on a straw, catching men's eyes and looking away again, though in my case they looked away first . . . And you'd think I would have escaped the old 'You're not going out like that!', with Dad being blind, but he always felt for necklines and hemlines on the doorstep and made me get changed into less horrendous outfits, if deemed necessary.

I look at him, his hands moving over the album, feeling the edges of the photographs under their transparent film. We seek to hide things from our fathers, don't we? We attempt to shield them from all those scrapes in the life of a daughter – the times we got so drunk we crawled up the road on our hands and knees; the time we called him from that phone box that was actually the bedsit of a man twenty years our senior; the dark things we are most ashamed of. It's to mothers we tell those stories – sometimes – and her whisper of 'We won't tell your father about this' is a hushed conspiracy between mother and daughter. Except my mother wasn't there.

Here's one of me and Cherry Lau, sitting on the step outside her parents' Chinese takeaway. She had to work there after school. I'd go and help out, loll around behind the counter and be surly to customers. We used to have such a laugh.

'Which one are you on now?'

'Me and Cherry Lau, you know, who lived next door?'

'Yes, I know,' says Dad. 'Sweet girl.'

She *was* a sweet girl. I feel so awful about how things ended with her. I mouth 'sorry' at the photo and turn to the next page, but it is empty. The last few blank pages of the album are stuck together in a clump, but there's always a sliver of yellowing paper peeping out, just before the back cover, so I peel it free of the last page to expose the paper flap, secured with the string that winds round the little cardboard button, and the set of faded photographs inside.

'The photos of you and Mum, before you had us,' I whisper. It's been a long time since I've seen them, but they always give me a jolt. They always make me feel stuff I really don't want to feel.

'Describe them,' says Dad, his face impassive.

'Well, there's the one of you at Covent Garden, by the flower market. You both look so young.' Sixteen, I think. Both my parents became parents at *sixteen* . . . 'You have flares on, and Mum's wearing the big T-shirt with a rainbow on it.' I clear my throat and try to sound jolly.

'Just before she had you,' says Dad. 'Best market in the world, back then,' he adds, with a quick smile. 'And we all loved the street performers, didn't we? Do they still have them?'

'I'm sure they do,' I say. I stare at Mum's face in this photo: so smiley, so full of fun, so alien. Her body, so full of me. The mound of me – not knowing how it would all turn out – is straining at the rainbow T-shirt, ready to burst forth. There's a general otherworldliness to these photos, I think. An unlikelihood. 'OK, here you are by the jeans stall in Camden, with the sign for the lock in the background,' I continue, my voice purposely light. 'You're both laughing and Mum has a feather in her hair.'

'I remember that.'

'And here you are on your wedding day.'

I remember this photo well. I remember how it makes my breath catch in my throat and my heart contract. Mum and Dad looking ridiculously young on the steps of St Peter's, the Italian church in Clerkenwell. Nana and Grandpa Larry to one side of them – tall and solemn and stoic – and Nonna and Papa on the other – small and proud and strained. Grandpa Larry died only a couple of years later – from lung disease; Nana Larry in 1975. What

47

do I say to Dad about this photo? What did I *always* say to him about the faces of the four parents and his boyish grin and Mum's pretty smile? I say how happy they all look. How hopeful. As if hope matters.

Dad nods. He places his forefinger to his lips and momentarily closes his eyes. 'Where's the photo of me with Jack Templeton outside the Roundhouse?' he asks, after a beat. 'When we went to see Blondie in 'seventy-eight?'

I'm happy to move on and flick through the faded photos. Some are a composite: a square photo with three or four smaller squares down the side, all with white borders. 'Here it is. You're wearing that jacket with the enormous collar and Jack looks like a proper dandy!'

'What a gig,' says Dad. The Roundhouse is literally just up the street from us. We hear the concerts sometimes, even through the closed window. I've never been there. 'Remember *Parallel Lines*, their album?'

'You used to play it all the time,' I say. *Before we lost the guide dogs,* I want to add, but I don't. 'You should put it on again.'

'Maybe,' says Dad. 'What about a picture of me by the Albert Hall?'

'Yes, that's here.'

'Describe it to me, Prue.'

'Well, you look sunburnt—' I say.

'Summer of 'seventy-six,' interrupts Dad. 'What a time to be alive! Aren't they saying this year's heatwave could be the longest since then?'

'I believe they are,' I reply. 'And you're stretched out on the grass opposite, the sun in your eyes. It looks like late afternoon.'

'Fabulous,' muses Dad. He leans back in his chair and closes his eyes as though he is back there, soaking up the sun outside the Albert Hall. He always was a sun worshipper. A man who would happily sit in a deckchair for hours on the beach at Southend, his top off and his trouser legs rolled up, in our early years – occasionally catapulting himself out of stripy canvas and crickety wood to fetch ice creams or help us make sandcastles with long foamy trenches dug back to the sea. Or he would enjoy enthusiastic, splashy paddles with Angela and me, standing in the shallows long after we had returned to our sandy kingdoms to stare at passing ships on the horizon, while moussey suds washed over his feet and the sun beat on his back.

Dad looks almost contented.

'Do you want to go out on some day trips?' I say softly but, to be quite honest, reluctantly. I have just the right inflection in my voice to let him know I don't really want to. 'Revisit some old haunts?'

'No,' says Dad, shaking his head, his eyes still closed. 'No, I don't think so.'

'OK.' I am relieved. Of course. Of course he doesn't want to! There, Verity. I've done what you asked. I've suggested it and he said 'no'.

'What about this one?' Dad has leant forward again and felt for another photo, curled at the edges. 'Describe this one to me, Prue.'

'It's you and me and Angela outside Papa and Nonna's *gelato* parlour in Clerkenwell,' I say.

'Go on.'

'Well, you've got your arm around us both and you're smiling and we're smiling, and I look about eight or nine, and Angela looks about six or seven, and you're wearing a white polo shirt and look all young, and the sun is in our faces. You can just about make out Nonna's face, in the window, behind the counter. She's got that headscarf on – the one with the big dots. And it's so sunny that you can't even really see the right-hand part of the photo and we just look . . . happy, I suppose.'

'Is it sunny today?' asks Dad, as I gaze at the three of

us outside Nonna and Papa's *gelato* shop, in Clerkenwell, and remember.

'Yes, it's sunny today. Ridiculously so.'

'And do you think it will be sunny tomorrow?'

'Yes, I think it's going to be sunny again tomorrow.'

He turns his face towards mine. 'Maybe we could,' he says.

'Could what?' I answer.

'Go out somewhere.'

'Really?'

He sighs and smiles and he looks a little strained, but hopeful. 'If it's a warm sunny day I'd quite like to feel the sun on my back and on my face.'

'Really?' I repeat. I feel a little panicked.

'Yes. We might not ever get another one – a heatwave. The summer of 'seventy-six and this one, and that might be it. Don't you think?'

'Yes. No.' I'm trying to gather my thoughts. I'm terrified.

'What do you say? Shall we have a day out?'

When Dad used to sit in deckchairs with rolled-up trouser legs, he could see. When we last went out properly, and not just to the very local doctor's surgery, Dad was guided by a calm and clever guide dog, not a grumpy, disillusioned daughter. And he was not grumpy *himself*, like he has been for so very long. Can Dad and I really do this? Can we have a day out? Will it be warm sun on our backs, or dozens of tripped-up kerbs, lots of swearing and staring faces, three falls and a trip to A & E . . .

'Well,' I say, looking at my father and glad he can't see the fear and anxiety that must be written all over my face. 'Where would you like to go?'

Dad smiles. 'I'd like to walk up to Camden.'

Chapter 7

It's thirty-two degrees. Dad and I are on the pavement outside The Palladian with the sun beating down on us like an angry torch. He's wearing navy shorts, a white Fred Perry shirt, trainers and a hat to cover his bald patch. I'm wearing a sundress unearthed from the back of my wardrobe and a scowl.

We're doing it. We're walking up to Camden this morning. I'm not relishing the thought of it. It's so bloody hot. I have my hair tied back in a ponytail, but my fringe is bothering me and my birthmark is already spoiling for a fight. It didn't play ball this morning, despite my down-pat, tried-and-tested routine of dabbing on green colour corrector with my finger, carefully working in a concealer with a brush, blending the edges with a sponge, and applying translucent powder. Then adding another layer of concealer and powder. Then a third layer. Sometimes a fourth. This morning I pushed all boats out by eschewing the fourth layer and doing my special contouring – dabbing a lighter concealer into the recessed parts of my birthmark and a darker concealer on to the raised parts, to create the optical illusion of flat skin. It can be a bit hit and miss, and this morning was very much 'miss'. I don't feel adequately disguised. My mask feels uncertain. It's going to slip, in this heat; everything's going to slip like a Hermès scarf off a French-polished coffee table.

'Lock the door, then,' says Dad.

He's grumpy; he's been grumpy all morning – is he already regretting this as much as I am? The street outside

51

The Palladian is busy and the people streaming past are already staring at the blind man and his coral-clad companion, and I worry if we step out we'll be swallowed up by them, carried along, out of control, but 'OK,' I say, and I lock the door and put the keys in my cross-body bag.

My sundress is a bright coral maxi dress I bought from *Loved Before* three or four years ago. It's been hanging in the wardrobe in Angela's old bedroom ever since. I've taken it out often, just to look at it. It's beautiful and it isn't really me (it should ideally be worn by a twenty-something Instagram influencer with Pinterest hair), but I feel I want to make an effort somehow, for this. This thing I don't really want to do. I'm not equipped to guide my father. I can't even guide myself through my own life to any satisfaction. I don't know what we're even doing here, with the sun beating down on us and a long road ahead. But this morning I really felt a need to take this beautiful maxi dress off its pretty padded hanger and put it on.

'Ready for the off, then?' says Dad gruffly.

It would be so easy to turn Dad around, step back into the cool, dusty lobby and head back up the stairs to The Palladian for a glass of cold lemon squash and a KitKat.

'Yes, ready,' I say.

Dad, who is standing to my left, places his hand on my left arm, just above the elbow and I straighten my arm. This is how we do it when I take him anywhere – the default positioning we slip into automatically. We start to walk slowly along the flank of the tube station, the closed windows of The Palladian above us and the dark red tiles of Chalk Farm tube station gleaming under bright sunlight.

'Do you want to pop into the Stop n' Shop for anything?' I ask him. I'm stalling, I know. My dress feels too swishy and rather ridiculous.

'No,' Dad says. 'But let me feel the tiles.'

We step closer and Dad places a flat palm on one of the oxblood tiles. I put my hand on another and it is hot to the touch. Dad looks like he is drawing energy from his tile. He loves this tube station – everything about it. The tiles, the arches, the ticket hall, the cornicing and the Arts and Crafts dado rail friezes, featuring the acanthus leaf. All the details people don't notice and he can't any more.

'Chalk Farm has the longest frontage,' he says, 'of all the underground stations in London – and the most tiles.'

When we lived in Clerkenwell, he'd bring Angela and me on the hour-long walk here, sometimes, and he'd point up at the iconic flat above the station and say, 'One day, I'd like to live there', like all the promise of the world was in The Palladian, which of course it wasn't. After the accident, he received a large amount of compensation, and when he heard from Jack Templeton that the flat was up for sale, back in 1982, he bought it, just like that, over the telephone. How sad it was that when he finally got to step inside, he couldn't see a bloody thing.

'Come on, then,' I say, with fake enthusiasm. Dad takes the back of my arm again and we walk away from the station and take the few steps to the edge of the pavement on Haverstock Hill. We have to cross in three sections; there are two islands in the road. I wait for the traffic to pass then I say, 'Kerb down, Dad,' and we cross.

'All right?' I ask him, as we cross to the first island.

'Well, I can't bloody well see anything, but yeah, I suppose so.'

It's going to be like this, then, is it? I think. Grumpy Bollocks on Tour? We cross to the second island. We must look quite conspicuous – Dad in his baseball cap and me in my coral dream and inadequate face paint. We reach the other side of the road – 'Kerb up!' – then

53

begin to carefully walk up Chalk Farm Road, heading for Camden.

Dad taps left right, left right, with his cane. We are ignored or stared at – briefly – or swerved around. Mostly ignored. It was so different when Dad had a guide dog. We always caused a bit of a stir, back then, especially on the school run – Dad rocking up with Sunny, all the school kids fussing round, the mums saying 'aww' . . . Angela revelled in it and I didn't. She would stand there in her pigtails and her little skirt, looking all proud; I was in the final year and would hate all the attention. Mums would look from dog to Dad to Angela to me; their eyes remaining on my face just a fraction too long before they smiled unsure half-smiles coated in sympathy and just a smidgeon of mild disgust.

'Careful,' I say, steering Dad to the left slightly. 'Lamp-post. Don't want to fall at the first hurdle.'

'I don't want to fall at all,' snaps Dad, 'and I refuse to walk into a lamp-post. What sort of cliché would that be?'

Is he *nervous*? I know he would never admit it if he was, but we both know he hasn't been further than the doctor's for years. When he had the dogs, he went everywhere. Did everything. Family glue, those guide dogs were. When a lovely lady came to The Palladian and took away our last dog, Folly, on a rainy day one autumn, and she trotted out the door so sweetly and so resignedly, it broke all three of our hearts, but Dad's shut down that day and we knew that was the end of the little life we had known. He became just a kernel of the man he was before. A man who retreated into his armchair without hope, and no desire to look for it again.

Not that I can talk.

'Is the Enterprise pub still here?' asks Dad.

'Yep, still here,' I say. God, we've got a long way to go.

'And the hi-fi shop?'

'Nope, that's gone. Do you need water yet, Dad?' I have a small bottle in my bag.

'We've only just left the flat, Prue; of course I don't!'

He *is* nervous. I haven't seen him this snappy for a long time. We both need to chill out, I think. It's only a seven-minute walk from Chalk Farm tube station to Camden Lock – we're acting like we're hiking to John o'Groat's. In a hurricane.

'Careful, Dad. Single file here.' Half of the pavement is gone, suddenly, cordoned off with scaffolding. There's a smooth little manoeuvre we employ for narrow paths, almost like a dance move. My left arm goes behind my back, for Dad to hold on to; he takes smaller steps not to tread on my heels, and we go single file.

'God bless you,' says an old man as we pass him under the scaffolding.

'Why, thank you, good sir,' says Dad, all Dickensian. I know he is being thoroughly sarcastic. He's always had this when he goes out: people blessing him left, right and centre. I've forgotten how 'blessed' Dad can be.

'OK, you can come back next to me,' I say to Dad, once the pavement opens up again.

'Keep going straight?' he asks as he returns to take my arm above the elbow.

'Keep going straight.'

We walk. Dad taps. My fringe sticks to my forehead.

'Whereabouts are we now, Prue?' Dad asks after a while.

'We're just coming past all the tattoo parlours.' The smell of food is beginning to come our way now; music starts to pump out of shop doorways. I wonder how many times he and Mum walked past these shops as teenagers. How many times they went jeans shopping.

There's a set of traffic lights we need to bear right at. As we wait, I spy a retro punk, leaning against the front window of an army-surplus shop. A middle-aged throw-back from the 80s. Bovver boots, safety pins, Mohican, the works. He must be boiling. He peels himself off the shop window and slouches indifferently down the road and the illuminated man on the crossing changes from red to green.

'Come on, then,' I say to Dad, and we cross. It's immediately busier and we need to slow our step. We start to get jostled a little, as the double act of our wide load takes up too much pavement; my right shoulder and Dad's left arm susceptible. A man stumbles against us, his hand landing on my wrist.

'Sorry.'

'That's OK.'

'We're here,' says Dad crabbily. 'I can smell burgers.'

Camden is basking in bright yellow sunshine and absolutely buzzing. Spirits are high, sunglasses are on; music is pumping from about six different places – Bob Marley, Rihanna's 'We Found Love', Paloma Faith covering the Mamas & the Papas . . . The smell of meat and onions and spices, of falafel and pizza and burritos, fills the air. There are dozens of tourists, pleasure-seekers and wanderers milling around, all soaking up the atmosphere of a very hot and sunny day in Camden Town, and we slowly make our way through them up to the bridge at Regent's Canal.

'Describe everything to me,' says Dad. He's so *terse*, I think. He's enjoying himself even less than I am.

'Oh gosh, I don't know where to start, Dad. There's just so much! OK, well, to our right is the Stables Market – food stalls and the like, I think. Lots of uneven cobble stones, so I don't think we can venture in.'

'OK.'

'There're people everywhere. Absolutely everywhere. Clusters of tourists. Couples holding hands. Teenagers.

A man carrying an Alsatian up the street, over his shoulder.'

'Really?'

'Yes, really.'

Dad tuts and shakes his head. He used to laugh when I described things for him. Sometimes, when I was young, I would embellish them or make things up – for fun – like saying I'd seen a dinosaur or a giant purple sunflower, making us both giggle. As a rebellious teen I would often refuse to describe anything and say 'nothing', when he asked me, even in the face of the most rich and abundant visual feasts. Today, I'm doing my best at becoming Dad's eyes, like Verity said, though Dad is hardly receptive. When we looked at the photos together, he seemed open, happy to talk, for once – now he is as closed again as the photo album itself.

'Oh, and there's a guy dressed as Elvis, at the orange juice stand.'

'Isn't there always?'

We arrive at the iron bridge, turn right at the towpath and go down to the locks. There are sloping flagstones to negotiate; areas of welcome shade. Volunteers are sweeping the lockside brickwork free of dust and weeds; a man is turning the lock of a narrow boat with a giant windlass. I describe everything to Dad as best I can: the canal boats waiting to pass through the lock; the green algae on the undisturbed sections of water; the weeping willow that arcs over the canal and nods in the sun. It's tranquil here, compared to the street. I came here quite a lot with my friend, Kemp, the photographer. He lived not far from here, in a houseboat at Wenlock Basin. I wonder if he's still there. He liked to take shots of the water and the weeping willow and the boats, and I would watch him and try not to blurt out that I loved him.

Dad nods as I speak, his face set and unreadable.

After a while we return to the bridge and continue down Camden High Street in the direction of Camden Town tube station, with the milling souvenir seekers dazzled by sunglasses and T-shirts and jewellery and Union Jack paraphernalia crammed below shop awnings under coloured buildings. Dad asks me if the record shop is still here.

'Which record shop?'

'Pete's Records? The other side of the road.'

I look. 'Yes, it's there.'

'Come on, then.'

We avoid a pair of chuggers in orange vests and cross the road to the record shop. Dad used to live for music. It used to be in the centre of our Venn diagram, if one existed for Dad and me: a common love, with architecture in the sole portion of Dad's circle, and absolutely nothing in mine. Dad has been a bit of a Mod since the late 70s, when he got swept up in the revival; he loves all that music and its tributaries. When he went blind in the summer of 1980, it was not long after the film *Quadrophenia* came out (he'd been to the cinema to see it three times with Jack Templeton), and when it was out on video he'd listen to it over and over again, reciting the dialogue. He had The Who soundtrack, too. *Quadrophenia* used to drive Angela and me mad.

Pete's Records is packed, with reggae music pounding through its aisles. Dad is partial to that as well – the roots of Mod, he says. I feel helplessly out of place in here, immediately. I always have, in Camden. It's far too cool for me. I used to come with my (short-lived) best friend, Georgina, from school, and when I did, I just used to agree with her about stuff, pretending I liked whatever she liked. Following her into places she wanted to go. Mooching in the doorways she wanted to mooch in. I've never had a 'scene', but if I did, Camden definitely wouldn't be it. My female singer-songwriters would fit in very well here, though, with their bare feet and their freedom and their roars of confidence; but I am nothing like them. They aren't afraid of fierce; they aren't afraid of ugly. I *am* afraid.

'Ska records, please,' says Dad. I look around and spot the handwritten sign, suspended from the ceiling. We stand at the correct rack and I leaf through the cardboard album sleeves of hundreds and hundreds of records. Vinyl records are making a comeback, apparently – they survived the CD and iPods and Spotify and iTunes – and video never did kill the radio star, after all.

'Who are you interested in?' I ask.

'Just read artists out to me,' he says.

I leaf through the records. 'OK, The Selecter, The Specials, this one is by Skarface.' I hold it up.

'French group. Crazy black-and-white illustrated cover?'

'Yes.'

He nods. 'Fantastic, fantastic. I've read about them. Give it to me.'

I hand him the record and he runs his hand over it. He reaches inside and pulls the record from its sleeve. Surely Dad doesn't want to *buy* anything? He hasn't used that turntable for years. He skirts a finger over the black vinyl, then slips it back into its sleeve, before handing it to me so I can slot it back into its alphabetical space.

'You should play your old records,' I say. 'I'd like to hear music in the flat again. Proper music, not just through headphones, and at a decent volume. Wouldn't *you*?'

'I don't know,' says Dad. He beetles his fingers over the top of a stack of records. Back and forward. Back and forward. A woman in green dreadlocks manoeuvres round his cane. 'OK,' he says finally. 'Let's move on.'

We shuffle out into the midday throng again, assaulted by the smells and the colour and the sounds and the heat of a busy Camden at lunchtime – the sun on our backs and reggae ringing in our ears.

'Shall we get something to eat?' I ask Dad.

'No. I'd like to go home now,' he says.

'What? Really?'

'Yes, really. I want to go back to the flat now, Prue.'

He has stopped still on the pavement. The milling people tut and swerve round us. A man in a suit and tie flashes me a sympathetic smile. I sigh. This has not been a success. We should never have come out or come this far. It's too difficult. Dad is too grumpy. Our comfort zone is dangerously out of reach. We're better in the flat, not talking. We've missed most of *This Morning* for this.

'OK,' I say, with a huge sigh of relief. 'Let's go home.'

Chapter 8

Dad and I don't walk back to Chalk Farm. We take the tube from Camden Town underground station – one stop on the Northern Line. Our carriage is fairly empty and we get seats next to each other, Dad's cane between us and not much else. He is silent, unwilling to talk. I let my eyes roam round the carriage. The guy opposite us is in a Choose Life T-shirt and has headphones on; he must have his volume cranked right up as I can hear what he's playing. It's not Wham!, as his T-shirt might suggest, but James Brown's 'Get Up'. Three other people in the carriage are tapping one or both feet in time to the beat; I look down and my foot is tapping, too.

'Our own gig,' remarks a young woman to my right, in a flagrant breach of people-don't-talk-to-strangers-on-the-tube protocol.

'Yes,' I reply.

Dad's feet do not tap; he is motionless and his eyes are closed until the tube pulls into Chalk Farm station. It's London: One, the Albertas: Nil, I muse. We gave it a go, but it was a big fat fail, this day-trip lark. We should never have put ourselves out there.

Back in the flat, I change out of my dress and into a pair of shorts and a T-shirt, then go to my chair. It's a relief to be back, far from the baffling crowds and the noise and the hurricane of life. Here with the window shut and the world outside muffled and at a comfortable arm's length, I can breathe again. My phone is in my hand; I've missed being on it and return to it like an old friend.

'Do you want a cup of tea?' asks Dad, from the kitchen.
'Yes, please.'

He seems relieved to be back, too. The baseball cap has been put away, probably for good, along with the notion we might ever venture out again. We are home and it's better if we stay that way.

Out of force of habit I check my messages and emails. None. I check WhatsApp. Nothing. I'm not sure why I even have the app. I click on to Facebook. My only Facebook Friends are Angela (reluctantly), a couple of people I used to work with at the Conference Centre, and a few from those lacklustre jobs after I was made redundant. Today on Facebook there's not a lot going on. Duncan in Bookings has a hangover; Florrie from the betting shop wants to know if anyone has seen her cat; Jane at the budget book depot has declared today 'Worst day ever' and has received a flurry of concerned 'You OK, hun?'s, which she is enigmatically ignoring, apart from a solitary, 'I'll pm you', to one lucky enquirer. And Sally Ann from the Co-op has cryptically 'checked in' to the local hospital without saying why. Oh, and my sister has a new pair of high-heeled sandals that apparently merit the caption, 'Give a girl the right shoes and she can conquer the world.'

'What shall we have for lunch?' calls Dad. 'I could rustle up a quick chicken parmigiana.'

'Yes please, sounds lovely.' I come off Facebook and head to Safari to update the news article about Philippa – I have it bookmarked now – and when it loads there's a new piece of information. A piece of information I read twice.

On the afternoon of her death, Philippa Helens had been out for an early celebratory lunch in Knightsbridge, on the eve of her thirtieth birthday.

'It'll be ready in twenty minutes,' calls Dad from the kitchen. 'I'm making a side dish of asparagus *crespelle*.'

'Fantastic,' I call back.

I read the short news article for a third time, concentrating on every word. I can hear Dad mumbling to himself in the kitchen over the sound of clanking pans and steam and taps running and things being taken out of and put back into cupboards. I rise from my chair and go and stand at the closed window. A man below drags a tartan shopping trolley into the mouth of the tube station. A pair of teenagers slouch with hands in pockets into the Stop n' Shop. And I remember a different tube station and the crowds there and I feel incredibly sad for a woman I've never met called Philippa Helens.

I also wonder at what point she let go of the balloon.

'There you go.'

Dad is behind me, standing at my chair and offering his iPad to me.

'I'm over here, Dad,' I say, walking back from the window. 'What have you got there?'

'It's a list,' he says, holding out his iPad to me with the 'Notes' app open, 'of all the other places I'd like to go to.'

'What?' I say. 'I thought you hated it today, going to Camden?'

He says nothing and continues to hold out the iPad. I take it and quickly read the list. Primrose Hill, Little Venice, St Dunstan in the East, Covent Garden, Liberty, the Albert Hall, the Shard, Kenwood House and the Albert Bridge.

'I'm really surprised,' I say. 'And it's quite a long list,' I add, scanning it again. 'In this order?'

He nods.

'What's St Dunstan in the East?'

'A hidden garden. The ruins of a church near Tower Hill. It's very beautiful.'

'You want to go to all these places?'

'Yes, I do.'

'I thought you hated going to Camden today,' I repeat.

'We can try again,' he says.

I stare at Dad's list of places. Some are walking distance. Some are tube journeys away. Can we really head back out there, to all these places? Can we make it there and back, unscathed? Can we *be* together, father and daughter, for all these trips, and forced to talk, to spend time in each other's company – properly? I really don't know if this is a good idea.

'OK, we can do this,' I say reluctantly.

'Great.' Dad reaches for the iPad and heads back into the kitchen. 'Lunch will be in ten minutes.'

I watch as he disappears through the doorway. Maybe Dad doesn't really mean it, this list. Maybe if I don't mention it again, he won't either. Maybe he'll forget about it. I just can't imagine it, after Camden. I can't imagine the pair of us walking around London and taking up space in the world, after all this time, like a couple of aliens landed from Mars. It's too strange. Too far from comfort.

I sit back down in my chair, click on Facebook again. I want to look up Philippa Helens. Distract myself from lists and proposed trips out and feeling like an alien . . . Oh, I have a Friend Request. Freddie Whitehorn – a boy I liked at school, who used to catch me staring at him until one time he said, 'Why are you so ugly?' and I blushed, and he just laughed and laughed for about five minutes, in Chemistry, until everyone joined in with him . . . He's probably taking the piss so I delete the request.

Philippa Helens . . . I find her. Her profile is still on here, although someone has edited it to RIP Philippa and added the years of her birth and death. It's incredibly sad. One hundred and two friends Philippa had, in total. She wasn't very active – her last post was over three weeks ago: a picture of a sunset that looks like a stock photo. It has a series of comments under it: 'Cool' and 'Where is this, hun?' and 'Never mind sunsets! Dating news please!' – she had replied to this comment with a smiley face. There are only three photos of her among all the posts. The one I saw online, on the news report; one with her in the midst of a group of laughing girls all holding cocktails; and an arty black-and-white shot of her with slicked-back hair and bare shoulders and sort of shadowy branches, like lace, all over her face and shoulders. One of those portrait shots done in a studio, I think. The sort of hideous thing I've avoided all my life. It is captioned, 'Truth'.

I still want to distract myself from lists and things I don't want to do, so I go to her Friends list and have a nose. There are lots of men and women her age: people drinking and at meals and smiling in sunglasses and posing for the camera. Young mums holding babies. Blokes atop mountains and in pubs and running in marathons. All going on with their lives without her. I scroll down, the faces all beginning to blur into one, when I stop at a photo of an older-looking man. He looks forty-something, his mouth is wide open and laughing; he has cropped hair, even teeth and a slightly crooked nose – broken, maybe? I stop because he is wearing a striking red and black Venetian mask. Clicking on his profile – Salvi Russo, he's called – Italian? – it says he's a performer. There's a photo of him wearing black and balancing precariously on a beam in front of what I'm sure is St Paul's Church at Covent Garden, and it has over a hundred likes. Indeed, he has over 3,000 friends – that's a lot, by anyone's standards. His posts are sporadic – photos of pints of beer on tables, a grinning selfie (*sans* mask, nice face, sort of cheeky) with a view of the Thames behind, a cat on a cushion – littered with comments like 'Nice one mate'. I wonder how this man knows Philippa. If he's an entertainer, perhaps they met at Ultra Laser; perhaps he dresses up as a clown, or something, and does kids' parties there.

Three thousand friends . . . how does that even happen? Everyone's got more friends than me, I think. I have none – in real life – but that's OK. Friends have not been a good thing for me. Either they betray you or you betray them – or they steal your heart, without even knowing it, and refuse to give it back.

I come off Facebook and go to help Dad set the table. I don't want things to change. Despite Verity Holmes and Dad's list and other people living their best lives with millions of friends, and others ending theirs because they can't see a way forward, except into the path of a speeding train . . . I want things to stay as they are, as stagnant as the algae on Camden's waterways. I want unwanted memories to be swept from my mind like stubborn weeds from the brickwork of the canal. I want stillness and calm, and for my blank heart to remain undisturbed.

I wander into the kitchen to get the salt and pepper and I chuck a little prayer out to the un-listening universe.

Can't things just stay the same?

Chapter 9

'Primrose Hill,' said Dad, over a breakfast of fruit and Greek yoghurt this morning.

'What about it?' I replied, suddenly studying the contents of my plate like I was a forensic scientist.

'It's the first place on my list,' said Dad. 'Shall we go this morning?'

'What time?' I muttered.

'Ten?'

'Ten? That's a bit early.'

'What else do you have planned?'

'Absolutely nothing.'

'Ten it is, then.'

I couldn't muster faking any enthusiasm. I couldn't *fake* pretending I wanted to walk the sweltering fifteen minutes to Primrose Hill with my father on a Friday morning while he grunted and uttered monosyllabic complaints; while he asked me to describe what I could see and I told him that I could see posh shops and nice trees and people sitting outside cafés on Regent's Park Road nursing coffees and *pains au chocolat*. I attempted to become his eyes, again, but I couldn't fake enthusiasm for this miserable jaunt when I want to hide, safe and unseen, in the flat and not put myself out there for inspection from the world and reflection in faces more normal than mine.

There's a bloke staring at me now. He's sitting on the bench closest to us at the top of Primrose Hill and staring at my face, despite its robust cover of make-up, like there's something about it that doesn't sit quite right with him. I resist the urge to stick my tongue out at him or, worse, alert the other inhabitants of Primrose Hill this morning – with a yell, possibly – that yes, he may have a normal face, unlike mine, but he also has a monstrous beer belly and a terrible haircut. Maybe *he* doesn't sit right with *me*.

I am looking down on the London skyscape and Dad is sitting next to me and working his way through a packet of Fruit Polos, which he peels carefully from the wrapper – and swigging from a bottle of water. I have chosen a bench in dappled shade; others are already out enjoying the full sun. Despite the early hour, there are people sprawled on picnic blankets, half dressed; pretty girls in bikini tops and cut-off shorts; a man with his shirtsleeves and his trouser legs rolled up; clusters of mums with buggies and babies and bottles and snacks; and a homeless woman, spread-eagled on the grass, a sparse grey blanket over her, despite the heat, and two discarded bottles of beer by her feet.

This morning a man on the radio said the heatwave is expected to go on for at least another three weeks.

'How's the view?' Dad asks. We've been here about twenty minutes.

'Good,' I say.

'You can still see the whole of London?'

'Yes.'

'New elements to the skyline, though,' he adds. 'The Shard, the Gherkin . . .'

'The Shard's on your list,' I say, hoping we don't get that far.

Dad nods. I feel guilty that he can't see the view. I feel guilty that I don't really want to be here and I don't want to go to the other places on his list. For some, the thought of a father and daughter wandering round London together would be rather wonderful; charming, almost. For *this* father and daughter, it's a challenge and a pain in the butt. At one point on our walk up here, Dad stumbled against me when he hit a bumpy paving stone and we both nearly staggered into the road like drunken rugby players on a pub crawl. And we're not exactly having *fun* or anything, are we? We are anti-fun. We are fun repellents.

We sit for a while, saying nothing. Eventually, Dad says, 'You can breathe up here. Is it busy? Are there lots of people here? I can hear children.'

'Yes, Dad, it's quite busy.' I describe as best I can the loungers and the sun-sprawlers and the gambolling toddlers.

He nods. 'People like to get out,' he says. 'In the summer. It can be so stifling indoors.' *Why do you never open the window, then?* I think. 'It's good to get away from the day-to-day,' he adds.

I don't agree with him about the day-to-day. I *like* the day-to-day. Doing nothing. Going nowhere. I like being in the flat so I can distract myself with the internet and social media and TV and music and movies. I don't want to breathe and think too much, out in the open air, but, 'Yeah,' I say.

'We sit in that flat too much, you know, you and me,' he continues. 'We should force ourselves to go to every place on that list, even if it kills us.'

It might well do, I think. 'Of course, Dad,' I say. 'Whatever you want.' Why isn't he grumpy today? Why isn't he saying, 'Let's go home now'? Is it simply because he wants to try again, like he said?

He takes a big breath of non-stifling, fresh air. 'This is quite nice,' he adds. 'Primrose Hill. Being amongst nature is nice.'

'Do you want to hug a tree?' I ask him.

'No, I don't want to hug a tree,' he says. 'Do you?'

'No, *I* don't.'

I don't even want to be here.

There's a blast of music in front of us, as a woman in shorts and T-shirt – mid forties, recovering from the school run? – accidentally turns her radio up too high. She turns it back down and waves a quick apology to us, before flipping on to her back and putting her face in the full, scorching sun. A basking iguana.

We carry on sitting for a bit. I look at the woman with the radio. She has wrinkles she has probably enjoyed gaining. She looks ordinary for her age. How I'd love to look *ordinary*.

'Are you too hot?' asks Dad.

'No, you?'

'No.' He unscrews the nozzle of silver paper he's twisted the Fruit Polos wrapper into and offers me one, which I take.

'People,' he says. 'People always say the same things to me.'

'Like what, Dad?'

'Like, "Bless you." Like, "How long have you been like that?" "How many fingers am I holding up?" And they're waggling their hand in front of my face – well, I presume that's what they're doing . . . That sort of stuff.'

'People are bloody idiots.'

'Or they talk too loudly, as though I'm deaf as well, or they say stupid things like, "You're my hero." Did people stare at us in Camden?'

'All the time, Dad.'

'Did you mind?'

'No,' I lie.

'You can't control other people,' says Dad. 'The only thing you have control over is yourself. How you react. How you deal with life.'

We haven't dealt with it very well, I think. I've never felt like I have any control. We have lived a life half lived. I don't know what to say in response to Dad's comment. All this

70

time I've wanted to talk to Dad – about real things – and now I don't know what to say.

We both fall silent. I gaze out over the London skyline, mesmerized by the top of the Shard catching the sun, like King Arthur's sword rising from the lake. I chomp noisily on my Fruit Polo, splintering it with my teeth, which I know will infuriate Dad as he likes to make his last, but he is pretending not to notice. The woman on the blanket flops on to her front again and fiddles with the dial on her radio, turning up the volume just enough so we get to endure Heart FM, and songs from the charts and a quiz where people have to guess sound effects. People come and people go, gathering up their belongings or plonking them down to create a little place for themselves, on this grassy hill that overlooks the whole of the city.

We sit for another forty-five minutes then we make our way back down, and home.

Chapter 10

It's a truth occasionally acknowledged that a father and a daughter who haven't been out of the house for years, or even much spoken to each other in the last thirty, will not necessarily re-bond over mung bean and Madagascan vanilla pod vegan gluten-free ice-cream.

'It's artisan, Dad,' I say. It's the following Monday and we're at Little Venice, place number two on Dad's London list. We've been here for what feels like days, although it's only 2 p.m. and we left the flat at twelve.

'It's revolting,' says Dad.

'Keep your voice down.' The hipster with the enormous beard who just sold it to us from a hatch cut out of a tiny tin caravan can probably still hear us.

'What would Nonna and Papa say at such an aberration?' complains Dad, as we walk away. 'Even the cone is inedible.'

'They would say it's not real ice cream,' I say. 'They would say, "Come to *Papa Alberta's* if you wanta da real ice cream!"'

'Yes, they would – but not in that terrible accent. And I asked for *vanilla*; heaven knows what this junk is!'

'It's not junk. It's the opposite of junk. It's super-healthy.'

'It's junk,' says Dad. 'Let me know when we pass a bloody bin.'

It's not going too well. The tube journey here was a nightmare; the crowds have been a nightmare. We have been jostled and bumped into; three people have tripped over Dad's cane; one has trodden on my foot; and a small child scooted between us on a pair of Heelys (which I'm not sure are even a thing any more) as we walked, Dad holding on to my arm, as though we were some kind of human arch at a skate park. We've walked up and down and looked at the boats. We've had a lunch of falafels with tahini sauce from a market stall. We've trudged backwards and forwards along a row of identical white-stucco four-storey mansions while I've made a fist of describing them to Dad and he's corrected me on my naming of several architectural features. Actually, that bit was all right. We were in the shade and there were fewer people gawping at us like constipated guppies.

We're now walking, with our ice creams, away from the hipster ice-cream seller in his shiny metallic food cart and towards an area of shade on the walkway adjacent to the canal. My scoops are wobbling precariously on their gluten-free cone. I remember, when I was a little girl, I was always dropping ice creams, often in the middle of the street, and Dad would never get cross with me but always buy me another one, and when I finished eating he would pull a big blue hanky from his trouser pocket and wipe my face laughingly with it.

'Let's sit here,' I say, guiding Dad to a picnic table that is half in mottled sunlight and half in the shade. I take the shade and both ice creams, depositing them in a nearby bin.

Dad sits down and exhales, stretching his legs in front of him. The waterway is busy this afternoon. Multicoloured houseboats are lined up along the edges of the canal. Dozens of them – I try not to think about houseboats, or friends with green scarves, or Polaroid pictures. Instead, I concentrate on a pleasure cruiser gliding down the centre, people in hats and sunglasses gazing out of its windows. Barges creep along the water, owners at their stern or bow looking as happy as people ever might. An approaching vessel startles by, sounding its horn. A woman sitting astride a barge that is coming the opposite way and heading languidly into its path shouts for a 'Cliff' and a Cliff appears from below deck with a rope in one hand and a beer in the other, and springs into action with what I believe to be a rudder and a do-or-die spirit. The two barges are saved from near collision with nary a cry of 'Easy mate!' and a couple of sharp intakes of breath between their owners.

'Argy bargy?' asks Dad.

'Almost,' I reply, and we are both in grave danger of cracking a smile.

'It's very busy,' says Dad. 'I came here a lot as a boy. And your mother and I used to walk here from Clerkenwell.'

'Did you?' I can't imagine him and Mum walking round here, looking at the boats. I can't imagine them doing anything I haven't seen in photographic evidence or viewed through the prism of my own memory.

'Yes. She liked it a lot here.'

'Right.' I don't want to talk about her. He never usually does either. But maybe he is flicking through the photo album of his memory, selecting images he likes. Does *he* like it here? I wonder. He hasn't really said. There has been a lot of grumbling and complaining. A lot of sighing. Still, we're here. We're out again. Without accident or incident, so far. Except revolting ice creams.

Another barge sounds a jovial horn. A child shrieks with delight at an over-enthusiastic dog. And a dragonfly levitates into view and hovers over Dad's thigh.

'Oh, a dragonfly,' I say.

'A dragonfly?' says Dad. 'Describe it to me please, Prue.'

'Oh, OK. Well, it's blue and it has four wings and—'

'What shape is it?'

'It has a long thin body, like a pipe – it looks too long for its wings to ever be able to hold it up. The body is bright blue with black markings. Its wings are almost see-through. They have veins in them, like leaves.' I've never looked this closely at a dragonfly before. It really is beautiful close up.

'What else?' Dad is frowning, like he is trying to imagine.

'Well, it has a blue head like a motorbike helmet and a bulbous sort of blue body underneath and . . . that's about it, really.'

Dad listens and nods. The dragonfly hovers for a minute then helicopters off, back to the canal.

'It's gone now.'

Dad nods again. 'That was a good description. You did a lovely picture of a butterfly once,' he says, 'when you were a kid. Didn't you win a prize for it?'

'Yes, I did,' I say. I liked art. As well as the benefits of it being a quiet activity in school – heads bent over desks, less bullying jibes – I liked the pencils and the charcoals and the pastels and the paints. I liked the way a brush wet with cobalt blue or vermillion red felt when it was stroked on to cartridge paper. How colour and lines transformed a blank paper into something new.

'You were a talented kid. So was Angela. All that craft stuff.'

'That was mainly her. All that terrible jewellery we made from those sets she got for Christmas,' I say. 'That weaving loom . . .'

'Yes, that's right. Some of that stuff was good!'

'Ha, hardly.'

'Well, I thought so. Remember that necklace you made me wear for a week, with the purple diamonds on it?'

'Yes.' I can still remember the smell of the glue. How we pushed those plastic 'jewels' into their metal clasps and folded the tiny claws around them. It was a necklace we would have made for Mum, had she still been around, but we gave it to Dad and he accepted it with laughter and good grace. He even wore it on the school run.

'Remember how every Christmas, you girls would go to Nonna and Papa's a few weeks before Christmas and plough through her Grattan catalogue? Write huge long lists of all the things you wanted?'

'Yes. Angela's lists were always way longer than mine, though.'

'She wanted a lot out of life.'

'Still does.'

We both smile.

'Great kids,' adds Dad, shaking his head.

'Yeah, we both used to be all right,' I said, and we were back then, when we were young – despite the abandonment, the sadness, the motherlessness . . . We all used to be a kind of all right.

'And you're not now?'

I shrug. 'I don't know.' Well, I do. Angela is both remote and imperious and I am a damaged soul, aren't I? An ugly adult, no longer able to hide behind whatever cuteness of childhood I could once muster. A flattened survivor of things I hadn't asked for. A willing and stupid victim of unrequited and unreturned love, with a cupid's arrow still sticking out of her back. Someone who is guilty of things both big and small.

I'm being dramatic, I know. It's a gift.

'You should take up art again,' says Dad. 'You were good at it.'

'Nah, I don't know,' I say. 'I don't think so.'

'Really?' He pauses. He pauses for quite a long time. Anyone seeing him from a distance would think he was looking out over the water, contemplating life. 'I'm scared, too,' he says finally. 'I'm scared all the time.' Where has this come from? I never said I was *scared*. And his words come across as purposely flippant, dismissive even. He doesn't *sound* scared. 'I guess we just have to keep on keeping on,' he adds. 'Take it one step at a time.'

'I guess so.' I look out across the water. I see the dragon-fly again, hovering by the flank of a houseboat. It hesitates, then levitates away.

I should be asking him if he really *is* scared and why – what I can do to help? I should ask him to talk to me, really talk to me. I don't believe he is as flippant as he sounds. I don't believe in his dismissiveness, or mine. But we're not there yet, are we?

Dad stands up, stretches out his shoulders in a giant shrug, turns his face towards mine. 'Anywhere we can get another ice cream?' he says. 'A normal one?'

'Well,' I say, looking around me, 'I think I can spy a Mr Whippy van over there.'

'Splendid.'

When we get home, Dad walks straight over to The Palladian window and opens it wide.

'Dad!' I exclaim. 'You've opened the window! Are you going to let your hair down on to the citizens of Chalk Farm?'

'No, just getting a little air in,' he says.

Progress, I think. We are no longer stifling. This is progress. I'm quite unnerved, I realize, at the thought of Dad being scared. I mean, yes, he's blind. Yes, he gave up on life when the guide dogs were no longer there to help him with day-to-day living. He's reclusive, elusive, shut down and shut off. But *scared*. I don't like the thought of it. People like Philippa are scared. People who are despairing are scared. I'm glad we brushed past the moment, shrugged it off. I'm not ready for such a moment with Dad.

I also think about the other things we talked about. After dinner – a delicious Tuscan stew with ciabatta bread and a leafy green salad – I wait until Dad nods off in his chair for an early-evening nap, then I go to the tall cupboard, reach under the photo album, and get out my paintings.

It's one of my secrets. I've been painting for about fifteen years. Portraits of Dad, mostly, as he sits in his chair, sometimes awake, sometimes sleeping. Sometimes a small smile plays around his lips as he uses his Braille reader. Sometimes he looks like a grumpy child, in repose. I try to capture the essence of him, his personality, his Italian-ness; what makes my dad my dad. I have other pictures I'm working on. Sketches. Line drawings. Faces I've copied from magazines. Faces that don't even exist, only in my mind. I've kept my brush-in-water-pot jangles and swishes – lovely sounds I haven't dared make – to a silent minimum. I haven't hummed as I've worked, or accidentally dropped any lids of paint tubes on to the floor. My painting has been a very hidden pursuit and I feel guilty – for the subterfuge and for the voyeurism, in particular – that I've sat painting my father and he's been totally unaware of it.

I haven't wanted him to know. Yes, I know he can't see my efforts, but he would have encouraged me to show someone and I haven't wanted to. They're not good enough.

I think that as I look at them again now – twelve or so portraits of Dad, in pencil, or oil paint, or watercolour, and the other sketches and paintings I've done. I look at them critically, each and every one. They're just not good enough.

I put them away again. Under the photo album in the tall cupboard. Some things we don't mention. Lots of things we keep hidden away. Still, it's a hobby. And a woman who sits in a flat for years on end doing bugger all needs a hobby.

Chapter 11

'Bloody hell, Dad, this is amazing!'

'I told you it was beautiful!'

'Yeah, but this, this . . . How come I've never heard of this place?'

'Not a lot of people have. It's one of London's best kept secrets.'

'But you remembered it.'

'Of course I remembered it!'

It's Wednesday. We nearly didn't come here today. To St Dunstan in the East. We were all ready to head out the door – me in a chambray sundress that has never seen the light of day; Dad in navy chinos and a black Fred Perry – when Dad said, 'Why are we doing this, Prue? I don't want to go out today.'

'Why not?' I said. 'You were looking forward to this – Dunstan in the Whatsit . . .'

'I'm not sure I can face it,' he said, hovering in the doorway and looking anxious. 'London, the crowds, the whole bloody *difficulty* of getting anywhere, Prue.'

He's scared, I thought. He told me he was scared and he is.

'Well, I think we should try,' I said perkily. It threw me, seeing him like that. I didn't like it. But I knew, suddenly, that I wanted to stick to Dad's list, to see it through, step by step. I knew we had a long way to go. I knew the road was going to be difficult, and stressful, but we were taking those steps, one at a time, and we were talking more, too. Just a little. I felt panicked at

79

the thought of that stopping, of us going back to the way we were.

'I don't know,' he said.

'Let's go. We've got water and we can pick up a few snacks en route, and we can stop any time we like . . .' I am trying to jolly him out the door. 'Let's go, Dad.'

Dad sighed. 'It's just so hard,' he said, his hand on the door frame as though he were about to pivot himself around and go back to his chair.

'I know. I know it is. But let's just go, shall we? See how we feel. Please don't be scared, Dad.'

I said it. The 's' word. I said it softly and I meant it kindly, to be received with a comprehension that I was being understanding, receptive, cajoling. But did Dad see it as a challenge? A hurdle to overcome? Something in him seemed to shift.

'OK, we'll see how we feel,' he said, letting his hand fall from the door frame. 'Let's go.'

'Good boy,' I replied.

He was quiet on the walk into Chalk Farm station. He was quiet on the tube. He was quiet on the sunny walk from Tower Hill to St Dunstan in the East, a beautiful courtyard garden flanked with the windowless remains of the tower and spire of a medieval church – destroyed by German bombs in the Second World War. Fairy-tale ivy trails run rampant over the Gothic window arches and blackened white stone edifices. Trees – rising unbidden and unchallenged between paving stones and ancient cobbles, their curious branches winding between the defiant arches and pillars – seek the sun. Peonies crouch in sprawling clusters and count themselves pretty in wild flowerbeds. It is the most secret of secret gardens and it is beautiful.

As we stepped inside, down a series of stone steps, and I gasped at the beauty of the place, Dad clutched at my arm.

'Is it still the same, Prue?' he asked me, almost frantic. 'I need to know it's the same!'

I described it to him, everything that I could see. Every detail of the blackened walls and the arches and the ivy. Every intricacy of the Gothic windows – proud and resolute and beautiful – as best I could. I told him about the Japanese tourists sitting in the stunning glassless stone frames and taking photos of each other. Of the couple entwined on the grass in one hallowed corner – a tangle of denim and white T-shirts – both reading books but reaching up to kiss each other at intervals. Of another couple, arms wrapped round each other, taking a selfie by the semicircle of benches in the courtyard.

'A place for lovers,' Dad says to me now, as we continue to walk slowly around the gardens. 'The most beautiful place in London.' He is serene now he knows it's just the same. He is smiling. 'The Great Fire of London got it first,' he adds. 'In sixteen sixty-six. Then the Nazis, of course. But beauty remains,' he says. 'Beauty remains.'

I look over at the face of the pretty girl in the corner reading Iris Murdoch, as she lies in her boyfriend's arms. His face when he looks at her. *This place is magical*, I think. An enchanted space that London keeps as its secret. A dream. It's for people like her. This girl. Beautiful, youthful, loved by somebody and full of her *own* dreams, who the universe nods at with a smile and sees to it that they mostly come true.

I see Philippa's face, in my mind – in that lace-effect photo – so beautiful and now gone from this earth. I fleetingly allow my mother's face to enter my thoughts – a flimsy, fragile image, sweet and smiling and (mistakenly) lovely, from my very early years – before banishing it. And then there's my own face. Beauty doesn't remain if you've never had it in the first place, I think. If you've never possessed it, you won't get to see it fade with the years, as life and sunlight gradually take their toll. Women like the one with the radio on Primrose Hill – whose every wrinkle is another day sipping from an oversized glass of pinot grigio in a beer garden or an afternoon on a 'hot lips' beach towel in Benidorm, while reading a James Herbert – get to see it fade. I just see my birthmark. Every day. In the mirror.

'Shall we?' says Dad. He takes my arm again and we carry on walking. Birds chatter in the trees intertwined with stone. A child laughs as a father places her inside a vacant window arch. I feel entranced but disquieted in this damaged but beautiful place, this relic that stands prettier than ever for its imperfections. It's clearly having an odd effect on me.

We walk. We walk around and around, and Dad trails his hand over the draping luxuriant ivy and we accidentally disturb a kissing couple half-concealed by foliage on a bench, and the man drops his giant pack of crisps and Dad says, 'Whoopsie,' and fumbles to pick them up and everyone laughs, and we walk and I describe everything to Dad and we walk some more. I think that I may never have seen this place, had Dad not shown it to me. And I would not have seen him look the way he does today. He looks almost happy, and I feel the merest glimmer of hope; a tiny shard of light piercing the darkness of our lives, that now we are out here, now we are talking, we could change our lives a little. Get closer. Throw off some of those chains that held us in The Palladian for so long. Will the list be a good thing, after all? I really don't know, but we'll see where it takes us, Dad and me. Maybe we could get there.

'Hello, Bertie.'

Dad and I are standing under the engraved stone architrave of an arch and I am looking up at its intricacies as

Dad explains Gothic medieval architecture to me. I freeze. I keep my eyes on the arch. The voice says, 'Hello, Bertie,' again.

Alberta – Albert – Bertie. It was a nickname that didn't take long to conjure up. It was a nickname I had loved. I daren't look behind me, where the voice is coming from. It sounds so strange to hear it, after all this time.

'*Bertie?*'

I still don't turn around. I am cursing myself for conjuring him up somehow, when I let that Polaroid fall from the photo album. I shouldn't have looked at it. I shouldn't have let my eyes fall on his face. I shouldn't have thought about him since. And remembered how it was.

I daren't turn around, but I have to.

'Hello, Kemp.'

Kemp. The boy I knew at school; nicknamed by Third Year consensus after both of Spandau Ballet's Kemp brothers for his zealous New Romantic phase – frilly shirts, pointy boots, the lot – showcased mostly at school discos, where he danced alone in corners. The man who is a brilliant photographer: landscapes, people, sunsets. Who spent most of his time at school holed up in the dark room of the Art Department. He's still one of *National Geographic*'s most in demand. He has a camera on him now, looped from his shoulder in a suede bag.

'I thought it was you.'

I haven't seen him for seven years, but he looks almost exactly the same – dusty jeans, work boots, a T-shirt boasting where he's been on his endless travels – Big Sur, apparently. Dishevelled was *always* his thing, when I finally became his friend, ten years ago, long after the New Romantic frills of school: scuffed boots and never-tucked-in-shirts and a series of terrible jackets even an Orwellian tramp would refuse, but it suited him. It still does. Today he is proper salt-and-pepper grey, weather-beaten around the edges; his face is craggy and crinkled, above a new and surprising beard, but when it crinkles into a slow smile those lighthouse eyes glow, just like they always did.

'How are you?'

'Good, thanks, really good, and you?'

I don't want to look him in the eye as I don't want him looking *me* in the eye. He is still beautiful; I am still ugly. Am I shaking? I hope I'm not shaking.

'Great, thanks. Just getting a few shots of this place. Isn't it amazing?'

'Yes, it is,' I say. I've tried not to think of him for the longest time, but I have. I always have. Kemp is why I can't listen to one of Bonnie Raitt's greatest hits. Kemp is why I don't like looking at houseboats or going to Camden or green scarves. Kemp is why I hide that Polaroid where I can't see it because if I see it, I'll remember I loved him. 'What a surprise.'

'This place, or bumping into me?'

'Both,' I say.

He smiles at me. I am shy. I am knocked sideways. I am suddenly and irretrievably in what is commonly known as a right old state. It is him and he is here. He is just the same. I *feel* the same, which is terrible. As I am still me. Not pretty. Not right. So far out of his league and romantic interest I'm on another continent, perhaps one of those he has roamed to, camera in hand. In the heat and dust. Far from anyone.

'Hello, Vince,' Kemp says to Dad, reaching out his hand for Dad to shake it. 'Kemp. Nice to see you again.'

'Likewise,' says Dad. They met a few times, why wouldn't they have? Kemp was my friend.

'We're on a day out,' I say. I am definitely trembling, on this fiercely hot morning, in my chambray dress, and hope to hell Kemp doesn't notice.

'Great,' he replies. 'Beautiful weather for it. It's nice to see you both. It's been a while,' he adds, looking at me in such an open, friendly way I want to bury my face in the ivy and leave it there.

'Yes, it has.' I want to avert my eyes, but I can't help drinking him in; his face, his hair, his biceps in that T-shirt. The chickenpox scar near his left eye I always had to restrain myself from stroking gently with my finger.

'Sorry I haven't been in touch.'

'What?' It was *me* who ghosted *him*, before it was even a thing. Who stopped returning all texts and phone calls. Who turned my face away from him for the safety of my heart. 'Don't be silly,' I add quickly. I can't read his face. Is he teasing me, because he knows it was me who dropped contact? Or is he just being Kemp, guileless and lovely, and sorry he hasn't been in touch when it's me who should be apologizing to him?

'You've been busy,' I add, which sounds stupid and like I'm accusing him of something, but I just mean I've seen his photos in magazines and that I've examined the small-print credits for his name and got that *feeling*, when I've seen it.

'Yeah.' Kemp laughs. He was always laughing. He had the kind of laugh that lit up his whole face and could go on for an hour, at a joke he'd heard three days before and was attempting to retell you. He pushes a reed of salt-and-pepper hair out of his eyes and tucks it behind his ear. 'I'm doing OK.'

He's still wearing those leather bands around his wrists. He's still got that silver necklace with the tiny half-pearl shell on it. He's a laid-back man. Handsome, ordinary, extraordinary. Like if the boy next door grew his hair down to his collar and got sexily scruffy and looked you in the eye one day, over the fence, in a way that suggested he not only knew all the dark contents of your soul but was going to have a go at dragging them into the light.

If only.

'Good,' I say. 'Good.'

'So, how are you keeping, Vince?' Kemp asks Dad.

'I'm keeping well,' says Dad. 'Prue here is taking me round London for the summer.'

'Fantastic,' says Kemp. 'One of the capital's best kept secrets, this place. I can't believe I haven't discovered it before.'

'Don't tell anyone about it,' says Dad.

'Ah,' says Kemp, with another laugh, 'better destroy my photos, then.'

Dad laughs too. He always did like Kemp. Not as much as I did, obviously.

The laughter hangs in the air for a while then, inevitably, fades away. We're left with nothing. Silence and regret – all mine – hang between us like a gossamer hammock. I feel I should break it, but I don't know what to say. What *could* I possibly say, after all these years? What *should* I say that won't give away how much he meant to me?

The silence goes on far too long.

'OK, well, nice to see you,' Kemp says eventually.

'And you.' I am brisk, pleasant. I can't look at him any longer.

'Really nice to see you,' he repeats. 'Bye, Vince.' He turns, shakes Dad's hand again, then turns back to me. 'OK, then.' He gives a small shrug. Runs one hand through his hair. 'Bye, Prue.' And, with a quick smile, Kemp bounds away from us, his camera swinging at his hip, and up the stone steps of St Dunstan in the East and out of my life again.

'Bye,' I whisper.

'Good to see him again, after all this time,' says Dad. 'Nice bloke. A good friend of yours, wasn't he, at the time?'

'Yes, he was.'

'No romance, though?'

'No, Dad, no romance.'

Of course there was no romance. Dad is forgetting who I am.

'Right, then,' he says, clapping his hands. 'Seen enough? Shall we go for a little wander around the area? Maybe head up to Monument?' He sounds so uncharacteristically *chirpy*.

'OK,' I say. I don't mind. I'd quite like to walk around a bit more. I'd like to clear my head, but I don't think I can – not now. All I can see is Kemp. All I can *think* is Kemp.

We come out of London's best kept secret and turn on to St Dunstan's Lane. We head towards St-Mary-at-Hill and Monument Square.

'Oh, I can see that couple again,' I say. 'On the other side of the road. The ones with the crisps.' They are still kissing. They have their arms round each other's waist and are kissing in an ungainly, grinning manner as they walk. The sort of kisses people would die for.

'That was very amusing,' says Dad. 'Are they in love, do you think?'

St Dunstan in the East has had a weird effect on Dad, too, I think. I glance at him and he has an odd look on his face. Contemplative. Lost somewhere, somehow.

'Yes, Dad, definitely in love.'

We walk up St-Mary-at-Hill in silence. Traffic is light and there are not many people around in this business district. They are all at work, like real people.

'You know . . . this is not what I wanted for you,' Dad says suddenly and rather quietly, his hand on my arm as we walk in tandem.

'What do you mean?' I ask him.

'This life without love.'

I want to stop walking but I carry on. I don't want to draw attention to the catastrophe of his words. *Please don't go there, Dad!* I cry to myself. Don't talk to me about love.

Not when I have just seen Kemp. Stop talking about people in love and all the things denied to me, and to us.

'That's very serious,' I say flippantly. 'Is this the Italian family thing?' I ask. 'The pressure to get married, have loads of bambinos, be in an apron by my age, well on the way to Nonna status, feeding everyone?'

'No, I don't mean all that,' he says. 'I mean *love*. Proper romantic love. Love for you in your life. It would be lovely for you to have someone. You need someone. You need a relationship. I wish you would open your eyes and see who's out there.'

'I don't need a relationship!' I protest. 'I don't need anybody! And there's no one *out there*, Dad! I've looked.' Yes, I've looked and I couldn't have who I saw and who I *loved*. 'And I'm quite bloody old now – it's all a bit late.'

'I'm sad for you.'

'Well, don't be! I'm all right, I promise you. Love is overrated, anyway.'

'Is it?' he asks.

'Why have *you* never dated again?' I ask. He's been without romantic love for a long time, too, I think. All that time since Mum. And, although I have asked him this before, I wait for his answer to see if it's different from his usual reply – that he 'can't be bothered'; that it would all be too much 'fuss and nonsense'.

'Well, I'm blind,' he replies. He has answered with this before, too. Sometimes I have said, 'So?' Often he has shrugged and changed the subject.

'I don't know,' he adds carefully. 'I suppose I was so disillusioned with the whole notion of it that for such a long time – after your mother – I simply didn't have the energy, and all the energy I had, I poured into you girls, which I don't regret for a second, by the way.'

'No,' I say. This is a new answer. And he's mentioned Mum in it, which is surprising.

'And then time just went on,' he adds. 'I became blind and time just went on.'

We walk. A bird clatters out of a tree wedged between two buildings and soars into the sky. Yes, I reflect; after our mother, *everything* changed. For Dad and for Angela and for me. Her absence sliced something into us that we then had to gather round, to fill. We had to be *more* than the gap she left, the three of us. We tried so hard to be, for a long time. To put all our energy into filling that giant, mother-shaped hole. 'But still. There might be someone out there for you now. You never know.'

'It's all a bit late,' Dad echoes, 'and we were talking about *you*.'

'Love is overrated,' I repeat.

There's a road sweeper on the pavement in front of us so I tell Dad we need to cross to the sunny side of the street. A white van waits for us to cross. We walk with the sun in our faces until we get to the junction with Monument Street. I'm sad I've just lied to Dad. I'm sad because love is not overrated at all. I know what it is and how much it hurts when you love someone who can never love you back. And I don't need to open my eyes to romance. I don't want to. I've seen who is out there and he can't be mine and never will, and now I've seen him again – this beautiful man in my memory and my heart, who I now have an up-to-date vision of to torture myself with – I feel a hollowness re-open in my soul that I know has the danger to swallow me alive.

'Thank you,' Dad says finally, as we stand by the column of the monument to commemorate the Great Fire of London and he has finished telling me of its provenance, of Christopher Wren and Dr Robert Hooke, who designed it. 'Thank you for bringing me out today, for forcing me out of the door. St Dunstan in the East . . . it's magical, isn't it? Did you think so?'

89

'It's one of the most magical places I've ever seen,' I reply. And I feel gutted, as gutted as the ruined church and its tower, destroyed by bombers in the Second World War, except part of it still stands (the beauty remains) and I have nothing still standing, just my memories of the past and the pain of the present and how much I hate myself for not being someone else, anyone else, who might be loved.

Chapter 12

Summer 1975

My mother left us when I was five and Angela was three. Dad was two years into his architecture degree. He told us, at first, that she'd gone away for a while on a 'little holiday'.

'And when will she come *back* from her holiday?' Angela had asked. Dad had picked us up from school and nursery – which was a surprise – and we'd had a snack of digestive biscuits and a Nesquik chocolate milk, and we were clinging on to Dad's legs once he'd told us about Mum's Holiday – like street urchins – while I patted Angela on the back with a consolatory hand. I'd overheard Dad on the phone to Nonna about an hour and a half before and had caught the words 'flighty' and 'hated to be tied down' and 'struggled with everything', amongst many more in Italian. I knew they were talking about Mum. Hadn't she told us herself how she'd run away from home three times as a child – with a cheese sandwich, an apple and a clean hankie in a tin lunchbox, each time – and once from school, one Thursday lunchtime, to go and watch The Beatles' rooftop concert at Savile Row?

'I really don't know,' Dad said, and that was that, for a while, but later I began to see my mother as a character in a series of vignettes – or as one of those cardboard dolls you cut out from a book and put paper outfits on by folding tabs around them – because every time she came back to us, she was a slightly different version of herself.

A month after she left – which to us had seemed like a lifetime – my mother breezed in as though she had just popped out to pick up a pint of milk; if popping out for a pint of milk involved a complete change in image and a personality transplant. Gone was the quiet but increasingly sullen mother who, in unremarkable clothes that smelled of Bold washing powder, unenthusiastically made us fish fingers, instant Smash and peas, followed by butterscotch Instant Whip. In her place was a laughing imp in flared jeans and a T-shirt that said 'Love' and showed her tummy; who had frizzy, crimped hair and a giant butterfly on her forehead courtesy of a pale blue bandanna, and who smelled like herbs. It was like our old mum had put her finger in an electric socket – something she had always shouted at us not to do – and had become a super-charged Mum, all lit-up inside.

Dad kept staring at her, as we all kind of stood around in the sitting room. He stared at her so much I thought she would laugh and say something funny to him, but she didn't. She only really talked to us.

She brought us a Sherbet Dip Dab each. I didn't even like Sherbet Dib Dabs but she seemed to have forgotten that. I licked the sherbet off carefully, trying not to let my tongue touch the liquorice. We were all sat on the sofa by then and Dad sat behind us, on a chair he'd brought in from the dining room, although there would have been room for him.

Mum had not really been on holiday. She'd been at her friend Janice's in Hoxton, she told us, not in France or Africa, places in my junior atlas I had imagined her exploring, in a big hat. But she wasn't coming back to us! She said she was sorry, but she wasn't! (Everything this new Mum said was in giant exclamation marks.) She was now going on a tour of Europe! *Europe!* In a van! She was breathless, her eyes were all wide and bright. Didn't we wish for her to have a lovely time?! She would miss us! She would send us a postcard! She got up from the sofa and squeezed Angela and me in a joint hug and the herb smell was even stronger and I didn't like it, and then she went out the door, blowing silly kisses at us, and the frayed hems of her jeans brushed the floor and reminded me of the brushes Nana Larry had on the bottom of all her doors.

After she had gone, Angela and I shrugged miserably at each other and Dad said a midge had flown into his eye and he had to get a tissue and then he put the tea on and he let us have Cherryade.

There were no postcards from the European tour. I did them myself, after a while. I went with Dad and bought a pack of blank postcards from Woolworths with my pocket money – for school, I said – and I drew a sun on the front of each, or a boat, or a beach umbrella and carefully pencilled silly things like 'I miss you' and 'Having a grate time!' on the back, in a childish approximation of our mother's handwriting, and stuck them through our letter box in secret. For Angela.

There were no postcards, no nothing, until 1977, which was when she next manifested.

It was summer again. Our mother's skin was tanned and she had a short dress on with weird and wonderful patterns all over it and leather flat boots that went up to her knees and had laces that criss-crossed up, like Eskimo boots. And her hair was even frizzier and she had a headband round her forehead and she looked very tired. She still laughed and smiled a lot, and she hugged us when she came in, but this time we sat on the sofa with Dad – with him in the middle and his arms round us – while she sat on a dining-room chair and stretched her Eskimo boots out in front of her.

She brought us a paper bag stuffed with Black Jacks and Fruit Salads, and she wouldn't stop talking. She told us she had been to lots of different countries and had been to music festivals and how much fun it had been and maybe she would take us to one, too, one day. And that she missed us so much and she would come and see us the next day, definitely. And she talked on and on, and after a while Dad got up from the sofa and started folding up some laundry he'd left in a basket, although he had already folded it, and then she left and Dad shut the door with a bit of a bang and Angela started to cry.

The next evening, when we had eaten all the Black Jacks and the Fruit Salads and the paper bag was in the bin and Mum hadn't come back again, Dad said, 'We'll get by,' or something like that.

We were sitting in a huddle at the bottom of the stairs and he had one arm round each of us, like Neptune with two wriggling fishes on his knees. Angela was wearing the crown she had made at school for Easter a few months before. It had cardboard Easter eggs stuck on to each point; she'd saved it – desperate to show it to Mum – but Mum had put her brown crochet bag on it, on the hall table, when she'd come, and squashed it.

'We'll manage on our own,' Dad said. 'I've got the pair of you, and you've got me. My love is going to be as big as a mum's and a dad's put together and it will wrap you up like an enormous blanket and we'll be safe and warm because we'll be together.'

'How big will that be?' asked Angela, her eyes all wide and her crown all crumpled. 'That love?'

'Well, as big as a blanket,' said Dad. 'I've just *said*.'

Angela frowned. 'That's not that big.'

'OK,' said Dad. 'As big as the *moon*. How about that?'

And we had a huge hug, where Angela and I pressed our faces into the warmth of his soft cotton T-shirt and Dad clasped his big, warm hands around us nice and tight.

In 1981, Mum came back as a punk. A rather startling one. I mean, a pair of ripped jeans scribbled on with a black biro, patent pointy black boots with buckles, a T-shirt with swinging chains and a black leather jacket proclaiming 'The Damned' on the back in white emulsion was not quite the look I expected from my mother, after the four long years since she last came to see us. She stood shaking in the doorway with a studded collar thing round her neck, which made her look like a scary bulldog we once saw on the school run; her hair was dyed burgundy and cut short into rock-hard spikes and she had a *lot* of black make-up on.

I was wearing a bra for the very first time. Lots of girls wore one already, in my new secondary school, and boys, with the unintentional goal of proving their immaturity by attempting to refute *yours*, found it hilarious to constantly ping the back of your blouse to see if there was a strap there. As I was laughed at enough already, I asked Dad for the money to buy a *Fame* rah-rah skirt, but instead went to Marks & Spencer on Oxford Street and bought myself a lightly padded teen bra, despite having next to nothing to put in it. I wondered if Mum would notice I was wearing it, under my Depeche Mode T-shirt, but I don't think she did. She didn't really notice us at all, and Angela and I spent most of the visit staring at *her*.

She was nervous, coming in, as she'd heard on the grapevine (I wasn't sure what kind of grapevine wound its way into the 'squats' of North London – not that I knew what they were – but Dad said she was living in one) about the 'whole blindness thing', as she put it, and she didn't know quite where to put herself.

'Oh, Vince,' she kept whining. 'Oh, Vince, I'm so sorry.'

She quickly became a very broken record. She repeated herself over and over, one whiny 'sorry' after another layering up, until the sitting room was a nauseating fog of them and Dad snapped, 'That's enough, Ellen!' She then became fascinated by Dad's first guide dog, Sunny. We'd had her for two months or so. She was amazing. Mum kept saying 'Awww' and 'Oh, would you look at her?' and 'Bless her little heart!', until I wanted to snap, 'That's enough, Ellen!' too.

Apart from that, Mum didn't have much to say. She didn't ask us how we were. She didn't ask me about my new school or how bullying the kids were, on a scale of one to ten (about a nine and a half), or about my bra. She just prattled on a bit about her new 'man', Dave, and how he was taking care of her in a little place on the Old Kent Road, all the time staring at Dad. How she was going to go down the Job Centre and get a job, just as soon as they got a permanent address; how she would soon be getting herself 'sorted' so she'd have the 'energy' to be in our lives more (how much energy did it take to be a mother? I wondered) and wouldn't that be great?

'You really can't see *anything*, Vince?' she drawled. Then, when he said 'no' – his face all set and weird-looking – she wheedled another, 'Aww, you poor thing', like Dad was a very old dog that was about to be put down. Eventually, she slouched after Dad like a punky scarecrow into the kitchen and there was lots of whispering and a loud, 'Oh clever, you! You know where the *kettle* is, Vince!' The kettle boiled but they didn't come out holding mugs of tea. Dad looked angry and Mum scuttled out the door, after flinging two packets of Flying Saucers at Angela and me and blowing us theatrical kisses.

We didn't see her again until 1984. There was only one more vignette to come. One more memory. One more character popped out from the book of her life, of which we knew so little and which she so absolutely wanted to keep us from reading, or even looking at the pictures. She remained a series of paper dolls to Angela and me: thin and without substance, unable to be pinned down or held on to; a papery wisp of a mother who fluttered in a wavering slipstream of her own design, always out of reach . . .

Chapter 13

I'm wearing a beautiful boho dress I bought from *Loved Before* last winter – another item acquired in a fit of imagining a lifestyle I don't and won't ever have and a dress I admired long before I felt brave enough to wear it. It's maxi length with an off-the-shoulder neckline – floral print. It's probably too young for me, but there you go. I look OK in it, if you squint your eyes quite tight and ignore the birthmark squatting above the dress, like a demon. If you don't squint, I probably look like a blemished Nana Mouskouri – and if you remember her then you're as old as me and there's no hope for either of us.

Dad and I are off to Covent Garden. The escalator at Chalk Farm is out of order so we take the stairs.

'Thirty-four spiral steps then a turning platform then twenty more flat ones,' says Dad and he counts them as we descend, his cane tap-tapping and his hand on the railing.

'How do you remember all this stuff?' I ask him.

'I just do,' he replies.

On the platform, the air that whooshes up the tunnel is hot and dry. As we walk to an empty space in order to wait for the train, Dad takes in a long deep breath of it, like he is actually relishing the thick, underground pollution filling his lungs. He seems cheery this morning. He wasn't scared on the threshold, before we came out. He seemed raring to go. Perhaps he is buoyed by our trip to St Dunstan in the East. Perhaps he is just getting used to being out in the world again.

'Eight stops to Covent Garden,' he says, 'changing at Leicester Square.'

The next place on the list. One of the busiest places in London. Even on a Monday. The tube we squeeze on to is sardined and crazy hot. Covent Garden tube station is absolutely packed. When we arrive, there're a million people choking the cramped barrier area: tourists; families with multitudes of swerving, meandering kids; people waiting for people or saying goodbye; gaggles of teenagers with bags over their shoulders, shouting at each other as they all have headphones on; a blind man and his daughter, just trying to make our way through them all, without injury, and out on to the street.

We turn right out of the station and head down to Covent Garden. James Street is also swarming with excited pedestrians and punctuated with those human statues: metallic frozen centurions and rigid Victorian ladies with parasols; a static, silver ballet dancer with fierce calves, sitting on a stool; a motionless Laurel and Hardy, in bronze. Each has a circle of gaping people around them, staring and staring, willing the spray-painted bodies to move and trying to get them to blink.

'The same as ever?' asks Dad as we walk down the street.

'Pretty much.'

I try to remember the detail he liked when I described the dragonfly. I try to be inventive, creative for him.

'There's a mass of people,' I say, 'hundreds of them, all ages. There's a lot of backpacks, shorts, vest tops, sandals. Some sunburnt shoulders. There's a man on rainbow roller-blades coming towards us. He's wearing a ginger wig and a huge pair of comedy headphones.' Surprisingly, the man high-fives me as he sails past; I actually slap my hand with his, then wipe it down my dress. 'There's a couple kissing outside a shop – why's everybody kissing all the time?' I move on – I don't want Dad banging on about love and romance again. 'A homeless woman asleep in a sunny doorway, inside a brown sleeping bag.' *Poor lady*, I think. *I wonder what her story is.* 'Just to our right is a man painted silver wearing a bowler hat and carrying a briefcase. He looks like he's running, late to work or something – one arm in front, one arm behind, one leg forward. He's really good. People are trying to make him laugh but he's not budging.'

'Remind me what a briefcase looks like,' says Dad.

'Oh, well, it's rectangular. It has a handle on the top and a fold-over flap with a gold clasp on it.'

'Yes, yes,' says Dad, his face creasing in concentration. 'Thank you. You're beginning to really see things, Prue.'

'Am I?' I answer.

'Yes. Open your eyes, *cucciolo*. Open your eyes and see what's out there.'

'Is this about men again?' I ask wearily. I won't think about Kemp, I just won't; I've done enough of that over the past few days. The new, weather-beaten, bearded Kemp; battered and chiselled by all the sun and wind and rain that has fallen on him since I last saw his amazing face. I have pushed him from me. I have shoved him inside that hollowness in my soul and plonked a paper bag over his head. And Dad has called me *cucciolo* – it means pup, or cub, or baby animal in Italian. A term of endearment. I may sound weary, but actually I am delighted.

'Possibly,' says Dad.

I nudge into him a little, kiss my shoulder against his. 'I'll try,' I say, just to humour him.

'Good.'

Ahead of us is the covered market, now a series of small shops. We came here quite a lot as kids. Before and after Dad went blind. The guide dogs always created quite a flurry. At the market we turn right and head for the grey stone square in front of St Paul's Church. People are lounging on the shallow steps, standing in clusters, shielding their eyes from the sun, guzzling from bottles of water, laughing and enjoying the afternoon. Crossing the square. Are we in a lull between street performers? There's always something going on here.

'We're at the square now, in front of St Paul's Church, Dad,' I say. 'It's very busy.'

'It doesn't feel quite so hot,' says Dad.

'The sun's gone behind a cloud.'

'I can't hear anyone performing.'

'No, it must be between shows.' We stop. I scour the square. 'OK, I can see a spot for us.'

We don't want to draw attention to ourselves; we want to blend in, if that's ever possible. We head towards the fat ribbed columns of St Paul's Church. We sit on the steps behind the 'stage' of the stone slabs; Dad stretches out his legs, places his cane parallel to them, I tuck mine underneath me, wrap the material of my dress around them. Adjust my sunglasses. A woman with loads of shopping bags plonks herself down next to Dad and gives him a warm smile he cannot see.

The sun pokes its head out from behind the cloud. A distant police siren wails. From his vantage point on the balustraded balcony of the Punch and Judy pub opposite, an early drinker holds a pint of beer aloft and gives a random whoop. I scan the crowd. A few people start chatting, gathering their things, making to move off . . . then there is a shout.

'It's OK, it's OK, I got this!'

Heads turn. To our left, at the far end of the church front, there's a man atop a unicycle, clinging to one of the stone pillars. His legs are paddling wildly; he's clutching the pillar in hilarious fashion. Children in the audience start to point and laugh.

'Don't take photos now, for goodness' sake!' he tells a woman with her phone in the air, which elicits a laugh that ripples round the crowd. The sun is fully back out and the audience is up for fun.

'What's happening?' asks Dad.

'A man on a unicycle clutching on to a pillar pretending he's terrified,' the woman next to Dad tells him.

'Ah.' He smiles and nods. He really does like to feel the sun on him, I think. He is positively *basking*.

The performer is lurching, pretending to almost fall. He is grinning his head off and lapping up all the laughter. 'OK, OK, I can do this!' With a shriek he lets go of the pillar and launches off into a wide circuit of the performance space, holding one arm outstretched like a preposterous Shakespearean actor, before collapsing back on to the pillar with an exaggerated sigh of relief. He recovers himself, eagle-eyeing the crowd as he does so.

'It's OK, madam, I think you've mastered the selfie stick!' he calls across to a woman pouting at herself in a magenta kaftan, who sheepishly puts her stick down.

'I think I'll do it again,' he says, setting off on another circuit. 'It's good to re-cycle.' There's a groan and a laugh, a few claps. He goes one way, then he goes backwards, his feet spinning on the pedals. He skims close to us – very close – before he returns to the pillar again. For just a second he makes eye contact with me and I blush. He looks exactly like his photo.

'What's he doing now?' asks Dad.

'Hanging off the pillar and pretending to be in trouble,' I say. There is more laughter, high-pitched giggling from children.

'What does he look like?'

Hmm, what does this man, Salvi Russo – for I know it *is* the man I saw on poor Philippa Helens' Facebook friends list – look like in the flesh? 'Er . . . he's not that tall, he's a little stocky, he has a slight bald patch at the back of his head, big expressive eyes.'

'Big expressive eyes . . . ?'

'Yes,' I say distractedly. I'm staring at them right now. There's a proper glint in them. 'He looks cheeky,' I conclude. Salvi is wearing black trousers, a clean white shirt and a waistcoat striped in purple and gold. He wears shoes that look like bowling shoes. I can see there's already quite a lot of money in his collection hat, lots of notes, overlapping the edges. People can't take their eyes off him and neither can I, which is quite surprising.

He comes away from the pillar now, forwards and backwards, pedalling like he is treading water. The sun has gone in again, behind a large cloud overlaid with grey.

'I need someone to come and help,' he calls out. 'Who would like to come and help me?'

About twenty-five hands shoot up. There is laughter amongst the crowd as most of the hands belong to women. He swivels round on his unicycle.

'You. There. The lady with the fringe and the long dress.'

Among all these people, he's looking straight at me. I freeze. I look behind me, desperately seeking another fringe but there isn't one. Oh God, *I'm* the lady with the fringe and the long dress.

'Yes, you.' Salvi is smiling above his waistcoat. He has a hand tucked in its front pocket, like Napoleon. One of his cheeky eyes gives me a wink.

I hesitantly point a reluctant finger at myself like a small child. Why me, for bloody hell's sake? There are hundreds of people here!

'Yes, you, with the terrified expression. Would you like to come up?'

'I don't know,' I say.

'Come on.' It's not a request but a command.

Dad looks amused and says, 'Go on then, Prue,' and,

like I'm hypnotized – because I really don't want to do this – I stand up, cross the ancient paving stones and turn to face Salvi Russo, the street performer. The sun has disappeared completely now – the sky a smattered grey and white lid above me. There's a breeze playing with the hem of my skirt. I wish my fringe was four inches longer.

'Where are you from?' Salvi is twinkling all over the place. His smile lights up his face, like it did in his profile photo. I do declare he is charisma on a unicycle.

'Chalk Farm.'

He grins. 'Ah, you have travelled far, my friend . . . Who are you here with?'

'My dad,' I say. God, I sound about twelve.

'The blind guy!' shouts out Dad, waving his cane in the air, and I am both astonished and mortified. What is he *doing*? Why is he bringing attention to himself like this? People are laughing and smiling at him. The woman with the shopping bags is in raptures.

'Nice to see you, sir!' calls back Salvi.

'Can't say the same!' Dad shouts back. Seriously, has a bit of sun turned the man into a deranged wise-cracker?

Salvi grins. 'Come a bit closer,' he says to me. Reluctantly I take four steps forward. 'What's your name?'

'Prue,' I say. 'Prudence.'

'Well, you're far too sensible for this, then,' he says. Only a few people laugh. Only a few know what 'prudence' means, I bet, and even fewer would remember the 'Dear Prudence' of The Beatles, the song my not-so-dear-departed mother named me after. '*Prue*. Nice name,' he considers. 'OK, Prue, I need your help. I want you to throw those three clubs up to me in turn.' In front of me, in the centre of the circle of people, are three juggler's clubs: orange and white in wide stripes.

'Club number one, please. Throw it to me.'

I walk towards the nearest club and go to pick it up.

'No, club number *one*, I said. That's club number three.'
The crowd laughs: of course, they are all identical.

I pick up the club and throw it, badly. He catches it.
There's a whoop from the crowd.

'Club number two, please.'

I pick one up. 'This one?' I say.

'Yes.'

'Are you sure?'

It's his turn to laugh. 'Yes, Prue.'

The way he says my name makes me feel something
quite unsuitable for my forty-eight years. I throw the club;
he catches it and juggles the pair of them, in front of him,
to a twirling rhythm. The crowd start to clap in time.

'Club number three.'

I throw the final club to him. The sky is graphite now,
above us. I feel a little chilly in my dress. Salvi juggles all
three clubs while treading water on the unicycle; pedals
spinning, that one wheel going backwards and forwards.
I wonder again how this man knows Philippa. Then I
wonder how long I should stand here for. Should I go
back and sit down? I look over to Dad and he is talking to
the woman with the shopping bags. I start walking slowly
to the edge of the performance area so I can make my
way back to him without too much of a fanfare.

'Where do you think *you're* going?'

I halt, contrite, and glance at Salvi, who has stopped
juggling and holds all three clubs in one hand. He is pinning me to the spot with narrowed eyes, eyebrows raised.
He is shaking his head in mock condemnation. I bite my
lip and know I probably look sheepish and stupid. A
caught-out schoolgirl. Then his face breaks into a grin
and he winks at me.

'*Naughty*,' he says and this cheeky reproach – so unexpected, so inappropriate, so *saucy*, even – plus the grin
and the way he is looking at me, sparks something inside

my body and my soul I'm not even sure I could quantify without sounding all unnecessary. I sense, I *see*, rather, here under grey London skies, amongst this crowd, an *edge* to this man – razor sharp and coal black, glittering almost – that pierces through my skin at this moment, like a slice of life that could be fully and exultingly lived.

'Watch,' he commands, and I am rendered as frozen as one of those metallic human statues, staring, spellbound, while Salvi finishes juggling the clubs, with a flourish, and turns to me again.

'Now you can be excused,' he says, and – there – the spell is broken. Did he *really* just call me 'naughty'? 'Thank you, Prue. Take a bow.'

I give a sarcastic little curtsy. I scoot back to Dad, who is clapping enthusiastically. 'Excruciating,' I say as I sit down, trying to hide under my fringe.

'It was fun,' he replies.

'You don't like fun.'

'Maybe I do,' he counters. 'Maybe I remember how it goes.'

After a few seconds, I dare to peep out from under my fringe again. 'Oh God, Dad,' I say, 'he's getting the fire sticks out!'

Salvi has a lighter in his hand and is up on the unicycle, lighting the third of three charcoal-grey fire sticks, two of which he holds in his mouth by the unlit ends. Their flames, caught in a heightening breeze, lick up towards his face, which he angles away. When they are all aflame, he takes each out of his mouth in turn and begins to juggle them, to another slow hand clap from the audience that gets louder and louder and quicker and quicker as the skies darken and darken. There's another loud police siren – it segues into a distant rumbling of thunder. Faster, faster, louder, louder. The orange flames leap and tumble; the sticks fly. Dad is joining in with the clapping and so am I. The rhythm of it is infectious. There's a louder, rather ominous clap of thunder and the crowd 'oohs' in mock horror, like we're at a firework display.

And then comes the rain. A sudden sheet of it, from nowhere; there were no fat warning-drops darkening stone slabs or plopping on bare forearms. It sweeps over the heads and the hats and the caps of the spectators and the tourists. Salvi jumps down from the unicycle. People clamber up with their backpacks and their carrier bags and their bottles of water and dash for shelter. We clamber up, too, and Dad grabs for the back of my left arm, at the elbow. We head for the covered market along with a hundred other people. We are swept along in a colourful sea of squeals and horrified laughter. A man presses against me. I feel Dad's hand release from my arm. I am pushed sideways, by a different man. He is wearing an orange T-shirt and has an American accent. He is yelling at some woman about 'fish and chips'. Where is Dad? I feel I'm about six people away from him now, maybe more – is he counting how many steps he has been pulled away from *me*?

I try to turn against the tide but the tide is strong; people weren't expecting to get rained on today, they are not dressed for it and they want shelter. Where *is* Dad? I can't see him. All I can see is bags and shoulders and arms and shorts and jeans and hair and people's backs. I trip on something, oh shit, how ridiculous – I'm falling! I hold out my arms to break my fall, see a flash of someone's ankles in bright red socks and then there is blackness.

107

Chapter 14

There's something on my eyes, something on my face. I'm sure my eyes are open but I can't see anything. I blink. A synthetic material brushes against my eyelids, it is cool and scratchy. I'm flat on my back, I realize. Laid out like a kipper. I wriggle my toes and my fingers; everything seems to be intact, although I appear to be half-submerged in a puddle.

'*Pardon*,' says a voice – French, if my C-grade O level serves me correctly – and something navy blue and plasticky is lifted from my face. I see a Hello Kitty fluffy toy swinging from a key chain, as a backpack goes floating up in the sullen air and on to someone's shoulder.

'I'll see to her. *Grazie.*'

A face appears in front of mine. Huge, amused eyes the colour of fir trees, wrinkled at the corners. Long eyelashes. A handsome mouth curled into a smile. A nose that looks like it may have been broken, once upon a time. If I flick my eyes down (and I don't want to), I know I will see a flash of purple and gold.

'Hi. You OK?'

'Yes.'

I sit up. I'm a few feet from the shelter of the covered market. I scan the crowds of people, all huddled under the archway. 'Where's my father?' I immediately ask.

'He's fine. He's over by the Moomin Shop being chatted up by a couple of pensioners.'

I follow the line of Salvi's pointed finger and yes, there is Dad, indeed surrounded by women – more than a couple, actually – who are talking animatedly into his face and clutching on to his arms. I wonder if they followed the golden rule of Approach, Introduce, Offer, like you're supposed to with blind people. Perhaps they *offered* to talk his ears off . . . Dad has his head thrown back and he is laughing, a sight I haven't seen for a long, long time. I'm so surprised to see it.

'We got separated. He's blind; we can't get separated,' I say.

'Here, let me help you up.' Salvi holds out his hand to me, closes it tightly around mine and pulls me up. The touch of his hand is confident, assured; so confident it borders on audacity.

'I'm Salvi,' he says. 'Salvi Russo.'

I know. 'I'm Prue,' I reply, although he already knows this.

He doesn't let go. He keeps his hand tightly around mine as he begins to guide me over to the Moomin Shop, and Dad. The rain has stopped as abruptly as it began. The sun is beginning to make itself known again, shy after its defection.

We're walking through all the people. We're getting some looks. Does it look weird that the Covent Garden street performer is pulling the show pony he drew from the crowds *through* the crowds? Will they think *I've* pulled? They must think I'm very lucky if I have. Close up, Salvi is still not handsome, but he has *something*: something magnetic, sexy; something that makes you want to never take your eyes off him. I try not to glance at him as often as I am.

'Your dad is not that old,' Salvi says, as we approach the Moomin Shop. He is smiling at me, his eyes casting themselves over my face and my body.

'He had me young,' I reply. 'At sixteen.' I wonder if Salvi is now calculating my age or whether it is announced on my face like a calling card. I also wonder about my birthmark. It has been rained on and had a Hello Kitty backpack scraped across it – is it still covered?

'Oh, right. Sixteen . . .' He nods and throws me another smile. 'And you're very pretty.'

'Shut up!' The words escape me like air. My impulse reaction. My knee-jerk.

'Shut *up*?' His eyes are sparkling at me. I shrug. I have never been called pretty in my life. Not once. Never. He can't possibly be sincere. 'It's true,' he says.

'Whatever,' I reply. 'I'm here, Dad!' I say to Dad as we come to a stop in front of him. Salvi is still holding my hand.

'I'm being entertained,' says Dad, smiling in the direction of my voice.

'Again?' lilts Salvi. 'Your daughter was flat on her back with someone's bag on her face,' he adds, and I am reminded of the boys at school always saying they would need to put a bag on my head, in order to do anything with me. 'She fell, in the scramble for shelter. I'm the juggler. I rescued her.'

'Entertained *further*, then,' says Dad. 'Are you all right, Prue?'

I hold out my free hand – Salvi still has the other one – and squeeze Dad's. 'A bit of a wet bottom, but yes, I'm fine. You?'

'Right as rain,' says Dad. 'I knew you'd find me. And there was no point me looking for *you* . . .' he jokes. 'These kind ladies escorted me to safety.'

'We can take you for lunch, if you like,' says one of the women, broad New York accent. 'You and your daughter. There's a fantastic Italian here.'

'That's a very kind offer,' says Dad, 'but we cannot impose, thank you.' Apart from looking briefly horrified at this suggestion, Dad appears perky; what's left of his hair is flattened by rain, but he has an animated look on his face I also haven't seen for a long time: an almost raffish air. It makes me want to giggle, suddenly. 'Prue and I have a table booked at Pizza Express,' he fibs.

'Only the best for us,' I quip.

I turn to look at Salvi and he is staring at me intently. I realize the wrong side of my face is closest to him. I want to get my hand and place it right over my cheek.

'Thank you,' I say to him, 'for helping me up.'

'Damsels in distress can never be ignored,' says Salvi. 'Or a pretty lady.' I wish he would stop saying that. 'So, I have to go now. It's been really nice meeting you,' he adds, still staring at me. 'Can I have your number?'

'What for?' Knee-jerk, again; that metaphorical knee is busy today.

Salvi looks amused. 'So I can call you. We could go out sometime.'

'Go out? Where?' Men don't ask for my number. Men *never* ask for my number.

'A bar, a restaurant, you know, like people do. Please may I have it?'

I fight the urge to look behind me again. For another woman with a fringe. Why is he asking me out? What does he want with me? *Really?*

'Yes, really.'

'Oh, for heaven's sake, give him your number,' says Dad. 'I'm starving and I want to get going.'

'You could be a serial killer,' I offer.

'I'm not a serial killer,' says Salvi, both mock wearily and with another wink. 'Honest. I just like the look of you.'

Those fir-green eyes are dancing. That smile curls at the edge of his lips. Would I be contemplating saying 'Yes' if he wasn't so mesmerizingly magnetic? Would I be thinking about saying it if he hadn't said I was pretty?

111

And wouldn't I be saying 'No' if I didn't feel that somehow, when my eyes opened, *there he was . . . ?*

'OK,' I say. I open my bag and scribble my mobile number on the back of the receipt for a bottle of water and a packet of Extra Strong Mints. Salvi folds the piece of paper and tucks it into the tiny pocket on his waistcoat.

'I'll call you,' he says, and I feel suddenly foolish and think, *Yeah right.* Just because Dad has been asking me to open my eyes to the world and its possibilities and I opened them and he was there, it doesn't mean he is going to call me. Just because I quite fancy him doesn't make him a man standing in what's left of my future, smiling on some kind of shimmering horizon. I fell prey to thinking that once – that there could be a man who held my happiness in his hand, like a throbbing heart. There wasn't.

As Dad and I walk away, his hand on my arm, I can still feel Salvi watching, those eyes boring into my back. We walk through the multiplied crowds, back past the silent human statues painted gold and silver and bronze, as the revived early-afternoon sun dries rainwater shallows on the cobbles and translucent speckles on shop windows. Dad's cane is suddenly magical: crowds part as it taps its path.

'I enjoyed that,' he says.

'Me too,' I say, 'apart from landing face up in the gutter.'

'*We are all in the gutter, but some of us are looking at the stars,*' say Dad.

'I know,' I say. 'Oscar Wilde.'

'It *was* fun,' he adds. 'Fun is something I wasn't sure I'd ever have again . . . you know?'

'I know, Dad.'

Dad has basked in the sun and been funny and *found* things funny and I have taken part in a street performance

112

with all eyes on me, and while I was lying in the gutter I looked up and saw Salvi. I can enjoy a little bit of hope, can't I? I can imagine there *might* be a shimmering horizon, somewhere, one day, for me ... That there is light and there are stars, with my name on them. And if that horizon and those stars dissolve to nothing, as they inevitably will, can't I enjoy this moment, when they are the flicker of a possibility?

'Are we nearly there?' asks Dad.

'Where, Dad?'

'The tube station?'

'Yes, we're here now.'

I have a sense, as we enter the tiny ticketing hall and shuffle with the crowd towards the entry barriers, that things have changed since we came through them earlier today. Shifted a little. I feel, for the first time in years, on the margins of hope. But hope, just like pride, can come before a fall. I'm not counting on the rogue mirror to the left of the barriers, a frameless square – pitted and dulled – which lurks as unconcerned passengers, their blank faces only to be written on by the afternoon, pass by. I don't reckon on catching my eye in it and realizing, with a jolt, that *I* can never be unconcerned. This waiting trap is not so pocked and murky that I can't see my concealer has been erased by both the Hello Kitty backpack and the rain. I am not so blinded by shiny new adventures that I can't witness, in this sudden looking-glass ambush, the streak, the flash, the burn of my birthmark – indelible and always there, no matter how I try to hide it.

Chapter 15

I had a sewing box when I was a kid, which Nonna bought me one birthday. It was hexagonal and had a creaky raffia lid with red and orange raffia flowers embroidered on it. She laughed when I unwrapped it, said she thought it was pretty and you never knew, I might find it useful. I had laughed, too. I wasn't really a sewing kind of girl. Crafts that involved sticking things? Yes. Cutting doll's hair into harsh asymmetric bobs? Yes. The contents of this box – everything a girl who likes sewing might need – went unused. Sorry, Nonna. But I found a purpose for that sewing box. I wrote secret notes to myself which I folded into small squares and hid under the soft material needle book and the clanking reels of cotton and the plump Japanese lady pincushion.

Some were in the form of questions: 'When will some-one love me?' (I meant *boys*, of course. My father loved me a lot, I knew that. His love was like a warm jumper I never wanted to take off.) 'Will it ever happen to me?' (Really bad pop song territory.) 'Will I ever be beautiful?' (A question with an absolute answer.) Sometimes they were whimsical statements, written in red or green, by one of those pens where you slide bars down to get dif-ferent colours: 'When I fall in love I shall sink like a stone.' (Terrible.) 'One day, the light of love will shine on me.' (Excruciating nonsense.)

I'm thinking of these embarrassing notes when the first of two surprising things happens on the journey home from Covent Garden. The first of the surprising things starts when the doors open at Oxford Circus and four men get on the tube, already grinning as they leap on board, a quartet of fizzing energy. They have instruments strapped to their fronts – a violin, a trumpet, an accordion and a set of spoons – and a square black box, which they place on the floor between the two sets of doors. The man with the spoons turns a knob on the box and, with a whine and a twang, the recognizable opening bars of 'La Bamba' strike up and the four men launch into it with great exuberance, the man with the spoons slapping them on his thighs and enthusiastically providing the vocals. It sounds great. I've always hated that song; it was one of three songs guaranteed to clear me from a dancefloor when I was a teenager: the other two were Lulu's 'Shout' and Phyllis Nelson's 'Move Closer'. Particularly that last one. Slow dances. Ugh. Dad used to come in with all the other dads to stand in the corner of the hall ten minutes before discos ended, despite all my pleading – the only father who couldn't see that *I* was the only one not snogging a boy in the middle of the dancefloor.

A few of my tragic notes were written after getting home from these soul-scouring school discos. The pen with the different colours would come out and I would scribble my questions, my hopes and my dreams, and secrete them at the bottom of the sewing box, far from anyone's eyes. Anyway, these men make 'La Bamba' sound bouncy and brilliant. Even the most hard-hearted tube-goers can't help but smile. The carriage is literally rocking.

The surprising thing is that Dad's foot starts tapping. There it is, Dad's right foot, in black Adidas Italias, tapping in time to 'La Bamba', on the floor, next to his cane. I look from the foot to the men with the spoons and the trumpet and the violin, then back again, and I smile too. It's some kind of miracle.

The second surprising thing is when I look at my phone just before we rumble into Chalk Farm station, there's a text there from Salvi.

Lovely to meet you, Prue. I'll call you tonight.

I should really believe this is some kind of joke. I should really believe that it *hasn't* been lovely to meet me, that he *won't* call me tonight. But I want him to. I want to imagine that he'll call me, that we'll go out, that he'll banish the returned ghost of Kemp; that I might fall in love and *sink like a stone*. I may not have my little notes any more, my dreams, however stupid, locked up in that sewing box, but I still keep them inside me, under the sharp needles and the clacking cotton reels of my hardened heart. It would be lovely to think this isn't a joke.

I put my phone back in my bag and Dad and I get off the train at Chalk Farm. The platform is empty. A crisp packet, whipped up from somewhere by the hot wind of the tunnel, flies up the walkway and grazes him in the face, on his right cheek, but he doesn't scowl; instead, he laughs, my dad laughs. This has been a good morning for him. I really do believe he has enjoyed himself. The lifts are working now and we glide up to floor level, the blind bloke and the daughter who has a text on her phone from a sexy street performer called Salvi, who hopefully isn't joking.

There's a third surprising thing. When we come out of Chalk Farm tube station, Kemp is on our street.

'Hello,' he says cheerily. He is slouching against the oxblood tiles just outside the Stop n' Shop, munching on what looks like a Crunchie ice cream.

'Hello,' I say suspiciously. 'What are *you* doing here?' I wasn't expecting to see him again. I don't *want* to see him again. What is he doing here, on our street?

116

'You look nice,' he says.

Hardly, I think. I've been flat on my back in a stampede. I'm hot and bothered. And when have I *ever* looked nice? 'So do you,' I say, to throw him. He does, though. He's wearing the ubiquitous jeans and boots. A 'Caracas' T-shirt. Scruffy and handsome, as per. I can't let it throw *me*.

'I knocked on your door, but you weren't in.'

'No, we're here,' I say. 'I mean, we've been out.'

He nods. 'Although, thinking about it, it's not like you haven't got form for not opening doors . . .' he says with a grin. I ignore him. 'Where've you been?'

'Covent Garden.'

'Nice,' he says. 'All right, Vince? How's it going?'

'Good, thank you,' says Dad. Somehow he seems to know Kemp is holding out his free hand to him, and they shake hands. Dad is smiling. He likes Kemp and is probably happy bumping into him again. I am not. The very sight of him is the undoing of me. 'Well, a bit tired, actually. It's been an entertaining morning.'

A silly part of me hopes Dad will mention I met a man this morning, and that he asked me out, then I realize this would be totally embarrassing.

'It's always really busy there,' agrees Kemp.

I'm looking at Dad; I don't want to look at Kemp. I have to look back at Kemp.

'You've got ice cream on your beard,' I say.

'Oops!' He wipes his chin with his hand. 'Gone?'

'Gone.' This exchange feels way too intimate. Like we're still good friends. I once wiped sauce off his chin with a napkin, in a restaurant, just like Dad used to wipe ice cream off mine. It felt natural, nice, even though I had wanted to lean forward and kiss him. I hate that I still have that urge, looking at him now. That I just want to kiss him.

117

'Oh,' he says, reaching into one of the back pockets of his jeans with that same free hand, 'this is that Diane Arbus biography you lent me.' He hands me a rather battered-looking paperback and reaches back into his pocket again, 'and this is one of your socks. You left it in the houseboat.'

'Oh,' I say, surprised, staring at the blue and yellow sock in his hand. '*Seven years* ago? You should have just chucked it.'

He shrugs. 'It's nice. It has stripes. I thought you might want it back.'

'Oh, right. Well, I don't have the other one any more so . . .'

'I'll chuck it,' says Kemp with a grin, tucking the sock into his front jeans pocket. He stands and looks at me. At Dad. Then back to me. 'Hey, did you get caught in that rain shower earlier?'

'Yes,' I say, running my thumb along the top edge of the paperback. I wonder why Kemp is talking about the weather again. We never talked about the weather or remarked how 'busy' places were. We talked about movies and television and art and photography and politics and life. He said he liked to hear my opinions on things, that I often had a different slant, and these different *slants* made him laugh. But I don't want to remember all that. He mentioned the rain shower, so instead I think of Salvi.

'Dreadful, wasn't it? Still we needed it – well, the grass did, anyway.' I look at him, bemused. What grass? 'Well, I won't keep you,' he says, popping the last bite of ice cream in his mouth and screwing up the wrapper in his hand. 'I was just passing and thought I'd say hi.'

'Well, hi,' I repeat, as though I didn't once secretly give this man my heart.

'Do you want to get together sometime, Prue?' he asks me quickly. 'For old times' sake?'

'No,' I reply, equally quickly. 'No, not really.'

'Prue!' scolds Dad.

'Oh!' Kemp laughs, surprised.

'How rude, Prue!' says Dad. 'And why are you saying "No"? You two were really good friends once upon a time.'

'Once upon a time was a very long time ago,' I mutter. 'People change. Things move on. Sorry if I sounded rude,' I add, like a child.

'Have *you* changed?' asks Kemp fixedly. 'Because I don't think *I* have.'

'Of course I have.' I shrug. 'Like I said, things move on, don't they?'

'Well, that's a shame,' says Kemp, and he looks at me in an odd way I can't read. Well, maybe I can read it. Maybe he needs a friend again. I *don't*. 'Would be a shame to never see you again, Bertie.'

'OK, well. Right, let's get you in, then, Dad. Time for lunch and a cuppa,' I say briskly. I can't look at Kemp any more and I don't want him looking at me. I need to get away, *again*.

'Maybe I'll bump into you again!' calls Kemp as I bustle Dad away and Kemp mooches off down the street, hands in pockets. 'See you!'

'Bye,' I call feebly and Dad and I stand at the doors to The Palladian and I rummage for my keys, and I wish and I wish and I wish for no more *bumping*, not from him, as – despite rain showers and Salvis and promised phone calls and eyes open – my stupid heart cannot bear it.

Chapter 16

Dad is tired tonight. He declines a leftover portion of his delicious tiramisu and a mug of frothy coffee, after dinner. He closes his eyes in his chair in front of the window I opened without his objection, and I gently take his headphones and put them on the table. He doesn't even stir when the phone rings.

It's Angela.

'Hello?' Her voice is shrill and chirpy, as clear as a bell. My 'hello' is a muffled trumpet, muted by pasta and tiramisu and blunted by waiting for my mobile phone to ring all night.

'I said I'd call back and here I am!'

'Here you are.' *About two weeks later . . .*

She sounds sunny and light. It speaks volumes, our tones, our light and shade. My unblemished, unburdened sister, brightened by love and Nova Scotia. Living her happy ending. And me, lumbered by life and insecurity.

'What have you been up to?'

A silly question, usually, and one she always twitters at me, but I could actually give her quite a good answer today. *Dad and I have been to all sorts of places around London and today we've been to Covent Garden and I've been asked out by an actual man.* I can't be bothered, though. And if he doesn't call, it won't be true. 'The usual. Nothing,' I say.

'OK. Warren and I have just bought a new swing set for the yard. The kids are out in it now. Adorable.'

'Wow,' I say. I have no idea what a swing set is. 'Great.' Angela always sounds so *free*, I think. She shrugged off the burden of Dad and me, let it fall like Dick Whitting-ton's knapsack to the ground, and ran. She made herself a man out of clay, in those pottery classes, fashioned it just how she wanted it and pressed herself against him to make an indelible impression. She has children – part of her, out there in the world. Well, in her back garden, at least. She has everything.

'It's really hot today. Thirty-two degrees.'

'Same here,' I say.

'Oh yes, the heatwave. I can't imagine London is very pleasant in it. It's going to be beautiful here. We're going to the jetty later, off to do some fishing.'

'Fabulous.' Angela seems to go fishing a lot, which amuses me. Another part of her wonderful Canadian life. I notice there's been no 'Thank you', for WhatsApping that crabbing photo . . . 'Actually, Dad and I have been out a couple of times ourselves,' I say, after all.

'Have you? You never go anywhere these days! Out where?'

'Covent Garden today. We went to Camden the other morning, too. And we've been to Primrose Hill, Little Ven-ice and St Dunstan in the East, as well.' Egg that pudding, why not? I think. *She* always does. 'I've been Dad's guide, I've become his eyes,' I say, mimicking Verity Holmes.

'Dunstan in the *what*?'

'The East. It's kind of a secret.'

'Oh, right, whatever. So, you've been out to places. This is astonishing. Has he been OK?'

'Up and down,' I say. 'But we seem to be heading in the right direction. This morning was fun.'

'*Fun?* Wow. Well, that's great. Really great. And so *sur-prising*!' There's a beat. She is obviously digesting this incredible news. 'So, where's next?'

'Liberty,' I say, thinking of the list. We might go in the next few days.

'Oh, right. He used to love that building. He went there with Nonna, or something, one day as a little boy – he told me. And he took *me* there once. I was only about three. One Saturday morning. I got told off by a man for running around.'

'Where was I?'

'Doing something with Mum.'

When was I ever doing something just with Mum? It was Angela who was thick as thieves with Mum, until she left. Angela who cried for her all the time, *after* she'd left. When she went to Janice's. When she went on her tour.

When she moved abroad to *Sweden*, where she's been since 1984 . . .

'Do you miss her?' asks Angela. She asks me this occasionally. I always say the same thing.

'No.'

'Do you ever wonder what she's doing, over there in Stockholm? How she's living her life?'

'No.'

'*I* do.'

'You shouldn't,' I say.

1984 was Mum's first and only visit to The Palladian, but she didn't come in. She slouched in the doorway unironically wearing her own, brand-new 'Choose Life' T-shirt belted over cycling shorts, topped by a curly perm. She'd brought half a packet of Opal Fruits and two Panda Pops and told us she was moving to Sweden, her ancestral home. That she was going to live with her cousin Torge, in Stockholm, the one who sold margarine for a living; that she was going to get a job and try to be a responsible adult.

I was fourteen at the time. I was soon to meet my friend Georgina and go to the fair at Finsbury Park. I had done my spiked hair and high-street make-up but was still in my dressing gown. Dad and I had been dancing to his Roxy Music album, when she rang on the doorbell, my bare feet planted on his slippers and my hands on his shoulders as we danced to 'Avalon' in that familiar father–daughter silhouette, although I was far too big for that, really. I answered the door and she said our old neighbours in Clerkenwell had told her where we'd moved to. That she'd come to tell us her news. I invited her in, but I didn't care that she only slouched in the doorway. I wasn't interested in her grand plans or her fresh start. I was pretty much over her by then – my heart, weary of her absence, had already formed its crust. Angela came and hugged her, she asked if she would write and Mum said 'yes'. Then she said she had to go. She had to make preparations; she had to pack. She asked if she could hug me and I said 'no', then she adjusted her belt, the buckle of which had swivelled round to the right, patted at her counterfeit curls and left.

'Definitely take him to Liberty,' Angela says, as though she hasn't just thrown the 'Do you miss her?' curveball into the conversation, and as though I hadn't told her Liberty was already on the list. 'And what about the gates of the Globe Theatre? Or St Paul's?' OK, now she was taking over. Why didn't *she* come back and do it?

'Yeah, maybe.'

'Oh, you should!' entreats Angela. 'Do make the effort! "Man cannot discover new oceans unless he has the courage to lose sight of the shore,"' she adds. 'Some French person said that.'

'Fascinating.' *Who needs Verity Holmes?* I think. *Who needs a sister like* Angela? My prickles are up. Dad and I both have them, but we're like cogs in a grumpy wheel: our prickles fit between each other's and somehow the cogs keep turning. With Angela, she's so smooth, so sunny, so bossy, I get the urge to dig my prickles right into her, but she's so infuriatingly *resistant*, and probably wouldn't even notice. Isn't it strange how once, a very long time ago, I would have done anything for my younger sibling, but now I want to put the phone down on her and give it the V sign?

Angela started writing to Mum a couple of weeks after she left for Stockholm. We found an address for cousin Torge in Mum's old address book and Angela bought air-mail letters from the post office and she wrote long, long letters to her, giving all her news, but Mum never replied. So, after a while, I intercepted Angela's letters, pretending to post them for her, and *I* replied. I got myself a Swedish pen pal from *Smash Hits* (I specified), I sent Sven a traveller's cheque I bought from Thomas Cook in Islington, so he would send me a stack of 'Stockholm' postcards and some stamps to England and for a year or so I sent Angela a series of postcards in a better approximation of Mum's handwriting but in a similar vein to the previous fake ones I'd engineered: 'I miss you!' 'Stockholm is great!' I couldn't risk longer missives, nor did I have the time. By the time she was thirteen, when she got fed up of the sub-standard responses and stopped doing it, Angela had written twenty letters Mum never answered and I had sent twelve rotten postcards.

'Can I speak to Dad, then?' Angela asks. 'Is he there?'

'Of course he's here.'

I walk over to Dad with the phone. 'Hey ... Rip Van Winkle, Angela's on the phone,' I say, gently touching his arm. His hair is all ruffled. He stirs and looks up at me.

'Ah. Thanks, love.' I hand the phone to him.

'Would you like a cup of tea?' I whisper.

He smiles. 'Are you making it?'

'Yes.'

'No, thanks, then.' He grins. On the small table between our chairs, my phone starts ringing. Dad puts the house phone to his ear.

'Hi, Dad!' I hear Angela cry. My golden sister, sunny and light from far away. I let my phone ring to a missed call; a mobile number I don't recognize has called me. The phone rings again. I wait a little, heart pounding, then I answer it.

'Hello?' Oops, I forget to adjust my tone. I sound as flat as I sounded to Angela. Maybe I need to fashion a big old boot out of the clay Angela made a man with and kick myself up my own arse.

'Hi!' Oh God, I didn't dare hope it was him, but it's Salvi. He's phoning me, like he said he would. 'So, it's the crazy street performer guy here! How are you doing?'

'I'm doing good.' Salvi's tone is upbeat – he's an *Angela* not a *Prudence*, isn't he? I try to sound more perky, to match him, but I am nervous. Really nervous. 'Thank you.'

'You got home OK?'

'Yes, we did.' I like the sound of his voice, through the phone. I like that he is talking to *me*.

'Good, good. So, let's go out? I'm free Wednesday night. Can you get into the West End? Soho? There's a bar on Hopkins Street called the Dickensian – do you know it? Dickens himself drank in there when he was writing *Hard Times*.'

'No, but I'm sure I can find it.' Oh, I'm *so* cool, I think. I could at least have pretended I have *something* else going on. A diary to check, maybe. A *life*.

'Great! See you there, eight o'clock? I'll look forward to it, Pruey.'

Did he say *Pruey*? Despite myself and my nervousness and my indignation at this liberty, I smile. Despite the fact he hasn't actually asked me if I *want* to go to this bar or given me the chance to say 'no', I find myself saying, 'Yes, me too, see you then,' before hanging up and placing my phone back on the table.

I stare at it, as though it's going to ring again and he'll laugh a cruel laugh, whilst lighting a cigarette and blowing smoke coolly out of an open window, or something, and say the whole thing has been a joke. If it doesn't, I'm going on a date for the first time in well, *ever*. I'm going to a bar called the Dickensian on Wednesday night with a complete stranger. I have to make myself look decent, I have to be witty and engaging. I have to be someone who might be of vague interest or attraction to another human being. I'm not sure I can do this! It's all well and good heading off on jolly day trips with my father; any mistakes we make – any stumbles, any falls – are just for us. On Wednesday, if I go, I'll be on my own. Exposed. I'll have to sit opposite someone and have him stare into my face like I'm a bloody show poodle and I don't know if I can.

He's a stranger, a *stranger*. Things with strangers haven't worked out too well for me in the past, especially those I felt attracted to and who took an interest in me. I met a man once on another very hot sunny day, in another country, and it didn't work out well *at all*.

Dad is still talking to Angela but a voice of my own is whispering in my ear, cold and rasping, 'Don't you remember? Don't you remember what happened in Tenerife?' I don't want to remember. I want to forget. Because it wasn't the first bad thing that happened to me . . . But I'll remember enough to be very careful with Salvi. I won't open the door too wide for him, in case he steps in too far; I won't drink too much or get too excited or let my guard drop to a dangerous level.

I pick up my phone again to start looking up the bar he mentioned.

Chapter 17

Salvi is not here. I've been stood up and it's no big surprise. Perhaps the whole thing has been a wind-up. I've heard of pigging; I've read about it on the internet – the girl who flew to Amsterdam to meet a man who'd courted her for weeks, only to be stood up for over two hours and eventually sent a text telling her it was all a joke, as apparently she was hideously ugly. I check my phone for a taunting text, confirmation I am a pig who is the butt of someone's enormous, ugly joke, but there's nothing.

I'm standing in front of what looks like a disused shop entrance in an outfit Maya helped me choose yesterday morning at *Loved Before*, which was very kind of her as it was crazy busy in there and she was dashing between rails and the back room like a beguiling bluebottle, in a silky sapphire midi dress. The outfit is a pair of grey skinny jeans and a glittery sort of drapey top – plus a pair of wedges I've had for yonks. The look I'm going for is not-trying-too-hard glam. Carefree-first-date smart-casual. It's a look I've never attempted before. I'm no Claudia Schiffer but I look OK.

This place is very Dickensian already. I half expect a fingerless-gloved Fagin type to haul up the shutters and scowl at me, or Bill Sikes and Bullseye to come lurking round the cobbled corner, in sudden fog. There is no plaque here saying anything about Dickens or *Hard Times*, though. Wasn't that the book when he referred to school children as 'empty vessels'? The one with the horrible

127

headmaster? I should have a plaque above *my* head: 'Here stands a terrified woman'. Because I am.

My phone chimes with a text. Salvi? He's going to be late, isn't he? Or he's not coming at all. Disappointment stabs at me. I hurriedly check my phone but it's not Salvi, it's Kemp.

> Hi, is this still your number or am I texting a complete stranger?

I stare at the text for a few seconds then bash out a reply. Well, I might as well reply, while I'm waiting. What does he want *now*?

> Hi, yes it is.

> Good! I finally upgraded from the Nokia, you'll be pleased to know!

> Well thank god for that! That thing was an embarrassment!

> Lots of my things were, according to you. My hat, my taste in music.

Well, that was *dreadful*, I think. *Rock ballads and Sade.*

> My batik wall hanging . . .

He adds a smiling-face emoji.

> Ha! I respond. I'm not feeling very *Ha!*, actually. I'm being stood up, probably.

> Anyway, let me know if you want to catch up properly.

There's a rattle and a loud clank behind me and the door next to the shutters slowly opens and a man hurries out, a hipster type: huge beard. I shove my phone back in my bag. The door hangs open, creaking on its Dickensian hinges. Do I carry on standing out here or do I go in? Is Salvi actually already in there, even though I was five minutes early?

I decide to go in and wait for him. I open the door and enter a short dark corridor, more like a tunnel, with moist walls and a weird smell: a combination of beer and beard oil, probably. At the end of the tunnel are six stone steps down to an archway and a podium with a stunningly beautiful girl standing behind it.

'Sorry, love.'

Someone pushes past me, a man in skinny jeans and a tight royal-blue jacket. His eyes alight on me fleetingly, then look away. I step up to the podium and find a list that's being checked with the tapping of a shell-pink nail is far more worthy of attention than I am. I haven't even been stood up yet but I can already feel my self-esteem scuttling back up the tunnel and into the light of the evening, like a rat. Eventually, 'Can I help you?' asks the beautiful girl. She looks like a brunette Bridget Bardot and has eyes like sapphires and smooth, smooth cheeks. She also looks like she has a gone-off haddock under her nose. Am I not the right look for this place? Too Dickensian for the aesthetics, despite the thick make-up I thought I was safe behind . . . ? Am I *Smike*?

'Well, I'm waiting for someone, but I'd like to wait inside, if that's OK.'

'Is there a table booked?'

'I don't know, maybe.'

'Name? Who are you meeting?'

'Salvi Russo?'

'Oh, Salvi,' she says breezily. 'He booked a table. You can go inside and wait.'

She turns, showing me her immaculately pert arse in her tight black dress, and leads me through the archway into a cramped and tiny low-ceilinged brick vault, damp and dusty and cobwebbed, but it's beautiful. There's a small bar set into the open brickwork at the end like a jewel, its optics glinting opal and amber. There are thick stubby candles in alcoves, fairy lights strung from the squat domed ceiling and oil lamps on each rough-hewn table. It's hot down here; womb-like. Romantic and seductive and perfect for assignations between spies and lovers, getting up to all sorts in the glow and the dark.

The beautiful girl shows me to a table.

'Thank you,' I say.

'Someone will be over shortly to take your drinks order.'

She glides off through the vault, watched by a thousand hungry eyes. I perch on a stool and place my bag under it. I have purposely chosen the stool facing away from the room, like I always do, and, as I read the menu, I turn my head every few seconds to check if Salvi's coming in.

It's a young crowd in here tonight. The hipster men are all accompanied by young beauties – giggling and chatting, twiddling strands of hair around their fingers, huddling together for selfies. I see one being taken by two young women and a man in the corner, the phone held high. One of the women has hair like spun vanilla and sooty eyebrows like overfed tadpoles. On her mate's phone she probably has bunny ears and a curtain of exploding love hearts raining down on her. I hate selfies. I have never knowingly been involved in one.

On my fifth head turn, with massive relief, I spot Salvi in the archway. He gives the beautiful girl at the podium a devilish smile and then he is laughing his way into the bar, touching arms and shoulders as he moves through the confined space, charming strangers with what look like gems of banter; gifts bestowed. He's wearing jeans, a tight white T-shirt with some kind of silky scarf tied loosely round his neck. He diverts suddenly and bounds to the corner where he hugs Vanilla Selfie Girl, who beams from the folds of his scarf. She knows him? Then he is off again, making his torch-lit way to me, the middle-aged woman hiding in plain candlelight.

'I'm not late, am I?' His hair is smoothed and parted, his face looks like it has seen moisturizer; he smells of lemons and musk and warm Italian nights.

'Well, technically you are,' I say, looking at the watch I'm not wearing with a bravado I'm not feeling. 'By ten minutes.'

He sits down, draws his stool up close to the table. Examines me. It's only the second time he's seen me. I *must* look better than that first time, when all my make-up was washed away. Now it is painstakingly applied, covering all my sins. So why does it seem like he is looking directly at my birthmark, like some men look at breasts? It's always been the face, with me. Curiosity. Trying to see what lies beneath. Their eyes stripping off all my layers one by one. Scraping off my skin. Gouging a track in it with a jagged nail . . .

'Are you all right?'

'Yes, I'm fine.'

'Nervous?'

Our faces are about three feet apart. I am on a date, on show, on audition: every single thing I say or do will be noted and calibrated, judged against Salvi's internal guide of what he's looking for.

'No,' I lie. 'I go on dates with virtual strangers virtually every night of the week.'

He laughs, his lips so soft-looking I wonder if I will get the chance to kiss them. *Highly unlikely.* 'Have you ordered anything yet? A drink?' He notes the empty table.

'No, not yet. I hadn't decided. I googled this place,' I add, trying to sound light and sparky. 'I couldn't find anything about Dickens writing *Hard Times* in here.'

'Of course he did! It's common knowledge.'

'There's no plaque.'

'You don't get a plaque just for drinking somewhere. He didn't *live* here. Come on, what would you like to drink?'

I scan the menu again, even though I have looked at it ten times already.

'I'll have a Copperfield Collins, please.' Gin. It could be the only way.

He gestures to a passing waitress and she stops at our table. She is very attractive, too. He orders my drink and a beer for himself.

'Olives and crudités?' she asks.

He nods. 'So,' he says, once she has gone. 'Have you had a good day?' I already feel he is just going through the motions. I already feel he is regretting asking me here. 'What is it you do?'

'Do?'

'Yes, you know, for a job?'

I should have prepared for this question. I should have prepared an answer for it so I don't sound like an utter loser. 'Nothing. I don't work. I'm sort of my father's carer.' Ugh. I hate that this falsehood rolls off my tongue so easily.

'Oh, it seemed like he can look after himself quite well.'

'Well, he can, but I just need to be there, you know?' *God, I'm boring*, I think. And I can't tell him the truth: that I gave up work because I wanted to run away from life; that I retreated from the world just like my father – but without his excuse – to sit on my backside and do nothing. I can see a great big cross hovering over Salvi's checklist as it is. 'How was *your* day?' I ask. 'Were you at Covent Garden again?'

'No, I was at the Old Bailey.'

I'm surprised. 'What, outside?'

'No, inside.'

'What, with the *unicycle*?'

He laughs again. His big green eyes dance and I feel warmth radiating off his skin. 'No, with a bunch of files and a wig. I'm a barrister; the street performer stuff is just something I do on the side.'

'Oh!' My view of him instantly shifts and he acquires a new, glossy layer – the sheen of stiff card; corporate, expensive. 'You're a barrister,' I repeat, like a total imbecile. 'You're a barrister as well as a street performer?'

'Yep, criminal defence – the street theatre is a nice release for me. In between defending serial killers. Well, this week it's a rapist. But I should get him off.'

'Oh, right.' I gulp a little, wishing I already had my drink. I fiddle with the food menu in front of me, picking at one corner. I'm trying to take this all in. He's a barrister who defends serious criminals. He's a street performer as a sideline. He's currently defending a *rapist*. He doesn't work at that Ultra Laser place as an entertainer. He didn't meet Philippa Helens there. 'Well, that's . . . unusual,' I say. *What is he doing here with me?*

'I'm a natural born show-off.' He shrugs. 'I always have been. I show off in court and I show off in Covent Garden, when I get the chance.' He sounds so delighted about it, all this showing off. So unapologetic. This man who rides a unicycle and juggles with *fire*.

'Do they know?'

'Who?'

'Your law firm.'

'Egon and Fuller? Oh yeah, they know how I get my kicks, but I'm the best barrister they've got, so they don't mind. They think it's a hoot, actually. As do I. All the fun of the fair,' he laughs.

'I don't like fairs,' I say. I wonder why on earth I'm telling him this. I also marvel at the utter banality and flatness of my conversation. He's so *confident*, I think. I have no idea how people get that way.

'Something bad happen to you at one?' he asks, looking at me curiously.

'No,' I lie. I peel a small fin of cardboard from the corner of the menu and roll it between my fingers. Of course, I won't tell him that something did, once. The night my mother showed up for the last time and I went to Finsbury Park with my sometime friend, Georgina. The first bad thing that happened to me. I check myself and smile brightly at Salvi. Try to lift myself. Try to look like someone he might be glad to be on a date with.

The waitress returns with our drinks plus a tiny double serving dish stuffed with green olives and slivers of red and yellow pepper. Salvi winks at her, grins at me. 'What would you like to continue with?' he asks. 'Shall we get a meat and cheese plate, and share?'

'Yes, please.' It's hopeless. My smile is hopeless. I have absolutely nothing to balance all this confidence with, nothing at all. *The barrister and the unemployed loser* . . . I'm an empty vessel . . . there you go, Dickens. I'm in the right place. Put that in your tankard and drink it. The waitress is staring at Salvi, but he is staring at me. I want to put my hand up to my face, but I worry I will rub off some of my careful make-up.

Once the waitress has gone, Salvi starts talking to me about some case he defended last month, a tale of a guilty-as-sin miscreant, aggravated burglary and driving into a cashpoint with some home-made armoured truck. He peppers his tale with jokes and enthusiastic bursts of laughter. Sometimes he closes his eyes.

'You don't mind defending those who are clearly guilty?' I ask. I feel like a robot, firing out a series of dull, robotic questions.

'Of course not.'

He treats it all so lightly, like it's a game. Perhaps that's what you have to do to work in law, I think. It's all theatre, I suppose, like the street performances.

'Here we are.' It's the waitress with the cheese and meats; I move my glass over a beer stain on the table to make room for the platter but I'm not sure I'll be able to eat a thing. I wonder how many other women Salvi may have brought here on a date. Women he may have picked out of the crowd to throw batons up to him, then brought to this dark, beautiful place. I'm sure they've all been a darned sight more interesting than me . . .

'How long has your dad been blind?' he asks. 'From birth?'

'No, thirty-eight years. He was just starting out as an architect when he had an accident and lost his sight.'

'Oh, that's tough.'

'Yes.'

'Still, there's a blind architect living in America, I believe; LA or somewhere. I read about him in the *Evening Standard*.'

'Hawaii,' I say. 'John Harrison Burrows. I've read about him too.' And I follow him on Twitter. And on Facebook. *I saw you on there.* (I'm never telling him this in a million years.)

'That's it. Knew it was somewhere beachy and American. Whereabouts in Chalk Farm do you live?'

'Above the tube station.'

'Hey, not The Palladian?'

'Yeah.'

'Wow, famous! I've read about that somewhere, too. I'd love to see inside sometime. Would you like another one? I'm going to the bar.'

'Oh, OK.' I look down at my cocktail and it is nearly gone. 'Yes, please.'

As he leaves the table, my phone rings. *Dad.* I'd forgotten we had a prearranged call, in case Salvi turned out to be a serial killer.

'Hi, Dad.'

'Say "yes" for, it's going OK; "no" for, I need to say I'm in hospital and you must come right away,' he whispers, in the voice of an Italian spy.

'Yes,' I say, although I'm really not sure. 'He's gone to the bar. We can talk.'

'Ah. That's good,' says Dad, in his normal voice. 'So, how's it going?'

'Good, good,' I say distractedly. 'He's a barrister, as well as a street performer. He's interesting.'

'Oh, right. How surprising. And that *is* interesting. Are you going to see him again?'

'It's way too early for that, Dad!' I can see Salvi at the bar, chatting to a woman in a black dress, who is laughing. My gut feeling is '*no*' . . .

'OK, well, enjoy yourself. Stay out as late as you like. Have you got your key?'

'Dad, I'm forty-eight, of course I've got my key.'

'Good. OK, bye then, love. Mind how you go.'

'Thanks. Bye, Dad.'

Salvi stops talking to the woman and returns to the table with two more drinks. Mine is ice cold and, again, delicious. I will sip this one more slowly.

'Did you ever study for anything?' He's really staring at me again. Staring at me and smiling. More questions.

'No, I left school at sixteen.' I hope my make-up isn't sliding off. I have powder, I have concealer and I have foundation in my bag. 'I've had lots of different jobs.' I think of the conference centre. Catering, Badging. The work trip to Tenerife, after which I switched departments for something more backroom. The *bad night* there. 'I worked for about twenty years in a conference centre. I was made redundant.'

'You could apply to another conference centre?'

'I'm a carer to my father.'

'Right.'

Salvi starts to talk and talk. He talks about the Old Bailey and Covent Garden and juggling skills and cases. He talks about films and TV and people in the news. I answer his questions. I try and fail to be witty. He is radium; a magnet. I am dull metal; tarnished. I am neither too drunk nor drunk enough. The jury is still out. But I know he won't want to see me again.

'Shall we go?' he says suddenly, finishing what I didn't know would be his final pint.

'OK.' What does this mean? *We*? I was expecting a polite rebuttal at the end of the night, a quick, 'Well, this was nice,' and I'd never see him again ... He's already standing up. He has fished keys out of his back pocket and holds them in his left hand.

I stand up, too. I reach for my bag from under the stool. I am wobbly on my wedges and my heart is not sure whether to thud or deflate.

'See ya, mate.' Salvi says this to at least four people as we make our way out. He kisses the beautiful girl at the desk on both cheeks. I stare at his bum, his biceps, the back of his neck. This will be the last I see of him, surely?

Outside in the dark, the air still humid, he looks up the street as though for a taxi. There are no taxis; the street is empty. A lone cyclist comes by, ringing his bell, although we are not in his way. Salvi is still looking up the street at nothing.

'Come here,' he says, turning to me suddenly and – how astonishing! – he draws me towards him, tucks his arms around me and leans down and kisses me. His lips are warm and surprising, and he tastes wonderful, and I close my eyes and surrender to this very unexpected moment, because that's what I am absolutely doing – surrendering. I'm not an experienced kisser. I don't really know what I'm doing. But it's a tender kiss. Exploring. Naughty. I surprise myself by wondering what it would be like to go to bed with him, and I'm wondering if he is wondering the same.

'I've got to go,' he says, pulling away from me.

What? 'Come here' and 'I've got to go' are bookends to this kiss? 'Oh?' I stammer. I am breathless, in the moment; a moment I hoped would be longer, or maybe even a lifetime.

'Yeah,' he says. *Yeah*, and in one smooth moment Salvi is raising his arm and hailing a cab that isn't there, but suddenly there *is* one and it's sailing down the road like a ship with its yellow light on top and it is pulling up to the kerb and I am being ushered in and Salvi is saying 'See you' and he shuts the door on me – the sliding door – with a clunk, well, it's a really stiff door and it takes three goes until he finally gets rid of me, and I find myself sitting like a small child in the back seat, small and small and small with disappointment, and the taxi pulls away and I see Salvi's face staring at me, from the night, his hand half-raised in an approximation of goodbye.

Chapter 18

Why are men never who you expect them to be? Why is there always *something* to trip you up or bring you down or leave you crying in the night? Why do you always have to be so very very careful?

I don't cry in the night over the fact that one minute Salvi and I were kissing on the street, the next I was in a taxi, alone, going home. I arrive home to find the lights off and Dad already retired for the night, and I take off my make-up and I put Savlon on my birthmark and I go to bed. Salvi kissed me, then he had to go. It was abrupt, it was incredibly disappointing, and it was startling, but it wasn't terrible. I've had terrible.

I've had really terrible.

Why does that other man come into my head now? That other man who hurt me? That stranger, in Tenerife? I lie in bed and watch the colours of a London night alight on my window then disappear, in a moving slide show. Why do I allow him to haunt my dreams, both awake and asleep?

I place a pillow over my head and block out the light, but it cannot block out everything. I've only ever told the story to one person – well, some of it, I don't even know how much – and I shouldn't have said anything, as I was tainted enough already and it was hardly a story that would make Kemp, my friend, fall in love with me. Why do I even continue to tell *myself* the story of what happened in the summer of 1996, in Tenerife? It was just a work trip. It was just a work trip to teach a badging system to a hotel on the coast.

I was good at Badging, at the conference centre in Highbury – printing, issuing, organizing – and that summer I was sent to Tenerife to train staff at a Spanish hotel on the same system. At twenty-six, I'd never been on a plane before – we'd never stretched to foreign holidays, as a family – and I loved the flight out. I liked being up in the air where everything stops and you are largely ignored; where fellow passengers only glance at you cursorily and cabin staff are trained not to flinch. I wondered how Angela had felt on her maiden flight to Nova Scotia; how *excited* she had been. Leaving us.

When we landed and I caught the bus to the resort hotel, I was disappointed. It was cloudy when I expected blue skies and dazzling sunshine; it was dry and somewhat commercial looking, not lush and exotic. There was bushy scrub, dusty roundabouts, random mountains with no purpose; two-storey buildings with shuttered apartments above, estate agents and restaurants boasting egg and chips below. It was dull and I felt dull there, after the excitement and promise of the flight. In the mornings I taught the badging system; in the afternoons I lay by the kidney-shaped pool behind the hotel. It was the school summer holidays so it was always busy, with lots of children. Lots of screeching and lots of splashing. I liked hearing them.

One afternoon, a rare sunny one towards the end of the trip, I put my minidress over my head, stretched out on my front on my sunlounger and, with my left cheek squished against its stiff fishing-net-like material, stared through the fretted squares to the chalky-white tiles below until a big toe with fine blond hairs on it appeared.

'Hello,' said a voice. European. Sing-song. 'Are you on your own?' The sort of thing an escaped murdering lunatic might ask.

'No,' I replied, raising my head and looking up from

140

under my dress. The man was very tall, silhouetted against the denim-blue sky. Glittering droplets of water on his body. Taut and honed. Silken-skinned. The kind of man the boys I liked at school probably grew up to be. 'No, I'm not. I'm here with my husband and seven children. They're just in the pool.'

I waved a finger airily towards the centre of the pool, where it was absolute carnage.

'Oh, OK.' I knew he didn't believe me. 'Would you like a drink?'

'I've got water,' I said, indicating the plastic bottle under the sunbed.

He sat down on the end of my sunlounger, tipping it so *my* end went up like a see-saw. Very presumptuous, I thought, but it was the type of thing men like him did. The kind of man who would shorten your name to a nickname before asking you if you minded. I sat up so the weight could shift to the end of the see-saw and balance return. He was quite good-looking, I thought. I wasn't sure why he was sitting on my sunlounger and asking me about drinks.

'Wouldn't you rather have a cocktail?' He was squinting at me, but I detected from the slits that his eyes were aquamarine blue. I squinted back at him, aware my birthmark was only covered by factor 50; that I was unmasked.

'OK, then,' I said.

We walked to the bar, which had a roof like a giant straw hat. He walked with his feet splayed out, like a duck, but had the kind of Tintin hair you wanted to play with and eyes that reflected the pool. A woman in mirrored sunglasses was singing in the bar – cumbersome, jazzed-up, synthesized versions of 'Hotel California' and 'Billie Jean' – as a beautiful girl I decided was Swedish danced alone in a floor-length white crochet maxi dress so everyone could see just how beautiful she was.

His name was Jonas. He was from Belgium. He was some kind of salesman. He asked me my name and what I was doing at the hotel. After a while, I wanted to get away from him. He had rather a high opinion of himself. An equally high tolerance for banal chat. I was uninspired but I drank three Tequila Sunrises.

The woman eventually finished singing and wheeled her gear away on a luggage trolley. I made my excuses, muttered something about going back to my book. I saw him loiter at the bar for a few minutes, from behind my sunglasses, back on my sunlounger, then he wandered off in the direction of the Sunrise restaurant.

Later that afternoon they closed the pool. A man in a white uniform went from chrome steps to chrome steps and joined them up with suspended crime-scene tape. The sun had gone in anyway, so I went upstairs.

My room had the kind of door that doesn't immediately swing shut after you, it just stays open. When I turned from putting my beach bag on a chair, Jonas was standing there, in the doorway.

'What are you doing?' I asked him, trying to sound nonchalant. Away from the pool I felt self-conscious in my bikini and sheer mini-dress and tugged at the hem.

'I wanted to know if you'd join me for dinner tonight.'

'Did you follow me up here?'

'Yes, I did. Well, no, not really. I asked which room you were in. At reception.'

'And they told you?'

He shrugged. 'I said you were a friend of mine; no big deal, is it?'

'No, I wouldn't like to go for dinner with you,' I said. *You're boring*, I wanted to add.

'That's a shame.'

The beautiful Swedish girl walked past, down the corridor – she must have been staying on my floor – but

Jonas didn't look at her, he didn't even glance in her direction. He only looked at me, so I changed my mind. I said I'd go for dinner with him.

We went for dinner in the à la carte restaurant – Mexican – and it was fine, and we had a laugh, actually, and he let me put tiny pinpricks in his ego, just for fun, and he seemed to quite enjoy it, as though it were a massive novelty, and I allowed myself the luxury of thinking that he looked at me with lust and interest and curiosity in his eyes. I had Badges again in the morning, after all. And after we had got through the best part of three bottles of wine, I took him back to the room he had followed me to earlier and this time he fucked me, just the once and terribly – so so terribly – and then I kicked him out.

I saw him, in the morning, although I didn't want to, as I was nursing a bruise as big as my birthmark on my inner thigh and a head that was constantly yelling, 'Stupid, stupid, stupid!' at me, and I had been, hadn't I? I was doing Badges and I had to walk from Meeting Room 2 to the lobby and he was waiting for me, outside the loos.

'Hey, beautiful,' he said.

'You hurt me,' I said.

'You let me.'

'I was drunk.'

'You didn't say "no".'

'I did say "no", at that point – and you know which point I am talking about. I said it until you *finished* – but you wouldn't get off me.'

'You let me,' he repeated.

'I could report you.'

'Are you going to?' I realized he was holding something in his right hand.

He knew the answer and so did I. Spanish police, all the shame, the interrogation and the hassle. I had invited him up to my room, hadn't I? He had only become rough

143

once he was actually inside me. He hadn't punched me in the face or pinned down my upper arms or worse. He had just pounded into me like a pile driver, kept going while I tried to rain ineffective punches down on his back and he held a garlicky hand over my mouth. I would not be believed. I couldn't really understand what had happened myself, let alone articulate it to strangers who were primed for every inconsistency in my story, every ambiguity. I knew the struggle to be believed – to tell my story in a clear, unambiguous way – would almost, *almost* be worse than what had taken place inside my room. And it would make it realer and realer and realer, and I didn't want that. I just wanted to forget it had happened.

He held up what was in his hand. It was a leaf. A red one, like it should belong to an English autumn or a New England fall, not a summer in Tenerife. A red leaf, who knows from what tree, heart shaped and folded down the middle so it looked like a veiny butterfly. He smiled and held the leaf out to me, by the stalk. I didn't take it.

'It looks like what's on your face.'

He was mumbling. I couldn't quite hear what he said.
'What?'

'It looks like what you have on your face,' he said and his eyes were pretending to be kind, but it was a trick. He was not kind. He was unkind and cruel. He was just like all those others. He was worse than all the others. And I knew exactly why he had done what he had done to me – recognized it with an uncomfortable familiarity – because he knew I didn't get many other offers, or *any* other offers; because he thought I should be *grateful* to be raped in my hotel room, during a badge-system-advising trip, to Tenerife.

I would not cry or give him the pleasure of seeing my anger. He was nothing to me. He would *be* nothing, in a day or two. When I would erase him, banish him from my memory, expel any trace of him – tell myself nothing had happened and I was OK. I took the leaf, scrunched it up in my hand and let it fall, in pieces, to the marble floor. Then I turned from him, went to my room to pack my case, put myself on a flight home and asked to change departments.

Chapter 19

Dad and I are outside Liberty. The sun is beating down for about the millionth day running and I have persuaded him into another hat – a baseball cap with 'New York' on it (not that either of us have ever been there; he bought it online from Next) – while I am stifling in a misjudged charity-shop khaki jumpsuit I thought could one day hold the power to make me look chic and current, but actually makes me look like a long past-it children's TV presenter.

'Architects hated Liberty,' says Dad, as I look up at the famous black-and-white timbered shop in the blazing hot sunshine. I *don't* have a cap on and can feel my face burning, despite my thick layer of suncream. 'They said it was for philistines. It's the finest example of Tudor Revival Arts and Crafts architecture in London and beyond,' he continues. 'Twenty-four thousand cubic metres of teak and solid oak timbers from two British naval ships – *HMS Hindustan* and *HMS Impregnable* – make up its frontage, and the store is the same height and length as the *Hindustan*.'

He sounds like he's reading from a website via his Braille display. He is grumpy again. The fun of Covent Garden has gone today and been replaced by surliness. I'm not really sure why. Perhaps it was the tube journey. A terrible twat in a tracksuit quipped, 'Look out, it's Andre Botticelli and Freddy Krueger's sister,' as we were going through the barriers.

'Andrea Bocelli,' I corrected him, *'mate,'* while shooting him a look that would freeze burning lava. 'And Freddy

Krueger doesn't *have* a sister.' I knew my make-up hadn't worked today; sometimes it just doesn't seem to *stick*. Then there was the pigeon that got on the tube at Mornington Crescent, causing great amusement to the other people on the carriage, but Dad got strangely snappy at even the mention of the word 'pigeon', wouldn't join in with the smiles and laughter and went all quiet on me.

Great Marlborough Street is busy and bustling this morning. 'The owner, Arthur Lasenby Liberty, literally wanted to dock a ship in the city streets,' adds Dad, sounding as excited as a fish reading the news.

'Excellent,' I say. Perhaps it's *my* grumpiness that has rubbed off on Dad. My mind is not on Great Marlborough Street, outside Liberty, this morning. It is still on the darkened street outside the Dickensian as a taxi draws up and a man looks at me with tenderness, then kisses me with passion and says goodbye.

Dad asked me this morning how it went, the date. I lied and said it was fine, but I expect he's not fooled. I didn't smile and laugh at the commuting pigeon, either. I stared morosely at my own reflection in the opposite window of the tube as we rattled here, disappointment scraping away at my insides with a metal spoon. No one expects a reflection of a middle-aged face in a tube window to be flattering but I looked blank, a non-person.

I wondered if Philippa Helens had stared at such a reflection of herself, on her final journey. If she literally couldn't stand the sight of herself. I read something new about her last night, actually, something quite strange: that on the Victoria Line leg of her tube journey from Knightsbridge, where she was due to change at Warren Street for the Northern Line, she was caught on CCTV getting off the train when it stopped at Oxford Circus, walking two carriages down the platform (with her balloon?), and getting on again before the doors re-closed.

'Arthur Liberty had a vision of an emporium with luxuries and fabrics from distant lands,' continues Dad rather morosely, 'and he borrowed two thousand pounds from his future father-in-law to make it happen. The loan was repaid in eighteen months.'

'Wonderful,' I say, a robot with a residual headache from two gin cocktails and one large measure of confusion. Maybe some paisley scarves and an assault of perfumes will distract me from what happened last night (dated, kissed, dismissed . . .), and today's sunshine will blast me from the darkness I felt in bed last night, when my memories crept over me like shadows.

'Shall we go in?'

Dad and I approach the main entrance, where overflowing blooms in metal pots spilling out on to the pavement welcome us into the fragrant, wood-panelled lobby with a heady bouquet. I realize I've never been inside this building before. It's beautiful. It's kind of cosy.

'Cheer up, Dad,' I say, and, 'everything will be all right,' I randomly add. Sod him, I think. No, not Dad. Sod Salvi. Yes, I shouldn't have put my head above the parapet only for it to be shot down but *sod him*. It was only one date. I'll get over it. I don't want to be a blank face in a tube-station window, numbed by some man.

'There are six floors and three atriums,' says Dad. We are trailing from the lobby behind a group of Japanese tourists and a woman with an enormous bottom, who sways it side to side like a water buffalo. People bustle round us on all sides; some staring, some uninterested, some very obviously *not* staring. 'All surrounded by smaller rooms. And I'm OK, Prue. I must have just got out of the wrong side of bed this morning. Check out the engraved pillars and the heraldic shields of Henry the Eighth's wives, if you can find them. There are also carved animals hidden all about the store.'

'OK, Dad.'

I look at him quizzically. He just looks *sad* today. I'll buck up. I have to. If I buck up then hopefully he will, too.

'Tell me the story,' I attempt, as we tap our way through the food hall, me guiding Dad away from the glass jars of all sorts of delights, set on low benches. 'Of when you came here as a kid.'

'OK,' says Dad. 'First, take me to a pillar with the engraving on so I can feel it, please.' I lead him over to a dark wood pillar, engraved with smooth, bulbous leaves, and I place his hand on it. 'Ah, yes, beautiful work,' he says. He glides his fingers over the leaves and down the pillar. Gives a sigh. I touch it, too, the glossy wood, here for over a hundred years. 'Well, I came here with Nonna – we'd come to the wholesalers in Ganton Street and we wandered in here, in awe – and she kept saying she shouldn't be in here, you know, that it was too smart, that she was just a *contadina* – a peasant.' He smiles a little at the memory. 'But she knew about the two ships, and the little windows between some of the wood panelling straight from the captain's quarters, and how the whole store had been designed to feel like a *home* and, well, I was just fasci-nated. I started looking around me and I thought about the flow of people and the flow of rooms and that it was beautiful and practical and really *said* something.' Dad is warming to his theme. I can see the small boy in him peering out, curious and excited about the world. I like that image. 'And then, years later, I was doing carpentry at the Barbican, and it was so, so different, but each building I worked on served the architect's vision of its *purpose* – the purpose of the people who would use it, you know?'

I nod. 'John Harrison Burrows,' I say.

'Who?'

'The blind architect. From Hawaii. He consults on libraries and centres for the blind and suggests things like using panels of differing lights, and textured surfaces, to aid people's navigation of spaces. Makes sure they serve the vision of their purpose.' I read that on the internet. I think I've paraphrased it quite well. Should I have brought him up, though, at this point? The blind architect?

'He's a clever guy, then,' says Dad. 'Let's go up to the second floor.' He takes his hand from the pillar and we head upstairs, then scoot up further, to the upper atrium. I describe scarves and artefacts and trinkets. Dark wood balustrades and panelling. There's a whispery kind of restraint in posh shops like this. A rarefied air. We mooch, we linger and we trace our fingers over slippery fabrics and run them through lace and buttons and pins. We don't smile a whole lot. We hardly talk. But we are here. Finally, I think we've been in every room.

'Hungry?' asks Dad.

'Hungry,' I agree.

We come out on Kingly Street. 'Is the clock still there?' asks Dad. 'Up on the arch?'

I look up. 'Yes.'

'"No minute gone comes ever back again, take heed and see ye nothing do in vain,"' says Dad. The inscription, black on gold, scrolling beneath the clock, is ignored by all the people wasting their lives below it. 'Take heed,' he repeats.

'Yes, Dad.'

We walk down Carnaby Street. It's so busy there is barely room on the pavement in front of us for Dad's tapping cane, and we shift like clams within a chattering sea of slow-moving people until a sudden commotion to our left causes a ripple. There's a bustle of people foraging round a hotel entrance, men with cameras jostling and crunching shoulders with each other, and a young woman steps out, flanked by bodyguards, her head down.

'What's going on?' asks Dad.

'Margot Robbie,' I say. I recognize her straight away. 'Actress. Very beautiful. She's come out of a hotel and is signing autographs by the looks of it.' There's a huddle of people around her, thrusting things under her nose. The flash of a silver pen.

'Yes, I've heard of her,' says Dad. 'Can you describe her?'

How can I describe such perfection? And do I want to? Do I want to list features so far from my own? Such beauty, when even a fragment of it has been denied to me? 'Well,' I say, 'she has large, almond-shaped eyes, full lips, an angular face that is contoured in all the right places. Cheekbones to die for. A smile to break a million hearts.'

Imagine being that beautiful, I think. To have people in *awe* of you because of how you look. To have your face stared at for all the right reasons. I would like to have that. Just for one day I'd like to step out of my front door and walk around London with people looking and looking for all the right reasons. Men, women, children – they say children and babies stare at the most beautiful faces the longest; well, I'd like to enrapture a baby in a pram, for a day. And one day would be enough. Honestly.

Margot is ushered away from the minions to a waiting car, the admirers closing round her like the Red Sea.

'She could have an awful personality,' says Dad, when it becomes safe to proceed and we are able to walk on in the dispersing slipstream of Margot followers. 'A black, black heart to counter-balance all that beauty.'

'I don't think so,' I say, and I briefly wonder if he's thinking of Mum, who was pretty rather than beautiful, but definitely turned out to have a heart blacker and more drug-addled than most. 'I've heard she's really nice. She's married.' As if that makes someone nice ... It doesn't always – remember that awful girl screaming 'I'm married!' at the end of *Muriel's Wedding*? Poor Muriel. I can relate to her a lot. And that awful girl was a bit like Angela.

Some people are so desperate to get married they'll marry anyone, and other people, like my mother and her black heart, just can't wait to escape marriage. Some people, like me, get neither.

Still, I bet Margot *is* really nice.

'How do you feel, these days, about your mother?' Dad asks, a couple of minutes later, once the tide has gone out on the crowd. Has he been reading my *mind*?

'I feel OK,' I say. Well, I do. My heart is stapled down where she is concerned. I know this is a protective mechanism, a defence, but it's true. My feelings are locked against her and I like them like that. Who wants to unlock them? Wallow in pain when it is nicely filed away. I'm fine.

'You don't get the urge to track her down?'

'Nope. Do you?'

'Not at all.'

'Do you miss her, Dad?'

I have never asked him this question. We don't do this. I look at him, as we walk, and I wait for an answer.

'No. I miss the *old* her, sometimes – I miss the old *life* I had with her – but I think that's more about me before I went blind, or my teenage years or even my childhood. I miss the *me* I used to be, I guess, rather than her – it's just that for quite a few years of being that *old me*, I was with her.'

'Yes, I understand. She's part of your history.' I'm sad he misses the person he used to be, incredibly sad.

'She is. And part of you and me and Angela, when things were good. And that's how I like to remember her. The person she became – the ugly person – doesn't exist for me. Even when I was first blind, when it was just us three, we didn't need her, did we?'

'No.' We were OK then, Dad and Angela and I, when we had the dogs. As good as it could get.

152

'She's not even out there, for me, if you know what I mean. But, for you, if you want to talk about her, you can, with me. I don't mind.'

'Thank you, Dad; I'll bear that in mind.'

I don't want to talk about her. I never have. But I'm glad Dad and I are talking. Like this. Can we ask each other all the questions we have not dared ask before? Is now the time to do it, as we walk the streets of London? I think of the clock in Liberty and its slogan: *No minute gone comes ever back again* . . . These minutes walking together may not come back again. What if they last just for this summer? What if we haven't said everything we want to say? I want to go further, to ask Dad if he's sad today, if he's still *scared*, but on this sunny, bustling street, something holds me back. Is it because deep down I want to tell him all of my truths – my fears and my memories – but I am afraid to? I don't know. But I like the feel of his hand on my arm. I like walking with him like this. And after lunch we're going to the Albert Hall and after that, we still have three places on the list, so you never know what the rest of the summer might hold.

'Table outside?'

We've stopped outside the steakhouse we booked. People are stacked on the pavement, under a huge awning, tucking into the most delicious-looking food.

'Perfect,' says Dad.

Chapter 20

We arrive at the Albert Hall at four o'clock. The sun is still high in the sky and renders the building a pinky-plum gateau, under skies of the purest blue.

'Is it still the same?' asks Dad.

'Still the same,' I reply. I wish he could see it; it breaks my heart that he can't. I haven't been here for years; I'd forgotten what a delightful surprise it is when it comes into your sights as you walk along Prince Consort Road, a terracotta confection rising to the sky. How it takes your breath away. We came here to perform in a school choir concert, Angela and I, not long before Dad went blind. We sang songs from *Joseph and the Amazing Technicolor Dreamcoat* in the auditorium, to an audience of adoring parents, and then afterwards Dad bought us a choc ice from one of the little bars and we came and stood outside with them, our backs against the brickwork, while Dad told us all about Prince Albert and the design of the Hall.

Today Dad and I climb the wide steps in front of the building then follow its curve to the right, along the lowest tier of this majestic layer cake, where the brickwork is creamy and embossed with heraldic shields. The sun has warmed the bricks to warm biscuits and Dad stops and places his hands on one like it's a talisman.

'I haven't been here since you girls were in that concert,' he says. 'It's been a long time.' Almost talking to himself, he adds, 'The Albert Hall was designed by two architects in the Royal Engineers and opened by Queen Victoria in 1871. It wasn't called the Albert Hall until after Albert died; it used to be called the Hall of Arts and Sciences.' They're probably the same facts he told me and Angela all those years ago. I wonder if we're standing in the same spot. 'The design was partly based on the Colosseum in Rome. The original dome was made in Manchester before being taken apart and transported to London.'

'It's so beautiful,' I say. 'I love the shape of it.'

'Its shape probably saved it from being bombed in the Second World War, you know. The German pilots used it as a landmark. Did you know it's oval, not circular?'

'No, I didn't know that.' Dad looks melancholic, with his hand on the warmth of the Albert Hall. I wish I could reach him, reach out to him, but I still don't know where to start.

We walk all the way around. Dad asks me to describe the building how I see it, so I talk about the gateau, the layers, the pinks and the plums. For the first time I notice the mosaic frieze that ribbons all the way around it, and Dad tells me it's called the Triumph of Art and Letters and what each panel of the mosaic depicts.

'Do you want to go inside?' I ask him, once we have done the full circumference.

'No, I don't think so. Let's head home now, Prue.'

We walk back to South Kensington tube station. Exhibition Road is busy. A woman in a pretty dress led by a guide dog walks towards us and there is so little space on the pavement that the dog, in its neon harness, brushes Dad's leg as he passes. It gives a muffled snort, as they continue on their way, a small elephantine trumpet.

'A guide dog,' Dad says, stifling a small sneeze.

'Yes,' I reply.

He is quiet for what seems like a very long time.

'I still miss them.'

'I know.'

'I never wanted to have to rely on anyone, Prue.'

'I know, Dad. Mind the kerb.' I guide him further over to the right, my heart contracting. This summer. This summer maybe everything we want to say *will* be said. Dad is talking. Dad is *talking to me*. We walk and I listen.

'You know, as soon as I became blind my goal was to qualify for a guide dog,' he says, smiling sadly into the lowering sun. 'You have to demonstrate you have sufficient mobility and orientation skills before they'll give you one, show you can travel safely and independently around the local area. So I practised. Nonna and Papa would take you to school and afterwards I would go out, bumble round the neighbourhood until I could convince the guide dog people I was OK. And then we got Sunny; do you remember her?'

'Yes, she was gorgeous.'

'She had a lovely temper. Do you remember how she would jump up to the box at pelican crossings and rest her paws on it to indicate to me where the button was?'

I smile. 'Yes, I remember.'

'She saved my life. Well, all three of you girls did. I began to head out with almost nothing to fear. I loved people's reactions. Knowing they were smiling at Sunny – I could feel a warmth radiating from people, you know? Not like now. The buggers.' I laugh. 'When the last dog, Folly, had to go, I . . . Well, you know there's a bereavement service now for losing a guide dog . . . ? Not in those days. I just internalized it; I couldn't talk to anyone. One day, when you were at school, I tried to go out alone again with just a cane but it was a disaster. I became disoriented and panicked. I barked – oh, the irony, Prue – at a woman who tried to help me, who grabbed my arm and tried to lead me off somewhere. I felt awful. I went back home and I couldn't go out again. I just couldn't do it. All because of a stupid allergy to dogs.' He shakes his head. He sounds angry and really Italian. 'It's ridiculous and I lost everything I had before. I'm so sorry. I'm sorry you have to lead me around now.'

'I'm not *leading you around*. We're out on a *trip*!'

'I can't even go down to the doctors on my own!'

'Dad, it's fine. I'm happy to take you where you need to go. I'm enjoying these trips! And losing the guide dogs, it's just one of those things. It wasn't your fault.'

He sighs, a deep deep sigh that makes me feel quite wretched. 'I know it wasn't, but it feels like it. It feels like it was my fault.'

We fall silent. I digest the story Dad has told me, the pain he has kept secret. It's hard for fathers and daughters to share the secrets of their hearts; but we have made a start, Dad and I. Now it's my turn, I know that. But I also know I am not brave enough to share my secrets with him. Not yet. But I want to. How I want to.

We're entering the long subway to the tube entrance now. I welcome the absence of sun. The echo of footsteps. It's cooler down here. There are flagstones underfoot, and glazed tan and cream tiles flanking the walls and the domed ceiling. A snaking line of chirruping school children in fluorescent bibs bounces ahead of us, as patiently smiling teachers punctuate the snake at intervals and occasionally pop a darting child back in.

'Children?' asks Dad.

'Yes,' I say. 'Maybe coming back from a school outing.'

There's a busker at the end of the tunnel, by the tube entrance, gruffing along to 'Wonderwall', with an accompanying mournful guitar. As the children pass him, he segues into 'Twinkle Twinkle Little Star', and starts to sing the nursery rhyme gently, plucking at the guitar like it's a lute. A child to the front of the snake joins in, lending his high, slightly out-of-tune voice to the husk of the busker's, and then another and another adds their voice – an escalating symphony – until the sweet pure voices of the children completely mask that of the busker and swell in the cool, echoing chamber of the tunnel. As they walk in time, now, to the music and sing so joyously, I breathe in the sweet sound of those voices like honeysuckle and I glance across at Dad and he is singing too – so softly I can barely make out the words – and he has tears in his eyes and I have tears in mine. And we're in step now, too, with the children, and as I also lend my voice to join in with this nursery rhyme that is as old as the hills and worlds far beyond them, one of the children turns from the tail end of the snake and holds her hand out to me, fingers spread, as though she is trailing them through a rippling stream, and she smiles at me, her face lit up like a beacon as though mine is – amazingly – a beacon to her, too, and I smile back, through my unchecked tears.

Chapter 21

When we get back to Chalk Farm, standing on the pavement outside the brown doors to The Palladian is a young man holding a blue plastic file and standing next to him is Kemp.

'Hi, Bertie,' says Kemp as we approach, and I remember I never replied to his final text, outside the Dickensian. 'This is my nephew, Ryan.' He gestures to the young man to step forward and shake Dad's hand. 'I promise you we have a reason for being here and I'm not just randomly loitering in the vicinity of your flat again.' He grins at me. I shake Ryan's hand and look at Kemp quizzically. 'Ryan's interested in The Palladian.'

'A little young to be a property shark,' I quip, thinking of all those brochures from speculating estate agents.

Kemp laughs. 'He's doing a sixth-form project on Leslie Green, the tube station architect,' he explains. 'I told him I knew someone who lived above one of his stations.'

'Leslie Green didn't actually design the flat,' I say. 'The Edwardians did.'

Kemp raises his eyebrows. 'No, but is it OK? If we come up and take a look around? Just a swift one? Ryan was too shy to come and knock on his own.'

'No I wasn't!' retorts Ryan, and I feel like Kemp wants to give him a comedy kick in the shins. I also feel this is a ruse for Kemp to see me again, but why? Why does he want to see me? I was just his friend and not a very good one, at that. Doesn't he have anyone better?

'Dad?' I ask, hoping he'll say 'no'.

'Fine with me,' Dad says with a shrug.

'Great!'

Kemp winks at me. I try to avoid his gaze. I don't want him looking at me. I don't want to keep seeing him. To be reminded that I loved him, but he couldn't love me. That he would never look at a woman like me in the way a woman wants to be looked at by a man she has regretfully fallen for and never got over. The damn fool idiot.

Ryan winks too, surprisingly, although despite this copied trait of his uncle's they look nothing alike – he is pale and placid-looking, with cropped blond hair and brown eyes. As he grins he shows sharpened teeth, like a cat's.

'Can you dust down your trousers a bit first, though?' I ask Kemp.

He laughs again. 'Yeah, sure. I've been underground.'

On the tube? I think. What's he been doing down there? Lying in a siding? He slaps tanned hands, edged at the wrists with those leather bands, in a show of dusting down his thighs, then he and Ryan follow Dad and me up the clanking metal staircase.

I take them straight through to the sitting room. 'Go wherever you like,' I say to Ryan. 'Take photos, whatever.' He wanders off in the direction of the kitchen and the remaining three of us stand awkwardly. Eventually Dad goes to sit in his chair.

'So,' says Kemp. He has never been inside The Palladian before. He knocked one morning after I decided I couldn't be friends with him any more – and had spent about a week ignoring his texts and phone calls. He knocked and I looked out of the window at him standing on the street below with his phone in his hand and I didn't answer. Eventually he went away. 'Lovely place,' he says, looking around him. 'Nice window,' he adds, wandering over to the Palladian window and running his hand over the painted wood of the sill. Dad is already reaching for his headphones. 'Hey, can I get a glass of water? I'll help myself. Kitchen?' He gestures, towards the door Ryan ambled through.

'Yes, of course.'

'Live, laugh, *bollocks*?' he whispers to me as he passes me, rubbing at the back of his head, and I blush.

I didn't really know Kemp at school. I mean, we were in the same art class, for GCSEs, but despite being generally smiley and quite bouncy, he was an enigma. A loner. He was always in the darkroom, emerging like an abashed vole with his shaggy New Romantic hair all messed up and a grin both joyous and sheepish, smelling of those weird chemicals and clutching photograph after photograph he had developed: people, buildings, animals, landscapes; everything. Colour, black-and-white, sepia. Not that I was watching.

He didn't seem to have any particular friends. There was one boy – David somebody – a peer-besmirched 'speccy runt', who he hung around with a lot but who moved away in the third year. Then there was just Kemp and his darkroom. I heard Kemp's mum was a hoarder, the sort they make programmes about now, and his dad an obsessive jigsaw doer, in a summerhouse at the bottom of the garden. That they had a cat they only allowed out on a piece of elastic, which stretched as far as that summerhouse and no further. No one really knew for sure, but it stopped him being popular. It deterred girls from finding him good-looking. His smiles were declared creepy and his bounciness viewed with suspicion. He had a cat on elastic.

I was not an enigma. I was viewed not with suspicion but with contempt. I was an ugly non-entity who did straight-up drawing, still life, painting onions and things. And I didn't see Kemp for many years, after we left school.

Then one day in my early twenties, not long before I got my first job at the conference centre, I bumped into him when I was waiting in a lay-by for Dave, the man in a blue van who picked me up every morning when we worked together going around pubs and leisure centres collecting cash from vending machines. Sheryl Crow wrote a song about a vending machine repairman once; in the song he picked her up when she was hitch-hiking and it was quirky and cool – he had a daughter named Easter and was surprisingly intellectual. Riding in the van with Dave was far from that. He ate stinky pasties, played Westlife CDs and had a daughter called Big Stacey. Anyway, one morning there was a whistle – not a wolf whistle but a 'Lookee here!' kind of whistle – and Kemp from school came bounding towards me. I'd just told a couple of giggling teenagers – identikit Impulse body spray and frosted-pink lipstick – who were giggling at my face from a nearby bus stop to 'Piss off!'

'Do you need any help?' he asked me.

'No, I've dispatched them, thanks,' I said.

He laughed. 'Good for you. Haverstock Comprehensive, right? Art class?'

'Yeah.'

At school it had intrigued me that Kemp was an outsider, like me, but always looked so cheerful about it, while I scowled and shuffled my way through classes, a ghost of the ghost I would become. *I* thought he was good-looking. I found his bounciness endearing. I liked seeing him dancing in the corner of school discos in his ruffly shirts and pointy boots. His smile, given out in the general direction of everyone and no one in particular.

I would have quite liked a cat on elastic.

'You did a lot of onions.'

'I did. And you were a really good photographer.'

'Thanks. I try to be. Sure you're OK?'

'Definitely. What, you're a photographer *now*?' I ask. 'As an actual job?'

'Yes,' said Kemp. 'I'm a photographer.'

'You always had a plan,' I said.

The lone boy in the dark room without any friends. The New Romantic fan who took brilliant pictures. It had all worked out for him.

He shrugged. Looked slightly amused. 'Yes, I guess I did. Well, see you,' he added, and just like that he bounded off again.

I didn't see him again until approximately fifteen years later. I was on a work's night out in Camden with the Bookings team from the conference centre, had drunk a whole bottle of rosé and was fending off the ill-conceived chat-up lines of a random Australian. Kemp was on a stag do for an editor at *National Geographic* and was wearing somebody else's very Jamiroquai-esque hat. Somehow we ended up chatting wildly at the bar, spring-boarding from people who hated us at school to art to Brit Pop and everything in between. Everyone *else* melted away, until it was just me and him, drinking and talking. Two former misfits in their late thirties; except I still *was* one.

I was raptured. I decided after twenty minutes he was the most amazing man in the world; he looked at me after about an hour and said, 'You know what, I think you'd make a really good friend, Prue Alberta.' And there we had it. I was Huck Finn to his Tom Sawyer. Charlie Brown to his Snoopy. David Somebody to his enigma. And that was how it began. Our wonderful, highly disappointing friendship. A friendship I had to take as all I could get, when I wanted so much more.

Kemp returns from the kitchen with the glass of water as I am ramming 'Bollocks' into a drawer. His jeans have dark sploshes on them. 'Sorry, you've got a fast tap. Some water went everywhere. I used a tea towel.'

'Don't worry,' I say. He was always accident prone. Always hitting his head on the door frame of his houseboat or cracking his shins on the side of the tables in the pub as he wound his way up to the front to do really bad karaoke to really bad power ballads. He grins at me. I want him to go away. I don't want to see his face because his face – his smile, the way his eyes crinkle when he laughs and the lines at the side of his mouth join in; that chickenpox scar I want to touch with my finger and smooth away – is what I love about him most of all.

'Are you still working at the conference centre?' he asks. He is leaning against the wall, feet crossed at the ankles. Relaxed. How can he always be so *relaxed*? I am a tightly wound spring, ready to unravel.

I hesitate. I really don't want to come across as a total loser. Not to this man. A man who I mostly met at night but who I always viewed as someone who walks on the sunny side of the street; who belongs on the sunny side of *life* . . . I got made redundant not long after I decided I couldn't have him in my life any more. When my heart was still breaking at the thought of never seeing him again, I was called into my own office and told I had managed so effectively and set up such a brilliant system, for all the tiers of staff below me, that I was no longer required.

'Prue's been looking after me,' says Dad and he settles back in his chair.

'Oh, right. Right,' says Kemp. 'That's excellent.'

After the night in Camden, Kemp took my number and he used to call me, about six o'clock, when I was on my way home from work, to ask me if I wanted to go to the pub. We'd meet in the tiny King's Arms near his houseboat, we'd drink too many Jack Daniel's and Cokes and eat salt-and-vinegar crisps and talk and talk and talk, and then we'd stagger, laughing usually to one of those recycled jokes of his he could never quite reach the punchline of, back to *Summer Breeze* and talk and drink more bourbon and talk and drink more bourbon. I found out he really *did* have a cat on elastic. That his mum *was* a hoarder and his dad an escapee jigsaw doer. That he slept, as a child, in a box room crammed with old magazines and plastic tubs rammed full of tat, and that his roaming the world as a photographer was his own escape, making up for the confines of his childhood. That he got into photography in the first place as a means to literally see beyond his stuffed and chaotic home life.

We drank too much, we realized that. We weren't teenagers any more, but we acted like them. No kids, no real responsibilities; lives that weren't entirely grown up. While we talked and talked, I realized we were never going to be more than friends. Sometimes I'd pass out on his bed, though, with him on the floor, and wake, a befuddled twit, in the early hours, to stare at him sleeping for a while, before making my way home.

'So, how are you?' he asks me. 'Really?'

'Fine, thanks.' I always say that, even if I'm not. People don't want to hear the truth, do they? That you are ill, or mightily pissed off with life, or dying inside. 'Fine, thanks' is the British way of saying, 'I can't *begin* to tell you how I'm really feeling . . .'

'And you? Are you still going away on photography assignments?'

During our friendship, Kemp went abroad on trips for *National Geographic* magazine; he came back again. We'd see each other for a while; then we wouldn't. That was a good thing. It kept me out of the danger zone. His lengthy absences gave me back enough control not to launch myself at him, weeping like a lunatic and making feverish declarations of undying love when he got back and nonchalantly invited me to the King's Arms again.

'Yes, I'm still off on my travels now and then. Got to make a living, you know.'

'Right. Great. Good.' He lived in another world and always had. A place of mystery and adventure and self-discovery. He would send me postcards, while he was away – of jungles and beaches and cities and desert plains. He would write 'Wish you were here!' but I knew he never meant that. There was something about me he liked enough to make me his friend, but he didn't wish I was *there*.

There were women, sometimes, in some of these places. A text would buzz on his phone, in the pub, and he would glance at it quickly and then turn his phone over. He told me he had occasional one-night things, in these far-flung locations. With women he would never see again but sometimes gave his number to. I would nod and smile, say things like 'Good for you' while dying inside. I hated the thought of him being lonely, but I hated those women more.

'What were you doing in the tube to get all dusty like that?' I ask. It's so hard to look at him. Every minute we ever spent together is the space between us he doesn't even notice.

He grins. 'I've been down at the Kingsway Exchange.'

'What on earth's that?'

He scratches at his chickenpox scar. 'A secret Cold War-era telephone exchange, below High Holborn. I'm between assignments so I'm doing a bit of urban exploring – you know, going into hidden places, disused and neglected buildings, former mental institutions, that kind of thing. Places where the public aren't allowed access. Taking photos. It's really interesting.'

'Oh right, sounds it.'

'What, you break in to places?' Dad interrupts. I realize his headphones are off again. He's halfway out of his chair, probably to get a drink.

'Not really *break in*,' says Kemp. We exchange looks. 'Well, kind of, but it's not illegal. It's just exploring, going where you're not allowed to go. It's fun. And I've been sent into some places by a couple of magazines. The rest, I go by myself. Hopefully I'll be able to sell the photos somewhere.' He pushes back his hair with his right hand. He tucks some of it behind an ear.

'All right to go in the bathroom?' Ryan is at the doorway.

'Not much to see in there, but yes, of course,' I say.

I'm standing too close to one of the side windows and the sun is coming in and hitting the left side of my face. I step forward and out of the sun. I turn my face from Kemp. Even now, I must hide all the worst parts of me from him. He has seen my birthmark, of course. Once we got caught in a rainstorm on the way back from the pub and I knew my make-up had run off; another night, in August, when there had been a terrible skiffle band at the pub we'd attempted to dance to, I sank one Jack Daniel's too many and threw up in his chemical toilet (the shame!) while he held my hair back. Afterwards, I looked in his tiny bathroom mirror and my birthmark was exposed and raw-looking, a mocking, witchy reminder he could never love me.

'Do you still live on the houseboat?' I ask, and I wish I hadn't as I am blushing again.

'No, I don't now. Another winter in that place almost did me in. I've got a flat in Primrose Hill. A studio – you know, the ones with a pull-down bed and no room to swing a rat.'

I smile. There were plenty of river rats in the houseboat days. Streaming on down the Thames or peering at us, curious from the bank, as we clambered drunkenly aboard *Summer Breeze*, their eyes shining in the dark.

'I've got a photo on my phone somewhere. I'll show you.'

He takes his phone from his jeans pocket, flicks to his

photos and hands it to me. Kemp's studio flat has the same kind of decor as the houseboat. A silly batik rug on the wall, bottle-green walls, a bed with a Thai gold and purple bedspread thing. A guitar he doesn't play slouching against a wall. A didgeridoo. I'm sure I can spy his tragic fisherman's hat, hung on a hook on a wall, just like it always was. Wherever he lays his hat that's his home, it seems. He has re-created the entire houseboat in flat form. I can understand why he moved. I remember all too well the houseboat in winter. Condensation on the tiny windows. Kemp's selection of blankets, including the treacherous electric one, with the frayed seams, which his grandmother had once owned. The other dangers in that houseboat: candles and Calor gas bottles and how close my heart was getting to a different kind of flame . . . Then I remember my sock. It *moved* with him?

'Very nice,' I say, handing the phone back. 'Cute.'

'I'll have to show you in person sometime.'

He looks at me, with those lighthouse eyes, and I pile on another blush. 'Maybe,' I say. This should not happen. I don't want to go where he lives, to see his things; his life. I took myself away from him for a reason and I won't put myself back there.

'Maybe?' echoes Kemp, teasing.

'I'm quite busy,' I say, shutting him down.

I stacked all the postcards he sent me in my knicker drawer, a pile of misery. When he told me he was going away again, that last time, seven years ago – to India; to the pink palaces of Jaipur and the white palaces of Udaipur – I knew that temporarily taking back control of my senses, while I chucked postcards in my knicker drawer, was not going to work for me any more. I knew, on the night he told me – a night where we escaped from the pub and ended up sitting on stone steps in the moonlight, and I'd looked at him and despaired at how much I loved him and how hopeless it all was – I had to end our beautiful friendship. Later that same night I quietly left his bed and his houseboat at 3 a.m., while he lay on the floor in jeans and black T-shirt, barefoot, sleeping – the most beautiful man I had ever known – and as I crept across his floor he opened his eyes and looked at me, a serene and almost tender look that made me want to cry.

'Just going to the loo,' I'd said, as he closed his eyes again and I silently said goodbye.

I simply cut him off. Stopped replying to his messages. Stopped answering his calls. I couldn't explain that his ridiculous friend had fallen in love with him, so I just had to ignore him. Walk away – swiftly – without looking back. I'll always remember his last message. It said, *Bertie! I don't know why you've gone, but I haven't. I'm still here. Take some time, if you need it. I'll be waiting.* But I didn't want him to *wait.* I wanted him to realize I could never see him again.

'I'm done.' Feline-toothed Ryan is back in the sitting room, clutching his plastic file. 'I got loads of photos.'

'Great, great,' says Kemp, still casually leaning against my wall, his feet crossed at the ankles, and making no move to go. He is sipping his water and looking all lovely and genial and good-natured. His hair is perfect. His eyes are kind. I'm trying not to meet them.

'I'm seeing Ellie at eight,' says Ryan.

'Yes, OK, we're off, then,' says Kemp, and he rights himself and hands me back the glass of water with a smiling 'thank you', and our fingers almost touch and I want to die.

'You're welcome,' I say.

'We'll see ourselves out. Thanks again, Vince, Prue. Don't be a stranger,' Kemp adds, to me. 'I mean it. Reply to my bloody texts.'

'Sorry,' I reply, a mere million millionth of what I actually want to say.

169

'Thanks,' chimes Ryan. 'Great place.' And off they go, shutting the door behind them, and I can hear them clattering down the metal stairs with Kemp ribbing Ryan about something and them both laughing and then they are out the brown doors and on the street below.

'Nice kid,' says Dad, from his chair. 'And Kemp really is a great guy. Why did you stop seeing him, again?'

I take Kemp's empty glass and walk into the kitchen.

'I had to,' I whisper to myself.

Chapter 22

Kemp was the only person I told my Cherry Lau story to. How we had stopped being friends after a house party one summer when we were seventeen. I'd been invited by some boys in Sixth Form – I'm not sure why. I think I'd told one of them to *'do* one' in the lunch queue earlier that week and they decided – *finally* – I was some weird strain of cool novelty.

It was the kind of house party where the parents were at a golf club dinner and someone would end up puking in the bushes of the neighbour's garden and teenagers 'got off' with each other (if they got lucky). I had my toothbrush in my back pocket because it was intimated I could stay over, and I brought Cherry Lau with me. If there was to be a *Carrie*-style bucket of pig's blood over my head as I walked in, she would get covered too and the humiliation would be shared. If there wasn't, there would be booze and we could sit in the corner and talk about people.

As it happened the humiliation was all hers.

I told Kemp in the pub one night. We'd had a skinful of Jack Daniel's and Cokes and he was trying to get stuff out of me. History kind of stuff. Stories. Anecdotes. I had a whole dubious pack to shuffle through that I really didn't want to share, but I'd had just enough bourbons to confess to this shameful one. How it was a very drunken party. That the bush-vomiting had started early, about nine o'clock. I didn't tell him a boy tried to stick his tongue down my throat at about ten o'clock, while we were

171

moshing to Madness in the hall, then burst out laughing and said, 'You'd look all right in the dark. I should have taken you down to the bottom of the garden.'

'Full moon and too many stars, arsehole,' I'd replied. 'You'd still see me.'

I told Kemp that at about midnight, Cherry and I were at the bottom of that garden, sitting on a swing chair and necking a bottle of Southern Comfort. We were talking to a group of idiot boys who were pretending to smoke weed. They were talking about going to the dog track the next day and although they hadn't asked or cared what we were doing, Cherry piped up with a Southern Comfort-ed slur that she had a family wedding tomorrow.

'What, a *Chinese* wedding?' asked one of the boys.

'Yes, my cousin.' She was so pissed her eyes were all over the place behind her thick glasses.

'What does that involve?'

'It's just a wedding,' she shrugged, 'there's nothing different about it. Oh, the bride wears a red dress and we drink tea and it goes on for two days and we give red envelopes with money in them to the newlyweds.'

This was the most she had ever spoken to a member of the opposite sex, I reckoned.

'Sounds stupid,' said one of the boys, and then the swing chair had lurched and Cherry had fallen off and her Madonna T-shirt got soaked from the damp night grass and she spilt her cup of Southern Comfort down the leg of what were already terrible jeans and everyone laughed, including her as she was so shit-faced she didn't care.

By 4 a.m. most people had left and about eight of us crashed out on the sitting-room carpet in spaces between spilt alcohol patches and fag butts and empty Twiglet packets. I had attempted to crash in the bathtub, thinking I wouldn't be disturbed as the toilet was in a separate room next door, but there was a manky soaking-wet towel lying in a puddle of something orange in the bottom, so the sitting room it was. My head was on a flowery cushion stained on one corner with red wine and I had pulled a smelly white cotton jacket with scrape-y buckles over me. I couldn't sleep, as a boy was snoring somewhere down near my left foot, so I got up and walked to the kitchen where Cherry was lying flat out asleep on the lino in front of the fridge, a bottle of Southern Comfort rolling near her head. Three boys were kneeling over Cherry and one, who we'd talked to in the garden, had a large black marker pen in his hand. Her glasses were off – I later spotted them on a kitchen worktop under a half-eaten piece of toast – but he'd already drawn them back on her, black and thick, great round circles around each eye, right into the socket, plus a black bridge across her nose and one chunky arm up to her left ear. The other boys were laughing.

'Problem, fuck-face?' he asked me as I stood in the doorway.

'No,' I said.

'Good. She'll still look better than you when I've finished. And *hers* will come off – eventually. It's permanent marker.'

The other boys laughed. The artist, his tongue out in concentration, steadily drew the second arm, up to her other ear. A 'Fuck you' came to my lips but I left it there. A strange feeling was coming over me. A feeling of relief, almost joy – that for once *it wasn't me*. Another victim was in town. He drew a comedy moustache above Cherry's top lip. I started to laugh, too. He drew two comedy clown cheeks on Cherry's and filled them in pitch black – she looked like a weird cherub suffering from the black plague. I laughed some more. The longer I laughed, the better I felt, and I liked that feeling. I was one of *them* and it felt good. I'd had a big fat target on my back since the day I was born, and now it was pinned to Cherry.

He turned to me and held the marker pen up in the air. 'Want to have a go?'

I hesitated. I was enjoying the laughing and I fancied him a bit, but did I want to draw on my best friend?

'OK,' I said. In my drunken logic – and because there wasn't a lot of space left – I thought I'd give her a beauty spot, like Elizabeth Taylor. She was a bit of an idol of ours; Cherry had a knackered old 'Girls World' styling head we used to muck about on and we often used to whack an Elizabeth Taylor beauty spot on it, as a finishing touch. So, I gave Cherry a nice one on the corner of her lips, mistakenly thinking I was both appeasing the boys and improving her look.

'What's that?' derided one of the boys.

'Beauty spot,' I defended.

'Can't really see it,' he judged.

'OK,' I said. And I made it bigger and bigger until it was a huge witch's wart.

In the morning Cherry went upstairs to go to the loo. There was no mirror in that bathroom, but when she came back down she noticed the constant giggling. I wasn't joining in with them now as I felt really bad, now I was sober. I was ashamed of myself. Harsh sunlight was coming in through the curtains that nobody had bothered to draw, illuminating my shame; my brief searing moment in the sun with these hateful arseholes.

'I'm going to call my dad to pick me up,' Cherry said.

I panicked then, so I took her up to the main bathroom and showed her her face in the mirror above the bath.

'I'm sorry,' I said.

She was horrified. She cried. And then she noticed the witchy beauty spot.

'A beauty spot?' she exclaimed, turning to me. 'Like Elizabeth Taylor?'

I blushed. I blushed a hungover crimson.

'Oh my God, you *joined in*,' she said. I went even redder. 'You think I'm just a stupid ugly little Chinese girl, too. I've got to go to a *wedding* today! How am I going to get this off?'

Tears came to my own eyes. I knew in that instant I had lost her as a friend and I totally deserved to.

'You of all people,' she said, and then she went downstairs and out of my life. She never called round for me again and when I went to visit her at the takeaway her dad said she wasn't there. Every time. And much later, if I ever reluctantly called in for sweet 'n' sour chicken and Dad's favourite Singapore noodles, and she was behind the counter, we'd have the most awful of small talk conversations, as she purposefully jabbed through *Cosmopolitan* magazine, and, if she looked up at me, I'd see the vestigial hatred in her eyes.

'Don't be too hard on yourself, Bertie,' Kemp said when I told him, sitting at that little table in that beautifully dark and cramped and cheerful pub.

'But I must be!' I said. 'After everything, I did *that* to her! It's unforgivable.' I remember tearing a beer mat into a hundred pieces, scattering them like confetti on the table.

'It was a long time ago; you were a teenager. I think you need to cut yourself some slack.'

'No, no,' I said. 'No slack. I don't deserve *slack*.' I was ashamed. I'd shown him a black part of myself when I'd been trying so hard to keep so much concealed. And now I had shown him, he knew exactly who I was. I wanted to forget I'd told this story and get another drink. I needed to be fun, night-time, pub-time Prue again. Grabbing his sunglasses from the table (he *always* had sunglasses on him), I put them on, tipped them on to the bridge of my nose and peered over the top at him. 'I demand more booze,' I said, in a poor attempt at a line from *Withnail and I*.

Kemp has left his sunglasses behind now. I can see them on the windowsill, left there from when he and Ryan came into the flat a few hours ago. I don't suppose he'll come back for them; he always had plenty of cheap pairs, for all that travelling.

Dad and I are in our chairs. Dad has his headphones on and is listening to a podcast on the modernism movement and London's tower blocks – so he tells me. I am idling on the internet again, trying to erase the new incarnation of Kemp from my mind.

I need a distraction. I need the equivalent of putting a cheeky pair of sunglasses on and having another drink. It's such a crying shame I won't be seeing Salvi again – he would have been more than a decent distraction. That charismatic, cheeky man with the swagger and the grin and the bad, black edge to him I feel could mirror me in a sharp, glittering way. I'd hoped he'd really like me. I'm still so disappointed that he didn't. I remember how he kissed me, how astonishing and remarkable and wonderful that was. How completely pointless.

I get up and go to the cupboard. I ease my sketchbook out from under the photo album and the *A–Z*. I turn to my latest fledgling portrait of Dad. I look at it critically. The nose is not right, the angle of the forehead is all wrong. He looks too old. But it's in pencil and I have a rubber. Or I can start again. I turn to a fresh page, run my fingers over the smooth cream cartridge paper. I get down my set of pencils and I start to sketch Dad again. I notice he has colours in the texture of his face you wouldn't expect – greens and blues and greys and ambers, depending where the light catches its contours. I need colour; I will use oil paints on this one. If you add Cadmium Red and Phthalo Blue to Burnt Sienna you get the most amazing rich brown that's the perfect shade for an Italian father's eyes.

First, though, I need to get the lines right and I concentrate and I sit and work for an hour, looking and looking and making marks on the page – some light and feather-like, some purposeful and considered – and when I hold the sketchbook away from me I am quite pleased.

There's a knock at the door. I put the sketchbook down and go to the window.

'Who's that?' asks Dad, from under the headphones.

'I don't know. I can't see anyone.'

Whoever it is must have tucked themselves right under the door frame. I really don't want to go down. I don't want to answer the door in a pair of Dad's old tracksuit bottoms and a shabby white vest – I look either like an extra from *The Sopranos*, betraying my Italian roots in a really shameful manner, or like something from *Rab C. Nesbitt*. No one knocks on our door at this time of night. I really hope it's not Kemp come back for his glasses.

After a few seconds there is another knock. I put the sketchbook back in the cupboard, huff the huff of those weary of the world and its cold-callers, and clank down the iron stairs in my bare feet to open the door to a grinning Salvi, who is standing there with a single tulip in his hand and his hair smarmed back. He's wearing a very snappy suit and shiny shoes and looks far too gorgeous for the middle-aged-Sicilian-mafia-moll-on-their-day-off who's just opened the door.

'Hello, Prue,' he says in a casual manner, like he didn't run out on me last night.

'Hello, Salvi,' I say. 'What are you up to?' I am carefully and equally casual – though actually, of course, I am bloody delighted he is here. At least I look the part: if an outfit ever said 'Couldn't care less' in capital letters, this is it.

'Seeing if you want to come out to play later,' says Salvi cheekily. He's actually got one hand on his hip. He looks like a naughty schoolboy. 'As I was in the neighbourhood.

I've been in Primrose Hill intimidating a witness-for-the-prosecution.'

He hands me the tulip, laughing at his own macabre joke, and I take it. 'Really?' I ask. I'm sure I should be saying something equally witty, but I can't think of anything. My heart is thundering in my casual chest too much.

'Yeah, want to see his blood? I have some on my handkerchief.'

'Er, no, you're all right.' I yank my vest down over my tracksuit bottoms. Try to look unruffled.

He laughs again, loud and bold. 'So, yeah, all in a day's work. Do you want to come out for dinner, around eight? Put your glad rags on?'

I look down at my sorry outfit, then back up at him. 'OK,' I say quickly, all pretence of not caring he is here gone. 'Yes, I'd like to.'

'Great. So, the famous Palladian,' he says, looking up at our kitchen window. 'Can I come up and take a look?' He already has one of his shiny feet over the threshold.

'Er . . .' I really don't want him to, but before I know it he is bounding up the clanking stairs behind me, two at a time, to the inner door. He's in the hall with me. He's in the sitting room. That's a really expensive suit he's got on, I think, as he stomps around, looking this way and that. I put the tulip on my chair and tap Dad on the shoulder.

'Dad? Dad, Salvi's here. We're going out later but he's just come for a quick look at the flat.'

Dad goes to get up. Salvi is admiring the cornicing, looking out of the Palladian window, picking things up and putting them back down again – including Kemp's sunglasses. His bum looks nice beneath the vents of his smart jacket. His shirt is pure white and very crisp still, for the end of the day.

'Hello, fella? How you doing?' he says in Dad's direction,

after he has examined my box of pencils and set them back on the table.

'Hello,' says Dad, from his chair. 'How are you?'

'Good, good, great actually. Really great. I wondered what this place looked like on the inside. How long you been here?'

'Thirty-six years.'

Salvi nods. 'Love it, love it,' he says. He wanders to the doorway of the kitchen, peeks his head inside, then does the same with the bedrooms and the bathroom. 'I feel a bit like an estate agent,' he laughs. 'I'll be getting my tape measure out in a minute. Right, well, I've got to shoot off. Meet you at Wotton's on the Strand, at eight, Prudence?'

'OK, yes, I'll be there.' Why not? Another place I'll need to look up, I think.

'Perfect. Like you,' he whispers. He has stepped forward so he is standing very close to me. I can smell cologne and the faint hint of beer. He kisses me on my good cheek and I squirm and pull away as politely as I can.

'He can't see us,' Salvi whispers, too loudly, and he trots out of the flat and down the stairs with a jaunty clatter and slams the brown doors behind him. I catch Dad frowning and raising an eyebrow I cannot mistake for anything but disapproval, but of course it is easy for me to ignore it.

I like Salvi and he appears to like me. I'm going on a second date when dating has always been a foreign land to me, for which I've had no passport.

And a distraction is a distraction, after all.

179

Chapter 23

Wotton's is cavernous and kaleidoscopic. Every colour in the spectrum – from shimmering amber to neon green to hot purple – has been elbowed and cajoled into this space, which, despite being huge and high-ceilinged, is jam-packed with a technicolour array of booths and banquettes and bars, in suede and leather and gold and steel, and presided over by two enormous multicoloured stained-glass murals. To the right, the mural runs floor to ceiling, with double-decker buses and cabs thundering along the Strand behind it to cast myriad and fluctuating shapes on to the faces packed and perched within. To the left, the glass mural is back-lit with panels of gold and red and green. Both are etched with a rainbow of hedonist creatures: drinkers and dancers and half-dressed revellers who raise glasses and snake arms around each other's waists in a tableau of sin and stained-glass.

The wall facing us as we walk in looks like a giant version of 'Simon', that retro game where you press the moulded coloured panels to follow a lit-up sequence. I get the crazy urge to go over and press my bum against one of the padded, lit-up squares, just to see what happens, but that would bring attention to myself. I'm exposed enough as it is, just being here, but I've laid it on thick, my make-up, and although Wotton's is brighter than the Dickensian, everyone around me looks flattered by the light here. I hope it will do the same for me.

Salvi was waiting outside. Eight o'clock on the dot. He was on his phone, smiling at something, leaning against the wall next to the entrance and wearing jeans and a white shirt, which as I got closer I realized was embroidered with tiny figures – cute divers in navy swimming trunks and 1950s bikini babes in sunglasses and turbans, lying on beach towels. When I was close enough for him to look up and smile, he simply took me by the hand and we walked into the bar.

The music is thumping as we make our way to our booth, and I smile at finding the pair of us stepping in time to Grace Jones' 'Slave to the Rhythm' – Salvi with a swagger, me with the uncertain step of a second-dater who's not exactly sure how the first date went. I hope I look OK. I'm wearing a jersey stretch cream midi dress with cap sleeves, slash hip pockets and a cowl neck – a dress I'd bought myself for my fortieth birthday but have never, ever worn. Salvi shows me to my seat, half of a purple velvet banquette, facing the stained-glass spectacle that flanks the Strand and I presume he will take the seat opposite – the waiting studded leather hardback chair – but he wedges himself next to me, his thigh flanking mine, denim to silky cream jersey, birthmark side.

'Good evening,' he says, and when I automatically turn to face him he leans from his side-saddle position and his eyelashes and his big warm smile come towards me and he kisses me. He smells of cinnamon and coconut. His lips are warm and soft and teasing and he holds them on mine for a few seconds, then his tongue edges forward and in my relief and joy at being out with him again, I find myself daring to meet it with mine, and before I know it we are doing the kind of snogging my dad never witnessed at school discos, the kind of 'Look at us' kissing only the drunk, smug or those with something to prove will exhibit.

When it's over, Salvi sits back in his seat and picks up the drinks menu, as though nothing has happened, and I sit back in mine, reeling. I wasn't expecting to be kissed at the beginning of the night and certainly not like this – it's like we just stepped from the end of last night's date straight into half-past midnight of this one.

'So, how are you?' asks Salvi, turning to me again, drinks menu in hand. As we were kissing, my forearm was angled against the edge of the table and resting in a puddle-patch of water – condensation of a former patron's drink? I soak up that dark water now with a left-behind, pristine napkin, pushing it to the corner of the table when sodden.

'Good, thanks. You? What was the lawyerly thing, really?'

'Someone I had to go and see. Papers to sign. Deathly dull, you know how it is.' Well, I really didn't. I wasn't a hot-shot criminal barrister. 'Hungry?'

'Yes, a little.'

'What would you like to drink? They do excellent cocktails.' Of course, he's been here before. He slides the menu over to me like he's a croupier at a casino, with the flat base of his hand. A performer's move. I wonder if everything with him is going to be a performance and what role I will play. I pick it up and scan the cocktail list.

'A pina colada, please.'

'You can't have that!' He shakes his head at me. 'That's so pedestrian. Have a Wotton Woo Woo. It's wonderful, trust me.'

The Woo Woo in the menu looks like a plumed bird of prey, it has fruit skewers and feathers and umbrellas spiking from it; a firework of a cocktail.

'OK, I'll give it a go.'

I hate that I have to continually turn my face in order to talk to him. Give him a full view of The Cheek. I try to look enigmatic but I've hardly got an enigmatic face. It's an open book, surely: you can read anything on my face; after all, it comes with its own map.

'Done anything nice today?'

'My father and I went to Liberty's and then to the Royal Albert Hall.'

'Oh, fantastic, fantastic. Much going on?'

'Where?'

'At the Albert Hall. Did you go to a concert?'

'No, Dad wanted to have a look at the outside.'

'A *look*?' Salvi laughs.

'You know what I mean. A feel for the place. He likes to touch the fabric of buildings. Brickwork, beams. That sort of thing.'

'Because he used to be an architect?'

'Yes.'

An attractive girl, the waitress, pitches up at the table – London seems to be heaving with them. 'Hi, Salvi,' she says – all boobs and tiny waist and big kohled eyes.

'Natalia,' he drawls idly, like he just screwed her last week.

'What are we having tonight?'

I fear he may lick his lips and say 'You', the way he is looking at her, so I decide to give her my best death stare – he won't notice as he's next to me – but she coolly ignores me. Girls like her always do.

'A Whiskey Sour, please, and this beautiful lady will have a Wotton Woo Woo.'

Natalia can't hide her derision. And I am finding it hard to conceal mine. He's taking the piss, isn't he? I have *never*, by any stretch of the imagination, been beautiful. Dad once had a record – 'When You're in Love with a Beautiful Woman', Dr Hook – I loved that song, but I knew the whole concept would always be beyond me. I gingerly touch my cheek, where the birthmark lies beneath. I want to scratch it off with my fingernails, bleach it, burn it, for it to be gone. I want a matching pair of smooth cheeks like everybody else. I want to be *Natalia*.

'Certainly. Nuts?'

'Why not, babe?'

'Great,' she exclaims and off she trots, wiggling her behind at Salvi.

'*Babe*?' I question.

'Everyone's "babe".' Salvi shrugs. 'I enjoyed it last night,' he adds. 'Did you get home OK?'

'Yes, thank you,' I say. I am bright, purposely chirpy. I am not going to acknowledge that he ran out on me. I am grateful to be here.

'You can't beat a London cab. Is that how you and Dad have been getting around? Taxi? Must be the easiest, you know, with him being the way he is.'

'No,' I say. 'We've been walking and taking the tube. Always a bit of an adventure,' I add wryly.

Salvi laughs. 'I bet. Wow, good for you. I was stuck in a tunnel for twenty minutes the other week – it made me an hour late for a briefing. The wig that had been roasting in my briefcase came out like sweaty roadkill!'

I laugh, but I'm going to ask him, I think. I'm going to ask him about Philippa. His Facebook friend. 'Did you hear about that poor girl who died on the underground a couple of weeks ago?' I say, ultra casually.

'Yeah, vaguely.' Not a flicker on his face, not a blink. 'There's always some idiot.'

'Philippa someone,' I add.

'Uh-huh.' His gaze wanders round the room then returns to land on me, his eyes blank. He doesn't know her, does he?

'It's terribly sad. She was only twenty-nine.'

'Yes, terribly sad.' He grins at me slowly, brushes a hand over the top of his head. Oh, he definitely doesn't know her – Philippa probably just heard of him as this eligible bachelor, read about one of his cases at Egon and Fuller, or a profile in a magazine, and Friend Requested

184

him, like people do. She was just one of his 3,015 and he was just one of her 102.

Our drinks arrive. My cocktail looks even more preposterous than its photo. I sip at it through a neon straw and it is savagely strong.

'Where's your mother?' Salvi asks, draining a third of his drink in one.

'What?' That's a very blunt question. Salvi's green eyes are glinting. What is he doing?

'Your mother. You live with your father and you've never mentioned her. Is she dead?'

'No, she's not dead. She lives in Sweden.'

'Do you mind?'

'No.'

I don't want to talk about my mother. I want to concentrate on the way Salvi is looking at me. He's looking right into my eyes. I notice flecks of navy and ochre in his eyes, fuchsia flashes reflected from a 2D woman doing the samba in the stained-glass opposite us. I feel half hypnotized. I wonder when he's going to kiss me again.

'You look beautiful when you're angry.'

'Oh, come on! You're having me on! I'm not beautiful!' I am pretending to be affronted now, as I'm not sure I am. I am tempted to be flattered, to believe his lie. And in approximately ten minutes, if I keep on drinking this cocktail, I will be drunk.

Salvi looks at me quizzically. He is smiling too, a smile I want to jump into and flail around in, for a while. 'How do you feel about your birthmark?'

My head snaps back. I feel I've been come at with a red-hot poker. My hand involuntarily goes up to my cheek. Why is he interested in my birthmark? I trusted he could barely see it in this kaleidoscopic light, but he's shoved it straight under the glare of a harsh bare bulb.

'Do we have to talk about that? How do I feel about it?

185

Good God!' Now I feel angry and hot – the bloody thing is going to flare like a beacon under all my make-up. 'I hate it! What do you think?'

'What I think,' he says evenly, ignoring my outburst, 'is that beauty is in the eye of the beholder. I think you're beautiful. And it gives you character.'

'I'd rather be character-less. Unnoticed. *Character* I'd rather not have, thank you very much.' The prickles are up; they are bristling, ready to pierce something. First my mother, now this! I want to get up from his side and go.

'I've upset you,' he says calmly. 'I was just interested. Look, let's order another round of drinks. Please. Don't be like that.'

He places his hand over mine again and turns to call a different waitress over. I am still smarting. I keep my other hand in front of my face, not touching it, though, as I don't want any make-up to come off.

The waitress comes over. Salvi orders the same again. 'I really like you,' he says, as he turns back to me. 'It was a stupid question. Please, let's just move on.'

'OK,' I say. 'We'll move on.' I can't have this evening ending in disaster and disappointment again, I just can't. 'Honestly!' I add, light as artificial air. 'Just because *you* like being the centre of attention. Hot-shot barrister and unicyclist!'

I have successfully lifted the mood and it floats upwards, taking us with it, to the atrium skylight in this place, where a big round yellow moon sits in its frame and laughs at us all. A double-decker bus thunders along the Strand, rattling the technicolour glass that divides us from it. A red prism descends on Salvi's face like a butterfly, then passes. He is grinning at my wit and my deflection, his eyes lit bright and kaleidoscopic; we are both relieved this moment has passed.

We eat. We talk and we drink and we laugh and we order more cocktails and more food arrives and we eat and we talk and I see a possibility, for us. For something to be happening here. I feel he won't run out on me again. I feel we have a spark between us, a pilot light that could inflame into sometime bigger and all-encompassing any second. I also definitely feel drunk.

'Shall we?'

A band is setting up on the small stage in front of the end wall with the lit-up panels. A guitar is being tuned, there's a sizzle from the drum kit, a squeak from the microphone – a spark created elsewhere; not just us. They launch into an enthusiastic 'Livin' la Vida Loca'.

I nod.

He leads me through the chattering tables and on to the dancefloor, where we are the first there. He starts dancing and I, shy but drunk, begin to sway from side to side. He is laughing at me, but not unkindly. His hand is still in mine, warm and nice.

'OK?'

'OK.'

We dance, while laughing at each other, awkwardly at first and then we start to really get into it and we are twirling and doing what we think are *all* the Latin moves and I haven't laughed like this for a long time. Ricky Martin segues into Prince – 'I Would Die 4 U' – and the hem of my dress is flippy and I like the way it feels as it flips. I am all bum and boobs and hips, but I don't care. I am cool girl in cool bar, dancing with cool guy. All those boys from a hundred years ago who didn't want me and would shout about the fact they didn't, to a laughing audience? They are gone. All those girls who thanked their lucky stars they didn't look like me and never hid their relief? They have slunk away. I am dancing with Salvi in the West End on a Thursday night and it feels utterly fantastic. What do they say? Just go with it. I'm five cocktails in and I'm beginning to believe I can.

We dance and we dance, song after song; there's a circle forming around us – admiring us. We're grinning in each other's faces; I'm basking in Salvi's reflected gaze. I feel free, freer than I ever have. I begin to feel a little bit beautiful. Just a little bit.

Salvi pulls me to the side of the dancefloor. We flag down and demolish another cocktail each then it's back into the arena again. Spinning and laughing. The band slows it down – they're playing an oldie – an *eighties* oldie. It's 'The Long Hot Summer' by The Style Council, when Paul Weller left Mod for Soul. It has always reminded me of teenage years, when long hot summers were to be endured, but now, now . . . Salvi pulls me towards him and I am the girl in hot pink in the window. I am one of the joyous, beautiful sinners. He holds me in his arms and I lean into his neck.

Suddenly his thumb comes from behind my head and towards my face like a weapon, and I wince. What is he doing? Is he going to wipe off my make-up? Expose my cheek and the real me that lies beneath? Just when I was feeling so amazing.

'Hey,' he says gently. He doesn't wipe anything off my cheek. He tenderly wipes just below my left eye, with a light yet firm touch. 'Your eye make-up is smudged,' he says. 'You're clearly having too much fun.'

'I really am,' I reply.

His grass-green eyes hold mine. I'm still in his arms, his face close to mine. I am spellbound. 'Can I take you home?'

Something is happening to me, when for all those years it hasn't because I have pushed the world away. Kept it locked outside. Kept all the light away. If I let it in, will Salvi notice the dark shadows of my soul? The black spots deep inside me as indelible and as un-scrubbable as my birthmark?

'Yes,' I say. 'Yes, you can take me home.'

'Fantastic,' he whispers into my ear. 'That's so fantastic.' I gaze at him. His eyes are like jewels in a rock warmed by the sun, his mouth an open-ended promise. The man is a complete and utter miracle. 'Let's go,' he says.

I am drunk, so bloody drunk – just the right side of staggering blindly about, bumping into people. I let Salvi lead me off the dancefloor and pull me through the dancing throng. Our waitress, from earlier – a sliver of black and white and blonde – is standing at the edge of the dancefloor and looks at us with curiosity. A look that says I am *punching*, that I had got my proverbial coat and pulled. I smile at her – conciliatory, patronizing – when do I ever get the chance to throw a patronizing glance at a pretty blonde? Never. Not like this.

A taxi is waiting outside like another small miracle on this miraculous night. Salvi opens the back door for me and I slip inside, on to the back seat; the windows are open and the night is coming in. Let everything in. I think. I want to be *flooded* with light and life until there's no room for any more. Salvi jumps in after me, plomps on the seat, leans forward and thunks the sliding door closed. He turns to me and takes my face in his hands, both hands, cupped round my face, and starts kissing me again. I press my breasts into his warm chest. My heart into his body. And as the taxi putters into a sprint, past another green set of traffic lights, another of my black spots turns light and dances off into the night.

Chapter 24

When I was about nine or ten, Angela and I went to stay with Nonna and Papa in a caravan somewhere near the white cliffs of Dover for the summer holidays and Nonna gave me an annual – I think it was *Bunty* – and I was obsessed with one of the comic-strip stories in it, reading it over and over, until, if someone had asked me to reproduce it, word by word and picture by picture, I could have done. It was about a young girl with blonde hair who had a hideous scar under her right eye which distorted that side of her face, and she was teased and taunted because of it, mercilessly. She cried every night, so one day she bought a mask – a black eye mask, a bit like Zorro's – and she ran away into the country and lived rough, like a gypsy, whilst wearing it; always. She had all sorts of adventures and forgot about her face, for many years, until one day the mask came off in one of her adventures and she happened to look into the reflection of a pond in the moonlight and she was beautiful. Just beautiful. I stared at that final panel of the story for ever. I wished so hard that this sequence of events – this story, told in black and white, in illustrations and speech bubbles – would happen to me. I wished and I wished and I wished, and of course it never did, but this morning, just a little, I feel like the girl in the final panel.

The scene is Salvi's flat. His open-plan sitting-room-slash-kitchen. One single corner lamp is still switched on. Two half-drained wine glasses and an empty bottle of red

190

sit on a trendy glass coffee table. And I am sitting on a high stool in one of Salvi's T-shirts while he's in the shower, and I'm drinking strong black coffee he has made in an actual cafetière, with my hair all tousled and half over my face and a big thumping headache.

'How's your coffee, madam?' Salvi emerges from the bedroom in a dark grey suit and tie.

'Perfect, thank you.' I hug my coffee mug like an actress and sip from it slowly.

I didn't sleep with him. It's not that I didn't want to; I did. I was ready to be arch seductress, fevered femme fatale – roles I have never taken on and have no clue about, but was ready to give a good go – as we tumbled through the door, kissing and kissing, but it didn't happen. Salvi pressed pause – to get us another drink, to fuss over preparing a bowl of trendy-looking snacks – and somehow we ended up sitting on his bed, the room spinning slightly, and then I was *in* that bed, somehow, and I have a vague memory of him tucking me in, the covers tight round me, like swaddling clothes, then waking at a very hungover 6.30 a.m., to him sitting on the side, staring at me.

His smile was gentle. He took a stray piece of hair stuck to my face and tucked it into the rest, he trailed a finger down my arm; he said I looked beautiful. I felt amazing. I felt looked after, cherished – almost; he looked at me like I was a precious porcelain doll in a box. Something exquisite. Something delicate and breakable. No one has made me feel like that before.

'I've got to go, I'm afraid.'

Salvi is grabbing briefcase, papers, keys.

'Already? It's not even seven yet.'

'Big case on.' Salvi comes over and plants a soft kiss on my lips. 'Thank you for a fantastic night, though,' he says.

'No need to run off, stay as long as you like. Just let yourself out, the door will lock behind you.'

'Oh, OK. Thank you.'

His gaze lingers on me. His eyes then flick over the breakfast bar.

'Ah. There it is.' He grabs his phone from beside me, half hidden under a napkin. 'You haven't touched this, have you?' he asks.

'Of course not! Why, you got something to hide?' I joke.

'No,' he says quickly. 'It's been playing up, that's all.' His eyes soften. 'I have to be careful with it.'

'I promise I haven't touched your phone,' I say sweetly.

'Bye,' he says, with a grin, and with another kiss and a look that makes me feel treasured and special, he is gone.

'Bye,' I whisper, as the door closes behind him.

I finish my coffee, place my mug in Salvi's sink and go to the bedroom to retrieve my dress and my shoes. I fold up Salvi's T-shirt and place it on top of his chest of drawers, then I snoop around a little, like they do in films. I'm not sure what I'm expecting to find – a gun in a drawer or a sealed letter to an unknown woman? There's nothing. Just suits and shoes and underwear and a couple of Jack Reacher books on a bedside table. It seems Salvi has nothing to hide. I even look on the top of his wardrobe – but it is dust free and there is no locked box of secrets. The only thing of remote interest I find, in the drawer of his bedside table, is a small stack of cards for somewhere called The Profilo Club. A purple card with simply the name and a website address on it. 'Profilo' is 'profile' in Italian: I imagine a swanky gentlemen's club full of Italian professionals all drinking grappa and talking about the Old Country. I take one of the cards – as a souvenir, I suppose – and slip it into the pocket of my dress then, once I've brushed my teeth with Salvi's toothbrush and rinsed it, it's time to leave.

I wash up for him, place the tea towel over the handle of the oven door and grab my bag. It's only as the door gently clicks behind me that I realize I have no idea when I'm going to see him again.

Chapter 25

'What's that tickling my calf?'

'A Womble. Orinoco, I think.'

The Northern Line is experiencing a few problems this afternoon. Dad and I have been stuck in the black soot of a tunnel for five minutes and counting, and people are starting to get restless. There's been a few 'Bloody hell's and a couple of 'Fuck's sake's. A child has asked 'Mummy, why are we stuck?' about fourteen times. A man with a violin case has sighed the sigh of a man who finds the world simply intolerable. Dad and I have seats, but it's really hot and oppressive and we're wedged in by a Stonehenge of enormous suitcases and a giant retro cuddly toy.

'I don't remember Wombles,' Dad frowns, but then he smiles vaguely in the approximate direction of Orinoco's owner. He – a boy in a red baseball cap and an *Avengers* T-shirt – pats Orinoco on the head and looks a bit worried, as children often do around blind people – it's that natural embarrassment he'll be able to hide when he's older. I smile at him, too.

'And what's that *smell*?' asks Dad.

'Ssh.'

For some unfathomable reason, the woman opposite us has pulled a glass jar from her bag and is tucking into the first of two huge stinky hardboiled eggs.

'Well, what is it?'

'Eggs,' I say, and I don't care if the woman has heard me. This isn't the time and definitely not the place for sulphuric treats from a specimen jar. Passengers are starting to catch each other's eyes, gurning resignedly at one another, because of the delay; hoping desperately no one will have a panic attack and need talking down. Dad, of course, is not catching anyone's eye but staring straight ahead with nothing but the feel of Orinoco's paw to distract him from this sauna of horror.

Why we're coming to London Bridge on a Saturday, I really don't know.

'Sorry.' A tombstone suitcase shunted by a fidgeting foot whacks me on the ankle.

'No problem.' I have plenty to distract me, in this dark tunnel. Plenty of lovely places for my mind to wander to. Every time I think of Thursday night I get that delicious shiver of excitement in my stomach and I love this feeling, unexpected and delicious. My phone is in my bag, latent and waiting. I'm willing for a text to arrive; something cheeky, an emoji would do – a little red devil or a winky face. A sign Salvi wants to see me again. I have my bag slightly open on my lap and my phone angled so I would see if it lights up – not that it would in this tunnel – but there's been nothing yet. Then again, it's only been twenty-eight hours and twenty-two minutes since I left his flat.

I can wait.

'Bloody hell,' says Dad, in a general kind of manner, and as soon as the second word is out of his mouth the tube lurches into action then anticlimactically begins to trundle very slowly through the tunnel. At last we reach London Bridge.

'Thank, Christ. Come on, then.' Dad is standing up before I am, feeling for my arm, and we are suctioned off the train – minding the gap with the best of them – into the marginally cooler air of the platform.

'All right?' I say as we walk toward the lifts.

'All right,' Dad says.

The platform is busy. Our train has expelled a lot of

people and we're all heading the same way. Dad's tapping cane seems to be annoying a few of them. One woman is stuck, revving, behind us; I can feel her aborted attempts to get past. She eventually takes a jeopardy-tinged swerve over the yellow line and scoots up the platform and out of sight.

When we turn into the hall where the escalators rise, there's the plaintive nasal sound of a saxophone weaving through the space like ether. A busker in an incongruous woolly hat and a *Sound of Music* T-shirt is performing Dire Straits' 'Romeo and Juliet'. This is incredibly romantic for a Saturday afternoon, I muse – I'm not sure many will find love at the bottom of the escalators at London Bridge tube station, but who knows? I drop 50p into his hat as we pass.

As the escalator takes us up, I check my phone and it chimes to signal the arrival of a text.

Beautiful night, Prue. Lunch on Sunday?

I quickly reply.

Tomorrow or NEXT Sunday?

And then feel incredibly foolish and overeager. Capitals, for God's sake! A text chimes in return.

2 pm, The Monastery on the Embankment. Not tomorrow. Next Sunday.

Oh, the shame . . . and that's ages away . . .

Great!

Still, I'm pleased. As well as being ridiculously keen to see Salvi again, The Monastery is one of *the* restaurants of the moment; I read about it in the *Mail* online. It's tiny and exclusive, with a waiting list as long as the Thames, and very very expensive. It's way out of my league and so is this man, probably. What the bloody hell am I going to wear?

'Who was that texting?' asks Dad as we queue for the barriers. 'Covent Garden Man?'

'Barrister man,' I correct.

'Bandits in striped trousers,' says Dad.

'I thought that was solicitors?'

'Yes, maybe it was. *You* would have made a good lawyer,' he adds.

'Barrister,' I correct, again. 'Really?'

'Yeah, you're very good at arguing the toss!'

I laugh, although my father is wrong. I could never stand up in front of people every day, performing like that. I could never have had a stellar career – something truly amazing. That was what my father was supposed to have done. He was the one with all the talent.

'He's taking me out for lunch next Sunday. The Monastery. Here, Dad, we're at the barrier. You go first.'

'That place still going?' Dad asks, once we are through. 'I remember that as a massive hot spot back in the sixties. It's a beautiful building – has been standing since 1521. Five central pillars and twelve arches. Designed around a central courtyard for the comings-and-goings of the monks.'

'*You* would have made a really excellent architect, Dad,' I say warmly.

'Don't you know it!' He laughs, but then a cloud comes across his face and I'm sorry for putting it there and as we walk through the concourse, to the exit, I say something I've never said before, 'I'm sorry things got cut short for you, Dad. Your career. Everything. I'm so sorry.'

'Thank you, love, I appreciate that.' It's hard to read my father's expression when his feelings are not reflected in his eyes. I can't see hurt in them now, for example, but I know that hurt is there. We keep walking. 'Sometimes I don't know if I'm more sad or angry about it, you know?' he says, and I am surprised, as he has never said anything like this to me before, either. 'I came so close to being an architect. I was qualified. I was ready. And then it all just slipped away. So easily. Maybe I *let* it slip away so easily—'

I jump in, feet first. 'It's not necessarily all over for you, you know. You could still do something, in architecture. Consultancy or research or teaching or—'

'What are you talking about?' He *is* angry, I think. 'You're not going to go on about that architect in Hawaii again, are you – that John somebody?'

'John Harrison Burrows,' I say weakly.

'I'm *blind*, Prue. I went blind a long time ago and the opportunities to do any of the stuff you're talking about also went a long time ago. I gave up, you know. I realize that. And I'm *sixty-four*. Like in The Beatles song.' I think of my mother; she would also be sixty-four. Does Dad think of that, too? 'I'm too old for anything. And I don't bloody live in Hawaii!'

'Norman Foster is over eighty.'

'Norman Foster is not blind and has been an architect for six decades! There is absolutely no comparison!'

'I know, sorry. I'm just saying. I'm just saying it's never too late, Dad.'

'Does that also apply to *you*?'

I fall silent. Dad does, too. We're on the final escalator up to street level. Near the top, he sighs, then in a voice so quiet I can barely hear him, he says, 'You know, if anyone should be sorry, it should be *me*.'

'Whatever for? Careful, Dad, we're at the top of the escalator. Step off – now – that's it.'

He retakes my arm.

'For going blind in the first place. For jabbering on like the young excited idiot I was and walking straight into that metal beam.'

198

'A metal beam that shouldn't have been there! A metal beam that defied all safety regulations. That was in breach of about a million things. It was an *accident*. An on-site contravention. You remember what they said in the compensation case! Don't blame yourself.'

'Oh, but I do,' he says. 'I *do*. I couldn't afford to go *blind*! Your mother had left, I was a single father – it was the stupidest thing that could ever have happened. And because of it I've brought you down, over all these years, and Angela's not here.'

'Oh, Angela was always going to abscond,' I say. 'That's just the kind of person she is. And if anyone's brought me down, it's me. I've done that all on my own. You really don't need to be sorry, Dad,' I add quietly. 'You've been a fantastic dad. Blind, or not bloody blind.'

'Thank you,' he says. We are out in the bright sunlight now, the Shard winking at us from across the street. 'Even if you don't mean it.'

'I do bloody mean it!'

My eyes adjust to the sun. Dad is wearing sunglasses, purely as sunscreen. 'My Peters and Lee look,' he said, as we left The Palladian, and I am old enough to get the reference.

'The Shard's just over there,' I say. 'About twenty feet away. It's magnificent, Dad.' Dad followed its construction. He's read about it from inception to completion. He's studied it for years. 'I'm getting that giddy feeling looking all the way to the top.'

'Describe it to me,' he says, as we walk towards it. 'I've listened to Steven Berkoff banging on about it on Vocal-Eyes, but I want to hear your description.'

'VocalEyes?'

'London Beyond Sight,' he says. 'A project where actors describe iconic London landmarks for the blind. I've

199

listened to all the luvvies waxing lyrical on some of the great buildings in London.'

I laugh. 'I'm not sure I'm going to be as lyrical as Steven Berkoff.'

'Good. I want it from *your* eyes.'

We've stopped now, on the pavement. People are snaking their way around us. 'OK, well, it's endless, majestic. It rises like a ship's mast, an obelisk, a tall and narrow pyramid, almost.' Oh, I'm doing well here. 'Yet there's something brittle about it, something piercing. It's grey and it's blue and it's white,' I say. 'The clouds and the sky are reflected in it, like it's a painting by Monet, or Constable.'

'A ship's mast,' says Dad, concentrating. 'Clouds by Monet . . . OK, OK, good, thank you, Prue.' He nods then squeezes the back of my arm. I'm pleased with myself. 'Right, let's walk all the way up to it.'

We cross the road and head for the main entrance, the corporate lobby beyond.

'OK, we're here.'

'I want to get close to the glass, how many more steps?'

'Three or four.'

'Guide me.'

I lead him a little to the right. 'We're here, Dad. Just reach out your hand straight in front of you.'

Dad takes the flat of his hand and places it against one of the glass panes. 'It's warm.'

'The sun's right on it.'

'Yes,' he says. 'Good,' he adds, like he has come home. And I realize that behind his sunglasses he is crying.

'Oh, Dad,' I say.

'I'm OK,' he says, and he stands there and he sighs and he smiles and I place my hand on his upper arm, slipping it under the hem of his T-shirt sleeve and I feel his firm, warm bicep. My lovely Dad.

'Why have we wasted so much time, Prue?' he says. 'Sitting in that flat day after day, when all this life – all this beauty – was out here?'

'I don't know, Dad. But we're out now, aren't we? We're here.'

'Yes, we're here.'

His hand is still on the pane of glass, as though he is drawing energy from it. He sighs again. 'I'm scared, Prue.'

'Why, Dad? Tell me why you are scared.'

'I'm starting to forget.'

'Forget . . . ?'

'What things look like, as I've been blind for so long. Objects, things, animals, shapes, even. Types of flowers. Colours. I can remember so many things – numbers of things, mainly, how many steps, things I've *read*, but some shapes now, some colours . . . I don't remember how a ship's mast looks. Or paintings by Monet. Or even clouds. Not really.'

'Oh, Dad. I'm so sorry; I'm an idiot, I—'

'It's not your fault.' He takes his hand from the glass. 'Your descriptions are excellent, Prue. But when you say there's a pigeon on the tube, I simply can't remember what a "pigeon" looks like. It's so strange, you know, to say the words but not see them in my head.' He sighs. 'For a long time I used to test myself every day. Go through a list of animals, say, in my head, one by one. Dog, cat, wolf, bear, rabbit, guinea pig, killer whale . . . I did it most days, for a long time. Then other days I forgot. And then I'd think, What was the point? Time is a killer, Prue – it is eroding my memory of all these *things* in life. Some of these animals don't exist for me, now, or they blur into one. I don't think I can see a difference in my head now between a dog and a wolf, for example.'

'Does it matter, Dad, if you don't know the difference?' I say, but I know that it does. To him. 'I could help you. I could describe those animals to you, explain the differences. Talk about lots of other things. Remind you.'

'I suppose so. If we carried on going out, if we talked more . . .'

'We can, Dad! We are doing that, aren't we? We're talking now.'

'There's so *many* things now, though. So many things I have forgotten.'

'We could *try*, though. What else can we do but try?'

Dad's confession has floored me. I want to cry for him. I want to stand on this street and weep for my father. He has never told me this. He is telling me secrets from deep down inside of him, when I have failed to reveal mine. He is starting to forget, when I remember everything but cannot put my worst memories into words.

I am still clinging on to his arm. A man in security uniform walks round us and disappears into the mouth of the Shard.

'You know, there are some things I'll *never* forget,' says Dad. 'Never in my life. And two of those are yours and Angela's faces when you were born.'

I attempt a laugh. 'Well, you would hardly forget mine, would you? I bet the massive birthmark was quite a surprise!'

'I'm not talking about that,' says Dad. 'Angela was all scrunched up, yelling at the world, making herself heard. You were quiet, after an initial yell. You just looked and looked – your eyes huge, as though you were saying, "OK, well, this is where I am now, is it?"'

'Did I already look pissed off?'

'No! You looked serene, all knowing.'

'I'm so glad you can't see me now.'

'Stop it, Prue. I don't need to see you. Seeing is not *knowing*. What you say and how you say it, how your personality is, that's more important than how you look.'

'But my personality is terrible,' I say, only half teasing (I won't mention Angela's).

'You're crazy, aren't you?' says Dad. 'You are a loving woman with a big heart. You have a lot of love to give and deserve to receive a lot of love in return. You just need to see that. You just need to see you can be happy.'

I have no answer to this. I think of Salvi. Is he someone who I could love and maybe have him love me in return? Is he my happiness, waiting at the end of the tunnel? I've never thought I deserve love. Not from my mother or my sister or from any man out there. Only from my father.

'Actually, I'm glad I can't see you,' continues Dad, 'as I know you'll have that look on your face right now that you had when you were a little girl. Cross and obstinate and disbelieving.'

'Maybe,' I say, although I know I am not looking like that. I'm sure, if I saw myself, that I would be looking a tiny bit *hopeful*.

'You were lovely as a child and you are lovely now,' he says softly. 'And that's the end of it.'

He feels for my hand and I take his – like a lifeline – and hold it tight, then he slips it from me and holds his arms out, as best he can, with the cane, and, in front of the Shard, as bemused and smiling pedestrians goldfish around us and restrain from saying 'Bless you', we hug. We haven't hugged for a very long time. I need this hug. Maybe he does, too. I hang on to my dad for dear life, here on the street, and it *is* a dear life we have been given, if we choose to see it, and we should make the most of it, while we are here, and not waste it sitting silently in the dark, with our eyes closed.

Eventually, Dad laughs, in my ear, a laugh of relief and of a little joy, I hope, and I laugh too and he takes my elbow and rights his cane and we set off again around the perimeter of the Shard, in the summer sun.

Chapter 26

'I left my sunglasses.'

Kemp is at the door this morning. I've just seen him from the window – Converse, jeans and a white T-shirt, standing on the pavement, hands in his back pockets – and now I am at the door I am continuing to ignore how the sight of him makes me feel, as I can't even begin to qualify it. Nostalgia, probably. Muscle memory for the potential of us, long expired? I expect so. I shouldn't get this slight jolt to the heart when I see him, I shouldn't be immediately remembering how he once made me feel. For goodness' sake, I have the memory of a hot man's warm lips on me that is mere days old and the excitement of an upcoming lunch date! I should be sticking to those things like a bloody limpet and nothing should be *jolting*.

'I know,' I say. 'I wasn't sure if you'd come back for them.'

'They're my varifocal ones,' he says. 'Ha, I sound old.'

'You *are* old.'

There's a noise from the stairs, behind me.

'*Prue?*'

'Yes, I'm here, Dad.'

Dad is clanking slowly down the metal steps, his hand on the railing. He insisted he didn't need my help. He insisted he was ready for the next trip on the list.

'Where're you off to now?' asks Kemp.

'Kenwood House, at Hampstead,' I mutter, looking at the ground.

'Oh, right. In that case, I can get them on the way back. My sunglasses.'

'The way back?' I snap my head up.

'Well, I'll come with you, shall I?' says Kemp. He's grinning at me and his eyes are all twinkly and mischievous. I know that look. It usually preceded a trilogy on the karaoke in the pub: Def Leppard, Aerosmith and Guns N' Roses. 'I could do with the walk.'

'It's about fifty minutes,' I say. I have worked out the route, with Dad. We're going to walk there and get the tube back. It's another beautiful day and I have been looking forward to it. Since we hugged, at the Shard, I've felt closer to him. I've felt that we can be there for each other. I hope for better days, and that this sunny Tuesday will be one of them.

'I know,' he says, and I have to look away. 'A nice long walk!' He's as excited as a three-month-old puppy, and just as bouncy. He's hopping from one foot to the other, in his Converse. 'Well, if that's OK with you, Prue? Vince?'

'Fine with me,' says Dad. 'And I'm sure Prue will be glad of the extra company,' he adds. 'Not just stuck with the blind old goat.'

'Dad!'

'Well . . .' says Dad, doing an exaggerated shrug, but it is not the 'blind old goat' I am objecting to. I don't want Kemp to come. I don't want to have to look at him for nearly an hour. Talk to him. Be reminded of all I felt for him. And that's just on the way . . . How am I going to feel when I get there?

'Great!' repeats Kemp.

I lock the door and we set off up the road, the three of us: Dad holding my arm as usual, Kemp the other side of me.

'It's a beautiful morning,' Kemp says.

'Yes.'

I begin describing things en route to Dad but, because

of what he said to me at the Shard, because of his confession, there in the midday sun, I'm careful to talk about shapes and the detailed form of things and I don't take for granted when I say 'a sparrow' or 'a post box' that he automatically remembers what I'm talking about. I paint a picture as best I can of people's houses and gardens and birds sitting on overhead cables. I describe the shredded cotton wool of clouds, in the distance. The shop fronts. People out of earshot who look mildly eccentric or interesting. I'm worried about Dad but he seems OK. He nods and smiles. I'm also self-conscious because Kemp is here. I become slightly monotone. I sound like I'm reading from a political party's manifesto leaflet.

'It's fantastic,' says Kemp. 'You two, coming out on these trips. Enjoying this wonderful summer in London together. You had an occasional sense of adventure, didn't you, Prue?'

'Did I? Oh, mind, Dad – wheelie bag oncoming!' The three of us migrate to the right of the pavement to let an old man with a battered tartan trolley bag past. He smiles his thanks at me, and I smile back.

'Yeah, I like to think so.' I ignore Kemp's inflection, keep my eye on the road ahead. 'My last trip was to America,' he continues, as we walk. 'To the wind farms of Arizona. It was really quite beautiful.'

'I know,' I admit. 'I saw the pictures.'

'She subscribes,' says Dad, and I want to dig him in the ribs, though I should never have said anything in the first place. Do I really want to confess to Kemp that I've been obsessing over his work for the past seven years?

'To *National Geographic*? That's cool.'

Oh God, I'm obsessing *now* about whether he's wondering where I keep them all. He wouldn't have seen them in the sitting room or the hall or the kitchen of The Palladian, when he and Ryan visited, because I keep them in stacks under my bed, like a love-struck teenager hoarding every copy of *Smash Hits* with Adam Ant on the cover.

'I've always been interested in wildlife and remote tribes,' I say breezily. 'I just never told you.'

'Right. Well, brilliant,' says Kemp, looking at me oddly. I see his odd look and I raise him an arched eyebrow. He counters it with an exaggeratedly furrowed brow, which can't help but make me laugh, then starts talking animatedly to Dad about the wind farms of Arizona and how he had the best hamburger ever in a little shack of a restaurant just outside Phoenix . . .

We finally get to Hampstead, then Hampstead Lane, and turn into the stone gateway for Kenwood House. It's a relief to get out of the sun and on to the wide shady paths of the grounds. It's a relief to be nearly there. Walking the streets of North London with a smiley bouncy Tigger you've always hidden your feelings from has been a bit of a challenge. I concentrated on Salvi, in the end. Re-conjured the feeling when he gazed upon me like a precious doll. Wondered if I would ever get to sleep with him. It helped me not to stare at Kemp's beard and despair at how handsome it makes him look. It helped me not to remember.

It's busy in the grounds of Kenwood House. There are families, and joggers – both lone and in packs – and couples young and old, strolling and pushing buggies and children running ahead of their parents, in shorts and sandals and T-shirts, tripping over, and blowing bubbles from those plastic tubes, and everybody looks content, or happy, even. They are enjoying a nice day out, in the summer sun. They are at leisure. At ease. They are making the most of the long hot summer because this is England and, like Dad says, who knows when we'll get one like this again?

'I haven't been here for a long time,' says Dad, as I tell

him we have reached the house. We are now crunching on gravel the colour of pearls. 'About forty years, I think.'

'Yep,' I say. 'I reckon you last brought Angela and me here when I was eight or nine.'

'And has it changed?'

'Not a jot.'

I describe the huge white Georgian house to him, with the pillars and the porch and the massive windows with their tiny panes Angela and I used to peer into. Its roof and its gables. How the expansive lawn rolls from the house, a green carpet, down to the large pond where Angela and I once trailed our fingers in the water and fed the ducks. How the good people of London are again on tartan waterproof-backed blankets, with their picnics and their snacks: families gathered to loll and laugh; couples entwined on the grass, a tangle of limbs and phones in back pockets and headphones and half-drunk bottles of water.

'Family, love and food,' says Dad. 'A great combination.'

'Yes,' I agree.

'And has it changed since *we* were here last, Bertie?' asks Kemp.

My heart stops. Just for a second. I hoped he wasn't going to bring it up. I hoped he wasn't going to say anything. But he has. Why wouldn't he? It's a night that means absolutely nothing to him, apart from a good laugh he once had, with a friend. A night about a million years ago.

'Remember how we climbed the wall, in the moonlight? Broke in? Walked up to the house?'

'We were really drunk,' I say, 'so not really.'

I look away from him, away from the house we sat in front of that night – as my heart broke into its final pieces – and down to the pond, where a man is having his photo taken with a gaggle of ducks. Of course, I remember everything about that night. Every tiny detail. We were in the King's Arms, as usual, when Kemp suddenly cried, 'Hey, let's get the bus to Hampstead Heath! It's Bonfire Night, isn't it? There'll be fireworks.' And I immediately got my coat from the back of my chair, as I would have gone anywhere with him. We ran up the street to the bus stop and waited ages for the bus and by the time we got to Hampstead Heath the fireworks had finished but Kemp declared he wanted to look at Kenwood House, in the moonlight, so we climbed the gate – very clumsily – and infiltrated the grounds, and made our way up the deserted winding paths to the house while Kemp told me elaborate ghost stories that became so funny and preposterous they ended with us both crying with laughter and shushing each other as the steam of our breath escaped into the cold night air.

'You *must* remember,' says Kemp, throwing me an odd look.

I do. I do. How can I forget? How we sat on the freezing stone steps at the front of the house and swigged out of the bottle of beer Kemp had smuggled out of the pub. How Kemp leapt up at one point and walked unsteadily backwards down the grassy bank to the pond, spreading his arms wide and calling out, 'They filmed *Notting Hill* here, you know? When Julia Roberts is shooting that Henry James movie. *I'm just a boy, prancing around in front of a permanently grumpy girl . . .*' How he returned to the steps and there our beautiful friendship ended.

'You broke *in*,' says Dad, sounding impressed. 'A precursor for all this urban exploring you're doing then, lad?'

'I guess so,' says Kemp. 'It can be magical being somewhere you're not supposed to be. It was the last night I saw you, Prue,' he adds, looking in my direction.

'Let's walk a little, round the perimeter of the house,' I say quickly. 'People keep having to walk around *us*.'

We walk, the three of us. As I describe sash windows and pillars and porticos to Dad, I know it's also magical, and heartbreaking, being with someone you're not supposed to be *with*. I was not supposed to be sitting so close to this amazing man, in the moonlight, in front of this beautiful house, in these wonderful grounds that had been shut up for the night. I was not supposed to feel the way I did about him. When Kemp returned from his *Notting Hill* backwards-walking shtick, he plonked himself back down on the steps and his right thigh, in those dusty jeans, was touching mine and I could feel the heat of him, but it was nothing compared to the heat that was soaring through me, the pain of knowing I loved him but he couldn't feel the same about me – ever. I was ugly, inside and out. I was not good, like him. I had too many black marks against me and he knew most of them.

'I'm going to India next month,' he told me, on that step. 'Jaipur and Udaipur. The palaces.'

'How lovely,' I replied. 'I bet you'll get some amazing photos.'

'Yeah, should be good,' he said. 'Have you been?'

'Where, to India? Of course I haven't!'

He nodded. He looked at me for a few seconds and then it seemed he might be about to say something else, but instead he turned and looked out over the darkness, beer in hand, dreaming of those places, I assumed; dreaming of the adventures he'd have. I stared and stared at the side of his face. I couldn't bear that he was going away again, without a care. Not missing me. Not wanting me. Not counting the days until he saw me again, like I did with him. I couldn't bear that I could only ever be his friend. Someone for jokes, and ghost stories, and drinks in the pub. Someone for everything but love.

I wanted and I wanted and I *wanted* to take that glorious, miraculous, warm and lovely face in my hands and kiss him and tell him I loved him. Instead, I just said, 'Kemp,' and he turned to me with a smile and said, 'What?' and I said, 'I'm cold, shall we go back now?'

I wasn't cold. I was burning inside, with the pain of a love that couldn't be returned, and I knew I couldn't go on feeling it. Not any more.

Dad's hand is tugging on my arm slightly. His right foot crunches on the gravel. 'Shall we go in the house now?' he asks.

'Yes, Dad.'

The three of us step into the entrance hall, where it is cool and smells of old houses, a smell Dad breathes in deeply as we go through the door and I pretend to do the same, but really I am taking a deep breath of relief. There are no memories in here, apart from the ones of Angela and I tearing through these rooms, giggling and excited (well, she was *tearing*; I was just in the slipstream), and staring, bored, at paintings and clomp-clomp-clomping in our sandals on the oak staircase, because it sounded nice and it was fun. There is no *Kemp* in here.

I spot a tactile map of the house on the wall, which I manoeuvre Dad to, and he runs his hand over it.

'Robert Adam designed much of Kenwood House,' he says. 'It was built in the seventeenth century and served as a residence for the Earls of Mansfield through the eighteenth and nineteenth centuries. It's kept today in its original condition, exactly *like* a house, for people to walk freely through and experience – a house with many priceless old masters and landscapes hanging on its walls, of course.'

It's just how I remember it: the wooden floors, the gorgeous winding staircases with their great acoustics, the richly patterned rugs, those imposing old masters. We start to make our way round. Dad and I lead; Kemp follows. There's a Braille guide in each room. Dad is impressed.

We trail through, room after room. I describe what I can see to Dad. The rich Aubusson rugs; the marble fireplaces and the cast-iron radiators; the window seats framed by heavy and pelmeted velvet curtains. The extensive artwork. I describe everything as carefully and concisely as I can. We enter the library, or great room. Here there is a stunningly pretty panelled and decorated domed ceiling, in pale pink and blue.

'Look up,' says Dad, 'at the cornicing. They've painted over some of the gilding, apparently, after extensive research of hundreds of forensic paint samples. Can you see it?'

I don't know what I'm looking at.

'A protective barrier between the old gilding and new paint, but the next generation of renovators will still be able to get to the gilded layer and—'

'Oh, it's Carina!' Kemp exclaims. 'Excuse me a moment.'

Looking away from the cornicing, I see him bounding over to a woman in a black shift dress and navy ballet pumps, who is staring up at one of the old masters. Her hair is a blond contained chignon; her arms are gilded with wide bronze cuffs; she has an enormous designer bag over one shoulder. She is one of *those* women – glossy, polished. The sort of woman that makes me feel like the last pumpkin in the bargain bucket at Halloween.

She looks delighted to see Kemp. They share a hug and two air kisses. I turn back to Dad and a portrait of a man sitting on a gold chair. I describe the painting to Dad: the colours – as best I can, hoping he can imagine them – the use of light and shade, the direction of the brushstrokes.

'Are you OK?' he asks me.

'Yes, absolutely fine. Why?'

'With Kemp being here, I mean. You seem a bit off.'

'I'm OK,' I say flippantly. 'I'm fine. Of course I'm fine.' I stare resolutely at the painting. I am not going to look over at Kemp and his polished *Carina*. He's never hugged *me* like that.

'You like him, don't you?'

'Everyone likes Kemp. What's *not* to like?'

'No, I mean *like* him.'

I move Dad on to another painting of another long-dead gentleman. Lots to describe here. A rather interesting hat.

'I *liked* him,' I say. 'We were friends. That's it.'

'If you say so.'

'I say so. Now, let me tell you about this painting—'

'Hmm.'

'What do you mean "hmm"? Are *you* OK, Dad?' I ask. I'm deflecting like crazy, but I also want to know. 'After what we talked about at the Shard? Are you OK today? Being out? Being here?'

'I'm fine, Prue,' says Dad. 'Nice subject change, by the way . . .' He smiles at me. 'You just have to keep on keeping on, you know? Isn't it all we can do? And I've got you, haven't I?' I think of our huge hug again, in front of the Shard. 'To keep me brave.'

'Brave?'

'To keep coming out again. To keep saying "yes". To take opportunities. To put myself out there even if it's scary. I want to ask you something.'

He already has, hasn't he? Asked me about Kemp. And I have fibbed. It's my default position, hiding my true feelings from Dad, isn't it? I've done it for so long. 'Go on.'

'You can take opportunities, can't you?'

'What do you mean?'

'You can say "yes" to things; you can put yourself out there. You could *look* for opportunities, if you wanted to. Develop your passions.'

'You've lost me.'

'I found your paintings,' says Dad.

'What paintings?'

213

'Come on, you know what I'm talking about! Ten or eleven pieces of A4 cartridge paper, curled at the corners or slightly crunchy – some of them – like they'd been made wet and then had dried – plus paintbrushes, paints, one of those trays with the thumb hole in it . . . I may not be able to see but I can *feel*.'

'When did you find those?' I rack my brains for when I may have left them out.

'About a year ago. You were out, on one of your occasional visits to a charity shop or something. You must have forgotten to put them away.'

'A *year* ago. You never mentioned it.'

'You obviously didn't want to tell me about them, so I didn't ask. Well, I asked you at Little Venice, about taking up art again. You brushed me off, if you excuse the pun. But I'm asking you now.'

'Well, yes, I've done some paintings.' I'm so cross with myself for inadvertently leaving them around; how could I have been so stupid?

'And are they good? Are you going to show them to anyone?'

I gently move Dad out of the way as a mother and son are trying to file past us.

'I don't know, and no.'

'You'll never know if they're good or not if you don't show them to someone.'

'Well, then I guess I'll never know.'

'Are you scared?'

I laugh. 'I'm not *scared*, Dad.'

'Really? I think you are. I think you're scared you'll be told they're good and I think you're scared you'll be told they're not.'

'I'm not scared,' I repeat.

'Well, then show them to someone.'

'I don't think so.'

'It might be time for some true bravery, Prue. It might be time for—'

'Dad . . .'

'Sorry about that,' says Kemp. He is back. Carina has gone. I see the final corner of her expansive bag disappearing round a door frame.

'Friend of yours?' I ask him.

'Kind of.'

I look at Dad, worried he is going to continue our conversation. He doesn't. He takes my arm and we carry on circling the room, with me continuing to describe the paintings to him in a half-hearted manner. I'm sorry Dad found mine, but it doesn't really matter, does it? I'm not going to show them to anyone. I'm not going to *do* anything about them.

Kemp trails after us. He studies the paintings in great detail. Well, he's an artist, isn't he? It's his kind of deal.

'There's a self-portrait of Rembrandt in the dining room,' he says to Dad and me, after a while. 'And after that shall we go and get some lunch?'

Chapter 27

We go to the Brew House café and sit outside in its pretty courtyard garden. I have a slice of coffee-and-walnut cake; Kemp has an enormous brownie. Dad orders a fresh ravioli dish and salad, which he has to wait ten minutes for but they offer to bring it over. We make small talk, mostly about the glorious weather, and I pour tea for us, and then Dad's lunch is delivered to him by a smiling woman in a pale blue apron.

'Enjoy,' she says, placing it in front of him.

'Thank you,' he says. 'It smells wonderful, just like the ravioli *san Marzano* Mama used to make. *Bellissimo!*'

She smiles. 'You're Italian?' she asks.

'*Si*,' replies Dad.

'Me too.'

'Ah,' says Dad, and they both give a silly little laugh.

She moves off to the next table to chat to the couple there. Dad takes a bite of his ravioli.

'Delicious,' he says. 'Compliments to the chef,' he comments to me and Kemp.

'The chef is me,' the woman giggles from the next table. 'Sorry,' she adds, turning back to us. 'I appear to be highly tuned to the slightest compliment.'

'So you should be.' Dad smiles. 'It really is wonderful. It's got a lovely lemony hint to it.'

'That's the lemon balm. We grow it here in the gardens.'

'I love lemon balm,' says Dad. 'I sometimes sprinkle it through a caprese salad.'

'Nice. And it's wonderful with fish,' she adds. 'There's

216

also plenty of basil and wild garlic in that dish, all grown here.'

'Wild garlic is the nectar of the gods,' offers Dad. 'I throw it in everything, from ribollita to pasta alla Norma . . .'

Kemp and I glance at each other.

'You cook?' asks the woman.

'Every night,' says Dad, turning his face in my direction. I grin sheepishly.

The chef tucks her hands in the front pocket of her apron. 'I can take you to our herb garden, when you've finished eating, and talk you through what we grow here, if you'd like.'

'I'm blind,' says Dad. 'And do you have the time?'

'I thought you might be,' she replies. 'And, yes I do, I'm on my break in twenty minutes.'

'I'd love to,' says Dad.

Kemp and I raise eyebrows at each other. Dad is saying 'yes', I think, yes to opportunities. He's giving me an out-and-out demonstration.

'*Perfetto*. Then I'll be back.'

And twenty minutes later she is, sans apron, and with a, 'Shall we?' Dad gets up from the table.

'I'll need to hold on to your arm,' he says.

'Absolutely fine,' says the woman, and Dad takes her arm and they wander out of the courtyard and in the direction of Kenwood House's kitchen gardens.

'Well, look at that,' remarks Kemp. 'Your dad's on a herby date.'

'It looks that way,' I laugh. I am quite astonished, really. Off he's gone, just like that. 'Funny the things people are interested in,' I add. 'I wouldn't know a basil from a brush.'

Kemp laughs too, and I realize we're sitting in the same positions we used to sit at, at our table in the pub. Except now we have tea not Jack Daniel's and Coke and I don't have a beer mat to tear to pieces, so I work on a napkin in between sipping at my tea and stabbing my finger at the remaining crumbs of my cake.

'Here, put your sunglasses on, Ted.'

There's an elderly couple at the next table. The man – white-haired and frail-looking – is blinking in the sunlight; the woman – soft platinum hair and pale eyes behind horn-rimmed glasses – rummages in her bag and tenderly places a pair of sunglasses on the old man's face, pushing them up his nose until they are in the right position.

'There,' she says.

'Thank you, Annie,' he replies. I watch as she cuts his piece of cake into neat slices and pushes the plate closer to him. He smiles at her. She winks back at him and says, 'It's a lovely sponge. Try some.' I glance at Kemp and he is looking at them too.

'I'd like to be like that, one day,' he says.

'What, not losing your sunglasses because someone else always has them in her bag?'

'No, well, yes – but no, in a couple like that. Look at how in love they are.'

'Yes,' I say. We watch as the woman gently wipes crumbs from the man's mouth with a napkin. She affectionately pats him on the chin with it, too, and his hand grabs hold of hers and holds it tight, for a few seconds, as they look into each other's eyes and smile the smile of the known and loved.

'How lovely to grow old with someone,' he says.

'Is it? I'm not sure I want someone to see me get old,' I say, with all due nonchalance, but I am not telling the truth as I think I would love this, this tender slipping into the night, whilst holding someone's hand – this love and companionship, to the very end.

'*I* would,' says Kemp, looking thoughtful. 'I think it would be wonderful. To have someone who sees everything. To have someone to call "home".'

'Better find someone, then,' I say. 'Before it's too late.'

'Charming!'

'Better just grab anyone you can.'

Kemp looks at me. 'Thanks very much,' he says slowly. 'I might just have to do that. Settle with just anyone so I won't be a lonely old fool.'

'Wherever you lay your hat . . .' I shrug.

I know he won't do this. I know he would only grow old with someone he deserves. Someone he would place very carefully in his heart, and keep safe. *Lucky cow*. 'Good plan.'

He raises his left eyebrow slightly at me. 'You know that woman, in the house, she was my ex-girlfriend.'

'Oh?' The napkin suddenly becomes completely fascinating.

'Yes. Carina. We went out for almost a year.'

The feigned nonchalance is still holding up. 'Why did you break up?'

'Well, she was lovely, but, ultimately, she was too linear for me.'

'Linear? I don't get it.'

'No mystery, nothing to unravel. Straightforward, open. Too nice. Too easy to get along with. Not for me.'

'Oh, right. You want someone you don't get along with? That's a bit weird.'

'No, not exactly that. I want someone who doesn't always agree with me. I want banter. I want someone who I feel there's constantly more to discover about. I want an onion.'

'You want an *onion*.'

'Yes.'

I have no idea what he's talking about.

'I miss you,' he says.

'What?'

'I said I miss you. I *missed* you. All this time.' I am looking up from the napkin. Into his face. His eyes. I have no

219

idea what they're saying to me. 'We had such a great time, you and me.'

I screw the napkin into a ball with my fist. Hold on to it tight. 'Why do you miss me? Have you still not got any friends?'

This is cruel and I immediately regret it. I think of David Somebody, the school friend who moved away. Kemp, the loner in the darkroom. The boy who always had a plan.

'Oh, Prue.' He is shaking his head. 'I have friends. I realized a long time ago I didn't want to live life on my own any more . . .' Well, that's evident, I think. He's had women, he's had girlfriends, of course he has . . . but at one time I was his only friend, I'm sure of it. It was just me and him, for a while. 'But *you* were the best friend I ever had.'

'Even more than David Somebody?'

He looks puzzled, then laughs. 'David Hopkins? My Geography buddy? Yes, even better than him. It's great having you back in my life.'

'Am I?' I enquire. 'Am I back in it?' I am looking into his eyes even though I don't want to. I am searching his face for answers when I'd rather be running away, away from here and him, across the immaculate lawns and over the walls of Kenwood House. To home and safety. To a place and time where I had never bumped into him again.

'Would you *like* to be?'

I place the screwed-up napkin on the table and watch it unfurl. 'I suppose so.'

'You *suppose* so?'

Yes, I *suppose* so, I want to say. Yes, I *suppose* it's OK for me to start seeing you – a *lot* – for you to keep turning up on my doorstep and appearing places, and bringing lost socks and forgotten memories and making me feel really terrible that you were the best friend I ever had but I had to let you go. Yes, I *suppose* I can stand it, but I can't. Not really. When have I ever?

I don't say anything. Kemp hesitates for a moment, pushes a hand through his hair. 'Does your dad still like Blondie?'

'I guess so, why?'

'They're playing at the Roundhouse next Friday night. I've got a few comps – tickets – my mate works for the promoters. Would you like some?'

I look at him. What is he asking me here? Is *he* going to this concert? Is this Kemp asking me to be in his life another day, on another trip out? Or is he just giving away tickets?

'He used to really like them, didn't he?' he presses. 'And it's so close to you, I thought . . .'

I look at him and all I can see is eyes and smile. He's just giving away tickets, isn't he? In a friendly gesture. As *friends* do.

'Yes, he did,' I say. I remember Dad's photo, him and his mate, Jack Templeton, at the Roundhouse, where he saw Blondie before. In 1978. I think about how I have *never* been, despite all the events that have been held there, over the years, and all the times we have shut the window on the music that escaped from its conical slate roof. I wonder if Dad would like to go. Now we were on our walkabout streak. Now he was – unlike me – being *brave*.

'How many would you like?'

Kemp looks bemused at how long I'm taking to answer. I'm still thinking. I'm thinking about everything. Then I think of Salvi. If Dad and I go, I could take him as well, maybe. Lord knows I need him in my life more than ever if I'm back in Kemp's, somehow. My *distraction*. Thank goodness for our upcoming lunch date at The Monastery on Sunday. Thank goodness for this man, Salvi – this charismatic, slightly bewildering man – who seems to like me. If Kemp's at the concert, too, I will have Salvi as an emotional balustrade. 'Three?'

Kemp slightly raises one eyebrow. 'Three? OK, done! Great. I'll drop round with them at some point.'

'OK, great, thank you.'

We sit in silence for a while, after this rather random and unclear exchange. Eventually Ted and Annie get up from their table. Ted is a little wobbly on his feet and Annie has to steady him before they set off. They take each other's hands and hold them fast as they walk through the café garden and out of sight, with Kemp and I both watching them go.

'Prue, I—'

'Oh look, Dad's back.'

Here he is with the nice chef woman and they are laughing at something and Dad has a great bundle of herbs in his left hand and she is carrying some sort of trug also full of leafy delights. She places Dad's other hand on the back of his chair, and he navigates it to sit down.

'Hope to see you again sometime,' she says, touching him lightly on the arm.

'Me too, Maria,' says Dad genially.

'Well, that was nice,' he says to Kemp and me, after she has disappeared back into the café. 'I've smelled about twenty-two different herbs and get to take some home for tonight's dinner.'

'And met your future wife,' I add cheekily. '*Maria.*'

'Ssh!' Dad puts his finger to his lips. 'She might hear you! And I haven't met my future wife!' Dad protests, but he is grinning, really grinning.

'You never know,' I laugh.

We finish our tea and leave the café and the grounds of Kenwood House and wend our way to Hampstead tube station. Kemp gets off at Belsize Park, saying he needs to buy more film for his camera. He missed me, I puzzle, as he waves cheerily at our departing train from the platform. I don't know why. He's glad I'm back in his life. *Do I want him to be back in mine?* I honestly don't know.

When we get back to Chalk Farm, I tell Dad we need milk and some more bread. Dad asks for the key; he is tired and wants to go ahead. He can manage by himself while I go to the Stop n' Shop.

There's a queue. Some bloke is arguing about cigarettes and alcohol. When I finally get to pay for my bread and milk, the same bloke is ranting to himself in the doorway, a bottle of vodka in his hand he is struggling to get open. He stares at me as I walk past, as though there's something wrong with me he can't quite fathom. I don't hang around for him to find out. As I come out of the shop and turn the corner of Chalk Farm station's apex, I hear music.

It's loud. Melodious. Familiar. It's the Kinks, 'Waterloo Sunset'. I look up, and the music is drifting down from the wide-open window of The Palladian. Dad has put it on. Dad must have lifted the creaky duck-egg-blue lid. Taken a record from a small stack on the little shelf underneath. Slipped it from its sleeve and placed it on the turntable. Felt for the edge of the record and lowered the needle. He must have felt the need for music. For melody. For the soft melancholic sound of Ray Davies' voice and his lyrics about the sweet, sweet end to another London day. And for it to fill our flat and drift through the open window and down to the street below.

Chapter 28

There is a dress. A dress I saw last time I came to *Loved Before*. A dress so floaty and romantic I would never have dared buy it, even to keep at the back of my wardrobe, unworn, for some unknown and never-arriving event. It's pale buttercup yellow, it has big white flowers on it, it is off-the-shoulder and mid-calf length and has ruffles and a low sexy wrap front – a bit English Rose meets Flamenco. It's in my size, I know, because I've looked at the label. I think it might be perfect for my lunch with Salvi.

It's busy at the dress agency this morning. Excited women of various ages are rifling through the racks and flicking nimble fingers between the necks of clicky hangers. There are rainbows of colours on the rails, teasing novel slivers of beads and sequins and gossamer fabrics, catching the light. A lot of new stock has come in. I hope my dress is still here. I've let the silky rayon slip through my fingers. I've failed to imagine any scenario where I could wear this amazing, seductive, sublime miracle of a dress, but now I have one, I need to find it.

I head to the rail. I can't see it, but the rail is concertinaed with rippling waves of dresses of all colours. I rifle through . . . yes! There it is, three dresses from the end, dragged wall-wards by two more robust beauties so I couldn't see it. I pull it out and wonder at its gorgeousness; I wonder where its previous owner wore it and how she could ever have said goodbye.

As soon as I put it over my head and zip it up, in the tiny changing room, I just know. It swings when I twist in it. It makes my boobs look great. The colour lights up the decent side of my face. It's perfect. I smile at myself, knowing this is the kind of romantic, summery froth of a dress that might just make Salvi want to rip it off with his teeth.

'That's beautiful,' says Maya, as I carry it like a precious child to the counter. She has escaped from the back room and is standing behind me. 'Please tell me you're getting it.'

'I certainly am.' I smile. I'm flushed, I know, from the over-warm changing room and the anticipation of me in this dress.

'Another hot date? Same man?'

'Yes, same man. We're going for lunch on Sunday. To The Monastery.'

'Ooh, fancy. Well, that's exciting. Shoes?'

'Shoes.' Ah, I had nothing that would go with this dress. The wedges wouldn't cut it. And *Loved Before* doesn't sell shoes.

'You'll have to go into the West End,' says Maya.

'Will I?'

'Yes, treat yourself to something gorgeous! Harvey Nics, Selfridges . . . beautiful shoes.'

'I suppose so,' I say. I never go shopping in the West End.

'That dress *needs* amazing shoes,' says Maya. 'Go to the West End and fall in love with some!'

'Thank you,' I say, looking into her kind smiling face. 'Maybe I will.'

I step out into the sunshine and hop straight on a bus that's heading to Oxford Circus. I head up to the top deck, sit about six rows back and look out of the window. London is sunny and sticky and in full-swing this morning. People are sauntering, jackets off, smiling at each other: things that don't happen in the winter. The bus

225

stops at traffic lights. Another pulls up alongside us, very close. I look down into the gap between the two buses and see a woman in an A-line denim skirt, sandals and an orange T-shirt squeeze through it, almost completely swivelled sideways, her tasselled beige bag tucked on her shoulder behind her. I watch her get on the other bus, through my viewfinder of thick, dusty dual glass. She looks like my mum, circa 1975 – *pre-flight*. Same shoulder-length hair, fashionable then, unfashionable now; that Farrah Fawcett flick. I watch her as she taps her Oyster card then she disappears and I see her reappear moments later on the top deck; she takes a seat halfway down, inches away from mine.

I thought I saw my actual mum once, getting on a bus, not long after her final visitation. There was some tatty cycling shorts and a perm; a confidence that looked chemical. I was crossing Oxford Street to the giant Top-shop on the corner, alone – when once I would have gone with Georgina, for trying-on sessions and some light coerced shoplifting – but instead I stepped on to the bus behind the woman I thought was my mother and fol-lowed her up the stairs to the top deck. It wasn't her. She was sitting three rows from the back and when I got there, I realized she had the wrong nose, the wrong chin, the wrong face. She wasn't my mum. I turned round and I got off the bus at the next stop, so angry with myself for thinking it was her, for that tiny part of my heart that let me down by hoping it was.

'Sorry, love.'

A big man with a small dog in his arms squeezes on to the seat next to me. I budge up. The woman on the other bus, even closer to me now, through the glass, is also nothing like my mother. Nothing at all. The man next to me shifts in his seat. He smells like bananas. The dog stares at me, doleful and suspicious.

Kemp says he misses me, but the fact that I don't miss my mum was another thing I told him, another black spot on my soul that I helpfully pointed out for his perusal. Another *reason* I could never expect him to be more than my friend. That's not normal, right? To not miss your mother? It hardly makes me someone to get romantically involved with. It makes me strange, off-kilter, someone to be suspicious of. Unlovely.

I uttered my confession the night of the skiffle band, when I got way too drunk. It was just before I threw up in Kemp's chemical toilet. Not long after, I think, I told him about Jonas, in Tenerife. Not all of it, but some of it, and I was so drunk I don't know exactly what I said, and I have no recollection of his reaction. But I said something, and I never dared bring it up again and when he tried to, I shut him down. I shut him down as quickly as when he tried to take a photo of me once, sitting at the tiny table in his houseboat, eating late-night sour cream-and-onion Pringles. His view of me in real life was bad enough; I didn't want it recorded – for him to witness my face and all that lay behind it when I wasn't even with him.

All these confessions were black marks against me. Cherry, how I felt about my mother, Jonas . . . They were my bad deeds, my unnatural thoughts, my shame and my errors in judgement. They were the dark and ugly waters of my past. The reasons – *more* reasons – that he could never love me. And I never even told him about Finsbury Park, where the black deeds all started, where I received my *tainting*, as a fourteen-year-old girl; where what happened to me became more indelible than my birthmark, more difficult to hide, more impossible to pretend it isn't still here.

The bus belches me out on to the street at Knightsbridge. I don't go to Selfridges or Harvey Nics; I don't have that much courage. Instead, I head into Zara, and

I'm intimidated as soon as I'm through the doors. They are all here: the mirrors and the *beautiful ones* – customers, shop assistants – and it's far too shiny and bright in here for me, so I keep my head down. I'm on a mission, after all. I walk past the line of changing cubicles to get to the shoe section – trying not to think about all the beautiful young girls, like dolls in boxes, inside them. The shoes twinkle under diamond lights and it doesn't take me long to find the perfect pair: pale gold, strappy sandals, high.

'They're stunning,' says a leggy brunette, all of about eighteen, with perfect skin, who is head-tilting at a pair of silver wedges. 'You should defo try those on.'

'I will,' I say. And when I do, sitting next to this ethereal creature on a faux-leather footstool and feeling like an absolute gargoyle, I smile. These are my Cinderella shoes. I have my Cinderella dress. I can be *that* girl. *That* woman. That woman who is going on a third date, ready to blow Salvi's mind. Gargoyle can scrub up, I think, with a little confidence and the right attitude. All you have to do is put it on.

When I let myself into the flat, I am surprised to see Ryan sitting in my chair talking to Dad.

'Hello, Ryan,' I say, failing to keep that surprise from my voice.

'Hi, Prue.' Ryan has grown a little bum-fluff moustache since I last saw him. He has an open file on his lap and is holding a biro. Taking notes.

'You answered the *door*?' I ask Dad.

'Yes.'

'Not knowing who it was?'

'Yes,' he says.

He's saying 'yes' again, I think. He's opening the door to himself and other people. I've said 'yes' too, though,

228

haven't I? I've said yes to new shoes and Salvi. I can *take* opportunities. The ones that I want to.

I go and put my handbag on the console table by the window. I start to unpack my bags. I want to describe my purchase to Dad. Talk about my new shoes. Talk about what it was like being in the West End . . .

Dad coughs. 'If you don't mind, we're rather busy here. Ryan's come for a bit more information on Leslie Green.'

'Wow, OK. Well, great.' I collect my bags up again. 'Kemp didn't come this time?'

'He knocked with me,' says Ryan. 'Now he's gone to a disused print works.'

'Of course he has.'

'Your dad makes amazing pasta.' He gestures at an empty plate to the right of him.

'I know. Doesn't he just?'

Dad coughs again.

'Well, have fun!' I say. I know when I'm not wanted. Ryan sits in my chair like Goldilocks and I am a grumpy bear – baby bear, probably – exiled to my bedroom by my own father. But, as I throw my bags on my bed and close the door, I am smiling. Dad has opened the door wide. Dad has let someone in. Dad has played music and now he is sitting with Ryan and talking about architecture. He's come a long way.

Chapter 29

'You look lovely.'

'Thank you.'

It's nowhere near two o'clock. It's Sunday. I've already got the dress on and the man seeing me in all its buttercup, Flamenco glory is not Salvi but Kemp, who is at the door brandishing three Blondie tickets in his hand. I've been ready since eleven. My make-up is done. I've just been waiting for the clock to tick round.

'Three tickets,' Kemp says, holding them out for me to take. 'You off out again? You and Vince?'

'No. Well, *I'm* going out. Not Dad. I'm going out for lunch.'

'Oh, anywhere nice?'

'The Monastery, at the Embankment?'

'Yes, I know it, interesting place.'

'Don't tell me, you've been burrowing around underneath it, sniffing at old habits or something.'

'Old habits die hard . . . Ha, no. Not yet, at any rate. Hot date?' he asks, eyebrows slightly raised.

'Well, it's a *date*,' I say. 'The temperature is yet to be determined.'

'I see. What time are you going?'

'Not until two.'

'Two o'clock?'

'Yes, two o'clock . . .'

'That's late.'

'Yes.'

'Right. OK.' He shuffles on to another foot. 'Look, do you fancy a quick drink before then, with me?'

'A drink? What for?'

'To catch up properly.'

Haven't we caught up *enough*? I think. You've been round the flat, I've had tea and cake with you, you've brought me back a sock, you've said ridiculous things like you miss me . . .

'I don't know,' I say.

'Oh, go on.'

Kemp has an almost pleading look on his face. Child-like. Plaintive, with that ever-present touch of mischief. Do I want him in my life again? Do I want him as a friend? He *was* a very good one, when I wasn't secretly lusting after him, in the moonlight. And I have a man in my life now – in the romantic sense – so I don't need to be yearning for Kemp to fulfil that role. I'm over all that now, aren't I? I have to be. I *need* to be. Perhaps I need a friend, too. Perhaps it would be nice.

And I'm nervous.

And I have time to kill.

And a drink would be good.

'All right,' I say. 'Let me just get my bag.'

'Too early for a JD and Coke?'

'Yes, I think so.' We are not those people any more, are we? Those eternal teenagers. Those pub and houseboat drinkers. I know he is joking.

'Prosecco?'

'OK, yes, please.'

'A glass of prosecco and a pint of Stella, please,' Kemp says to the pretty waitress standing at our table. We're on a pavement table in St Martin's Court, in the shade. Kemp has his legs stretched out under the table; I have mine tucked back, under my chair. On the way here we talked about movies and books and the dreadful state of current music. We talked about politics, art, television and photography. We talked about how we like the tube in the winter because it's always warm down there, but how it's an absolute sweatbox in the summer. I hoped I wasn't sweating. I hoped my make-up stayed fast. I thought that maybe, yes, Kemp and I really could be friends again.

Kemp makes a joke with the waitress about sitting in the drinks fridge, or something, to escape the heat. She laughs, genuinely amused. I remember him in the King's Arms, laughing with the old barman, Frank. One foot, in scruffy work boots, on the scaffolding of a stool. Keeping everyone smiling. Making everyone laugh. Dousing people in that special Kemp sunlight. Once she has gone, he steeples his fingers, rests his chin on them and smiles at me.

'So . . .' he says.

'So,' I reply.

'Who's the boyfriend?'

'He's not my boyfriend,' I say, feeling about twelve and smoothing the skirt of my dress over my knees. The waitress returns with the drinks.

'Thank you,' says Kemp. He helps her take the drinks and the napkins and the nuts off the tray and put them on the table. I sip from my rather large glass of prosecco.

'It's only our third date,' I add. I'm playing it down. It's our third date and we have kissed and I've lain in Salvi's bed and he has told me I'm beautiful.

'Ah, I see. Well, I hope your third date goes well, at two o'clock, at The Monastery. By four o'clock you might have fallen for him.'

'It's not the falling, it's the getting up again,' I say. I'm not really sure what I mean so I sip more of my prosecco

232

and study a mark on the tablecloth until it is rubbed off by my forefinger and my annoying blushes disappear with it. 'Anyway, how about you? Anyone on the scene since Linear Carina? Girlfriends, lovers, whatever?'

'No, not really,' he says. 'I met someone on my last trip. Arizona. A woman called Sarah.' Another one. I already hate her. Yeah, yeah, we're just friends, or could be, but still . . . 'She was OK, not . . . *complicated* enough for me, really.'

'Complicated? What were you looking for, a Rubik's cube?'

'No, an onion.'

'*Onions* again.'

'I like people with layers,' he says, and he is looking at me so intently I feel at least three of mine are in danger of dissolving and disappearing into the ether, which is disconcerting and very puzzling. '*You're* an onion.'

'Well, you don't want *me*!' I scoff, laughing just a little too loudly.

'Maybe I do,' he says quietly. And the look in his eyes makes my heart beat fast but my head knows with absolute clarity this is a trick. Some kind of huge and horrible trick. I give him my best 'what-the-fuck' look with a 'what-the-fuck' open-palm hand gesture thrown in. I mean, really, *what the fuck?*

'You're a surprising person,' he adds. 'And I don't just want to catch up. I want to talk to you about a few things.'

'OK . . .'

'The first is to do with something your dad showed me.'

'My *dad*? What are you talking about?'

Kemp smiles. A slow smile that reaches the crinkles at his eyes. 'He showed me your paintings. When I knocked with Ryan again the other day – you know, when Ryan saw your dad about more research – he invited me up and showed them to me.'

233

'He had no business showing you those!'

'Well, he did. He wanted my opinion. They're really good, Prue!'

'Oh. Right. He shouldn't have showed you.'

Kemp shrugs. 'They're really good,' he repeats. 'I took some photos of them.'

'Oh, God . . .' I mutter, embarrassed. 'Why on earth did you do that?'

'I might show them to someone else.'

'Please don't.'

'I might do,' repeats Kemp. He's looking at me intently again. 'Now let's talk about another thing. Something about us. About the past. About India.' He takes a deep breath. Runs a hand through his unruly hair. 'I was going to ask you to come with me that time. When I went all those years ago. To Jaipur and Udaipur.'

'Oh, come on!'

He doesn't take his eyes off me. 'I was. I was going to ask you to come with me.'

I set my prosecco down on the table. I've somehow drunk half of it and feel a bit pissed already, as I haven't eaten anything today yet. *Not entirely grown up.* I drum my fingers against the side of the glass. 'I think I'd like another drink. Shall we get another round?'

'Not yet.'

'OK.'

'I had something for you, in the drawer of my bedside table.'

'My sock?' I enquire.

'No, not your bloody sock!' He sighs. 'It was a hat.'

'A *hat*?'

'Remember my fisherman's hat? The one I always took travelling with me?'

'Yes, of course I do, because it was tragic.'

'I bought you one as well.'

'Oh!' I swiftly glug more of my prosecco. 'I look really bad in hats,' I say.

He ignores me. 'I was going to give it to you, the morning after we went up to Kenwood House. Our trespassing adventure.' He smiles. 'I thought about asking you to come with me while we were sitting outside, actually, but I was still worried, at that point, about ruining the friendship, about spoiling what we had, that if you said "no" it would change everything and be awful – but in the middle of the night I woke up and I saw you, creeping across the floor of the houseboat, and I knew I had to. I knew I had to ask you.'

'This all sounds very dramatic,' I say flippantly, but my heart is yammering. 'You know I wouldn't have been able to go anyway, because of the conference centre. Well, who knew they were going to get rid of me? And why would me coming with you ruin our friendship? Us wandering round ancient ruins, or capering through the streets in a rickshaw, or sharing a curry at a makeshift plastic table in some back-of-beyond backstreet?' I am rambling, but the images are close to hand; they are something I had often fantasized about, after all. 'Friends on tour . . .'

'Yeah, well, you see, the "friends" thing wasn't really working for me any more.' Kemp picks up his pint and takes a sip. Sets it down again. 'I'd started to see you as more than a friend.'

'Right.'

What is he saying to me? What is he *actually* saying? I drain the dregs of my prosecco.

'I had started to get feelings for you.'

'What sort of feelings?'

Kemp looks ambushed. He taps at his pint glass. 'Well, like I said, feelings that I saw you as more than a friend. But I didn't get a chance to ask you, because you ran out on me. I knocked for you a few days later. I brought the hat. I'm sure you were in, but you didn't come down. You didn't reply to any of my calls, or my texts. You just disappeared on me. I knocked one more time, just before I flew to Mumbai, then I gave up. There is a limit to my thick skin, you know, when it has been carved into. Well, more like hacked at with a great big knife . . .'

He grins at me, but my mind is whirling and whirling like the cogs have been electro-charged. Like a big fat light bulb has been switched on in my head, throwing everything he's just uttered into sharp relief. I understand. The images I once indulged in – of us in a rickshaw or eating a pavement curry – were not the ones he had in mind. The look he gave me in the middle of the night, on the houseboat, which I had mistaken for tender friendship and briefly, almost imagined – mere seconds ago – as something sweetly and infinitely more heart-soaring (fool!) – was very much something else.

'I get what you're saying.'

'You do?' He looks relieved. 'Well, that's—'

'May I summarize?'

'Er . . . OK . . . if you wish.'

'Right. So. What happened was, you decided you really fancied girls with huge birthmarks on their faces, after all.'

'Well, I—'

'Or there's always paper bags, isn't there?'

'What?'

'Let me finish. You decided because I was there, available, around all the time, clearly desperate for anyone, *anyone* at all – it would be pretty easy to slip things up a gear and make what we had going on "Friends with Benefits".' Oh, I get it all right. My face. My black marks. The stuff I had told him about Jonas. My mother. Cherry. How dark my recesses were. 'After all, you knew my history. You knew what you were dealing with.' Thank goodness I had never told him about the night at Finsbury Park . . . 'And you—'

'Prue, you're not listening, I—'

'Shut up, Kemp! And you were getting lonely, on all these trips. Yes, you had the odd one-night stand, the odd short-term thing, but you were looking for some kind of effort-free on-tap booty call. Some convenient ever-ready shack-up. You thought I would say "yes". You *knew* I was so *ugly* I would jump at any offer going. You knew how much I *liked* you.' My face is hot. My anger is hotter. I know my voice is too loud. 'Well, screw you; you never got to ask! I'm *glad* you never got to ask. Because I would have said "no". And now you're back again, like a very bad penny, and you've broken up with someone. You're bored, you're lonely. Are you looking for another easy booty call? Is that what this is? This "miss you" rubbish, this turning up everywhere? You're full of utter shit, Kemp.'

He is trying to reach a hand across the table towards me. I want to jab it with the pepper pot. 'Prue, you're being ridiculous . . . and how much you *like* me. I didn't know—'

'I've got to go.'

I am standing up. I let my chair scrape back on the pavement with a horrific clatter.

'No, you don't,' he says calmly. 'It's only half one and The Monastery's only ten minutes up the road.'

'I want to get there early. I need to get there early and . . . sort myself out. Sort my make-up out. And I've got a blister and I need to . . .' What on earth am I even saying?

'That's a shame.' Kemp is *infuriatingly* calm, gazing steadily at me in the face of my righteous rage and my overwhelming desire to flee. 'I wish you would stay. I wish you would listen to me.'

'I've got to go,' I repeat, then after what seems like a

slightly drunken (on my part), silence-weighted eternity, Kemp stands up too, pushing his chair back, and I reach for my bag and my glass – empty – tips over, heading for the salt pot. I go to grab it at the same time he does. His fingers touch mine and it would be like coming home, except this is not my home and could never be. Our friendship was a sham and whatever *this* is, today, is even worse. 'Bye, Kemp.'

I lurch down to grab my bag from under my chair and turn on my unsteady blister-free heels and head off down the pavement, in my lovely buttercup-yellow dress, without looking back.

'Bertie!' he calls after me. 'You're always walking away! Always disappearing on me. I'll see you soon, OK? And we can try to have this conversation again! I'm not giving up on you!'

'Not if I see you first!' I call back.

Chapter 30

The courtyard of The Monastery must be one of the most beautiful places in London to dine in, I think, as I stand a little unsteadily at its entrance, and *definitely* one of the most exclusive, as it's absolutely tiny. Accessed by a damp, dark passageway I'm glad I researched first on Google Maps – a wafer slotted between an old-fashioned cobbler's and a South African deli – the courtyard has cloisters on all four sides (each with three arches bowed with plump and weeping wisteria); a yellow flagstone floor both cracked and polished by centuries of shuffling monks' feet; a scattering of round stone planters stuffed with miniature palms; and, apparently, an incredible survival instinct, as it's all that remains of the original, much larger Cassinese de Londres Monastery the Luftwaffe bombed to smithereens in the Second World War.

Half the quadrangle is currently in bright sunshine, the other half in shade. The courtyard is beautifully open to the elements; the squared-off sky an azure blue above us – and by 'us' I mean a suited-and-booted maître d' who is standing next to me and tutting into a leather clipboard because I am early.

'Follow me, madam.'

With a tap on the clipboard and a condescending sigh, the maître d' reluctantly walks me through the courtyard to the table Salvi has booked – one of only ten in the restaurant, which Google says in the winter are moved to The Orangery in the minuscule modern annexe I can spy through one of the arches.

The heels of my gold sandals skitter precariously on the flagstones. The skirt of my dress flips nicely against my legs. I'm glad I'm here early: I want to sit and catch my breath and try to sober up. Drunk at lunchtime before you've even had the lunch is not a good look.

The table is in the sunny half of the courtyard and when the maître d' goes to pull out the chair on the side facing the sun I say, 'Actually, can I . . . ?' and scoot round to the chair that allows me to have my back to the sun and a view of one of the cloisters.

'Thank you,' I say, as he tuts under his breath and lifts the chair back for me, and I try not to think of Kemp pushing back his, before, when he stood up, and how I fled, yet again. Self-preservation, my old friend . . .

The cloister and its wisteria are lovely. A waitress comes over and I order a sparkling water with loads of ice and lemon. I guzzle it down like a buffalo at a watering hole, staring at the wisteria. I think about ordering another, then I decide I don't want to be sober, after all. I order a large glass of white wine. At quarter past two, a hand plomps on my right shoulder and Salvi is at my ear.

'Hello, you,' he says and he swizzes round to his side of the table and drops into his seat; a quick move, like a fox jumping into a brook. He does look a little vulpine today, actually – sharp and cheeky. Up to no good. He's wearing a black shirt, silky in texture, many buttons undone, with black jeans and black loafers.

'Hello, yourself.'

'Been waiting long?'

'No, not really.'

'Hey, you're facing the wrong way.' He's up again. 'You can't come to The Monastery and face the wall. Here, swap with me, then you can look out over the courtyard.'

'Thank you,' I say, taking his just vacated seat as he takes mine, but this is far from what I mean. As I sit in my

240

new seat, the sun, above the arches of the opposite cloisters, is right in my face, like a searchlight; I didn't even bring my sunglasses.

'So, how are we? Have we had a good week? What did you do this morning?' he adds genially. Warmth radiates off his skin, as does his cologne, sweet and musky. His eyes are a penetrating green. 'Anything nice?'

'No, not really, just getting ready.' Damn, why the hell am I telling him it took me the whole morning to get ready for this date? Schoolgirl error, and Lord knows I've made those before . . .

'You *look* ready,' he says. 'You look great.'

'Thank you.' I blush. The waitress reappears. She looked a bit surly when she served me; now she is all smiles.

'Can I take your drinks order, Salvi?'

Of *course*. He is known here.

'Sure, lovely. A bottle of Sancerre, please. And a Coke.'

The waitress nods and sweeps away my empty glass.

'A Coke?' I ask.

'Oh, I'm not drinking. I've got the car parked further up the Embankment. I'll take you for a spin in it after. Hey, the food's fantastic here,' he adds. 'I know the menu like the back of my hand. Shall I just order for the both of us?'

I nod, and he flicks swiftly through the parchment pages of the massive menu. 'Yep, yep, yep. OK, done. You'll love it, Prue – it's really special.' He slaps the menu shut then pats it twice with a brace of rigid fingers, as if sealing a deal with the universe.

The waitress returns with the drinks. A Coke with ice and lemon is placed in front of Salvi and a chilled bottle of Sancerre, sporting delicious beads of condensation, is placed in an ice bucket to my right. I'd put my head in it if I could; I'm so hot. A glass is poured for me. The wine is crisp and delicious.

241

Salvi reels off an order of lobster bisque and spicy courgette fritter shards and steak with chunky chips and salsa
verde and side orders of julienne carrots and sautéed broc-
coli and asparagus tips. As the waitress smiles and bobs
and walks away he looks at me curiously and says, 'How
many glasses of wine did you have before I got here?'

Oh. That's a funny question. I feel exposed or, worse,
like I am on the stand, being cross-examined. I don't
want him to think I sat here waiting for him knocking
back the sauce, like Dorothy Parker, so I blurt out, inad-
visably, 'Well, one here, and I did go for a quick drink
with a friend, before.'

'Oh? Male or female?'

'Female,' I say quickly. I don't want to think about
Kemp, and his Indian booty call or him seeing my paintings or anything about him.

'Do you have a lot of friends?'

'No. Do you?' I remember Facebook and the three
thousand, including Philippa Helens. Why did she move
down two carriages? I wonder. When did she let go of her
balloon with the little bow in the string? When did she
decide enough was enough and she had to let it *all* go?

'Yes,' says Salvi.

Salvi didn't know Philippa, I remember. She was just
an insignificant face he'd never even noticed, one of
thousands of thumbnails on a Friends list that was utterly
meaningless. Is that how she felt? Just a face in the crowd
there was no purpose being in? Just another snapshot of
a person among many others in the world, going nowhere?

I hope the wine is not making me morose. Salvi turns
to look across the courtyard and I swear I see him winking at a woman three tables down.

'Are you OK?' he asks, turning back.

'I'm a bit hot.'

'It's nice to sit with your face in the sun, isn't it?'

'Not really.' I drink more of my wine, in an attempt to flip my mood. I need to be brighter, more breezy, much more interesting and more *interested* in him. 'So, how are you?' I ask. 'How's your case going? And work in general?'

'Well, I've hired a new clerk, Jennifer Dixon,' he says, as though I should remotely know who that is. 'I've been going over some things with her this week. She's pretty sharp.'

'What kind of things?' I suddenly feel as dull as the dullest dullard; that if Jennifer Dixon is *sharp*, I am a sat-upon loaf of bread.

'Notes for a new case tomorrow. Domestic violence. High provocation. We're expecting it to go on for weeks.'

'Sounds interesting,' I say. *I have no further questions, Your Honour*, I think; I know nothing whatsoever about the law. The word 'provocation' has seeped into my brain, though, like cold mercury. What does he mean: the victim, male or female, asked for it? He'll get his client off because the other person *deserved* it? I think about rape trials. About men like Jonas, in Tenerife, who choose how they operate with clear and careful minds, so those they abuse are led into muddied and confusing waters of their own, unable to get things straight no matter how many times they relive them. What sort of a witness would I be to his crime? Would Salvi tear *me* apart if he was the defence counsel for that particular male scum? I know the answer to this. That's why I didn't report it.

'It could so easily have been a murder case,' he says with a regretful sigh, as though he has thoroughly missed out. 'Hey, did you know there was a murder here once, in one of the cloisters?'

'No, I didn't.' Wine is not good for me, I think. I am definitely morose.

'It was one of the monks,' Salvi continues. 'His throat

was slit. Over there, I think.' He turns and points with his thumb to the middle arch of the cloister behind him, across the courtyard, where the wisteria is heavy and weeping. 'Struck down by one of his own.'

'Another monk did it?'

'Yes. The motive was never determined. Jealousy? The stir-craziness of being shut in here, no wine, no women. Who knows? Grim, though, eh?' He grins. 'Although it adds a certain magic to the place.'

'Magic?'

'Well, you know . . . mystery, tragedy, intrigue, a monk's robe, steeped in blood, dragging across the flagstones . . . I love all that stuff.'

I take a deep glug of my wine. 'You love *tragedy*?'

'You know what I mean. Tragedy and the twists and turns of fate . . . it's *exciting*.' Salvi sits back in his chair like he has said a Great Thing. 'So here we are, Prue,' he adds, with a wink. 'Lunching in a place of both abject beauty and downright ugliness.'

I'm horrified. I'm sure he is staring at my left cheek. I move my hand up to my face and rest my fingers on my nose so my palm covers my birthmark. God knows what state it's in. I haven't checked it since I left the flat and now it is burning in the sun under three layers of foundation and a thin coating of SPF 50.

'It *is* very pretty here,' I say. I really want to divert from ugliness. I don't want to think about the murdered monk, blood on his robes, over in the cloisters, bleeding to death. Tragedy. And least of all my face. My birthmark is scalding to the touch now. I really want to swap seats again with Salvi, but I daren't ask.

Food arrives. Two waiters bring bowls of soup and a wide shallow dish of courgette fritters, plus a huge bread basket, filling our table with them.

'Ah, brilliant,' exclaims Salvi, his big eyes lighting up.

He is a man who devours, I think. Who devours life when I have always just picked at it, like a bird.

He encourages me to start with the steaming bowl of lobster bisque I would ordinarily find delicious but I am so so hot. I slurp at it half-heartedly and drink more wine. I feel slightly ill, in my lovely buttercup dress with the big white flowers, as Salvi chatters on, in his lovely position with his back to the sun, a carousel of life and personality. He is dazzle to my dull; sparkle to my leaden apathy. Why did he say that about 'downright ugliness'? I feel I can't recover from it. I feel I can't recover from what Kemp said, either. That he wanted me. Because I was ugly and available.

When the soup bowls have been pushed to one side, mine barely touched, Salvi looks at me from across the table – my face a blazing fire – and says, 'I like you. I like you very much.'

'Do you?' My stomach flips a little, from its position of low-slung wallowing in my ugliness.

'Yes.'

'What's in it for you?' I ask.

'What's *in* it for me?' he laughs, his head back and his mouth wide open, and I wish he would stop laughing and lean across the table and kiss me as I need to be kissed, right now. I really, really need to. '*You* are what's in it for me. You, Prudence.'

I am drunk, I realize. Proper wobbly, no-return drunk. The sun in my face is becoming unbearable. My cheeks are so fucking hot. I want him to either kiss me or let me run from here, into shade and air. I don't want the three further courses. I don't want any more wine.

'I think you're beautiful,' he says.

He's staring right at my left cheek again, but instead of saying 'Shut up!' or 'Don't be stupid!', I decide to say 'Thank you' as I really really want to believe he means it,

245

and he smiles at me as though that dress is just slipping off and flying clean away and I am already in his bed, which is where I want to be, all my rough edges cloaked in desire and magic and the mystical and the conundrum that is this man, Salvi Russo. I want him and I want him to want *me*. My choice.

A breeze is picking up, in the courtyard – edges of table-cloths are being lifted; hems of dresses are fluttering. I look up and there are some frayed clouds in the sky now, drifting in apparent innocence across the azure oblong ceiling above us. The starters are cleared away and the main course appears. I try a tiny bit of the steak and it's delicious. The half-shade in the courtyard is slowly creeping over table-cloths and cutlery and faces now – a stealthy eclipse. It sweeps like a monk's robe over the courtyard until the whole of it is engulfed and our table, too, is in shade.

'Oh, no more sun,' says Salvi, looking incredibly disappointed.

'Yes.' I exhale slowly, so relieved the sun has disap-peared behind a scud of grey cloud. We used to cloud watch, Angela and I on sunny days, except I was always doing the reverse: hoping a bundle of cotton wool would block the mocking yellow circle that highlighted the worst of me all too clearly.

'Do you want the rest of that?' Salvi asks, eyeing my steak.

'No, you can have it.'

Salvi slides his plate over and I plop the remainder of my steak, raw and bloody, on to it. The sky continues to darken and one corner of our tablecloth flips up on to Salvi's plate and immediately soaks up a little of the blood puddled there, as he eats.

'Can I come back to yours after this?' I ask. The blood seeping up the white of the tablecloth has almost reached his little finger. There is a crash and the tinkle of glass

246

behind us, accompanied by an 'Oh fuck, Jeffrey!' from a Patsy Stone blonde in a jade two-piece – the rising breeze has toppled a champagne flute off a neighbouring table. It's almost dark now in the courtyard, cool and delicious and dark.

Salvi nods. He lays down his knife and fork and calls over the waitress. I offer to pay half but he waves me down. He tips generously and we stand up and he takes my hand in his as he guides me through the tables and out through the arch of the cloister that leads to the dark passageway, between the cobbler's and the deli, and as we come out on to the street the skies are furiously grey and the wind has really whipped up: a strange, hot wind that attacks and disarrays the ruffles of my dress and detonates my hair.

'From the Sahara,' says Salvi, and I remember the summer winds we sometimes get, which coat cars with dust so they are photographed for eerie-looking pictures in the newspapers and everybody can't stop talking about it, but nobody minds, really, as these rare, random winds from the Sahara make England feel – just fleetingly – exotic and Arabian. 'My car's this way.'

Chapter 31

Monday morning dawns hot and bright. From Salvi's bedroom window all I can see is a square of royal-blue sky and the trail of an aeroplane.

'Yep, yep, Dino. That's all done.' Salvi's in the kitchen. On the phone. It must be his landline as his mobile is on the bedside table beside me. The tap is running. The cafetière is being filled. Mugs are clanked from the cupboard. 'Yep, sorted. Ha, no. But you know how it is. Good image for the club, though. Yeah. Yeah, mate. No, no, I'll see you there. Yes, absolutely fine. OK, mate, yeah, have a good one.'

The bed is unmade. I am a little undone; despite the black satin sheet wrapped round my left leg and trailing over my naked stomach.

We didn't sleep together.

Salvi drove too fast, way too fast, in his Aston Martin something-or-other, all turquoise and leather, on the way here. It frightened me. Initially, we purred through the streets, Salvi courteously letting drivers out, braking evenly at traffic lights, humming along to the radio, driving executively, but somewhere near his flat, on a more open stretch of road, the car surged forward, and Salvi turned up the radio – the song 'Halo' by Texas; its soaring instrumental break with all those strings, in the middle, an interlude and a crescendo – and laughed at my terrified protests as we scalded along at a terrifying speed, flying past the identical black doors of elegant townhouses, streaking towards the end of the street and a looming set of red traffic lights . . .

'Fucking hell!' I cried, as we came to a high-performance but very sudden stop, my heart hammering in its incandescent cage.

Salvi laughed. He reached across me and snapped down the tan leather sun visor. There was a mirror on the underside, winking at me, a little light above it.

'Look,' he said. 'It really put the colour in your cheeks.'

'Is that a joke?' I snapped. My face in the small mirror was flushed, with fear and fury. My eyes were wide, my make-up a little smudged. My birthmark, that rocky terrain, was covered but crusty-looking – always there, always there. But I was glowing, somehow. I looked alive.

'Come here,' he said, and I found myself leaning towards him and I knew when we kissed my anger would seep right out of me and fly from the open car window up to the dark, Saharan sky.

He kissed me and I forgot the fear and the danger. He kissed me again as we pulled up to his building and as we tumbled through his front door and up his stairs. He kissed me as my dress was flung to the floor, like a rag; he kissed me as he threw me back on his bed and I prayed he'd consume every part of me until there was nothing of me left and someone else, hopefully, was in her place. My choice. My choice.

I'm still here. He didn't touch me. As I lay back on his bed, naked and ready – to be devoured, swallowed up; erased, not loved, but erased – he stopped. He just stopped and looked at me. Smiled at me. Pulled the satin sheet up over my body and tucked it around me, like a shroud. Then he smoothed his hand slowly and gently down the bad side of my face, while I lay breathless, and told me I was something else, that I was really something else.

'Don't you want to sleep with me?' I asked; begging, pitiful. I needed him. I needed the validation. I needed him to need me.

'No, I'm going to save you,' he said, and I didn't know what he meant, and I was so disappointed, as he was supposed to be my miracle, my promise of something – yes, I did crave to be loved, I did – I wanted love and romance and happiness, all the things that other, normal-looking people obtained so easily. But then he said, 'Bad girl,' so tenderly I was confused and humiliated and happy, all at the same time, and he sat down beside me and stroked my hair and the side of my face and gazed at me until I fell asleep – too early, way too early – and I eventually let the disappointment ebb from me like the tide from an abandoned beach at the end of a long summer's day.

'What are you thinking?' he asks, from the doorway now, a white towel wrapped round his waist and a coffee mug in his hand. It's early; it's only about 6.15.

'I'm thinking this is usually something a woman asks a man,' I say. 'And the man is usually thinking nothing at all, or about the football scores, or what time dinner is.'

Salvi laughs. 'What else?' he asks.

I want to say, I'm wondering why you don't want to sleep with me, why you have brought me back to your flat twice now to simply put me to bed. Instead, I say, 'I'm thinking you're way too cool for me,' which is also true. Everything about Salvi is, isn't? His career, the street performing, friends called Dino . . . Dino must be another Italian professional, I muse. A member of The Profilo, that gentlemen's club. Maybe he's a barrister too.

'Probably,' Salvi laughs. 'What would you like for breakfast?'

'You?' I hazard, shifting my body slightly so the sheet rides further up my leg and a black silky corner slips from my stomach.

'You can make scrambled eggs,' he says. 'Eggs are in the fridge.' He goes to the wardrobe and pulls a white shirt from it. A dark suit. A serious tie.

'You've got to go already?' *Disappointment*. Again. It spreads through my body like ink.

'Busy day in court.' He quickly dresses. He's now on the edge of the bed, putting his shoes on. I want to reach out and slip my hand under his expensive cotton shirt to touch his back, but I think better of it. It's OK; he's busy, he's important. He doesn't have to sleep with me if he doesn't want to. I just feel ashamed that I've asked him to. That I've invited him to take a part of me, but have been rejected.

'Right, that's me,' Salvi says, standing up. 'You can let yourself out, like before.'

He walks from the bedroom and into the kitchen. I hear him pick up his keys and zip them into his briefcase.

'Wait,' I call, from my satin shroud. 'When will I see you again?'

He flicks his head back round the bedroom door and grins at me. 'I'll call you,' he says.

Chapter 32

The landline phone rings, making me jump. It's been ultra-quiet in The Palladian this evening, after a day of not doing very much at all (since I arrived back from Salvi's flat at 10 a.m., all I've done is guzzle water, read about the life and times of Jackie Onassis and slump in my chair, ruminating on the excitement and confusion that is Salvi Russo). A day brought to an ennui-filled conclusion by a light early supper of bruschetta with cured ham and mozzarella, and I've been dozing fitfully in my chair since about six o'clock. Dad has been comatose since about five. He opens his eyes, too, at the jolt of the phone.

'Angela?' he suggests.

'It hasn't been three months,' I counter, going to the phone in no hurry and hoping whoever it is will ring off before I get there. 'Perhaps it's PPI. Remember how Nonna got so fed up with cold-callers she used to hang up every single phone call she got, even if it was her own friends or the doctor's surgery?'

'Yes, I remember,' says Dad. 'Answer it, then, in case it *is* Angela.'

'Hello?' I say into the phone.

'Oh, I thought you weren't going to bother answering,' says a cool voice. It's her. 'You sound tired.'

I want to say, 'I was up all last night, shagging', even though I wasn't – what exactly *was* last night? – but instead I say, 'Do I? You sound chipper, as usual. Just come across a new cupcake recipe?'

'No,' says Angela. 'How's Dad?'

'He's good, thanks. To what do we owe the pleasure?'

She ignores me. 'Been out anywhere else?'

'Yeah,' I say absent-mindedly. 'Liberty and the Albert Hall and the Shard. Do you want to speak to Dad?'

'Not just yet. Any news?'

'Like what?' She never asks for *news*. 'We've been to the Albert Hall and Liberty and the Shard,' I repeat. I won't tell her anything about Salvi. My sister and I don't have that kind of relationship. We have the kind of relationship that if I told her the miracle that I've met someone, she'd bang on about Warren for twenty-five minutes without a breath, both to convince herself she still likes him and to maintain her one-upmanship.

'*I've* got some news,' she says.

Well, this is no surprise. There's always something to boast about or to be a *drama llama* over: a milestone reached at school or nursery for one of her kids; an altercation with another Alpha Mom at the school gate in which she emerged indignant and victorious – most of which is already on Facebook.

'I'm going to write to Mum in Sweden,' she says. 'To Torge's address, if he's still there.'

'*Are* you?' Now this is unexpected. Angela never says anything unexpected on the phone; I could pretty much write every line of every conversation, like a script. 'Why?' I take the phone into the bedroom. 'Just checking a label of something of mine, for Angela,' I call out to Dad. 'Why are you going to write to her?' I ask.

'I realized something the other day,' she says. She suddenly sounds a little breathless. 'That my two girls are the same ages we were when Mum left that first time. For her little "holiday". It shook me, actually. Made me hold on to them really tight. But I want to write to her. Find out if she's happy.'

253

'Why do you care if she's happy? I doubt she's sitting there musing that about *us*.'

'She might be,' says Angela, and I know she is pouting. That, whatever her age, she will always be pouting about something. 'She might be thinking about us all the time but be too scared to get in touch.'

'I doubt it,' I say. 'I think it's all too late.'

'You never know.' Angela sounds clipped, like she's been rehearsing this. 'I want to reach out, as they say these days.'

'Like the Four Tops? I wouldn't bother.' My bullet-proof heart is very cold beneath its crust today. Although other parts of me are very warm indeed. For Salvi.

'OK, well, I've already sent it. The letter. A couple of weeks back.'

'Oh. What on earth did you say?'

'I said I hoped she was well and gave her my address if she wanted to get in touch.'

'Well,' I say. 'I suppose you never know.' I think of all the letters Angela wrote before and all the stupid post-cards I sent her to stop her crying. Maybe I shouldn't have done. Maybe I should have erased all hope way back then, so it couldn't resurface now. Angela may be under the misapprehension we have a mother who *replies*.

'Well, good luck,' I say.

'You don't need to sound so stroppy about it. I can do what I like. "Doing your own thing is a generous act" – Barbara Sher said that.'

'Never heard of her. And of course you can. Haven't you always?'

Angela tuts, then gives a huge weary sigh. 'You sound desperately unhappy, Prue. But *haven't you always*?'

'Actually, I'm not,' I say. 'I'm very happy indeed, as it happens.' I'm not sure if this is true, or not. 'I guess you're the one who's unhappy if you're writing to Mum again.'

'Don't you feel there's something missing in your life?'

'There's loads of stuff missing!' I laugh. 'Though I'm working on it. But Ellen is not one of them.'

'Don't call her Ellen.'

'She's lucky I'm mentioning her at all! You think she mentions *our* names? Tells people she has daughters? I bet she doesn't, because then those people might ask her what we're up to and her answer – "I have absolutely no clue. I don't even know what they look like any more" – might shock people.'

'You don't miss her.' A flat statement.

'No.' An equally flat statement. 'Why are you always asking me this?' Our mother's simply a missing jigsaw piece, I think, of a puzzle that makes just as much sense without it. The corner of a square that suddenly became a triangle, and so what? 'Anyway, do you want to speak to Dad?'

I am already up and out of the bedroom and taking the phone over to him in the sitting room.

'Yes, please,' she says, clipped and affronted. 'Warren has bought a new sailboat. I'm hoping Dad might love to hear all about it.'

I imagine Angela's neat, backward-slanting handwriting on an airmail envelope. Her fingerprint on the licked stamp to Sweden. A hopeful missive forwarded by cousin Torge and delivered to the mailbox of a tiny apartment above a sweet Swedish bakery. A shard from the past piercing Mum's present like a poisoned dart piercing a balloon.

'Angela,' I say to Dad.

'Thanks, Prue.'

I return to my chair and look across to the window where dusk is now descending over London. Things are changing. Dad and I go out together now. Angela has written to our mother. And I sort of have a man called Salvi.

I check my mobile but there is nothing from him. Nothing at all, and, although it's only been a few hours since I was with him, I have the sudden gripping, choking fear I may never hear from him again. That, like my mother, he is gone. This is how it's going to be with him, I realize. Never knowing what's going to happen. He has set a spell into suspension – of black satin sheets and fast cars and the promise of something – a spell that hangs in the night; a tangible portent, a beautiful destiny. And if it is my destiny then it is one edged in both dark and light, as this is how I feel when I am with him – picked up and laid down; illuminated then plunged into darkness.

He's part of it all, isn't he? The darkness of my life that was set in motion on a night over thirty years ago – a night of brash lights and jangled music and all the fun of the fair – when I was a teenage hopeful: of being loved, of being looked at with desire, of being part of something, like everyone else. But I am not like everyone else. I am a motherless paper-bag girl, a girl not to be loved but chosen as a plaything, a booty call. Salvi wants me. I hope. I want him to want me. He's my choice when not much else has been in my life.

I check my phone again. There is nothing.

Chapter 33

It's 9.30 am and Dad and I are at Central Hall, Westminster. We're sitting second row from the back in the George Thomas room, which boasts lemon-and-white panelled walls, a large empty fireplace, several chandeliers, a sumptuous blue carpet and, currently, lots of very intelligent-looking, earnest architect types. Dad is opening a packet of Fruit Pastilles. I am looking at a screen that says, 'Architects, Bring Me Your Ears'.

We've come to a talk. We haven't been out for a few days as Dad has had a summer cold, but he found out about this on the internet. Expressed an interest to come. It's an hour-long presentation by an architect called Lawrence P. Sullivan, who wants to ask how sound can and should influence British design.

'"Sound is one of our primary senses",' reads Dad, from the Braille brochure on his lap he picked up in the lobby. '"Yet architects tend to focus almost exclusively on the visible, without paying attention to the other senses. Sullivan explains why architects need to use their ears and not just their eyes." Should be fantastic. Did you bring a book?'

'No, why?'

'You might get bored. Not really your scene, is it?'

'I'll be all right. And is it *your* scene?' I ask. 'Your scene again?'

'It's always been my scene. Fruit Pastille?'

I take one and Dad puts the packet back in his pocket. 'No, I mean to actually get involved in. Come on, Dad, the subject matter! Architects using their other senses. It's right up your street! Or it could be.'

'One step at a time,' says Dad, and I take this as a small Dad Hint not to bang on about him becoming any sort of a blind architect again, especially as John Harrison Burrows, the one from Hawaii, is featured in the brochure. There's a short interview with him. A couple of photos. I see Dad trace his finger over that page of his Braille version now, but he says nothing.

There's an air of anticipation in the room, an intellectual frisson slightly disturbed by the man next to us, who is noisily unveiling a huge foil pack of sandwiches that look worryingly like corned beef and piccalilli. Even more worryingly, he appears to be holding them out to Dad.

'No, thank you,' I say on Dad's behalf. 'You're being offered someone's picnic,' I whisper to him.

'No, thank you,' he whispers back. The man shrugs and takes an enormous bite out of one of the sandwiches. He has an interesting face, I think, like a basset hound, from the side. He would be great to draw.

Finally, Lawrence P. Sullivan – a unit of a man in an immaculate suit – takes to the podium, welcomes us on this fine Thursday morning and begins to talk, in great detail, about modern architecture and the employment of the senses. Dad nods. He smiles. Mr Sullivan's enthusiasm is palpable. You could reach out and take hold of his passion; it surrounds him like a chunky aura. I think about passion, about art; about my paintings. Am I passionate? Could I let my art become a proper passion, something I bring out to the light, like Dad said: show people, share with people? Or do I keep it as hidden as my heart?

I know the answer. I'll probably keep it hidden. I wish it *was* hidden. I hate that Kemp has seen my work. I hate that he has photos of it on his phone. I don't want to put myself out there. I never have done. I may be traipsing all over London now but my confidence is far from sauntering about, troubling anyone. My heart (and my art) is better off under lock and key.

I feel unsettled, out of kilter: Salvi hasn't contacted me in three days, leaving me in perilous limbo; hanging off a rickety rope bridge over a churning river of my own insecurities. A letter is winging its way to my mother, breaking the seal of silence she has spun between her and her daughters for so long; I fear it will shatter, like glass. And Kemp was going to invite me to India to be his friend with benefits. I see no benefit in that at all, as I loved him. I don't want to be his friend with *anything* and I can't even be his friend at *all*, any more. I wish Dad and I had never gone to beautiful St Dunstan in the East; I wish I had never seen Kemp there – returned, handsome, not ever able to love me.

Lawrence P. Sullivan is talking about a community project in Canada. I look at Dad and he is enraptured. He is nodding at things I don't understand. Words of wisdom about sound textures and sonics and acoustics. Basset Man next to us is still providing his own sound textures by tinkering with his scratchy-foiled wares. Astoundingly, he proffers them to Dad again.

'My Dad's blind,' I whisper across, in the hope of erasing the tireless sandwich-offering and the irritated look on the man's face at Dad's non-acknowledgement.

'Oh, you're *blind*!' shouts the man, causing a lot of people to turn round and a few to shush. 'I thought you were just *rude*!'

'I try not to be both at the same time,' says Dad.

The lights are dimming. Dad and I settle back in our seats. There's going to be a film. It is set in sunny California, where a man walks through a new museum, explaining how the architect designed it the way he did. There are interviews. There is uplifting music. It's pretty interesting, actually. I am not bored, like Dad predicted. As the architect is interviewed about absorption acoustics and his use of voice-activated technology, I am surprised by Dad feeling for my hand and placing his own warmly on top of it, in the dark. His sturdy hand, with the neat fingernails. The hand I used to hold, crossing the road, when I was a small child and he was the one to guide me. The hand with which he used to pull the big blue hanky from his pocket when I had ice cream over my face. The hand that wiped away the few and only tears I cried following my mother leaving – tears he discovered in the airing cupboard where I had retreated for a silent sob about an hour after Angela and I had sat on his lap like wriggling fishes.

'Thank you for coming with me,' he whispers, and I smile, in the dark, with him holding my hand. 'You're a good girl.'

My heart lurches; rises then falls. At these words. These words. Dad used to say them to me when I was that little girl. He would say them when I reached up to give him a kiss on the cheek or gave him his flask of coffee when he set off for days studying to be an architect. He would say them when I fed one of the guide dogs, or brushed their vanilla coats with a special two-sided brush. He would say them when I danced on his feet; even when I was too big to do so. And he would say them when I told him my childish secrets – how I had been laughed at at school or how I had won a prize for a painting of a butterfly. He said it was good for me to share my secrets with him, that it would always make me feel better.

He hasn't called me a 'good girl' for a long, long time and I am horrified that tears start to fall, in the dark of this panelled room. That they silently track through my make-up and my artfully applied edifice. That they are unstoppable.

I have not been a good girl to my dad. I have let him down. I have sat with him in that flat year after year, indulging him in his isolation, being glad of it so I could wallow there, too, in mine. I have let him fade, as I have faded. I have let him disappear, as I wanted to disappear. Even when I worked, when I was a reluctant part of the world, I made no effort to bring Dad out of the flat and out of himself – I made no roads to try to encourage an embrace of the world, or this life, from either of us.

I've had a lacklustre career, which stalled. I've not ful-filled any kind of potential because there was never any there. I've painted but not let anyone see. I'm a purposely blank canvas I have let other people write on. I've not been a good girl since that first secret – the night at Fins-bury Park, when I was fourteen and so desperate to be wanted by someone, to be looked at for the right reasons, that I let a bad thing happen. A bad thing that became a catalyst for so many other things in my life and the reason I was marked out to Jonas, in Tenerife: an easy target.

On screen, the Californian architect is now showing us around his sprawling home. He has floor-to-ceiling glass everywhere. He has light and tranquillity. He is introdu-cing his Sound Room. He talks about something called The Golden Ratio.

My tears continue to fall. A long time ago, Kemp came into my life and unwittingly showed me what love was, and it was a pretty picture laid out on a piece of cartridge paper – beautiful, but not to be touched, and, like a paint-ing, one-sided. It was never something for me. Love was never something that could be returned. Until Salvi . . . maybe. Successful, charismatic Salvi. And now I am a bad girl – again – because I have offered it to him on a plate and he has said 'no'.

And Kemp wants me for one thing and not everything, like I wanted of him.

That bad thing. That first bad thing, that first bad night. I can't escape it. I can't ever get away from it. I *invited* that bad thing in, when I was fourteen. I asked for it, didn't I? I'm a good girl gone bad who bad things happen to and I deserve them.

I don't want to remember it now – that encounter, that night – as tears pitch down my face, unchecked. I don't want to remember. But as I close my eyes I am back there. I am back there, that summer's evening, and I can taste the candyfloss on my lips and smell the kerosene and the danger.

Chapter 34

Summer 1984

'All right, Roo?'
   'Yeah.'
   'Where first?'
   'Waltzer?'
   My friend Georgina and I strode into the fair at Finsbury Park to the mangle of four loud and colliding bassy pop songs (UB40, Bob Marley, A-ha and Mel and Kim, as far as I could make out), and the intoxicating stink of candyfloss and kerosene. There was a buzz in the air, competing neon lights; excitement. It was warm enough that we didn't need jackets over our black-and-white-striped T-shirts emblazoned with 'Blondie'. It was clear to anyone we were a double act, a duo, a force to be reckoned with. We were identical, apart from the obvious; our hair short and on-trend, our dark blue jeans with red piping down the sides skin-tight, and our demeanour defensive.
   I felt pretty good, or as good as it got for me. I had new boots – pointy, cone heel, kick arse, should there have been any arses that needed kicking. Two coats of Heather Shimmer lipstick, the tube a bullet in the pocket of my jeans, ready for reapplication. Glittery eyeshadow under brows shaped to death and slicked with Vaseline to make them both *neat and iridescent*, something I had read about in *Vogue* in the waiting room at the laser clinic, as I flicked

through the pages of the beautiful people. And bags of slapped-on confidence, dredged from nowhere like mud from a dirty river, that I willed to be as thick and all-concealing as my foundation.

'Let's get some candyfloss first.'

'OK.'

We stomped past the stall where you threw rings over ducks to win an enormous cuddly hippo with nails for eyes. It was busy everywhere, already. Flashes of fairground neon in red, yellow, royal blue, green and pink illuminated people's faces, making them look flushed, excited, up for it. Teenagers eyed each other up. A boy in a green bomber jacket chucked me a crooked grin that I returned with a sassy smirk under my aggressively winged eyes. *Fantastic.*

We passed the Hall of Mirrors to 'Don't You Want Me' and I caught a glimpse of myself in one of them – stretched to seven feet of bendy elastic with arms that seemed to be coming out of my feet but, apart from that, I looked all right. My hair was Studio-Lined into a truculent pixie cut Annie Lennox would be proud of. My mask was as impenetrable as I could get it, with the high-street make-up I could get my hands on. My dug-up halo of confidence may have had a fuzzy border and been likely to collapse at any moment, but it was there. From a distance, I could have passed for pretty.

'We'll go to the one by the Hearts and Diamonds.'

'OK.'

Georgina was my best friend. My only friend, actually. She had a steel-hard glare to rival mine. The ability to dispatch jeering school mates with a curt 'Fuck off!' She had been my friend for precisely four months, three days and six hours. Before that, I hadn't had one. I was not the sort of girl other girls wanted to be seen with. I was not popular. I was not funny. Actually, I *was* funny, but my sense of humour seemed to be an acquired taste. I was certainly not pretty. It wasn't the *greatest* truth – not to be pretty – when you're fourteen, but hey, other truths are worse. Mum used to lie to me about it all the time – when she *was* our mum. She'd tell me I was lovely, but I wasn't. Her words meant little. *She* meant little. She'd meant little again earlier this evening, when she'd visited us, meaning she was faithless, groundless, insubstantial ... for the very last time. And I was ugly. I was a freak with a stellar line in eye-rolls and that steely stare that could strike you dead at twenty paces. I could see people off, if they started. And Georgina could, too. We made an excellent team.

'Medium or large, Roo?' asked Georgina as we watched the floss swirl round the stainless-steel pan. Something being made out of nothing. Sustenance out of air. My family and my friends called me Roo. I liked that. It was much better than Prudence or The Prude, or The Freak or *Ugly Fucker* – all names thrown at me across the play-ground or in the dinner queue when I was minding my own business adding to the slops bin or getting seconds of cornflake tart and custard. School kids could be *so* charming, couldn't they? Other girls got dates and snogs and phone calls in the evening that they took while sit-ting on the stairs in the hall, the curly phone cord wrapped round their eager fingers; I got, 'What happened to your face, freak?' or, 'Did someone punch you at birth?' What joy, being a slightly plump North London schoolgirl with a massive heart-shaped birthmark on my face, lurking tonight like a stamped-on mouse under three layers of Maybelline's finest (colour-matched for me in Boots by a simpering blonde in a white coat) and a supplementary slick of Rimmel's Hide the Blemish.

'Large.' I was chewing gum, too. I didn't really like it but it seemed required, for the copycat pals. I took it out of my mouth and flicked it off my finger on to the grass. We took our candyfloss and tramped off, in the pursuit of good times. Cone heels on damp grass; floss sizzled between eager tongue and scrubbed teeth. I was hoping things might change that night, just temporarily, in all the distraction of the neon and the pop and the fun of the fair. Perhaps, for one night, I could forget who I was.

'Oh my.' Georgina had stopped. Her mouth was hanging open; a melting cloud of floss was threatening to fall to the ground. 'Shaun's working!'

I stopped, too. 'Who's Shaun?'

'Shaun on the Waltzer. He's *fit*.'

The Waltzer was coming to a stop. Grinning teenagers shouted, 'Oh my *God!*' to each other and scampered from their bucket-like carriages under flashing lavender and emerald-green lights. A tanned, skinny man in tight black jeans and an even tighter black vest was riding one of the slowing Waltzer tubs like a Roman chariot racer, one black Monkey Boot up on the silver rim so it looked like a purple lightning bolt was casually coming out of his foot. Shaun was typical of the type who work the Waltzers. A bit sexy. A bit scary. The sort of bloke who would usually have sneered at my face then turned away in disgust, but my Hide-the-Blemish/Maybelline combo was cement-thick that evening and sometimes miracles do happen.

'Oh Lord, he's coming over!'

Georgina wedged a shaft of hair behind one ear. I chucked my candyfloss on the ground and slotted my hands into the back pockets of my jeans as though I was not excited. Shaun loped over, a scraggy cigarette of man.

'All right, Georgie?' he said, but he was looking at me. My instinct was to raise a hand to my cheek, like I always did, but both were frozen like clams in the back pockets of my jeans. I scratched a bright pink, shell-hard nail

266

against the smooth card of the tube ticket we had bought at Chalk Farm.

'Yeah.'

'Who's this, then?'

Shaun had a tiny mole beneath his left eye. It was cute, unlike my affliction. I prayed he couldn't see my birthmark; he was dissecting my face with laser-like precision and I was afraid I hadn't covered my heart-shaped monstrosity enough. He was looking at my winged eyeliner, wasn't he? My glitter eyeshadow? I also prayed I wouldn't blush, as then my birthmark would have shown itself with the efficiency of nuclear-reactive radium.

'Roo,' I said.

'Roo. What sort of a name is that?'

He smelled of dodgy rolled-up fags and generator diesel. His eyes were dark brown, almost black. I didn't answer but I shrugged. I was a little frightened of him. He looked knowing, like he really knew *everything*. His eyes were wrinkled top and bottom, even when he wasn't smiling. A flash of red neon glanced across his face and lingered there for a moment, making him look devilish. I felt a blush cast across my face and Shaun laughed. It was a deep and throaty laugh cracked with a thousand furiously sucked-on cigarettes.

'Do you think she likes me?' he asked Georgina.

'She'd like anyone,' laughed back Georgina, which I thought was a bit cheeky of her – my usual defender – but I needed her as my only friend so I didn't pick her up on it. Instead, I slid my right hand from my back pocket and absently chewed the hangnail of my little finger. I had a silly silver plastic ring below the second knuckle, from one of last year's Christmas crackers. Dad had found it in one of the drawers of the sideboard, before I left the flat – while he was tidying up – and, after pressing each of my fingers to work out which it would fit best, had put

267

it on me, saying it might look pretty. It kept rotating and catching on the inside of my next finger. I flicked it off and let it fall to the grass. Dad wouldn't know. He had threatened to come here tonight; said he used to love the fair and might come to wander round and soak up the atmosphere. I hoped he wouldn't.

'Let's see,' said Shaun, and I didn't know what that meant, but without warning Georgina pushed me on to him, causing me to stumble against his concave chest. My hand thumped against hot skin, tight under ribbed cotton. My little finger, now free of its plastic collar, was millimetres away from a hard, jutting nipple. I could feel Shaun's skinny heart beating. My other hand, startled out of its pocket, floated near a left bicep, which was smooth and almost painful looking; he had a tattoo there – an anchor – faded, with indistinct edges. I wished my birthmark was faded and indistinct. It was throbbing under the make-up and my flushed face, trying to push itself to the surface. I didn't want to be exposed. 'Fancy it?' he asked.

'Fancy what?' I tried to sound cool. George Michael was singing about his careless whisper to the thudding beat of Frankie Goes to Hollywood's 'Relax'. The air around us was hot and charged.

'Something,' he said and, winking at Georgina, he thrust a callused hand in mine. Signet rings chafed against my palm, scratching. I wished I still had my plastic ring, to somehow counter-attack. Closer, Shaun smelled of alcohol, pure nicotine and danger. He had a missing tooth, on the bottom. He pulled me – quite roughly – round the back of the Waltzer. I was giggling but I couldn't see Georgina any more and wondered if she was going to go on the Hearts and Diamonds without me. A generator was chuntering and vibrating, issuing the smell of diesel or kerosene I knew would make me feel sick after a while. But I didn't care. He liked me. He wanted to do something with me. Was he going to kiss me? I hoped so. My heart was pounding under my T-shirt. Something exciting was finally happening to me. *Something*, despite my face and my fears.

He was breathing into my face. My back was against the generator. It was warm and pitted with a meteor shower of rust. 'You ever played chicken?'

'Chicken Square?' This was a game we had used to play in Clerkenwell, growing up, and still played, sometimes, by our school. A bunch of eight or so kids had to cycle around each other, in a square of tarmac, marked off by tar lines, staying within the square and fully mobile; if you put your foot down on the ground you were out. If you came to a wobbly, screechy stop because some little shit had cut you up and laughed at you when you fell off your bike, calling you an ugly witch, you were also out.

'What the hell's "Chicken Square"?' He looked borderline-angry, mocking. Shaun didn't look pleased with me now and I imagined it didn't take much.

'Oh, nothing.' I needed to backtrack, keep the momentum going here; not put my bloody foot down.

He snarled at me, his deep voice a further three octaves lower. 'Chicken is I touch you, as far down as you dare. Do you want to?'

Touch me? I didn't know, I thought, because I didn't know what that involved, and I was scared to ask. Why wasn't he going to kiss me, like I wanted? Why did he have to *touch* me? Still, I was curious. I'd never had a boy so much as hold my hand. They were too busy staring at me; huddling in packs as I walked by – laughter escaping them like gas from one of the Bunsen burners in Chemistry; telling me with uncontained mirth that they would need to put a bag on my head to do what they didn't want to do to me.

Shaun grabbed my hand again, squeezed it and it hurt a little. My dad was the only one who held my hand or put stupid rings on it. But I would let Shaun do whatever this 'chicken' thing was. 'OK,' I said.

'Lean back and close your eyes,' he growled. I was already leaning back. I pressed my back further into the stinky rust, knowing my Blondie T-shirt would probably be stained, but it was OK, as I had been stained all my life. The smell of kerosene caught at the back of my throat; I wanted to cough but I wasn't going to. Nothing would spoil this moment. Shaun liked me, didn't he? If he wanted to *do stuff* with me?

Shaun placed his forefinger in the middle of my forehead. I could smell it, above me; it stunk of cigarettes and something pungent I couldn't identify. He moved it very slowly down the centre of my forehead, his other fingers and thumb splayed out, like the prongs of a fork, and his palm descending like a red road map over the top part of my face. The finger journeyed between my neat and iridescent eyebrows (I was the furthest from the pages of *Vogue* I had ever been) and slid down on to the bridge of my nose. It reeked, but I didn't want it taken away. I wanted it to keep going. The finger moved further down and Shaun held it on the tip of my nose for a few seconds, giving me cause to repress a giggle, before he ski-jumped it off to land in the cleft above my top lip. I held my breath. This felt so strange and intimate. I could have reached out with my tongue and touched that finger if I had wanted to. Tasted how bad it stank. He paused for a few seconds. I wanted to open my eyes and lock them with his, to see what that felt like, but I didn't dare. The finger dragged down to the space between my top and bottom lips and I was still not breathing. He pushed my bottom lip down slightly, let it softly ping back. This was sexy, wasn't it?

'OK?' he said, gruff.

'Yeah.' My breathing was laboured, I felt giddyingly out of control.

'Want to say "chicken"?'

'No.'

The finger had moved on, to the cleft of my chin – I had a spot there, also thickly covered – I wanted him to avoid it. He sped up a little now, his finger travelling over the mound of my chin and down the plane of my neck. He was accelerating, searching for something new. He stopped his finger in the hollow above my sternum; I had a pulse in that silky notch I'd never noticed before. The finger moved on, pressing flat on T-shirt cotton, against my breastbone, then into the slightly sweaty ravine of fabric between my breasts. It was probably on the 'O' of Blondie; I didn't dare look. Underneath, I was wearing a pretty bra, one my mother had left behind when she first left, which now fit me. I couldn't think about her now. Her 'Choose Life' nonsense. Her endless running away. Panda Pops. Margarine. *Sweden.*

Shaun stopped above the band of bra beneath my breasts. I knew there was a little embroidered rosebud sewn to it, with a pink heart at its centre. His fag breath was in my face. My heart was pounding; my eyes still closed. I felt weightless but also that I was tethered, against that generator and on that dry grass. I wondered where Georgina was. The finger set off again, down towards my stomach, which I instinctively pulled in. Too many doughnuts, too many sweets, on the way home from school. That's when I'd met Georgina, on the way home from school; she'd nicked a bag of sherbet off me then we'd got talking. She was different, like me. We *got* each other. Shaun's finger was travelling lower, down my stomach, as though squelching through mud. Through my T-shirt it rested in the fleshy pool of my belly button for a

271

few seconds. I didn't like my belly button being touched but I let him touch it. I wanted this revolting, sexy man to touch me. His hand was now at the top of my jeans. He circled the edge of the brass jeans button, popping it free of the buttonhole, then he pulled down the zip below it; fast, abruptly. He was breathing in my right ear as his hand waited at the bottom of the zip, a claw.

'What are you doing?' My words were involuntary. My eyes were wide open.

He sneer-smiled. 'Do you want me to stop?'

'No?' I answered, but it was also a question. I didn't know.

He smelled really horrible now. Bad breath, booze, ciggies – I didn't want him to kiss me any more. His hand moved up from the bottom of the zip and that same grubby forefinger nudged inside the elastic at the top of my knickers; dirty against my pale virgin flesh, my chub of chunky flesh. I was wearing knickers with a pink and green flower on the front. He pinged the elastic; he was grinning right in my face, his mouth moments from mine, his eyes black like he couldn't really see me. His finger began to push slowly downwards, puckering the eighty per cent cotton, twenty per cent polyester.

I gasped. 'Chicken,' I said.

'What's that?' he murmured and he removed his finger from burrowing through pale pink cotton blend and in one swift movement cupped me; his whole hand a clutching dirty bear's paw, his thumb bent and pressed into the skin at my pubic bone, his fingers curling under me and clutching me underneath. He had me in a grubby vice; his forefinger and the one next to it squeezed down hard where they found themselves. I froze.

'Chicken,' I said. Louder. I wanted him to stop. This was not what I wanted. I tried to shift my body backwards, away from him, but there was nowhere to go.

'Sorry? Can't hear anything.' His other hand was pinning me against the rust, by my right shoulder. It hurt my neck. He pressed his fingers down harder. And his horrible thumb.

'Chicken!' I shouted. 'Chicken! Stop, please! Chicken!'

I sounded ridiculous and he laughed at me. He didn't stop. He left his pressing hand where it was, the *vice*, and I was reminded of hideous woodwork lessons, where I had been humiliated in so many other ways, but he took his shoulder-pinning hand and raised it to my face. With a closed-mouth smile, he dragged two rough fingers down my left cheek and when he held them away from me I could see a smear of Hide the Blemish, shade 1.

'What we got under here, then?' he asked, his breath hot and fetid, and I was terrified for a second he meant under my knickers. 'Hiding a little secret, are we? Let me see.' His other hand still cupping me tight, he spat on his forefinger and scrubbed hard at my face, scouring the Maybelline off my birthmark until a half-moon of beige foundation was wedged under his already filthy nail. 'Oh, that's a beauty,' he said, staring at my birthmark and tipping his head from side to side as though admiring it. 'A pretty little thing, ain't ya? You should be grateful,' he spat in my ear. 'No one else will want to do *anything* to you, with that face.'

He laughed that husky, cigarette-coated laugh and I tried to whip my head away from him, but he was still pinning me to the generator. I thrashed from side to side. 'Stop, stop!' I shouted, right into his wizened, smirking face and I intended to carry on shouting it, louder and louder, until he got irritated enough to let me go.

'Roo?' called a voice. 'Roo, are you there?'

My heart froze. I whipped my head in the direction of the voice and was horrified to see my dad – red Fred Perry polo shirt, Adidas Italias, a bridled Labrador sniffing at the damp grass – standing over at the back of the Hearts and Diamonds; delighted teenagers strapped on to padded playing cards screaming above him. He was tapping his cane on the grass in front of him and reaching his other arm, usually holding on to Milly, out in front of him, his palm outstretched, grabbing at the air. 'Is that you, love? Are you there? Are you all right? What's going on?'

I remained frozen. I knew Dad couldn't see me but I felt ashamed, so ashamed. All those times he had stood in the corner of discos waiting for me while I wished I had been doing something with someone, and now here he was and what was happening was bad, very bad.

'Roo?'

I kept my mouth shut. If I spoke again Dad would come running forward, Milly surprised and excited, by his side, I knew he would, and I couldn't have him getting into a confrontation with Shaun. I had to protect Dad. I had to protect myself. I drew my knee back as far as it could go with the rusty generator behind me stopping its trajectory and I rammed it at the zip of Shaun's fly.

The knee was chubby; it was ineffectual. Shaun laughed again, full and throaty in my face. I would never forget his smell. He squeezed his hand around me, one more time, his fingers like pincers – I knew I would be bruised – then, with a smoker's husk, and a quick final desultory ping of my knickers, he removed his grisly paw and unpinned me. I staggered away to the left, humiliated and silently weeping, leaving Shaun leaning insouciantly against the generator and my dad standing there, at the back of the Hearts and Diamonds, under a sign saying, 'This ride may not be suitable for those with a medical condition.' In a matter of moments, I would compose myself and come round the other way to get him, as though nothing had happened and the girl shouting 'Stop!' round the back wasn't me. In a day or two, I'd pretend what happened that night hadn't scarred me as much as my birthmark always had and always would. But then, to the mournful tap-tapping of my dad's cane, mangled with Wham!'s 'Freedom' and the imagined laughter of my former best friend, I ran.

Chapter 35

'It's finished, Prue. Shall we go?'

I realize there has been some clapping, which is just dying down. I realize my eyes are still closed. I open them, jolt myself back to the present. The lights have come up. People have begun to gather their belongings. The man next to us re-wraps what's left of his sandwiches in cratered tin foil. Places them in a canvas rucksack.

'Yes, Dad.'

I don't want to gather anything to me. I want to stand up and shake my body and mind until I am clear of my memories, like a dog whipping itself into a car-wash-brush of a tornado after an escapade in a muddy river. Dad's cane has ended up under his chair so I retrieve it for him. I brush down my denim skirt although there is nothing to brush away. I put a hand to my face and wonder how badly my tears have eroded my make-up.

'Were you bored senseless, love?' Dad asks, as we stand.

'No. No, not at all.'

We make our way out of the room, walk through the lobby and I guide Dad down the stone steps and back on to the street. It's fiercely sunny already. It's as hot as a furnace. I'm glad of the light.

'So you enjoyed it?' I ask Dad, as we head for the tube.

'Yes, it was very interesting.'

'Would you go to another?'

'Yes, I think I might. If you'd come with me again.'

'Of course I would.'

Would I come and sit in the dark with Dad again? Let him take my hand and have my memories flood me like poison? Yes, I would – for him. I want to do right by Dad. To continue bringing him out into the world. To stand blinking with him on the pavement, like two moles emerging from the hibernation of a very long winter. To be good for him.

'You know,' he says, as we near Westminster station, 'I've listened to some podcasts and things, over the years, read articles, but to be present in a room and feel a person's – an architect's – *enthusiasm*; well, that was quite something. I was surprised by it.'

'*Inspired* by it, too?' I venture to ask. 'For the future?'

'Don't push it.' Dad grins. 'But maybe.'

'That's great, Dad,' I say. 'Really great.'

'It's all thanks to you, Prue.'

'I don't think so.' It was Dad who came up with the list. Dad who instigated coming today. Dad who suggested the walk to Camden. Dad who's been brave and can say 'yes'. Dad who has pushed us back out into the world. While I was crying in the dark, my father was inspired, for the first time in years. While I was trapped in the past, Dad took a possible and hopeful step into the future. I wish I could do the same. I wish for so many things.

My phone buzzes in my pocket. It's a text in capital letters suggesting I've suffered whiplash when I don't even own a car. Of course it's not Salvi texting me. He is not interested. He is too *interesting*, too successful, too charming, too present in the world for me. Then why did he offer to save me? What is he saving me for? I wish I could get it back, that feeling I had with him on the first night in his flat. That I was precious, that I was beautiful. I want that back so I can be a good girl again.

'Tomorrow night is Blondie,' Dad says, as we navigate the barriers at Westminster station.

'Yes. You're still OK about going?'

When I first asked Dad, he was taken aback. Then he shook his head and laughed and said, 'Blondie, eh? I did really love them, back in the day. Especially Debbie Harry.'

'Who *didn't* love Debbie Harry?' I said.

'What a night me and Jack Templeton had back in nineteen seventy-eight . . .' he mused, and then he added he was a little worried about the hundreds of people who'd be there, and I said that it'd be OK, that I would look after him. And I thought Salvi would be there to look after him, too, but he doesn't even know about it. I forgot to mention it when we had the lunch and the evening and the morning, and since then he hasn't called me. If we went out again, I'd be *that* girl again. The one he looked at with tenderness in his eyes. I wouldn't ask him to sleep with me; I wouldn't ask him for anything. I'd be exactly who he wanted.

I'll text him. When we get back to The Palladian, where the three Blondie tickets are in the drawer of the console table, waiting, I do just that. This is not the Dark Ages and women can ask men out to things. We can put ourselves forward. We can be brave. And I'm thinking of tomorrow night, and the possibility of Salvi's arms around me at the concert. The possibility that he does really like me, after all. And me getting that feeling back.

Do you want to go and see Blondie tomorrow night?

There's no answer. An hour sludges by, like treacle down a plate. I try to read an article about Frida Kahlo but I can't concentrate. At the end of that leaden hour, I have a mad idea. I could go and present his ticket to him. I could go to the Old Bailey and wait for Salvi to come out, for his lunch break, catch him outside. Then he's got to come.

'Dad, I'm going out again for a bit,' I announce. 'Is that OK?'

'Sure, love. Where are you off to?'

'Just to my charity shops. Won't be long.'

'OK, pet, mind how you go.'

I've stood here for fifteen minutes, over the road from the Old Bailey, by the fountain, and there've been lots of coming and goings, but no sign of Salvi. I'm thinking about leaving. I feel foolish. My insecurities are starting to sweep across me again, like the shade in the courtyard of The Monastery. I look down the street. A car passes me, a woman staring out of the passenger window. I watch the car round the corner and disappear.

When I turn back, there's Salvi, standing outside the grand, arched entrance with a young colleague, a woman, short brown hair, gamine, with the look of Mia Farrow, though this woman is tall and willowy. Is it Jennifer Dixon, the new clerk he mentioned? She's not quite how I imagined. She is wearing enormous Jackie-O sunglasses that cover half her face. She is wearing capri pants and perilously high heels. Yet, she and Salvi look friendly. She tilts her face down towards his and he gives her a kiss on the cheek, lingering perhaps a little too long. He takes a finger and raises her sunglasses a little, at one outer rim. She shakes her head, a little cross, and pushes them back down again. Then she walks away and gets into a cab that sweeps in to pick her up.

I'm already crossing the road.

'Salvi! Salvi, hi!' I am slightly out of breath with nerves. I've dressed up for this. I'm wearing the jacket, again, plus a cotton fifties skirt (not a London bus in sight) and a cute white capped-sleeve top. I hope I look a little like Audrey Hepburn, not a budget chorus member from *Hairspray*. I had this whole ad hoc meeting in my mind as

279

a rather romantic encounter. Me dashing to meet him, him looking surprised and delighted, his face breaking into a great big grin and his eyes lighting up. Us going for an impromptu cosy lunch somewhere, in a deep dark bar where barristers hang out. A bottle of red wine and a few furtive snogs. His hands underneath the jacket, moving down to my waist . . .

'What are you doing here?' His eyes are narrowed and glacial and he looks at me as though I am a piece of dirt on the bottom of his shiny, prohibitively expensive shoe. A carbuncle on the face of a cherub. A blight on the world. My heart chills, humiliated and confused and fallen. I'm back there again, aren't I? Back in that place. The look on his face and his cold words conjure up the look and the words of every boy and every girl who ever threw taunts at me. The stares. The scowls. The cruel laughter. *Ugly. Pig. Put a bag on it.* I feel both the claw of Shaun the Waltzer charioteer and the heavy press of Jonas's body on mine in that hotel bed in Tenerife. Why is Salvi looking at me in such a terrible way?

'I know you're busy, but I thought I'd come and meet you for a quick lunch? Maybe.' I'm stuttering, stammering; an instant wreck. 'Did you get my text about the Blondie tickets? I've got yours here. I hope you can come with me – it should be great . . .'

My voice trails off. He looks at the ticket in my hand as though it's a turd and at me as though I am a mad witch who has just escaped a drowning. I shrivel under this look on his face until I *feel* exactly like a wizened witch, decrepit and desiccated. Twisted and hideous. Beauty truly is in the eye of the beholder and if the beholder is looking at you the way Salvi is looking at me right now, then you are ugly, ugly, ugly.

'Thank you,' he says finally, his voice so quiet I can barely hear it above the traffic. 'Yes, I did get your text.'

He sighs and looks at his watch. 'I haven't got time for lunch, I'm afraid, is that OK?'

'Yes, that's OK,' I say brightly. 'Of course it is. I'm sorry for bothering you.' Now I sound like a meek bloody below-stairs housemaid, chastised for daring to arrive at Master's chamber five minutes early, to ask if she can draw his morning bath.

He looks at me again, a detached stare, like he's seeing me for the first time – curious, almost – then, to my utter, utter relief, his face breaks into a belated smile and the sun comes back out.

'I'd love to come. When is it?' I hand him the ticket. 'Tomorrow night, yes, I can make it.'

'Great,' I say. 'That's really great.'

He puts the ticket in his inside jacket pocket and goes to give me a kiss on the cheek, my bad side, but I'm so grateful he has given me this crumb, I let him. He won't have his hands inside my jacket this lunchtime, we won't be snogging over a wonderfully neglected bowl of arrabiata and a savoured bottle of Merlot – so I let him kiss my bad cheek. He smiles at me after the kiss, a clipped, finite, professional smile I sense he reserves for his clients in court or, worse, his opponents. I have the terrible feeling, yet again, that's the last I'll see of that ticket, and of him, but then he corrects his smile into something a little less disarming and the sun comes out again.

'Bye.' He is already walking away. There's a whole line of cabs now, at the kerb. He leans in through the window of the first one and says what sounds like 'Capaldi's' – is that the name of a restaurant? – and he gets in, sliding the door shut, settling straight down to look at something on his phone and the cab sets off in the wake of the previous one.

Chapter 36

Dad and I are heading to the Roundhouse. We're going pretty early; the concert starts at eight and it's only just gone seven. We'll get in, have a drink, meet Salvi, get ourselves a good position on the floor. I want Dad to feel as relaxed as possible.

It's fairly busy out and about this evening. As it's the end to another glorious day, people are wandering to restaurants, heading to bars, lingering outside pubs where they've been all afternoon. They and we are in good spirits. Dad's cane taps rhythmically as we walk. He's been playing Blondie's *Greatest Hits* on the old record player all afternoon. He's told me three or four times how much he's looking forward to tonight. I am, too, as Salvi's coming. And I'm excited to be going to the Roundhouse, at last.

'Twat!'

'Uh-oh,' I say. We are passing a small, busy pub. Men and women are huddled at and standing around picnic tables out front, laughing and drinking, but a couple with matching hostile glares are squaring up to each other further along the pavement. Beer is sloshing from his pint glass; she is brandishing a huge goblet of red wine.

'Oh, *do* fucking shut up, there's a love.'

I automatically swerve Dad over and bring us to an alarmed halt as the woman wallops the man on his bicep, where a bright, apparently freshly done tattoo of a tiger's head stares out from under a wrapping of cling film.

'Aargh! You *bitch*!'

The couple start screaming at each other.

'Oh dear,' says Dad, still holding my arm. I'm glad he can't see the spittle flying from the woman's mouth; her grubby pink vest top falling off her shoulder to reveal a purple bra strap, or the man's face, a canine snarl.

The pair stumble off the kerb in front of us. There's a shout from one of their mates to 'Get out of the bloody road!' They tussle a little, drunken and ineffectively, like kids in a playground, or sumo wrestlers, then the woman trips on what looks like her own foot, in red wedged peep-toes, and stumbles forward like an ungainly fla-mingo, her head slam-landing on the man's chest. He catches her by the elbows and she rests her head there awhile then she suddenly starts to cackle hysterically. His meaty face, too, breaks into a laugh.

'You stupid cow!'

'Oh, fuck off!' And, as they laugh, the man rams his arm across her shoulders like the top bar of medieval stocks, forcing his good lady into the gurning, temporary stoop of a hunchback, and frogmarches her good-naturedly back into the pub.

'Some people love a good old barney,' I comment, as the delighted onlookers trail into the pub behind the rec-onciled couple.

'Some people shouldn't be together,' says Dad.

We resume our walk, Dad's cane tapping; my feet, in new flat sandals, clacking; my mind going to lots of places.

'Angela is writing to Mum.'

'Is she? In Sweden?' We keep walking, but I can tell by the change in the rhythm of the tapping that Dad is surprised.

'Yeah, she's already sent a letter. To Torge's address. She hopes it will get forwarded. Surely Mum's not still living with Torge after all this time?'

'I doubt it.'

'Angela wants to "reach out". She wants to find out if Mum's happy or not.'

Dad pulls a face. 'I'm not sure your mother is capable of that,' he says. 'But you never know. How do you feel about Angela writing?'

I shrug. 'I don't feel anything one way or another. I've always just been happy with you.'

Dad looks pleased. 'Have you? The blind bloke . . . ?'

'Yes, the blind bloke . . .' I have been. I have been happy just with him. Despite all the other layers of unhappiness my life has been wrapped in. I've never said this to Dad before. 'How about you?'

'I think it's up to Angela,' Dad says.

I have more questions. Other things I want to say.

'Dad . . . ?'

'Yes?'

'Do you think that you and Mum shouldn't have been together? Do you think it was doomed from the start; that *she* was?'

Dad pauses. And, *Was I?* I wonder. Was I doomed from the start, too? But I am not my mother, I think. Yes, I have distanced, yes, I have removed myself from situations and from people, but I am not her. I don't think I possess quite her level of *froideur*. Or her addiction. Or her selfishness. When I disappeared from life, I didn't keep popping back, to tease and to betray.

'Yes,' he says finally, 'I don't think it was ever going to work. But I really hoped it would as I loved her. I loved her a lot, considering we were two bewildered kids, pregnant and married at sixteen. And she loved me, too, for a while. But she felt suffocated.'

'Did you?'

'No, not suffocated. I felt I had to step up. Make something of myself. Provide for my family. I had to become a man. Cheeky little Vince Alberta, a husband and a father at sixteen! Who could ever have imagined it! Could you imagine being a parent at sixteen?'

'No,' I say. I manoeuvre us under an overhanging branch. I never imagined being a parent at all.

'Neither of us got the life we had expected,' Dad says thoughtfully. 'Although I expected better of *her*, for a long time. I expected her to *try*. I expected her to try to keep on loving us, but she just didn't have it in her. It's best if Angela doesn't expect a reply from your mother,' he adds. 'I don't want her getting hurt, or disappointed. I don't think she should have written to her . . .'

'Bertie!'

We're at the Roundhouse. From outside a bar opposite, Kemp detaches himself from a cluster of men in jeans and band T-shirts, holding pints, and bounds across the road to us.

'I was hoping I'd see you. You're on your way into the concert, right? Hi, Vince.' He reaches out and shakes Dad's hand.

'I'm guessing *you* are,' I say. He's wearing a *Parallel Lines* T-shirt with a charcoal linen shirt over the top. 'I didn't know if you were coming or not.'

I hoped he wasn't. After that drink with him, I hoped he was never intending to come to this concert. That he gave me tickets just because they were spare. But here he is. And he was hoping to *see us*. I remember what he said about not giving up on me and he must mean it. I mean, I was so angry with him, yet here he is, with a big smile on his face, once again. He doesn't look even remotely discombobulated by the fact that he's confessed to asking me to be his fuck buddy. He must be remarkably thick-skinned, after all.

'Yes, of course I was. I'll walk in with you.'

'What about your mates?'

285

'I'll see them in there. *See you in there!*' he shouts to them. He is answered with some thumbs-ups and a couple of ironic salutes. Where did he *get* them all from? I wonder.

'My new neighbours,' he says, 'most of them. I met them in my new local.'

'Oh, right.'

He's had his beard trimmed since I last saw him; and his hair is a bit neater at the sides and the piece that falls into his eyes doesn't fall down so far. I wonder what his new pub is like and whether it's anything like ours used to be.

'How was your lunch at The Monastery?' he asks, as we join a small queue of people waiting to go through the Roadhouse doors.

'Oh, great, thanks.' I then fall silent. I have nothing else to say. I'm hardly going to go into *details*. Kemp is looking at me, so I look away. I want him to know I'm still angry.

'Been anywhere you shouldn't have, lad?' Dad pipes up, across me, as we start to shuffle forward. 'You know – the trespassing lark?'

'Yes, a couple of places, since I last saw you, Vince,' answers Kemp and I think of Dad showing him my paintings and feel slightly sick. 'A disused police station and an old orphanage, in Buckinghamshire, that's been closed since the eighties.'

'Sounds fascinating,' says Dad.

'They really were, and I've got loads more coming up. On Tuesday I'm off to another derelict psychiatric hospital and next Saturday I'm going to the Hornsey Wood Reservoir, underneath Finsbury Park.'

'Hornsey Wood?'

'Yeah.'

'I know that place,' says Dad. 'I went down there once

when I was qualifying. It's a fine example of Victorian architecture. I like to read up on it sometimes. Can I come with you?'

'What?' I say, in the middle of them both, as we take another couple of steps in the queue. Dad and Kemp have been batting across me like jovial players in a tennis match. 'What are you talking about, Dad? What even is it? Like, a sewage works? You can't go there!'

'It's a *reservoir*,' says Dad, 'and people go down there all the time. People like Kemp – urban warriors or whatever they're called.' Kemp grins, and I find myself shaking my head disapprovingly at him, but when he winks back at me, I abruptly stop. 'Plus, they filmed scenes from the *Sherlock Holmes* and *Paddington* movies there. It's perfectly safe. I'd like to go. Can I join you, Kemp?'

'You can't go to a bloody underground reservoir, Dad!' I cry. 'You're *blind*, and it sounds really dangerous!'

'"Avoiding danger is no safer in the long run than exposure,"' says Dad, tapping his cane on the ground. 'Helen Keller said that. And she was *blind* as well, you know.'

'What's your point?' I ask.

'My point is we can't stay in all the time, avoiding things. I've realized that recently.' He beams in my direction. 'I'd like to go down there. You don't have to parachute in or anything, Prue. There's a hatch and a ladder.'

'I don't know,' says Kemp, finally able to get a word in. 'Prue might be right. It might be wise not to do that one, Vince. Sorry, mate. Perhaps you can come somewhere else with me.'

'Oh, *sciocchezze*!' replies Dad. 'Tush! I could wait up top for you. You could go down and then come back up and describe it all to me. Maybe you'd even let me sit and dangle my feet down the hatch, so I can soak up the atmosphere.

287

Have pity on the poor old blind boy and let him soak up a bit of the atmosphere,' he pleads dramatically, in the voice of a randomly Italian Dickensian waif.

I can't help but laugh and so does Kemp. A woman in front of us in the queue turns round and smiles at us. 'Well, I suppose it wouldn't do any harm for you to sit at the mouth of the entrance,' Kemp says finally. 'If Prue thinks it's all right for you to come on a trip with me.'

'Prue is not my bloody keeper!' exclaims Dad. 'If I want to go, I'll go!'

'All right, Dad,' I joke. 'Don't forget who's been guiding you all round London! Be careful, or I could start describing things to you that aren't there again, like I did when I was a kid . . . Oh look, there's a pink dinosaur!'

'Very funny.'

'Well,' says Kemp, 'what do you think, Prue?'

'As Dad's *keeper* I suppose it would be OK,' I say. I make sure to give Kemp a look that says, *I still hate you.*

'All right, then, you're on, Vince. I'll take you to Hornsey Wood. But you can't mess about.'

'Wouldn't dream of it,' says Dad cheekily. 'That's settled, then.'

I shake my head. 'Such a sucker for Victorian architecture,' I say.

Kemp raises his eyebrows at me and smiles. I raise mine back at him and resist the urge to stick out my tongue. We move slowly forward in the queue, and the lowering sun continues its warm swansong over the buildings of London.

Chapter 37

'Bloody brilliant. Bloody, bloody brilliant.'

The beautiful thing about my dad being at the Round-house tonight is that, for him – apart from all the subsequent records they've released since then, of course – it could still be 1978. Dad is here. Blondie is here. The sublime Deborah Harry, rocking a red cold-shoulder dress with a low-slung wide belt and a whole lot of attitude – is here. And the crowd is *loving* it. The atmosphere is so electric and the music is so blisteringly loud, it courses through us like liquid nitrogen. The floor is jumping and that conical roof is being raised to the heavens by transcendent punky pop. We are here, at last, and it is magical.

There was a slight wobble as we came in, when Dad was momentarily daunted at the noise, at the moving body of people. He hesitated at the threshold of the main auditorium. I could see his hand was shaking slightly on his cane, but 'Let's do this,' he muttered, and now – *now* – he is dancing, actually dancing. We're standing by a pillar and Dad's cane is leaning against it unattended, and he is dancing to 'Atomic' and singing along with great and unadulterated gusto. Who knew? Who knew Dad would ever enjoy music again, let alone *dance*? I can't stop look-ing at him. I can't stop looking at my dad dancing.

In between searching the venue for Salvi, of course. He's missed at least three songs. I keep trying to catch his face among the crowd but I can't see him anywhere. Now and then, when I think I do, it's always someone else. A stranger. Nobody that I want as my miracle. There's a woman in front of me with ridiculously shiny red hair and she keeps getting in my way whenever I look towards the exits and the bars. Where *is* he? I keep looking at my phone, too, but there's radio silence.

'This is great,' says Kemp, his hands in his pockets, jigging around like a coiled spring. I'm trying to ignore him. Why is he still hanging around with us? Where are his mates?

'I love this one!' cries Dad, as 'Union City Blue' strikes up and Debbie caresses the mic. He starts dancing again.

'Brilliant, Dad!' I am looking, looking. So many people, so many heads and T-shirts and shirts and jackets and hair. The woman in front of me flicks her shiny red hair again, and I can't see past her.

'Are you all right?' asks Kemp.

'Yeah, yeah, I'm fine, thanks,' I say impatiently. Oh, there he is. There's Salvi, coming from the other direction. I can see his hair, his face in profile as it flashes between the moving heads of others. Relief seeps into me like candlelight. Salvi's here, he wants to be with me; everything is going to be OK.

'Hi, Prue. So sorry I'm late. I had a thing that turned into another thing. You know how it is.' I don't. My life was empty of both meaning and events until I met him. He's standing in front of me wearing a black T-shirt, black jeans, black boots. He's about the coolest person in this place. 'You're looking lovely.'

'Thank you, I've been shopping.' I can't seem to stay out of real shops these days. I've been to Zara and to Mango and to Wallis. I've even been to Topshop, Oxford Circus. I almost baulked at the top of the escalators as I had a sudden horrible memory of Georgina laughing at me in one of the changing rooms and saying I wasn't 'really pulling off' the dress we were about to shoplift, but I did it. And it's all for him.

'Hello, again,' says Salvi to Dad.

'Salvi,' says Dad.

Salvi looks at Kemp. 'This is Kemp,' I offer reluctantly. 'An old friend of mine.'

Kemp puts his hand forward and Salvi shakes it. 'Nice to meet you,' he says.

'Likewise,' says Salvi with a trace of steel. There's an awkward silence then Salvi says, 'Right then, my beauty, I'm just going to get myself a pint.'

'OK,' I say. I don't want him to go to the bar. He's only just got here. I want him to stand behind me and circle his arms gently round my body and for us to listen to Blondie together.

'See you shortly.' Salvi pulls me towards him suddenly and clutches at my waist, a bit too tightly. He kisses me loudly on the cheek, my good one. He smells fantastic. He squeezes my bum. He traces a hand down my left arm, then he is away into the crowd, a dark shadow. I realize he hasn't asked anyone else if they want something.

'So that's the mime artist, then,' Kemp says to me, about two songs later. I'm dancing to 'Heart of Glass' and waiting for Salvi, who's been gone ages.

'The mime artist?'

'Vince has just told me he's a street performer. And don't mime artists dress all in black like that?'

'He's a barrister,' I say.

'Oh right, sorry.' He doesn't *sound* sorry.

'Thank you again for the tickets,' I add, in brittle tones. I wish Kemp would just go away.

'*Looks* like a mime artist . . .'

'Oh, shut up!' I turn away from him to talk to Dad. 'All right, Dad? Enjoying yourself?'

'Yes!' he shouts above the music, and it makes me feel so incredibly happy, how Dad is tonight. 'I can't believe I've been such an idiot!'

'How do you mean?'

'Missing out on music for so long. To miss out on *this*. It's fantastic, Prue. Thank you for bringing me out again.' Does he mean out on another trip, or out again after such a long time sitting in The Palladian, with me, doing nothing? It doesn't matter. What matters is Dad is out in the world again, when the world has been closed off to him for so long. He is swaying in time to the music, a look of sheer bliss planted on his face.

'I've turned a corner, Roo!' he cries. 'I've turned a bloody corner!'

He has called me Roo. My dad is dancing at a concert in a room packed with people and he has called me Roo again. He *has* turned a corner. We have turned one together.

'Oh, Dad,' I say, and we have a dancing, laughing hug, here in the crowd, to Blondie. We've turned a corner and have found our way back to each other again, haven't we? This summer. Almost all the way back.

I stay close to Dad for another whole song. I refuse to look at Kemp. I refuse to look towards the bar. Well, I do a couple of times and there's no sign of Salvi. God knows what he's doing – changing a barrel? Oh, there – I can see him. His head is bent; I can see the cute little bald patch. He's in conversation with that shiny redhead, at least that's what it looks like. She has a curtain of red hair flopping down over one eye and she's peering up from under it and laughing. Does he know her? Are they just having a bit of banter at the bar, the way strangers do? Has he just said something charming and funny to her?

He's turning away from her, a smile still on his face. He's pushing through the crowd, a full pint glass in his hand.

'You didn't get a drink for anyone else?' I ask him, when he's back at my side.

'I wouldn't have been able to carry four.'

'I could have come with you.'

Salvi shrugs. He sips at his pint. He doesn't put his arm back round me. He seems preoccupied. He gets his phone out of his pocket and stares at it. He looks at his watch, then in the direction of the bar. He's twitchy.

'Work?' I ask.

'Yeah.' He awards me a businesslike smile.

'You should switch off your phone sometimes. Try to relax.'

'Not possible, darling.' He gives me another smile and I wonder if it is indiscriminately universal: to other barristers, criminals, girlfriends . . . Yet this is the first time he's called me 'darling'. 'Come here,' he says, and he wraps his free arm round me and whispers in my ear. 'I'll try to relax, with you. You certainly help. You're good for me.'

He turns my face towards him and kisses me, a lingering peck. Then he faces the stage, drinks his beer, and starts to dance, which makes me laugh as he really gets into it. For a glorious, glittering ten minutes he is all mine. Dancing, laughing, whispering things in my ear. Singing along to Blondie. Happiness once again sweeps my body.

'Little boys' room,' he whispers and the glittering minutes are over, as he goes off again, and doesn't come back, not for a really long time, although I'm sure I've seen him exit the Gents, a black shape that got engulfed by the dancers and the drinkers. Goodness knows where he is or who he is talking to. Not Shiny Hair, at least; she is back in front of me, bobbing among the tide with that floppy curtain of hair over one eye. Dad is in his own world – a happy one, still – and Kemp has finally buggered off to his friends, who are over by the main entrance.

'Would you like a drink, Dad?' I ask him. He is swaying happily to 'The Tide Is High'.

'Yes, love, a bottle of water, please.'

'Will you be all right while I go to the bar?'

'Absolutely fine.'

When I get there, having squeezed through the crowd, Kemp is leaning against it, one scruffy boot up on the rail at the bottom and a twenty-pound note in his hand.

'Are you waiting in line?'

'Yes, I'm waiting in line.'

'That sounds loaded.'

'Does it? Where's your boyfriend?'

'In the Gents.'

'He's an interesting character.'

'What does that mean?'

'Nothing much. Just that he's interesting.'

'You sound critical.'

'Should I be?'

'OK, then, you sound *cryptic*.'

'Maybe I'm jealous.'

'Not this again!'

'Not what again?'

'The whole stupid friends with benefits thing.'

'Come on! You're way off the mark with that and you know it!'

'Am I?'

'Are you happy with that guy?'

'Why?'

'Because I don't like him.'

'It's got nothing to do with you.'

'There's something about him when he looks at you that I don't like.'

'As I said, it's nothing to do with you . . .' I'm bloody annoyed. I turn away, fumble in my bag for my purse. I don't want to look at him and his fucking earnest eyes.

He grabs my hand. 'Prue—'

'Everything all right here, darling?' Salvi is standing next to me. His eyes are shining. He looks super-charged. I briefly wonder if he's been somewhere and taken something.

'Hi, yes, of course it is. I was just getting Dad and me a drink.'

'I'll get these,' says Salvi. He pulls me towards him, away from Kemp, who is swallowed into the waiting crowd. Salvi gestures to one of the bar staff. As he carries the drinks through the crowd I hold on to the back pocket of his jeans like an elephant in the procession in *Dumbo*. When we get back to Dad, he's chatting to a girl in a pink tracksuit, her hair teased into top knots. I hand Dad his water and sip my vodka and lime. Then I finally get my wish. To Blondie's encore, a haunting slow version of 'Call Me', Salvi stands behind me and snakes his arms all the way around my waist and laces his fingers together above my belt buckle. He kisses me on the neck. We stand like this for a while, then he pivots me round like a ballerina in a jewellery box and starts kissing me, snogging. Tongues. It's a little too much. I know Dad is blind and can't see us, but it makes me feel uncomfortable that he is right there, standing close to me on the left-hand side. And I make the huge mistake of catching Kemp's eye, standing with his mates, over by the exit, before he turns away. People are starting to stare.

'Prudence, Prudence, Prudence, don't be such a prude,' Salvi whispers in my ear and I freeze, as that's what the poisonous boys at school used to say. I feel that old poison seeping into me, filling me up, flooding the skin beneath my birthmark. 'You should be *so* fucking grateful . . .'

'What did you say?'

I break away from him. I take my left hand and place it on his chest, pushing slightly.

He laughs. 'Hey, hey, I'm joking, I'm joking; I didn't mean anything by it.'

'You said I should be fucking grateful! What did you mean?' I feel cold, quite cold. Shaun said this to me, when my back was up against that rusty generator at the fair at

Finsbury Park. Jonas, in Tenerife, insinuated something similar when he was holding that fucking leaf. Why is Salvi saying this to me?

He laughs again. 'I simply meant you should be grateful someone wants you so much, that they want to keep kissing you, right in full view of a room full of people. That *I* want you so much. And I do, I do want you so very very much, dear Prudence.'

'Funny way of showing it, so far,' I say hotly, my hand still pressed against him.

'Oh, darling,' he says, still laughing. He removes my hand, he nuzzles his face into my neck, he snakes those arms around me, pulling me in close again. 'You'll never know how grateful *I* am. You're so wonderful . . . you're so wonderful in so many ways, you know I can't get enough of you . . . Come on, don't be cross with me; you know how much I like you . . . We're so good for each other, you and I. Come on, darling . . .'

I give in. I give in to the nuzzling and the cooed words and the promise he might be right for me but, as he caresses my neck and holds me tight, whispering over and over again how much he likes me, I wonder what this rollercoaster is that this man has put me on, without strapping me in. Why I am hurtling all over the place, flung from one side of my seat to the other. I have no idea if an up or a down is happening next, with this man. I have no idea where we're heading.

But I know I don't want to get off.

Chapter 38

On the way out, Dad has a fall. According to him, it was his 'own stupid fault'. It wasn't. It was the fault of a drunken bloody idiot who wasn't looking where he was going and tripped over Dad's cane. This made Dad lose his balance and he went into an un-rectifiable wobble I couldn't hold him from, and he staggered backwards, against a young couple who were talking about geocaching, and on to the floor. Salvi helps him up.

'Are you all right, boss?'

'Yes, thank you, Salvi, fine, fine.' Dad is dusting off his palms as I retrieve his cane from under the feet of exiting punters at the side of the entrance lobby, where it has half-skittered under a radiator.

'You haven't hurt yourself, Dad?' I ask, concerned.

'No, I'm absolutely fine. Right as rain.'

'Are *you* all right?' Dad turns to the space behind him, but the young couple patting themselves down are beside us now.

'No, we're OK, all fine. So sorry,' they say, as the British do. 'No harm done.'

'Come on, let's get out of here,' says Salvi. He goes to take Dad's arm.

'No, no, you're all right, lad. Roo?'

'I'm here, Dad.' Dad finds the back of my left arm, just above the elbow, and we set off towards the exit, Salvi hanging just behind us with his arm hovering at the small of my back. People give our weird trio a wide berth, a clearing opens up before us; the parting of the

Red Sea. I didn't see Kemp again; he must have left before we did.

'Silly old twit,' says Dad as we pass through the final space of the lobby.

'Who, you or that other bloke?'

Dad gives a snort of laughter. Salvi reaches forward and tries to retake my hand but I want to keep it free, just in case. I can't not catch Dad again.

'Are you sure you didn't hurt your leg, Dad?'

'No, no, I'm really all right. We'll check it out when we get home.'

Except I was hoping to go home with Salvi. I was hoping to drop Dad off then travel with him to his flat. I glance behind and Salvi is on his phone. He taps away on it as we walk.

'Actually, I've got to go,' he says, now walking level with us.

'Go? Where?'

'Got to see a man about a case, crucial evidence. Pre-arranged meeting in the area.'

'In the *area*? It's Camden at eleven o'clock on a Friday night! I thought we could drop Dad off at The Palladian and go on somewhere.' *Like your bed.*

'Another time?' He's looking at his phone again. Tap, tap, tapping at something. Those fingers should be on *me*!

'Really?' Disappointment is knifing me in the chest, its blade rusty and flaking; twisting. Why is this man always running away from me? Is it because my focus is on Dad; because I wouldn't hold his hand? Is Salvi a petty child? Has he *invented* this thing, this meeting? I don't really know what to think any more.

'Yes. Nature of the job, and all that. I'll call you,' Salvi says, and he kisses me very briefly on the cheek – the bad one – so lightly I can barely feel it, and he nods at Dad, although Dad cannot see him. 'See you.'

'Bye,' I say flatly, and he is going, the escape artist, out of the exit behind a group of middle-aged bikers with ZZ Top beards and matching Blondie bandannas. He is running out on me again. Something or someone better to do. Something better to see. As I watch him speeding through the exit, he turns once to catch my eye and mouths what I think is 'I'll make it up to you', and just as the back of his head disappears through the doorway, flanked by denim and leather, I see a shiny flash of red.

Outside on the pavement, the night air is warm and muggy. The stars above us are diamanté studs to my disappointment. The moon a mocking orb. I steer Dad clear of a pile of McDonald's cartons and wrappers, and around a smashed beer bottle.

'So, you had a good night, Dad, apart from that last bit?' I say, as we start to walk home. 'You *are* OK, aren't you?'

'For pity's sake, I'm fine!' exclaims Dad warmly. 'And yes, I did, pet. A really good time. Did you?'

'Yes, very much.' This *is* true; I enjoyed the concert, I *love* that Dad and I have turned that corner, yet all I can think about is Salvi pushing through that exit. The flash of red. The flash to my heart of disappointment, fear and envy.

'Kemp is very good company. I like that boy.'

Why is Dad talking about Kemp? I can only focus on Salvi. Red hair on black sheets.

'Yes.'

'Is it serious, you and that man?'

'Why are you calling him "that man"? You sound Victorian.'

'I'm not sure about him; I wonder how much you are.'

'Oh! Well, you haven't had a lot to go on, so far,' I say. I feel the chasm opening up between Dad and me again. A fracture, creaking with disapproval and unsaid

299

things. I haven't got a lot to go on, either, have I, when it comes to Salvi? I haven't got a particularly compelling defence to make, should one be required. 'What are you not sure about?'

'Well, for one,' says Dad, 'he has never shaken my hand. That's just basic politeness, unless he thinks it doesn't extend to blind people. Two, he's very full of himself. I had a conversation with him, towards the end, when you went to the loo. It was very illuminating. He talks about himself to the exclusion of everything else. He's full of stories, and I bet I shouldn't believe half of them. Three, he kept calling me "sir", which to be honest is worse than being "blessed" all the time. And "boss". I didn't like it.'

'What's wrong with "boss"? That's quite nice!'

'He's as obsequious as Uriah Heep. Cold, with it. He's a performer, Prue, and I'm not sure what *this* particular performance is all about. With you.'

'Right.'

'I'm just telling you how I see it . . .'

'Right. Er . . . weren't you the one telling me to go looking for love, to open my eyes to it?'

Dad sighs. 'Look, everyone knows if you're blind the other senses get sharpened. Isn't that the kind of bollocks everyone spouts? Well, I can *smell* this bloke is a bullshitter, and I can suss a patronizer at fifty paces. I just don't like him, Prue, especially when you compare him to Kemp.'

'I don't want to compare him to Kemp!' I retort. 'Salvi is . . . more complex.'

'Complex is often shorthand for "arsehole".'

'Dad!'

'I'm being serious. I think he's a wrong'un.'

'Now you sound like a weird cockney. Let's just agree to disagree, shall we? After all, you've met him for – what? – two minutes, and I've had four whole dates.' Four dates and what do I really know about him? Is Dad

right? Is Salvi the worst kind of complicated? The hurting kind?

'If he's telling you who he is – listen. If he's showing
you who he is – see it.'

'Maybe it's too late,' I mutter.

'What did you say?'

'Nothing, Dad, nothing.'

We're almost home. I get the keys out of my bag ready
to unlock the double brown doors.

'Come on, then,' I say, helping Dad over the threshold.

'Cup of tea and a KitKat?'

'You know me so well, Dad.' Yes, I think, Dad knows
me well, but he can't know everything. He can't know my
heart – what's really, truly inside it. He doesn't know that
Salvi is supposed to save me. He doesn't know my secrets.
He doesn't know the things I yearn for in the present to
erase the past.

Because I have never told him.

Chapter 39

'How's tricks?' Angela asks, at nine o'clock five evenings later, when she calls again. Dad and I have eaten and I was just about to settle down with a blog article about Eva Peron, some Alanis Morissette and my misery.

'I don't have any tricks,' I say. Why on earth is she calling again?

'You know what I mean. What's new?'

'We went to see Blondie,' I say flatly. I am absent-mindedly scrolling down Alanis's tracks on my phone to find the most soul-scouring.

'Who did?'

'Me and Dad and a couple of friends.'

'Dad went to a *concert*? And with what *friends*?'

'Just a couple of people I've met.' I'm not telling her about Salvi – it's been five whole days and he still hasn't called. Five days of phone-checking and teeth-gnashing and disenchantment – and I never told her about Kemp.

'What did you wear?'

'Clothes.'

'Oh well, good.' There is silence; I wonder if the phone has gone dead. 'So . . . I didn't hear back.'

'Back?'

'From Mum.'

'It hasn't been that long.'

'No.'

'Were you really expecting to?'

'I don't know. No. I don't think so. I still feel quite disappointed, though.'

'She moved to Sweden,' I say. *To be a Swedish drug addict.* 'Despite her occasional crappy visits, she didn't want to be in our lives any more. I don't know why you'd think she'd suddenly want to be, again, just because she gets a letter.'

'Maybe she hasn't got it yet. Maybe she'll never get it.'

'Maybe.'

'I'm going to keep on trying. I'm going to call the consulate there. Or the British ambassador or something. See if they can help me find her.'

'Good luck with that.'

'You sound like you don't *want* to find her.'

'No, I think *she's* a missing person who doesn't want to be found.' I sigh. 'She moved to Sweden to escape us and that's where she wants to stay, undetected. I don't think she's going to welcome being tracked down, and Dad feels the same.'

'What? What has Dad said about it?'

I sigh again, wishing I hadn't said anything. 'Well, not that much. Just that you shouldn't expect a reply from her.'

'Right.'

There's a devil on my shoulder, patting me there. I'm trying to ignore it, but I can't. I can't help myself. *I'm* disappointed and angry and let down, too. About a million different things. '*You* left too, you know. It seems *you* don't want to be found either.'

'What? What do you mean I don't want to be found?'

'You left too,' I repeat. I am despondent and numb enough to bring this up now, after all these years. I just don't care about putting it out there.

'I don't know what you're getting at.'

I sigh again. 'I get the impression you'd prefer to have no contact with us at all. That you want to be free of us. Free of me and Dad. You *left* to be free of us, after all.'

'It wasn't like that.'

'What was it like, then?'

'I was nineteen, a grown woman. I was just making my way in the world.'

'A way that involved plotting your escape at a local college full of foreign students and buggering off to the furthest place you could manage!'

'That's unfair!'

'I don't think so. I think you were positively Machiavellian about it. Actually, your timing was pretty horrendous, if I remember rightly.' I am bitter. I am as sour as an underripe lemon. I move into the kitchen and run myself a glass of water. 'But leaving is soooo easy, isn't it, if you're the one who's going?'

'I don't believe this! Prue, for God's sake!' Angela falls silent, well, apart from the fact I can hear her positively seething down the phone. 'Do you know *why* I left?'

'Who is it on the phone?' Damn, Dad must have taken off his headphones.

'PPI!' I call out. 'Hold on a minute,' I say to my sister. I take the phone into the bedroom and shut the door. 'There's no big mystery, Angela,' I whisper. 'You left because you were selfish, because you wanted to have fun and be free. You left me and Dad, with a clear conscience and no regrets, because the guide dogs had gone. You *left* us so I could be there for Dad and you didn't have to be. So you wouldn't have to worry about him being blind or what that meant for all of us any more. You left me at the coal face, *Angela*, and it was really bloody hard.'

'That's *really* not true.'

'I think it is! And when you left, you left so *completely*. It's like Dad and I didn't exist for you any more. Like we *don't* exist. You've closed your eyes to our lives. You just hear our voices, every three months, when you can bear to. Even when you came over for those awful visits, it was

304

like you weren't really with us. Whereas I could probably write a thesis on *your* life: how wonderful Warren and the girls are, what your backyard looks like, the kind of cakes you can buy at the idyllic little bakery down on the shore. I can picture your life, Angela; I can picture every aspect of it.'

'You never phone *me*,' says Angela quietly. 'And I know I don't phone very often. I *have* closed myself off to you and Dad, I admit it. You're both so miserable when I phone up, although I try to be happy and chirpy. *Positive.* I make the effort, but you have nothing to say . . . You don't sound like you particularly want to talk to *me* . . . Can I speak now? Can I tell you why I left?'

I sit down on my bed. 'Go on then.'

There is silence. Then I hear her take a deep breath. 'It had nothing to do with not being there for Dad,' she says quietly. 'It wasn't that at all. It was because of how it *was* with us, once the guide dogs had gone. How everything slipped into a kind of despair.'

'*Despair?* What do you know about *despair?*'

'Let me finish! *Please!* Ever since our last dog, Folly, trotted out of The Palladian with that woman, it was a soulless existence in that flat – Dad so depressed and all his cheerful hope gone; you fighting your own demons, as always. It's like you both just gave up! I felt I was being gradually swallowed up by it all. Our home life. I ran away because I couldn't bear it. I missed the three of us. I had missed Mum for so many years and now I was missing the two of you as well, because it was like you were both there but yet you weren't. I missed the fun and happiness we used to have. I missed everything.'

At home, in The Palladian – behind closed doors – we *had* known fun and our own brand of happiness, before the guide dogs had to go. The hole Mum left in our lives had been closed over by the three of us until it wasn't visible any more and its seams remained invisible, despite Dad going blind. Despite the things that had happened to me. When the dogs left, didn't that hole we'd closed over open up and swallow Dad into it, with me jumping in willingly after him? Isn't that something I've always known?

'I had to make my own life,' she continues. 'Some kind of life. Because our life in London was life in the dark.'

'You left when we needed you most,' I say to her. 'We needed your sunniness to pick us up and stop us falling into that darkness – but you took it away.'

For much of my life, I've wanted to keep the light from me. I've slouched along, living it with headlights at half-beam. I let something bad happen to me as a teenager. I was raped, in my twenties, by a man who saw that distance and breached it, with lamps turned down low and an insidious force that nearly destroyed me. I've wanted to talk, but not about the things that matter. Did Angela feel the light go out on her, too? I thought she was OK, that she was immune to everything. That her determined self-centredness shielded her from any despair; that she remained carefree, doing her own thing, until doing her own thing meant leaving us.

Have I always been so wrapped up in my own issues that I just couldn't see what was really going on with her?

'I had to,' she says quietly. 'I just had to. Something else happened around that time, you know. Before I left.'

'Something else?'

'Mum came back.'

'She came back in nineteen eighty-four ... The time with the Opal Fruits and the Choose Life T-shirt . . .' The day of Finsbury Park. 'That was the last time.'

'No,' says Angela. 'She came back again in nineteen ninety. I was eighteen. You and Dad were out – a doctor's appointment or something. I was so surprised to see her.

306

I opened the door and she was wearing normal clothes, for once. Jeans and a lilac T-shirt with buttons down the front and a pair of trainers, but she looked awful. Like, worse than she ever had. She was, what, thirty-six? But she looked about seventy. She had massive bags under the eyes and her face was all wrinkly and she looked drawn and ill. I think I actually winced. And she made no sense whatsoever – you know what she was like. Muttered something about the ferry, you know, back to Sweden – "the boat" she kept calling it, and giggling – and about money and did I have any. In fact, that's pretty much all she kept saying – did I have any money? Did I have any money? – and when I said "no" she got angry and she whacked her own head on the door frame and she called me a bitch.' There's a huge sigh down the line, all the way from Canada and my sister. 'She actually called me a bitch, Prue. And I was frightened. So, I shut the door on her, and I watched from the window as she walked away, and I knew then that the mother she should have been was never coming back. That any dream I'd had of that was gone. So, I might as well be gone too.'

'Bloody hell, Angela! Why didn't you tell us she'd come again?'

'What was the point? I didn't even want to talk about it. All I knew was I didn't want to be in London when she next came for a pathetic, self-pitying visit. That I had to make sure I wasn't there. That I was a long long way away. So, yes, I *did* go to that college for the foreign students. I *was* looking for an escape route. And then I found Warren. And a career. I was aimless in London, Prue. I'd scraped through my A levels but I had no clue what to do next. I had no direction, no drive.'

Angela and I have never talked about this stuff before. How directionless we were. How we drifted through school with no purpose. Angela's escape finally gave her one, while I continued drifting in a boat with no oars and no rudder, apart from my truncated career at the conference centre, where I was eventually kicked overboard. She didn't have to go quite so *far*, but that's Angela for you. And I realize she *had* to go; that I had been blind to just how badly our life in The Palladian – in London – had affected her.

'If you'd *seen* her, Prue! I knew then, there was no hope for her. If she hadn't grown up and got herself sorted out by thirty-six, I knew she never would.'

'I was already long done with her,' I say. 'But I knew you still had hope.'

'Not after that.'

'But you have some now?'

'It's been nearly thirty years, Prue. Things may have changed.'

'Maybe.'

There is silence again – this time, silence from London all the way to Canada and back again.

'I'm sorry,' I say. And I am. I am so so sorry. 'I'm sorry that I didn't realize that you were feeling like that, when you left London. I'm sorry you felt you had no choice but to go.'

'I'm sorry I could never explain,' says Angela. 'I'm sorry I've been absent for so long, in every way.'

I sigh. But in that sigh is a little bit of relief and a little bit of hope. 'We never talk like this,' I say.

'No,' says Angela. 'I'm glad we are. I miss you.'

'What did you say?'

Angela laughs. 'I miss you! I've always missed you, and when I've spoken to you and Dad recently you've been . . . different, both of you. You've been going out on those trips; you seem, suddenly, to be getting closer again, after all this time. It's making me really miss you both!'

'*Miss* us! I can't really believe this, Angela!' I'm teasing now, and it feels nice.

308

'Yeah,' she says, and I can hear the smile in her voice and I can picture her shrugging, just like the teenage Angela used to do. 'Do you think you two would ever come over here for a visit?'

'I don't know,' I say. 'I'm not sure I can get Dad on a plane.'

'He's not bloody Mr T, Prue.'

I laugh. *The A-Team* was one of our favourites. How we loved it when a plan came together. 'We'll think about it,' I say.

'Good. So, can I talk to him now?' she asks. 'To be honest, I'm exhausted after talking to you.'

We both laugh. 'Of course.'

'We'll speak again, Roo,' she says. 'Properly. Like we have today.'

'Yes, Angela Pangela,' I reply, 'we'll speak again.'

Chapter 40

Dad and I sit in silence. Dusk falls. It will be bedtime soon. He spoke to Angela for half an hour. There was a little laughter. Dad cracked a couple of jokes. I'm still digesting everything she said to me. How she had no choice but to go, as life was darker than night. How all her hopes about Mum were seemingly extinguished, yet she still has reserves for more, all these years later. I thought I knew my sister so well but now it feels as though I have never seen her clearly at all. I need to re-shape her, in my mind. Adjust my view. She has appeared as many things to me over the decades: sunny playmate and surly teenager; arch deserter and selfish escapee; irritating Tiger Mom and boastful Canadian wife . . . But perhaps all along she was just my *sister*. And she was hurting, like I was, though I was too blind and wrapped up in myself to see it. We were *all* hurting. And she missed me.

A man out on the street calls for 'Dasheep' but it sounds like Dasheep is not going to show up. There's the slam of a door, a blast of heavy rap music from a car whizzing past, a fox knocking over a wheelie bin: the sounds of the streets of London. My lullaby – now accompanied by the strange and new sensation of me missing Angela.

I get Dad a beer. I sip at mine. At twenty past ten the doorbell goes.

'Who on earth's that?' asks Dad. We are about to start on some honey-roast peanuts.

'God knows,' I say, but my heart is suddenly thumping

in my chest and hoping against hope that it's Salvi. That he is at my door, as laid-back and unrepentant as ever and ready to sweep away the ignored-presumed-dumped melancholy he so casually unloaded on me.

'Prue, hi.' He's leaning casually on the door frame, one elbow propped against it. Sometimes you get what you wish for. 'I wanted to see if you were free on Saturday night.'

Salvi stares from my face to my chest, to my face again. No mention of him running out on me at the end of Blondie. The radio silence. He couldn't look more relaxed, while I am ramrod straight, heart yammering. Fingers rigid on the other side of the door frame.

'I might be.' I know I am blushing, the redness sweeping into my birthmark and making it inflamed. There's no point trying to hide it. I know, at the sight of him, that I instantly forgive him. That I want him. I *am* grateful. I am forty-eight years old; there are limited chances for me left, in this life, and I want to live it. I want to live it on the edge – *his* edge – standing on a precipice at the top of a tall building, my arms outstretched over a winking night skyline, vulnerable and precarious but knowing I won't fall, as he is standing next to me. I'm so happy he is on my doorstep. That he has come back.

'The fair's on, at Finsbury Park. I'd like to take you.'

'Oh, right.' I'm on that edge already, then. Shaking. Looking down.

'I know you said you don't like fairs, but you'll be going with *me*.' He shrugs merrily. 'It'll be fun!'

I gulp nervously and hope he doesn't notice. The Finsbury Park fair. I had vowed never to go back there again. The bright lights, the smell, the music. The grip of that man . . . But *he* won't be there, will he? I'll be with Salvi, like he said, if I agree to go. I'll be safe, won't I? And maybe I can erase that night from my past. Do it over, somehow, with him by my side.

'Yes. Fancy it? Your local fair? Shame to miss it.' He's grinning at me. The running out on me, the ghosting – none of it has touched him. He's back again, asking me out, not a care in the world . . . *Saturday night*? Isn't that when Dad and Kemp are going to that stupid reservoir?

I have one final chance to say 'no'. Call his bluff and say, 'No, thank you,' to his picking me up and putting me down. His mind games and escapology. And all the fun of the fair. *No, thank you, Salvi.*

'OK,' I say. 'Sounds great.'

'Fabulous. I'll meet you by the Ferris wheel at six thirty.'

'Yes, OK.'

'See you then, Prue.'

'Bye, Salvi.'

I close the door. As I come back into the living room, Dad looks up from his podcast and removes his headphones.

'Who was that?'

'Salvi.'

He nods.

'I'm seeing him on Saturday night. The fair at Finsbury Park. While you and Kemp are messing around at that reservoir, sitting in hatches, I'll be on the Ferris wheel.' Better to be out in the open, I think. No secrets. For once. Although I can't really see me on the Ferris wheel . . .

'Sounds good.'

'I know you don't like him, Dad, but tough cheese. You know?'

Dad smiles. It was an expression I used when I was young. Tough cheese. It went nicely with 'bog off' and 'wotcha' . . . the lingo of seventies and eighties kids.

'You're a grown-up, you can see whoever you like.'

I sit down in my chair. Reach for the packet of peanuts. 'Thanks. So, the last place on your list, Albert Bridge?' I say, feeling relieved, charitable; wanting to appease. Dad had mentioned Albert Bridge earlier in the week but such was my Salvi slump, I hadn't wanted to go. 'When shall we take a trip there?'

'Saturday? Might as well make a day of it, gallivanting around?'

'Albert Bridge in the afternoon and Finsbury Park in the evening?' I suggest.

'Why not?'

'OK, that's a date,' I say. 'Saturday it is.'

Chapter 41

'The Albert Bridge was built in 1873,' Dad tells me, 'as a cable-stayed bridge that turned out to be structurally unsound, so it was modified with suspension bridge elements by Sir Joseph Bazalgette between 1874 and 1888.'

'Uh-huh.'

'And, in 1973, two concrete piers were added, transforming the central span into a single-beam bridge and making it an unusual hybrid of three different styles. Am I boring you yet?'

'No, Dad.' His touch on my arm is light. My steps, sandals on pavement, are satisfying. 'But I had no idea there was so much to be said about bridges.'

'There's *always* a lot to be said about bridges.'

Dad and I are walking up Chelsea Embankment, on approach to Albert Bridge; the sun is blazing above us. The air is perfectly still; there is no breeze this early afternoon to disturb the languid heat. There's no birdsong either. London's flocks are quiet, choosing to keep counsel on the world, and summer itself seems suspended, hanging on its own blistering falsehood that it is endless. That days like this are simply all there is.

'Albert Bridge is possibly my favourite,' continues Dad. We got the bus here; Dad fancied it. We manged it without any problems. 'Although Tower Bridge comes close. Funny that Angela lives in her very own Albert Bridge.'

'Albert Bridge, Nova Scotia, Canada . . .' I say. 'How very far away that seems.'

She's probably waking up about now, I think, jumped on

by her daughters, brought tea and toast by Warren, in the life she moulded for herself when she ran *towards* life – a whole and happy one. Can Dad and I join her there? Can we make the trip to Nova Scotia? Could we wake up in Albert Bridge, too, wander down to the quay, eat pancakes at Missy's Diner (I've been googling) and sip afternoon tea on the swing chair on the veranda while the nieces I've shamefully ignored play at our feet? Could we sit and talk to Angela on that veranda until dusk falls and everything we want to say has been said? Maybe we could. Maybe we could re-create the little family we once knew and wrap our arms around its new members. I also wonder if Angela's going to sit on that veranda later today and make a call to the British Embassy in Stockholm, looking for our mother.

'Is the sign still there?' asks Dad.

'What sign?'

'The sign about soldiers breaking their step. You'll see it on the tollbooth.'

We are almost at the bridge. The river is busy – boats and barges and a couple of pleasure cruisers, their windows glinting in the unblinking sun, glide under the bridge in both directions. We arrive at the left tollbooth of an octagonal pair standing sentry at the gateway to the bridge. There's a Royal Borough of Kensington and Chelsea sign on one of the panels, in pink and purple.

'*Albert Bridge Notice,*' I read out. '*All troops must break step when marching over this bridge.* Why was that, then, Dad?'

'Bad vibrations.'

'Eh?'

'Walkers have a natural tendency to match their steps to each other, and when they all walk in unison it causes vibrations. It happened at the Millennium Bridge, when it opened – remember? Pedestrians fell spontaneously into step – thousands of them – and everything got a bit wobbly.'

315

'Yes, I remember. Oh, that's interesting.'

What did the troops do instead of marching? I wonder. Saunter, hands in pockets? A little light whistling?
Did it unnerve them not to march in time with each
other?

We're on the bridge now.

'Let me tell you about all the boats on the Thames this
afternoon,' I say to Dad.

'Go for it.'

'Well, they're mostly barges – low, flat-bottomed
affairs; a couple of tourist cruisers – blue and white, with
lots of windows, the sun reflecting off them; some small
motorboats; the river police . . . a big brown dog on the
back of some sort of dinghy . . .' I'm reminded yet again
of Kemp's houseboat, how many of my emotions were
contained in that thing. 'There's also an old-fashioned
tugboat, red and black, complete with a seagull perched
on its cabin and a man in a woolly hat.'

'Good, good. It does sound really beautiful,' Dad says,
but I worry he doesn't remember what a seagull looks
like, or a tugboat, or anything else I am talking about.

'Sorry, am I describing too many things at once?'

'No,' says Dad, smiling, 'not at all. I get the overall
picture.'

I hope I really *am* painting pictures for him, in my
flawed clumsy way. We *are* closer now, Angela is right.
The corner has definitely been turned this London summer: these trips out have given us the chance to talk,
really talk again, and try to walk in each other's shoes . . .
to a point. We have stopped short, though. *I* have stopped
short. There are confessions, just like Angela's last night,
that still lie dormant, locked away. Things that need to be
said. Will I ever be able to describe the hidden corners of
my heart to my father? Can I ever turn that rusty key and
let them spill out?

'Oh, lamp-post coming up.' I steer Dad away from it. 'How long is the bridge, Dad?'

'Seven hundred and ten feet.'

Dad's touch at my arm is now feather-light. He'll be able to go further on his own soon. There'll be no stopping him; no breaking step. I hope he has a good time with Kemp tonight, nosing at the reservoir. Sitting in the hatch or whatever he plans to do. And I'm looking forward to meeting Salvi tonight. My outfit is planned, the butterflies in my stomach are all lined up. He wants to see me again! Life truly is full of small miracles.

'I had an interesting chat with Angela before you spoke to her the other night,' I say. If I am not quite ready to make confessions of my own, I can start with my sister's.

'When you shut yourself in your bedroom? I *knew* that wasn't PPI!'

'Yes. She told me something. She said she left London because it was so dark and depressing at home. With us two.' I laugh, but I feel incredibly sad. 'I think it was, though, don't you? It *was* dark. She was struggling. She had to go. Mum came to visit from Sweden once, in nineteen ninety – when Angela was at home by herself. She said Mum looked worse than ever. That she was quite abusive, asking for money. It was another reason Angela went to Canada . . . because she knew however many visits there were, or how long she waited around, Mum was never going to change.'

'Oh. She came back again,' says Dad, frowning. 'I wish I'd known that. Poor Angela. Your mother . . .' He doesn't finish his sentence. He looks so downcast. We keep in step, his hand weightier again on the back of my arm. My eyes are on the bridge as it extends into the distance. 'And yes, those were dark days. I never considered how dark they were for Angela. That she was struggling. I don't know what to say.'

317

'You don't need to say anything, Dad. You can't change how things were, or what happened. But I do feel . . . *better* now she's told me. I thought all this time she left because of what she *wanted* – a husband, a certain lifestyle, an adventure – not because of how she *felt*.'

Dad nods. 'All these years,' he says. 'All these years. So many things have remained unspoken!' He sounds angry suddenly. Should I not have told him? He exhales – an enormous sigh that carries into the still air and over the water. 'I've never been able to *reach* Angela,' he adds quietly, 'despite all those phone calls, although the last couple have seemed a little lighter, somehow. Do you feel *you* have?'

'No, Dad.'

'Do you think it's too late for us to reach her now?'

He squeezes my arm; there is a real entreaty in that touch. I feel pain in it.

'No, I don't think it's too late. She made a start on reaching out to us. Maybe we could go out there one day, to visit her? Her and Warren and the kids? What do you say?'

'Well,' says Dad, 'it would be a big step. I mean, I've only been to a few places in London, with you. A trip to Canada! But maybe we could.'

'We can think about it.' I'm glad I've told him, despite the pain of the utterance. We *could* go to Canada. We could go to Angela. When I dream of holidays, I dream of something tropical, but I would like to see my sister. 'Shall we think about it?'

He nods. 'Let's do that.'

The bridge is busy. A baby in a red pushchair is coming towards us – snug under a bar of swinging cuddly toys; bare feet kicking upwards – and she has a perfect face, the softest pinkish skin and a turned-up nose and big, wondering eyes. She fixes those huge eyes on me and she grins, and I smile back.

318

'Single file, for a minute, Dad,' I say and Dad drops behind me.

'Angela didn't hear back from Mum,' I say to him, over my shoulder. 'She's going to keep trying. She's going to ring up the consulate, or something. I get the impression she's not going to give up.'

'I'm sorry to hear that.' Dad's frown is back. I don't know if he's sorry about Mum not getting in touch, or that Angela is going to continue to try. The baby glides past us up the bridge in her red cocoon, waving a pudgy pink foot at me. Dad returns to my side and we fall into step. He sighs again. 'I just wanted to keep you girls close to me, you know,' he says. 'Safe. Protected. Because in the end you were all I ever needed. And I ended up driving you both away.'

'*I* didn't go away, Dad! I've always been here.'

'You did go away, Prue! And so did I. Even though we've sat in that same room together, year after year, the space between us could not have been wider. We closed off from each other and the world, you know we did!'

'I know,' I agree. 'I know.' That wide space. Between us. Between Angela and us. The things we should have said. The secrets we could have told. And I was not safe; I was not protected. But he never knew.

A boat clanks under the bridge. Its horn sounds. A child stops on the bridge and waves at it happily. Life on the river goes on. Life in London goes on. The world keeps spinning round and all my secrets stay hidden, unless I decide it's time.

I look at Dad. At his face, with a thousand different emotions flickering across it. I want to be in the same room as him, father and daughter, and not two strangers, who were never brave enough to tell their stories. He has told me some of his, while we've been out this summer, walking around London. I have told him nothing of mine.

I think it might be time. I don't want there to be a wide blank space between my father and me. I don't want there to be long-kept secrets. I would like to tell him my truth, like Angela has finally done. I would like to tell him who I am.

'I want to tell you something, Dad,' I say. 'Two things, actually.'

Our feet are walking in time, not enough to make the bridge wobble but I *do* feel wobbly.

'Go on,' says Dad.

'It's bad things. And the first thing brought about the second thing, I believe. It brought everything *since*.'

'I'm a little confused, but I can take it.' Dad looks uneasy, concerned. 'Go on, love.'

I take a deep breath. Then another one. Dad waits. 'OK. Firstly, when I was fourteen, a man working at Finsbury Park fair . . . abused me.' The words rush out of me, a torrent. 'He . . . he grabbed me where he shouldn't have done and he pinned me to a generator and didn't let me go. You were there, Dad. You came round to look for me.'

Dad stops walking. 'What do you mean, grabbed you where he shouldn't have done?' he asks. Pain flashes across his face. 'Was this when I had Milly? When I came to the fair and your friend Georgina sent me round to you?' It's his turn now to take a deep breath. It's almost a gulp. 'I remember . . . I thought I heard you shouting, but you appeared a couple of minutes later and said it hadn't been you?'

'Yes, that was then, Dad. It *was* me.'

'Well, what did this man do to you? Tell me!'

'Oh Dad, I can't go into detail, but . . . but his hand was sort of like a vice, on my . . . knickers, on the outside. It wasn't that bad but . . .'

'It was *bad*!' exclaims Dad, his voice raised. 'Why didn't

you tell me? How could you have pretended everything was OK? I could have done something!'

'You couldn't have done anything, Dad. And I was fine, really, except for being very angry, for a time and maybe for ever.' I grin sardonically, but of course he cannot see it.

'I could have *done something*,' repeats Dad. His face is red and the hand on his cane is clenched, knuckles straining. 'I could have done something, Prue.'

'No,' I say. 'It was all down to me. I . . . I was so happy that someone was interested in me. I shouldn't have gone round the back with him. I thought he liked me. But he made me a victim. I made *myself* a victim – or that's how I've always seen it. And when the second thing happened, I felt that "victim" was a label I wore, a sign above my head – that I was marked out . . .'

'I'm afraid to hear it. This second thing.' I can see tears threatening at the corner of Dad's eyes. I may regret telling him these things. The first and the second. But he has revealed the layers of his heart to me – about his blindness, the guide dogs, his love for Angela and me. He has stepped out into the world. He has listened to a talk at Central Hall Westminster. He has danced to Blondie. If we are to truly know each other again, I must tell him.

'Can we stop a minute?'

We both put our hands on the railing and feel the breeze from the river caress our faces. A party cruise is going under the bridge; people are whooping and raising plastic champagne flutes in the air.

'Back when I was twenty-six, I . . . I was . . . well . . . I was sort of raped.'

'Good God, Prue!' Dad pulls back from me, letting his cane fall to the railing, and grips both my hands. He grips them tight as the boats ebb and rock beneath us, going their merry way under the bridge. 'Prue, Prue, I—'

'The thing is, I don't exactly know if I was or not and that's almost the worst thing, that I don't know for sure. Remember I went to Tenerife that summer, in nineteen ninety-six? To train staff at that hotel, in badging?'

'Yes, I remember.'

'That's where it happened. I met this man, from Belgium. He seemed nice, at first. He wasn't.' I hang on to Dad's hands for dear life, anger rising. I don't know what to say next. If I had been raped in the way lots of people imagine it – the monster in the shadows, the evil attacker following down a dark alley – it would be more clear-cut; I would be the victim, he would be the perpetrator. I wouldn't feel so much guilt that I'd got myself into that situation – *again* – or maybe I still would. Maybe anyone this has happened to – from a violent attack on the street, to a 'no' in a living room, to a 'I'll let you finish because it's easier than trying to get you off me' in their own bed – feels that same guilt; I don't know. That they could have done more to make it not happen to them. That they could have done *less* – to not make them wonder every day if they asked for this, when how could anyone *ask* for that?'

'What happened, pet?'

'I slept with him . . . but it turned bad . . .'

'He hurt you?'

'He was . . . rough . . .' I say. 'He was rough. And he wouldn't stop.'

'Then you were raped.'

'Sometimes I don't know, Dad. I don't know. It's all such a tangle, in my mind. I go over it again and again because I just don't know. I invited him in. I invited them both *in*.'

'You were raped,' says Dad, squeezing my hands. 'And he did it in such a way that you would be trapped in doubt and confusion about it. I'm so sorry, love. I'm so, so sorry.'

I let go of Dad's hands and I stumble into his arms, breathing in the warm skin at his neck, that smell of Imperial Leather soap and washing powder. I can feel the tears on his cheeks on mine. I can feel his heart beating.

'I don't want to be trapped any more,' I whisper.

'It's not your fault,' he whispers back. 'None of it is your fault.' He strokes my back and clutches me tight. My dad. My lovely dad. Eventually he pulls away from me and his eyes are red and watery.

'I remember now, when you got back from that trip,' he says, a waver to his voice. 'You were very withdrawn at times, but at other times very over-bright and chatty. I thought you were just exhausted. But I also remember you changed departments not long after that, didn't you?'

'Yes. I had to. I couldn't do the badging thing any more; I had to shake off all the memories that came with it. I resigned, Dad, long before I was actually made redundant from that place. I resigned from my life and I've *been* resigned my whole life, to who I am.'

'Roo.' He is hugging me again. '*Roo*. I'm sorry you went through all that alone, both those things, though each time I was right there. I was right there . . . I'm so sorry I didn't know.'

I press my hands to my eyes and wipe away my tears. 'I didn't want to upset you, to make things worse.' But I knew not telling him, all these years, had made *me* worse.

Dad clasps me tight to him again and whispers again, 'I'm sorry I didn't know.'

'I knew after the first time that no one would ever love me,' I sob. 'I knew then exactly how people would always see me. As ugly. As not good enough.'

'Then you knew wrong,' says Dad. 'You are *beautiful*. You didn't deserve those things to happen to you.'

'I'm ugly, Dad! I'm ugly inside and out! I should always have known it.'

'Stop, *cucciolo*! I know I haven't seen your face since you were ten years old, but you were beautiful then and I know you are beautiful now. You have always been so very very *lovely*. Inside *and* out.'

'You're only saying that because you're my dad,' I sniff, through my sobs.

'I'm saying it for lots of reasons. That's only one of them. Nothing is too big to overcome, pet. You're strong, I know you are. You just don't realize it yet.'

We both fall silent. I look out over the water. I've told him. I've told my dad. And it hurt to tell him but now I do feel as though the chains around my heart have been loosened a little; that he has held them in his hands and shaken them free.

'Are you OK?' he asks me, placing his hands on my shoulders. 'Do you think you can be OK?'

'I can be better,' I say. 'Better now I've told you. Shall we walk again?'

He nods and I retrieve his cane from the railing, and we set off, our footsteps in unison. A barge hoots; a bird calls in flight above us and is answered by another. The birds are talking once more.

'I hate the thought of you being hurt,' says Dad. 'I hate the thought of *either* of you girls being hurt. If I can stop that happening, then I will.'

'I know, Dad, I know.' He looks like he is wrestling with himself, somehow. He is biting his lip, face contorted. 'Are *you* OK?'

'Yes. No. I think I've got something to tell *you* now.'

'Have you?'

'Yes.' That biting at the lip again. The tapping of his cane. The rhythmic stepping of our feet. An elderly motorbike splutters past us, its driver in leather and goggles. 'Your mother is not in Sweden.'

We break our step. Well, I stop, and because Dad is

holding on to my elbow he has to stop too. 'What? What do you mean she's not in Sweden?'

A jogging man with headphones circles round us. 'Pardon me,' he says, American accent.

'She's in London. She never went to Sweden. She's been here all along. Well, apart from that bloody hippy trip around Europe . . .'

'I don't understand. She didn't go to Sweden? She just made that up?'

'*I* made it up.'

'Dad, you've lost me. You need to explain what you're talking about.'

We have stopped dead on the bridge and are in the way of everyone. I steer Dad over to the railing again and this time *I* grip it tight, my knuckles whitening as they push against my skin.

Dad takes a breath. His eyes are still red-rimmed. 'I couldn't have her coming in and out of your lives like that, so infrequently. It just wasn't fair.'

'Go on . . .'

He sighs and rubs at his eyes. 'I tracked her down, sometimes, in between those visits, to a squat or a horrible bedsit – she'd refuse to get her act together, refuse to come and see you. Other times I feared she was dead. You know, when your mother first left she told me she wanted some time off, to be free of everything, and I told her, yes, "go". I said, "Do what you need to do." I was young but I loved her so fiercely, so determinedly – determined that we were going to make it work, this marriage. I thought we'd be together for ever – how naïve was that? I thought this was a temporary wobble. Yes, she might need to do this – go away for a while – but then she would come back and everything would be all right.'

I had thought so too, hadn't I?

'Let's walk again,' I say, peeling my hands from the

railing and letting Dad take my arm. I need to move, to be in motion, and there's a gap in the stream of people ambling along the bridge. We set off, once more, our steps in sync.

'So, I got the bus with her,' resumes Dad, 'helped her take some stuff to Janice's, who was waiting for her with two bottles of beer and a cigarette. I never thought, when I dropped her off, that this was the beginning of her screwing up her life. Destroying part of yours. The drugs, calling herself Starflower . . .'

'*Starflower*? I don't remember that,' I say.

'Maybe she spared you that bit . . .' He turns his head and smiles at me, and I try to smile back. 'In nineteen eighty-four I found her in another grotty dosshouse and I told her I couldn't have it any more, you girls waiting and hoping and wondering, and that she must come and see you and tell you both she was moving to Sweden.'

'Choose Life,' I whisper to myself. 'And of course we believed her.'

'I was so angry with her!' cries Dad. 'I said, "I don't want them looking for you on every street corner, thinking they see you getting on every bus, or going into a shop. Thinking you're going to turn up on the doorstep."' He sighs. 'I wanted you to think she was far away so there was no hope, Prue. You and Angela. Because it's the hope that kills you.'

One foot is going in front of the other. Dad and I are still in step. I wonder if the hope had killed him, in the early days after Mum left. Each time she didn't turn up. Every time he tracked her down to another dosshouse. All the times he missed her and had to be everything to us, because she was gone. 'All this time,' I say. 'All these years and she was in *London*!'

'Yes. Look, I'm telling you this now because I don't want Angela to carry on trying to find her. Ringing the consulate, emailing places in Sweden . . . hurt by the disappointment when her mother doesn't reply . . . I don't want *you* hurt. I don't want you hurt ever again.'

I've stopped walking again. He was hurt; we've all been hurt. My mother is in London and has been here all along. I'm not sure where to insert this information in my life, where it slots. Does it make any difference? Does it make any difference that she was in the same city as us rather than one thousands of miles away? That she was shooting up in a grimy bedsit in London instead of a skinny Stockholm townhouse with a snowy front step? That she will grow old under London's streetlights and not beneath Sweden's midnight sun? I feel unsteady, and that the bridge under my feet may collapse at any minute.

'Are you OK?' says Dad.

'Yes,' I fib. 'I'm OK. Thank you for telling me. And thank you for the lie.' I'm trying to stay upright, on this bridge. I'm trying not to crash. 'I know you were only trying to protect us.'

'I'm sorry I couldn't protect you from *everything*,' replies Dad, tears in his eyes. 'Everything that's ever happened to you. I'm so so sorry.'

We carry on walking. One foot in front of the other. Dad's cane. My sandals. We're nearing the end of the bridge. Sparrows chirp at each other and a mum tells off a child for dropping an ice-lolly stick into the water.

'Shall we go and get an ice cream, Dad?' I ask him.

'Yes, please. I'd like that.'

Chapter 42

The unburdened father and daughter buy *gelato*, we wander around Chelsea and we carry on with our afternoon in the sunshine, cloaking our revealed secrets in chatter about mint chocolate chip versus *passionate* and the weather, but the more we prattle on, the quieter I know we are inside. The more burdened, after all. Our hearts are still and our minds full, and we are wondering. We are wondering what it cost the other to conceal our secrets for so long, how hard we tried to protect each other, the private pains we suffered for keeping our counsel. Was it a mistake to reveal those secrets now? Have we hurt each other irrevocably with them? A dad knowing his daughter has been abused, and he wasn't able to see it? A daughter who was shielded by her father in a thirty-four-year-long lie, who had an absent mother living in the same city all along? I am wondering a lot of things right now. But I feel my father and I are both thinking the same thing – that we are beginning to truly know each other again, after all these years, although we are yet to calculate the cost.

Eventually, we get the bus back to Chalk Farm and it expels us on to the pavement, hot and slightly weary. It's two hours before I'm meeting Salvi at Finsbury Park, half an hour before Kemp arrives to pick Dad up for their trip to the reservoir.

'Where does she live? Our mother?' I ask Dad. We're the other side of the road to the brown double doors. We're waiting to cross Haverstock Hill to the first island.

There's a beat. 'Haringey, I think.'

'Haringey!' That's only about five miles away. I feel an immediate sense of my throat tightening, of claustrophobia almost. 'Do you know whereabouts?'

'No.'

I notice a moment's hesitation in his voice, in the configuration of his facial features; just a tiny one – a chink appearing between two curtains closed against sunlight. 'Dad?'

'There have been rumours,' he says. 'About where she works.'

'Rumours? Rumours from where?'

'Remember that volunteer who used to come round and try to take me out? The one I was sent by the council?'

'From about five years ago? The one you always sent packing?'

'Yes. Him. *Tom.*'

Tom grew up in our road in Clerkenwell. When he used to try to pick Dad up from The Palladian, he'd come upstairs, plonk himself in one of our chairs and not stop going on about it. How he used to knock and ask Mum for one of those Ice Pops she was always giving out, or play 'Chicken Square' with us. He was a weedy-looking thing who rode a Grifter. 'Yes, I remember him.'

'The last time he came round, before he finally gave up – you were at work, I think – he told me he'd seen her, or thought he'd seen her, *Ellen.* Working in a shop in Muswell Hill. Said he never forgets a face.'

'Even from decades before? What sort of shop?'

'A travel agency. It's . . . well, from what he said, it's near your clinic, where they do the lasers. Where I used to take you.'

'A travel agent's,' I say slowly and carefully, as though I'm drunk but trying to pretend I'm not. As though I can cope with the fact my brain and my mouth have turned to cotton wool.

We're still at the kerb. People behind us tut but then notice my dad's cane and say 'Sorry' or smile at us. I don't smile at them. We're teetering on the edge. *I'm* teetering on the edge. My mother works in the travel agent's two doors from *Loved Before*. She works the other side of the laser clinic that has never been any use to me. And she has never been any use to me either, but she has been there, all this time.

'Why are we not crossing, Prue?' Dad's cane is tapping on the kerb. His Adidas Italias scuffle impatiently. He knows how close we are to home.

'She works near one of my shops. One of the clothes shops I always go to. Only two doors away.'

'Oh. Have you seen her? You haven't seen her, have you?'

'No, of course I haven't seen her!'

I feel angry. I feel we have been tricked, my sister and I – Angela, who cried for our mother over and over again, and me, who didn't. I feel a fool that I've been mere feet away from her and I didn't know. That while I was browsing dresses in *Loved Before* she was very close at hand and we could have passed on that street and she could have *seen* me, and I would have seen her. Without preparation. Without warning.

I have been so so close to her – a woman hiding in plain sight – and I simply didn't know.

'Kerb down,' I say, and Dad and I cross the street to the first island. 'Kerb up,' I say as we arrive there. 'Kerb down,' I say again, when we step off it. We reach the pavement outside The Palladian. We're at the brown doors. I'm putting my key in the lock.

'Are you all right, Prue?'

'Perfectly, Dad,' I reply.

'I'm sorry,' he says, and the expression on his face is so full of contrition and anguish and hope and love, I almost hug him like I never want to let him go and tell him it's OK, that it doesn't matter, but instead, after I open the brown door and we go up the iron stairs and into the flat, I walk to the cupboard in the sitting room and rifle under the photo album and the sketchbook and Dad's old *A–Z* and pull out my old square sewing box, the one with the creaky lid and the red and orange raffia flowers on the top.

'What are you up to?' asks Dad hesitantly.

I feel for a stack of pale blue, thin envelopes, edged in red and blue chevrons and secured with a faded elastic band, from under the material needle book and the cotton reels and the Japanese lady pincushion, and I place it carefully in my bag, between my purse and my powder compact.

'I'm going to see her.'

Chapter 43

Chalk Farm tube station is packed. Loads of people are crammed into the ticket hall, sweaty and complaining because it has just been announced there are no south-bound trains, due to a signalling problem at Morden.

'Don't even bother, love,' says a man in a Bart Simpson vest top, and I step straight out again, back on to the pavement and the unrelenting late-afternoon sunshine. There are no black cabs in sight. Shall I get a bus? I can't bear to wait for one. There's a massive queue at the bus stop and everyone at it looks hot and murderous. I'll have to walk. It's about five miles. I can walk it. I'm fired up enough. Or I could try and get an Uber? I'll walk *and* try to get an Uber. I get my phone out of my bag, sliding it past the stack of Angela's blue airmail envelopes, and click on to the app.

'Bertie!'

Kemp is coming up the pavement towards me. He's wearing a blue checked shirt over a white T-shirt. Ubiquitous jeans and boots. He looks all perky and handsome, precisely what I don't need right now. I keep my head down, pretend I haven't seen him.

'Bertie!' He's standing right in front of me.

'Please would you stop bloody calling me that! Why are you so early?' I tap my destination into the app. My nearest available driver is Derek, Ford Mondeo, eight minutes away.

'I'm just early.' He shrugs. 'Well, actually, I wanted to talk to you. You look awful, by the way. Where are you going?'

I look up. 'Thanks. None of your business. I've got an appointment.'

'What sort of appointment?' I recognize that blue checked shirt. He often wore it to the pub.

'Mind your own business,' I repeat.

He's not moving. I'm going to have to swerve round him. I want him to bugger off. I slalom round him, but he grabs my arm – firmly but gently – and stops me in my tracks. His arm is tanned. The sleeves of his shirt are rolled up. I don't want his hand on me.

'You look upset,' he says. 'Maybe I can help, if you need to talk.'

'No. I told you, I have an appointment!'

I extricate his hand from my arm and start walking away from him, swiftly, my phone still in my hand. Derek is now seven minutes away. Kemp is on my left, walking at pace beside me, his hair flopping over his forehead. *Bugger off, just bugger off*, I mutter in my mind. Why can't people just bugger off?

'Can we talk about something?'

'Not right now.'

'About your paintings?'

'Not that again!' I'm striding but he's matching my pace.

'I've just been to see a friend of mine about them.'

'What?'

Derek is five minutes away. He's still on Malden Road.

'They deserve to be seen. They should be hanging in a gallery. I've just come from my mate Col's gallery in Old Street and I showed him the photos I took. Of your work.'

I almost drop my phone. It slides into my elbow and Kemp catches it and hands it back to me, with a smile. I have to look at his face. We're still walking fast. I check

333

my phone once more. Six minutes again? For God's sake, hurry up, Derek!

'Don't you want to know what he said?'

'Not really.'

'You don't want to know?'

'No, I don't want to know!'

'You're still angry with me, aren't you? About that stupid friends with benefits thing?' He veers past a couple sharing a huge panini. 'You really don't see it, do you, Prue?'

'No, I guess I don't.' I am walking so fast now I think I might take off into a run and run for my life.

'Oh, come on, slow down. I'm sweating cobs here.'

'I don't want to slow down.'

'Then shall I tell you what *I* want?'

'It does seem to be all about you, so yes, if you must.'

'I want you.'

A tourist pushes past us with a backpack. Hello Kitty, like the one I had on my face when I met Salvi. Mysterious, intoxicating Salvi. The right man for me. The right man for me.

'Yeah, you said.' I check my phone again. Thank God. Derek is three minutes away.

'You're always seeing things the wrong way! Right – bloody hell, you walk fast. Look, I'm going to say something, and I want you to listen. Actually *listen*. I don't want you to say you don't believe me, or throw it back in my face, or twist it, or say it's only because of this, that or the other, or some other crap you like to come spouting out with – which is one of the reasons I'm going to say this, actually – that you're a colossal, infuriating pain in the arse, yet somehow . . .' I dare a sideways look at him and he gives me a sheepish grin. I jerk my head frontwards again. 'I'm going to say this, and I want you to listen and then you can go away to whatever this mysterious

334

appointment is, and you can think about it. But don't take too long, OK? Because there's less life left for us both than there's already been, you know? So, I want to say this and then, well, we'll see. OK?'

'OK.' I don't mean it. I just want him to stop talking.

'So, just please stop a minute!'

'I don't want to stop.'

'Would you just *stop*?' He turns and grabs both of my arms, not tight, but determinedly, and we come to a halt, on the pavement. A man with a messenger bag almost crashes into us. A boy on a scooter goes into cruise mode to avoid us, muttering, 'Bloody idiots.' Kemp's hair is damp on his forehead but his eyes are shining.

'I love you.'

'Oh, fuck off, Kemp!'

He laughs, astonished. '"Fuck off!" I tell you I love you and that's all you've got to say to me?' He is looking right in my eyes with ones I once wanted to drown myself in.

'Yes, it is,' I say. The touch of his fingers are hot on my arms. I want to shake them off, but I don't want to.

'Well, then I'll tell you again.'

'Go on, then.'

'I love you.' The notification beep – Uber – goes off on my phone but I ignore it. Well, I don't ignore it completely – I look down quickly to see that Derek is two minutes away. 'Do I need to say it *again*?'

'Probably.' I look up, stare at the half-pearl shell of his necklace, on its leather cord, for a moment, then I decide I *will* shake him off and I carry on walking again, my mind racing faster than my feet.

He catches up with me. 'God, you're infuriating. I *love* you. I love you. You're *home* for me, Prue. And not because I'm getting old and want to bloody *settle* for anyone I can just grab to grow old with. Or because I want – or *ever* wanted – some friends-with-benefits, unsatisfactory, shallow, surface bollocks. I called the world home for many years; it was what I wanted. Until you. You're home for me because you're the person I want to come home *to*, from my trips. I want to turn the key in the door – any door – and have you there . . . or be waiting when *you* turn the key and come in; it doesn't matter which way round it is. I want to take you with me when I do go away, if you'd like to. I want a life with you. I want to wake up with you in the morning and have you irritating me at night and it to just go on, until almost for ever. I want to grow old with you, Bertie! I want your *sock back* in my bloody sock drawer!' I realize we have come to a stop again, somehow. That I am just staring at him, here in the hot sun, out on the streets of London. 'Do you understand what I'm saying? Are you *listening* to me?'

Of course I'm not. I feel like I can't even see him. The sun is in my eyes and the thought that my mother is a few miles down the road is a bloated poisonous mushroom filling every corner of my brain. I don't have room for this. Not right now. 'No,' I say.

Kemp shakes his head. 'Come on, Prue. It's you. It's *just you*. Every time I look at you, I just think, Yeah. *Her.*'

'I've got a date tonight. You're too late,' I say. I don't want to believe him. I don't want to believe a word of it. I don't want to be almost crying and willing, *willing* my tears to dissolve before they fall down my face.

'He's not right for you, that Salvi. I know from the way he looks at you, Prue.' Kemp takes both my hands and holds them fast. 'Look, ever since I met you, you've been wearing a mask. And I don't mean the make-up – don't look at me like that! – you know I've never had any issue with your birthmark – and don't *ever* mention paper bags again, do you hear me? The mask you've been wearing is that bullshit mask you put on every day that says, "Keep your distance from me; don't touch me, don't love me."'

I flip. 'Why would you *love* me? I am angry and I am aimless and I am ugly, with ugly secrets! I don't deserve you. I didn't even deserve you as a *friend*. And you don't deserve *me*!'

'They are not ugly secrets once you've shared them,' says Kemp gently. 'They are just things that happened to you. Things in your past. They don't make you less beautiful to me. They don't alter how I see you. And I *want* to see you. To see all of you, to *know* all of you. Always.'

He looks at me. He just looks. I can't see clearly enough to read him. I don't *want* to read him. I'm scared to. But there's something there in his eyes that speaks of tenderness, of love, that speaks of something I have been searching for my whole life. I look away. I can see Derek, just up the road; that's his registration number. I march towards the car.

'I deserve you!' shouts Kemp. 'Your past, your present and your future. Most of *all*, your future. There's still plenty of it left and I'm right here to share it with you, if you'd only look at me! I *deserve* you, Prue! *I deserve you!*' Kemp shouts so loudly that people on the pavement around him turn their heads and a white van beeps, from the middle of the road, and a man with no top on calls out, 'You go get her, pal!'

I turn back, one last time. 'I've got to go, Kemp! I've really got to go. Derek is here.'

'Who the fuck's Derek?' calls back Kemp. I open the back door of Derek's Mondeo and get in. 'I'm coming over to see you again tomorrow, Bertie!' shouts Kemp. I can hear him through the open window. 'I'm not giving up! Think about what I've said.'

'No!' I shout back, a petulant child in my mask. 'I don't want to!'

'Impossible!' says Kemp to the man with no top on, who's further up in the line of traffic now, and the man shrugs and raises both palms up and Derek pulls away with an undramatic splutter and I don't look back any more.

Chapter 44

The tinkling bell isn't working at *Loved Before* this afternoon.

'It overheated,' says Maya as I walk in. It's quiet in the shop; there's only an hour or so until it closes. 'Too much sun, apparently,' she adds, with a smile. 'We don't normally see you on a Saturday. We've got some new dresses in, if you're interested.'

I wander over and have a look at them, without seeing them. Maya has followed me. She looks nice today; she's wearing white dungarees with a black floral top underneath.

'This pink one's lovely,' she says, pulling out a floaty midi dress from the rail. It's a bit like the one I wore to lunch with Salvi at The Monastery. Not as pretty, though. Not quite as sexy.

'Yes, it's nice. Thank you.' I give it a cursory glance and hang it back up with the others. I am shaking slightly. Now I'm so close, I'm stalling for time. I'm hiding out. I walked in here, almost on automatic pilot, but I need to come out of here, walk past the clinic and into the shop next door. To *her*. 'Actually,' I say, not looking at Maya, 'I didn't come to look at clothes today. I've got something I want to ask you. It's a bit random but please bear with me.'

'Oh?' Maya smiles. 'Ask away. If I can help you, I will.'

'Do you know Ellen who works in the travel agent's?'

'*Ellen who works at the travel agent's* . . . Jameson's? Two doors down?' I nod. 'No, I don't know the staff there. Why do you ask?'

339

I feel slightly deranged. Why am I in here, talking to Maya? Stalling for time so pathetically?

'I don't know. Well, I *do* know. Ellen's my mum.'

What a strange sentence. *Ellen's my mum.* And what a strange thing to say to Maya.

'Right, right.' Maya is looking at me with such puzzlement and such kindness on her face, I can't bear it. I feel like I don't even belong to my own body right now.

'I need to speak to her,' I blurt out. 'I haven't seen her for a really long time.' I have a thought. 'What time do they close?'

'I think they close at seven on a Saturday ... So, OK ... Well, do you want me to come with you? To Jameson's? I can lock up for a moment.'

I'm so tempted by Maya's offer. To say 'yes, please' and let her handhold me through what I need to do. 'No. No. Thank you. Thank you for the offer, though. It's OK. I'm being silly. Sorry.'

'Are you sure? Are you sure you're OK?'

'Yes, I'm going to go now.' I have to go. I *have* to do this. I have to do this for Angela. 'Thank you, Maya.'

'I'm here anytime, you know, if you want to talk? I'm always here.'

'Thank you. Thank you so much. I'd like that.' I *would* like that, I think. I like Maya. I head to the door.

'Take care, won't you?'

'I will, thank you. And I'm fine, I promise. I'll see you again soon.'

I leave the shop and Maya looking both bemused and concerned and walk the two doors to the travel agent's. There's a woman at the desk. She is not my mum. There's a laugh and a door opens at the back of the shop and a different woman walks out.

'Hello,' I say.

She is short, like me, and is wearing an A-line black

skirt and a pair of silver flat sandals and a dark grey sleeveless T-shirt and she has the same hairstyle as me, including the fringe, except her hair is a stripy palette of blonde and grey highlights. She's not a hippy or a punk or an eighties Wham! fan. She looks a little like she did when we were young.

'Hello,' she says. Actually, she looks like she's seen a ghost, which is what is happening here, after all. I am a ghost, and she is a ghost to me.

'Hello,' I say again. I know she knows it's me. I mean, there's no mistaking me, is there? I could be immediately pulled from any line-up. I'm amazed she looks so familiar, though. I thought she'd be all drug-addled, starey-eyed and Starflowered; wizened and ruined by substance abuse. But her eyes are clear and her face is relatively unlined. It doesn't tally with Angela's description of her from 1990. Of *Starflower*. Age and recreational drug use have clearly been kind to her, after all.

'Would you like to go and get a coffee with me?' I ask. 'Can you take half an hour off?'

A half-hour audience with my mother. Half an hour after thirty-four years. It's not much to ask, is it? And I think it will be enough.

'Can you hold the fort here?' my mother asks the woman at the desk and the woman nods. 'I'll just get my bag,' she adds, and she turns and goes back through the end door. I wonder if there's a window at the back, an escape hatch, so she can run away again. Is she now squeezing her body through a narrow gap and preparing to leg it down the road? Does she have a hippy friend waiting for her in a 1970s getaway van?

She reappears. I walk to the exit and she follows. We slip out the door and we are walking down the street.

'How did you know I was here?'

It's so weird hearing her voice, the same one that used to

tell us to eat up all our fishfingers or do up our shoes. It's perhaps a little huskier, but I would know it anywhere.

'You look nice grey,' I say. 'Grey-y blonde. It suits you.' I deliberately don't answer her question. I don't have any explaining to do; she does.

'Thanks, it's been like this for ages.'

'So, you've been here for years, then? At the shop. And in Haringey?' I try not to sound bitter and disgusted. I try to sound like I'm just making small talk.

'Yes, I've always lived in Haringey.'

Well, not always, I think. There were all those squats, and once you lived with us. 'How long have you worked at that travel agent's?'

'Six years.' Such a quiet voice, I can barely hear what she is saying. 'I—'

'Let's go in here,' I say.

We stop outside Harry's, the coffee shop near the key cutter's. It always looks cosy, whenever I walk past. Workmen on a break supping tea. Teenage girls enjoying a cheese-and-ham toastie during a college lunchbreak. Mothers and daughters chatting over a coffee and a bun.

'What would you like?' I ask her. 'Sit down and I'll get it.'

'Just a tea, please,' she says. 'Two sugars.'

'You can put your own sugar in,' I say, pointing to the sachets on the table.

She nods, then looks away. I spot tears coming into her eyes and she sees me notice them, wipes them away with her hand and says, 'Sorry. It's just such a long time since I've seen you.'

'Yes,' I say. I can't be trusted to speak so I go to the counter and order two teas.

'Are you well?' she asks, as I sit back down with the drinks. Her absence, for all those years, settles on the table between us like thick fog.

342

'Yes, thank you.'

'And Angela?'

'Alive and well and living in Canada,' I say chirpily. There's a sharp bit at the edge of the table, where some Formica has peeled off and is grazing my arm, but I don't move my arm away.

She nods. 'And your father?'

Hasn't she got more to say about Angela living in Canada? That's quite a big deal! 'Still blind,' I say. 'You found that quite hilarious, once upon a time.'

'I wasn't well.'

'No. Angela said she saw you in nineteen ninety. That you were in a right state. She moved to Canada after that. You know, Canada? That big place above America?'

'I know Angela lives in Canada,' she says quietly and she smiles. It's a turned-down smile. Her mouth never used to do that.

'Oh? How do you know that?'

She looks at me, her gaze even and steady. Her eyes are exactly the same colour as mine. 'I came to see you both, one evening, in the summer of nineteen ninety-six. Neither of you were there so I went next door, to the Chinese takeaway. I saw a girl there, she was about your age – I mean the age you would have been at the time. She was behind the counter, reading the newspaper. I asked if she knew you and I asked her where you were – you and Angela. She told me Angela had moved to Canada and you were working in Spain.'

Cherry Lau, I think. It was Cherry that she saw. I'd been in the week before Tenerife, I expect, for Dad's Singapore noodles, and had probably mumbled something about my trip in one of our awkward conversations. And I bet it wasn't a newspaper, I bet it was *Cosmopolitan*.

'Both girls living abroad!' continues Ellen. 'I was a little surprised you'd left your father, but he had the guide dogs and, knowing Vince, he'd encouraged you both to be go-getters, to make something of yourselves—'

'Dad didn't have the guide dogs then,' I say flatly. 'He became allergic to them. He said goodbye to the last one in nineteen ninety, a few months before you came to see Angela that time. You know, the time you called her a bitch.'

She looks like I have just slapped her. 'Yes, I did. Fuck, that was awful!' Her hand is over her mouth but something about that 'Fuck' makes me think that in another life I could warm to her, just a little. 'I didn't realize about the dogs, but I wasn't capable of realizing much, at that time. I—'

'And I wasn't *living* abroad. I'd gone to Tenerife for a week, for work.'

'Oh. The girl said you were working in Spain. Well, that was a huge misunderstanding,' she says. She looks quite shocked. What exactly had Cherry Lau said? I wondered. Had she misunderstood what *I'd* said, in one of our usual half-listened to, excruciating exchanges, or had she been deliberately ambiguous? 'I immediately thought I'd lost both of you, then, that it was too late. I thought you'd both literally *gone* places. I was clean then, you know. I had been clean, actually, since the early nineties. After I'd seen Angela that time . . . Well, I knew I had to stop. I went to France for a few years. To a kind of retreat, a commune. I sorted myself out, with help. Then I moved back. I felt I didn't deserve to ever see either of you again – I was frightened to, to be honest, but in nineteen ninety-six, I came.'

'So you never went to Sweden, but you went to France,' I say.

'Yes.'

'And you didn't try again, after that? To come to The Palladian? To see Dad, or try to get addresses for us, although obviously I was there all along.'

'I thought you were gone. I saw it as my punishment. I knew I didn't deserve you. That I never had. I didn't come back again. I continued with my life, what it was. It's such a surprise to see you now. I never expected to.'

'I was quite surprised, too,' I say. 'I walk past that travel agent's all the time.'

'I'm so sorry for everything.'

'Sorry is just a word.'

She nods. 'Can I explain myself?' she says. She is fiddling with the sugar sachet; she has spilled some on the table but makes no attempt to clear it up and nor do I. 'I presume that's why you came to see me, why we're here?'

'I don't know,' I say. I'm not sure I want an explanation; there's nothing new to know, is there? My mother was a drug addict. 'Well, we haven't got long so make it potted. They'll be needing you back.' I look at my watch like a foreman of a factory.

'Oh, it's a short story,' she says. Someone walks past us – a lady in a red mac, despite the weather, and in her downdraught I get a waft of the perfume I think Ellen is wearing. I know it, but at the same time I don't. 'I had to go; you know that, don't you? I just had to. I was twenty-one; I'd had you when I was sixteen.'

'Yes, it was very young,' I say with a tight smile. 'But it happens. And you were married. Things were stable. You had a good future with Dad and it was getting better. He was going to be an architect.'

'I *had* to get married,' says Ellen. 'There was no choice in the matter. There was so much shame back then. There was no other course of action. Especially with *our* parents.' She smiles at me but I can't bring myself to return it.

'I know all this,' I say. 'That you were just two kids who got yourselves in trouble and marriage was the only answer.'

'Vince Alberta . . .' she muses, and I feel like she has

345

stepped out of the café and into her past. 'He was certainly something else . . . sixteen, cocky as hell, a smile that could light up a school hall . . . I thought I loved him, I suppose, but who really loves anyone at sixteen? You're more likely to love a pet rabbit or your favourite skirt.'

'Or The Beatles.'

'Or The Beatles.' She gives me another smile I don't mirror.

'We got married two months before you were born – those ridiculous photos, everyone trying to look happy when mostly we were just feeling numb, all of us. I was supposed to go to secretarial college; I was supposed to have a life! But my life was all mapped out for me: housewife and mother. I just plodded on, I suppose. Plodded on with my life.'

'You're not a *plodder*, though,' I say. 'You like running away.'

She ignores me and I almost admire her for it. 'I wasn't happy. I found it so hard. And then your dad – well, your dad had left school at sixteen, become a carpenter. We knew our places – we knew the life that had been set for us – but then he got this idea to go to college, to become an architect. I couldn't see it happening, not at all, when he first talked about it, but he did it, he made it happen, and he was studying and all excited and had this future ahead of him and it was all going to be so great, except it wasn't going to be that great for *me*. I was going to be the one to facilitate that marvellous career. Be behind the scenes, supporting. Doing the housewife and mother stuff. It was all going to be brilliant for him, but nothing was ever going to change for *me*.'

'Same for many women all over the country in those days,' I say, disloyal to womankind in my bitterness. 'Supporting men in their careers. And you could still have gone to secretarial college, once we were older.'

'Those other women *knew* they had married men like that. Ambitious. Successful. I had married cheeky little Vince Alberta. I thought we were going to be equal – him a working man, grafting in a job he didn't particularly enjoy, and the same for me . . . at home.' *Thanks*, I think. 'Secretarial college would hardly have been the giddy heights, would it, even if I had ended up managing to go? I've always known my limitations. Your dad was making something of himself and I knew I never could. He was going to *change*. I was frightened of that, what it meant for me.'

'You could have waited,' I repeat. 'Saw how things panned out.' I get it. She was jealous of my father, of his future, his ambition and his mind – all of which she'd had no inkling of when she was screwing cheeky Vince Alberta behind the *gelato* shop (probably) on a Thursday afternoon. She resented his successful future – the future, ironically, he never got to have.

'I may have waited for ever,' she says. 'While my parents were alive I would never have left. But they both died. They were—'

'They died and you took your chance.'

'I wouldn't put it quite like that—'

'*I* would. You took your chance and you escaped it all,' I say. 'Dad, us. You became a hippy bumming round Europe, and then a druggie in London. It was hardly better than what you had, was it?'

'No,' she says. 'I've wasted a huge part of my life. Whatever reasons I give doesn't excuse that I have behaved terribly and lost everything. That I have been despicable.'

I drum my fingers on the Formica, pull a virgin napkin over a tea stain. 'Hey, if only Dad had gone blind earlier,' I add sarcastically, 'then you both could have *suffered* together and everything would have been all right.'

'I'm so sorry Vince is blind,' she says. 'But I would

never have escaped how he saw me. The disappointment from him, that was always there. When I took drugs . . . well . . . I was part of something. I felt I belonged. No one was ever disappointed with me.'

'That's because everyone was always off their faces!'

She laughs and I remember that laugh. From long ago. But I think about what she's saying – that Dad was disappointed in her. He had told me he loved her fiercely, that he was determined to make the marriage work. Did she view that ferocity as a directive for her to do better, to *be* better? To not *struggle* or be flighty? That she was a kind of enforced and failing work-in-progress for him?

'Yes, there is that.' She turns her untouched teacup in its saucer and I fear I might suddenly feel sorry for her because I understand. I understand that how you perceive people looking at you – looking at you in a certain way – can destroy you. 'Maybe if I'd been older, I would have worked out a way to deal with that disappointment, or to change things in my own life, but that disappointment destroyed me.'

'So it was never my face?'

'What do you mean?'

'My face? Was part of you leaving ever because of my face?' I fear I might cry and I absolutely must not. I must not cry in front of this woman. I have not cried for her for forty-three years and I'm not about to start now.

'Of course not!' She looks shocked. 'I loved your face. I've missed your face. I've missed *both* your faces. You were both amazing girls. *Amazing* girls.' I swallow down my tears and place both hands flat on the table, to steady myself. 'It was a pity I only ever had it in me to be the opposite of anything even *close* to amazing.'

I take a deep breath. 'Angela wrote to you,' I say. 'She wrote you these.' I take the stack of airmail letters out of my bag and put it on the table, among all the spilt sugar granules. 'There were a couple more that she sent to Sweden, before I intercepted them – we found Torge's address in your old book – and of course you never replied, so I started to reply for you. I did it for over a year. I wrote *as* you on fake postcards I posted to Angela from the letter box at the bottom of the street.'

'What on earth did you say?' She is fingering the letters without looking at them. She is looking at me.

'Not much.' I smile weakly. 'Not much at all. We don't have them any more – I think Angela threw them away.'

She nods. She is looking down at the letters now and her face crumples at the sight of Angela's childish handwriting on the top envelope. There are doodles, too, some swirly flourishes in the corners, some flowers and rainbows. Angela's *hope* is in those doodles. My mother takes the elastic band off and leafs through them in turn, soft tears falling on delicate pale blue. 'I'm sure you made a better *me* than I could ever have been. Can I have these?'

'Yes.' I feel pity and sadness and I don't like these emotions. I am already walking away, in my mind. I have already got up and left this table with the two still-full cups and the spilt sugar and am out on the sunlit street, making my way back home.

I stand up. 'I'm going to go now,' I say. 'Angela has been trying to get in contact with you. Her number, in Canada, is on the back of the last letter.' I had scribbled it there whilst in the back of Derek's taxi. 'Maybe you could give her a call. Oh, and if you do, please don't mention the postcards you never sent. Or that you only have Angela's letters *now*. It would break her heart.'

I think we both realize the irony of this. That hearts were already broken, long ago.

'No, I won't. And yes, I'll do that. Thank you. And you? Could I give you a call?' She looks at me and I see

349

her whole life and some of mine in her eyes. I see regret and I see longing. I see something that looks a little like love.

'I haven't written my number down,' I say quickly.

'Might you come back again? To the travel agent's?'

'I don't know.'

'It's a miracle to me that you've found me,' she says quietly. 'That you've come to see me. That we've talked like this. Could we see it that we've found each other now, maybe? That there's still a chance . . . of something? Will you at least think about it?'

'I'll think about it,' I say. And I pick up my bag and I walk out of the café and I am back on the street in the still bright sunshine, heading for home.

Chapter 45

Dad, of course, is not at The Palladian. I knew he would already have left, with Kemp, for Hornsey Wood Reservoir. I need to see him. I need to tell him that I'm not angry now, that I understand a mess of a mother – a too-young, fleeing, disappointed and disappointing mother – would have been worse than no mother at all. That I know he was shielding us from hurt. That our mother may have been in the shadows of our lives all along, without us knowing – but she was better there, than out in the light.

I don't blame Dad for keeping their secret. This painful, justified secret he engineered and instigated. He did it for us, and at least Angela will have her answer now – she will finally get the *reply* she's been searching for, all this time. Who my mother is, and where she has been. If she has thought about us, cried for us. Seen our faces in her dreams. I have never sought a reply, but I know the one she gave me in the café was incomplete, full of gaps and blanks and missing pieces. Do I want them filled in? Angela may seek to read between the lines of the letters our mother never wrote or sent, from a Sweden she never lived in. Angela may want to re-start a dialogue with *Ellen* – resurrect a relationship, a lost life. Do I? Do I want to go searching behind shadows for more answers? When my answer has always been Dad?

He has been both father and mother to us. All those years ago, he kept the ship sailing when the seas were rough and the skies dark, keeping the light in our lives when the sun seemed far from us all, and though he left that helm a long time ago, when the guide dogs went, and he and I both, eventually, withdrew from the world and sat in our chairs – the window and our hearts closed – he has still been there, my dad. He has always been there.

I don't know about my mother, not yet. If there *is* still a chance for something. But I'll seek Dad out tonight. My constant, my source of light. The reservoir is just beyond the fair, if I can find it. I'll meet Salvi, then I'll go and look for Dad and Kemp. *Kemp* . . . oh God, I can't think about him right now. He said he loved me. This is the sort of miracle I would have prayed for seven years ago. For him to say I meant more to him. That those times in the houseboat were not just drunken conversations and power ballads. That it wasn't just me who was sinking and sinking . . .

I couldn't see him, when he was talking; I couldn't listen to him, out on the street like that, when I was rushing to my mother. I don't know what to think about it all. He loves me? That just doesn't make *sense*. How can he love me? How can he now be reflecting back at me the feelings I've had for him for so long and kept so far out of sight? This is huge. A huge, hunkering ball of bewilderment I need to stand back from and view clearly, when I feel at the moment nothing much is clear. And what about Salvi? Salvi is the man I have obsessed over recently, have imagined as my future and allowed to light up my life. If Kemp loves me, then how can Salvi be my miracle?

I need to see him. Salvi. Once I see Salvi's face I'll know. I'll know what to do.

When I get to Finsbury Park, in through the arched entrance of the fair, lit by giant bulbs from a starlet's mirror, I feel light-headed. Of course I have been to fair-ish kinds of places over the past years: a seaside pier on a work's trip (jolly from the local sandwich factory), an indoor bowling alley that had arcade games and its own carousel (jolly from the bookies); but I never thought I'd be back *here* again – with the clanging music, the flashing lights, the whirring machinery, the smell of kerosene and candyfloss and hot dogs – and the memories. Telling Dad about that awful encounter with Shaun only this afternoon has hardly helped. I remember how upset he was, so helpless in hindsight. It's a big thing to tell a father. I can't wait to see him.

The only thing that's different about the look and feel of this fair from the one in my teenage memory – they haven't really moved *on*, have they? – is the music. It's Dua Lipa and Ed Sheeran and Taylor Swift all trying to out-do each other under flashing neon, instead of eighties cheese. A bored youth slumps at the gate of the Ferris wheel, where I'm to meet Salvi, mouthing along to 'New Rules' and pretending not to despise the children that are flashing their wristbands at her. I think of Philippa, in the laser place where she worked – another assaulting sensory overload, I expect, under a confining roof. At least here you can see the night sky and the stars above the jangle of coloured metal and the lights. I can breathe this time, I think. I'm not fourteen any more. I'm a grown woman who makes her own decisions and is in control. Maybe Philippa couldn't breathe – anywhere. Maybe she just couldn't see the night sky and the stars, no matter how hard she looked.

Salvi is not here. I look into the surrounding crowd, I double-check the long queue; I even look skywards to the mini-gondola capsules of the Ferris wheel and half expect him to be hanging out of one, laughing, greeting me with a shout and a bottle of beer. A woman and a young boy shove past me to get to the queue. She glares at me: I am in the way. I feel exposed, waiting here. Why am I always waiting for him?

There are two lads over by the red cab where the

operator sits. They are all snarls and crew cuts and basketball vests; baggy track pants and monstrous bright white trainers. They keep looking over at me. I move away from the Ferris wheel. Perhaps there's been a misunderstanding; perhaps Salvi meant somewhere else. I wander over to the other side, to the distorted mirrors attraction. I go from each like a crab. Here I am tall and stretched and thin, a pin head. Now I am short and squat, sat upon. Then I have hilarious lanky legs, but a squashed body and no neck. In the last one I just see my face.

'Tricked you!' says a sign above it. 'This is YOU!' *Charming.* My foundation is still on – just. My eyes are a little wild. I look a bit like I did in the mirror of Salvi's car. In the corner of this mirror I spy the back of his head. There he is. He pulls his phone from his jeans pocket then he turns round. For a moment Salvi doesn't see me. He looks serious, his eyes are cold. Then he spots my face in the mirror and his breaks into a smile.

'Prue! How you doing?' He saunters over, kisses me on the cheek – the wrong one.

'Good, thanks.'

His eyes are a rich green in the lowering sun that chequers through the rides and the stalls, his smile wide and mischievous. He has cut himself shaving and there is a small red nick on his chin.

'This is Dino,' he says.

I hadn't noticed there was a man lurking behind him: a very tall, gangly man, with freckles and sandy hair and an almost safari-like outfit of beige chinos and beige T-shirt. Beige suede shoes. He doesn't look very Italian but he's quite attractive, if you like the pale and interesting colonial jungle-explorer look. Dr Livingstone, I presume?

'What are you doing?'

Dino has stepped forward and quickly holds up his phone to take a photo of me and Salvi. I can't imagine it will be a very good one. Salvi smiley and confident; me nervous and caught-out.

'Sorry,' says Dino, in a thick Scottish accent. 'I thought it might be nice to get a picture of Salvi and his new girlfriend.'

'You could at least say "hello" first,' I argue. I don't like the look of him. He looks as shady as the rainforest palm leaves I imagine him pushing through in that outfit.

'Sorry,' he repeats, putting his phone in his pocket. He steps forward, goes to kiss me on the cheek – bad one, also – but I recoil and stick my hand out for him to shake, instead. 'Hello,' he adds.

'I wanted him to meet you,' says Salvi.

'Oh?'

'So he could see you. See who you were.'

'Why? Have you been talking about me? All good, I hope?'

Salvi smirks. Dino nods. He stares at me as though I am a curiosity behind glass. A museum piece. I get the uneasy sensation I've met him before. That he already knows me, somehow.

'Let's go on the ghost train,' says Salvi. 'Thoroughly spook ourselves.' He places his hand on my right shoulder. Presses down. Steers me past loud stalls and gathered bald blokes holding beers; threads me through excited coiffed and gelled teenagers, half-running to the next ride. Dino trails behind.

'Get in the back, Dino.'

Salvi and I sit in the front of the first black-and-silver carriage of the ghost train. Dino folds his long limbs into the one behind. A toothless ghoul clamps the bar down on us. Salvi presses his hand down on my left thigh.

'Are you frightened?' he asks me, close to my face.

'Of course not,' I laugh, but this is not entirely true.

It's an old-fashioned ride, a bit crap. It involves bashing

355

through several sets of black double doors, a lot of woo-
ing and cackling from recorded witches, skeletons
hanging from the ceiling. I get water sprayed at me at one
point. Something tickles my face and I have a horrible
feeling it's Dino's hand. Salvi and Dino are both laughing, when I whip my head round, their faces green and
mocking in the fluorescent gloaming.

When we get off, Salvi clamps his arm down on my
shoulders, just like the bar on our carriage. He weighs
on me, as we walk – Dino behind – claiming ownership,
bearing down. I'm reminded of the arguing couple outside the pub on the way to the Roundhouse, but that man
at least showed affection in his gesture. This feels like a
statement of *intent*. Am I Salvi's girlfriend? Do I want to
be? *I love you*. That's what Kemp said. I can see his face
now. I also said once I saw Salvi's face I would *know*. I
glance at him as we walk. I try to appraise him carefully.
Sometimes he looks so cold, like he just turns on warmth
when he thinks he needs to. When it suits him. I worry I
could badly cut myself on his edge, that sharp glittering
side to him he has shown me so many times. What did
Dad say? *If he shows you who he is, see it.* Has he *shown* me?
Have I just not been looking properly?

'All right, darling?' asks Salvi, pressing my body into
the ground with his arm.

'Great!' I smile.

'Even though you don't like fairs?'

'I'm fine.'

I get the sudden impression he has brought me here on
purpose, to a place I said I didn't care for. That he wants
me to feel and admit to some sort of fear. I look at him
again. This is a man who doesn't shake hands or say
'sorry'. This is a man who runs out on me all the time, who
sometimes looks at me with contempt, who has told me I
should be 'fucking grateful'. Who has picked me up and

dropped me whenever he feels like it. Push and pull, that's how it's been with him. Push and pull. This is not the man who has told me that he loves me, on the street. That I am 'home' for him. This is a man who I believe, suddenly, enjoys manipulating people. I've been focusing on the wrong man, haven't I? I have had tunnel vision down absolutely the wrong tunnel. I've made a mistake.

'My father's here somewhere,' I fib, 'I need to go and find him.'

Salvi is not my destiny. He may have been set on the path I walk on, but I don't *have* to walk on that path. I can get off, and I can walk away from this man who is not my miracle and towards the one I never dared believe could be the best thing in my life. I need to find my father and Kemp and tell them both how much they mean to me. I need to get away.

'Not just yet,' says the manipulative boyfriend with the weighing-down arm. It grips me tighter; it holds me fast. 'Let's have a go on the Hook-a-Duck. And then how about the Crooked House? Someone got locked in one of those things once. They weren't discovered for fifteen hours. Dino likes the Crooked House, don't you, Dino?'

'Yeah,' says Dino. 'I like a lot of things.' He flashes me a charming smile.

'Are you a barrister, too?' I ask him weakly. I feel if I attempt conversation, I won't feel so panicked – so trapped.

'No,' he says. 'I'm a driver. For a soft-drinks company.'

'Oh, right.'

Salvi's grip bears on me like an anchor. We keep walking. Salvi steers me towards the stall with the giant yellow ducks, with hooks in their heads. I see those two boys again, over by the peeling and chipped fortune teller's head in the glass box – the boys in the white trainers and basketball vests. I wish I had the strength to struggle free of Salvi's grasp and break away. I wish I could shake off the fourteen-year-old girl inside.

Salvi hands the man – a grinning bulldog in a retro *Dukes of Hazzard* T-shirt – a twenty-pound note.

'No change, mate; I'll have to go and get you some.'

Salvi dismisses him with a wave of the hand. 'Play on, good fellow. We'll sort that after.'

Dino and I step back and watch as Salvi expertly hooks three ducks and claims his prize.

'Cuddly Shrek, blow-up Sponge Bob or a balloon?' grunts the man.

'Balloon,' says Salvi, and he points to a huge hot-pink one, heart shaped, high up on the stuffed hanging rack. It has 'Kiss me' on it, in a pair of red lips. I don't want this balloon. I don't want Salvi to kiss me. I want to escape and go to my dad, and to Kemp. But I feel strangely powerless.

The bulldog hooks down the balloon and hands it to Salvi. He immediately steps forward and bonks Dino on the head with it, then Dino grabs it, pulls it to his chest, laughing. 'Kiss me,' he says to me, in a saliva-y lisp.

'I need to go now,' I say weakly.

'Hang on,' says Salvi. He takes the end of the string and ties it into a small bow, double knot. 'Just prettying it up,' he says and he takes the balloon from Dino by the string and hands it to me, while my spinning world stops.

Chapter 46

'Philippa,' I say, trying hard to catch my breath.

'What?'

'Philippa's balloon.'

I stare at the balloon I'm holding. Hers was the one with 'Happy 30th' on it; the one she had on the tube. The one abandoned and bobbing over everyone's heads, its string trailing across people's shoulders. Salvi bought her that balloon and he tied a bow in the end to 'pretty it up' and he gave it to her, didn't he? He knew Philippa. Why did he lie about it? He saw her that day. He saw her and gave her that balloon. And then she died.

'You *did* know Philippa Helens, didn't you?'

'Who?' He's looking at me all innocent, all incredulous. As though I'm crazy.

'Philippa Helens. She died on the underground. She jumped under a train. You were out with her the afternoon she died.'

'What the hell are you talking about?'

My mind is whirring. Was she his girlfriend? Had he been to her birthday celebrations that day? She was young and pretty, not quite thirty; I am forty-eight with a huge birthmark. If she was his last romantic interest before me, then why me *next*?

'You knew Philippa Helens. Was she your girlfriend?'

'Hey, mate! I've got your change here.' It's the bulldog, from the corner of the stall. Salvi wanders over to him, looking as unconcerned as I've ever seen him. He's always like that, isn't he? Unconcerned. So unconcerned he didn't care his girlfriend went under a train, if she *was* that. Maybe she was just a friend. Something is nagging at me at the edges of my brain. Something that connects us. Me and Philippa.

'I'm going, mate!' Dino calls out to Salvi. He obviously doesn't like where this conversation is going. 'See you around. Look out for my post on the club later,' he adds, with a wink. 'I got nice and close.'

'All right, mate,' Salvi calls back, but there's a warning look in his eyes, directed at his friend. *Post on the club. Nice and close.* What does that mean? And if he means The Pro-filo Club – that card I found – why would Dino be a member? He's not Italian *or* a professional. What kind of a club actually is it?

Dino lopes off and Salvi turns away to banter with the bulldog, laughing about goldfish in plastic bags on buses, or something. Delaying coming back to me because of what I might say? Philippa and me, Philippa and me. What is it? I think of the other two women I have seen Salvi interact with, the women I have fretted over. The woman with the overly shiny red hair flopping over one eye; the colleague he kissed, with the oversized sunglasses. I turn my back on the stall. I take my phone from my pocket and check the photos of Philippa I have saved. The one from the news report . . . Philippa with her friends and cocktails . . . I go to the last one, the only close-up picture of her, the black-and-white photo where she has the shadows of branches on her face, like lace. I look and look at this photo, while Kylie is 'Spinning Around' and the smell of candyfloss burns my nostrils, until I realize one of the shadows of the branches is not a branch at all, but a long, searing scar.

There is a laugh behind me. I turn and Bulldog is laughing heartily and slapping Salvi on the back while Salvi grins like the cat that got the cream. Salvi has cer-tain tastes, doesn't he? I think I know what they are. He has a taste for the scarred and the ugly. Philippa had a scar on her face. I have a birthmark on mine. Is that woman's floppy red hair hiding a scar or facial disfigurement, too? And the colleague outside the Old Bailey. She has something too, doesn't she, under those huge sunglasses? Something that caught Salvi's eye and put her in his gaze. A gaze with a smile that is actually a taunt. I realize now why Philippa moved down two carriages. Someone was staring at her, weren't they? Making her feel uncomfortable. And I realize exactly how Salvi could have gone from *her to me*: because he was moving to his next victim, project, item of curiosity. I was the next bearded lady. The next freak. The next woman with the kind of face Salvi really likes.

'You knew Philippa,' I say, when Salvi finally makes his way back. I am shaking and grip my hands together, fingers entwined, so he won't notice. 'And you were with her the afternoon she died. What happened, Salvi? Were you in a relationship with her?'

He rams his change into his front jeans pocket. Checks his watch. 'Anyone who jumps under a train is nothing to do with me,' he says cheerily. 'Stupid cow.'

'So you knew her?'

He sighs, looks inconvenienced. 'Come out of the way,' he says. There's a straggly group of teenagers trying to weave past us. Salvi sweeps me by the shoulder down the side of the stall, into the shaded grass channel between Hook-a-Duck and Tin Can Alley. 'Yes, I knew her. A few randoms went out for her birthday lunch and I was one of them.'

'You were dating her.'

A smirk. 'I might have been.'

'You were dating her because of how she looked.' I clasp my fingers tighter, try to steady my voice. Salvi's face is in shadow.

361

He laughs. 'Doesn't everyone date everyone because of how they look?'

'She had a scar on her face? A really big one. The approximate length of my birthmark, I'd guess. You date women with facial disfigurements, don't you? That's why you're with me. That's why you asked me out in the first place.' Damn, my voice is all trembly. My face is probably bright red. But I have to get these words out.

'I don't know what you mean.' But Salvi grins, and that smirk tells me everything. He looks proud of himself. He is still performing; but now the performance is owning his evil and displaying it like a trophy.

'Yes, you do. You date people with facial imperfections – it makes you feel, what, powerful? That you can pick them up whenever you feel like it because they're so grateful and desperate? Or do they make *you* feel less ugly? Less ugly on the inside.'

I see it now: how ugly he is. It's not an *edge* he has, it's a gaping black hole. He *collects* trophies, doesn't he? *Profilo* is Italian for *profiles*. Faces. Salvi runs a website for him and Dino and God knows who else, to look at photos of scarred and facially disfigured women. It is far from a club for *gentlemen*. And I am on there. Dino will post the photo he took of me today, but I am already on there, I know it.

I am pretty certain Salvi took photos of my face while I was sleeping.

'What happened on that lunch? For her birthday. Did you do something? Did you upset her?'

'Not that I know of. You're ridiculous!' says Salvi, still grinning, still laughing. 'Hey, what's wrong with you?' He steps towards me, hand raised, and I know he is going to stroke my cheek.

'Don't touch me,' I say, still trying to steady my voice. I feel hemmed in here, between the stalls. 'I can see you for exactly who you are. Did you say something to her on the day she died? To Philippa? After you bought her that balloon?'

'You're ridiculous,' Salvi repeats. 'If only you could see yourself! Who knows why she topped herself? It's nothing to do with me. People shouldn't be so sensitive.'

I know that he said something to her, or that she found out something, maybe about The Profilo. I can feel it; I can taste it. I can see it on his face and in his eyes.

'I think you need help,' I whisper.

He laughs again. He laughs like he has done many times before; just now, and in the bar, in the restaurant, at The Monastery and, just like that, his mask drops and the laugh turns into a snarl. He grabs me by the throat and shoves me against the side of Tin Can Alley, on to bright yellow studded metal where rows of rounded peaks dig into my back.

'I don't need any *help*,' he spits. 'I'm a barrister. I'm rich. I have women lined up. You're the one who needs help. You're the *freak*. Did you think what we had was real?' He says this with utter scorn. 'That we would stay together, trot off into the sunset holding hands. Life is uglier than that, *darling,* much uglier.'

He's really hurting me. I'm struggling to breathe. My voice doesn't sound like mine. 'You are nothing,' I wheeze. 'You are no kind of man at all. You don't have any power over me.' But he does, doesn't he? He has his hands round my throat. He has reeled me in; seduced me – thrown me up in the air like one of his street performer batons, and then left me to fall. He has hurt me, like the others. He has power.

He squeezes a little harder. 'What are you going to do, dear Prudence? Kill yourself? Go and throw yourself under the Waltzer or something? Who would miss you? Your pathetic blind father? That sap, Kemp? He won't stick around, will he, not for you. Who would, *freak*?'

There's a girl, suddenly walking past us, down this untrodden space between stalls; too close. She stops dead in front of us, surprised and horrified; her face coming into hyper-vivid focus, like a cartoon: coppery frizzy hair, a round face pocked with acne scars, thick milk-bottle glasses. Salvi, brazen, raises his eyebrows at her, in both challenge and a kind of twisted seduction, then, piercing her with his gaze – her eyes caught in his look terrified, yet strangely captivated – he releases me.

I take a large gulping breath and clutch at my throat, rubbing it. Salvi seems breathless too, his own eyes bulging, *his* neck red.

'All right, darlin'?' he says to the girl with the glasses, frozen before us.

'Piss off!' she shouts – his spell broken – and she rushes past, from shade into sunlight, and is gone. Salvi and I stare at each other for a few noiseless seconds, our eyes locked on each other's faces. I see now exactly how he looks at me. Exactly how he always has. I see disgust and objectification. I see fetishizing and displacement. I don't need anyone looking at me like that. I don't want anyone looking at me like that ever again. With the blood pounding in my veins and my heart yearning for refuge, I turn from him and I flee into the jangling music and the lights and the excited screams of those enjoying the safe danger of a summer funfair in London.

Chapter 47

I am in a flat area of the park, which borders Seven Sisters Road and is surrounded by trees, heading for the children's playground. The entrance to the reservoir is somewhere around here; Dad talked me through a map he brought up on his iPad a few days ago, when I pretended to be interested, but I remember enough.

I search for the hatch, while furiously dispatching hot smarting tears from my eyes. Somewhere behind me, in the distant hum and clang and blaze of the fair, Salvi lurks among neon and noise. He wouldn't follow me, surely? He is done with me? The grass is dry and parched here; cut very short and patchy in places, long and tufty in others. Those same two boys are at the playground – basketball vests – one of them is on the swings; the other is lolling against one of the posts, smoking. What are they doing here? Perhaps *they* are following me. Not letting me forget my ugliness; my freakdom. There is no sign of Dad. He is not sitting in a hatch at the entrance to the reservoir, his legs dangling down, his back angled so his face catches the last of the day's sun. I can't even see the hatch. I'm not sure where I'm supposed to be looking. I feel exposed, foolish and fearful, here in this field, searching like a hunchback for a square-foot hole in the ground among the piebald grass.

The two boys have moved to the see-saw now; they are flicking something at each other, laughing, but their eyes are on me. I wipe the tears from my face with the back of my hand. There's a shout of laughter from one of them – over-exaggerated and ultra-loud. The other one yells, 'Yeah, bro!'

I refuse to look over. I can't catch their eye. Right now, I just want to see the hatch. There's something orange in the grass – I step forward to take a look. Dad's headphones. Perhaps he and Kemp have been and gone already and Dad dropped them. No, here is the entrance, behind a bank of tufty grass, an open oblong in the ground bordered with a flat concrete frame; its thick metal hatch lying on the grass beside it. If Dad and Kemp had left, the hatch wouldn't be open. Are they down there? I drop on to my knees and peer over the top rung of a metal ladder – a series of rusty orange bars set like staples into the peachy-amber brickwork below the hatch. At the base of the ladder I can see four or five descending concrete steps, then there is darkness. I call.

'Hello? Dad, Kemp?'

There is no answer. I call again, then lean back on my haunches and scan the lines of trees beyond me, in case I see Dad and Kemp disappearing into them. No. But I see those two lads advancing from the playground, in my direction, with horrible matching gaits – all shoulders and spite. I *need* to see Kemp. I *need* to see my dad. It's utter madness, but I decide I need to climb down the ladder, as far as the top concrete step, and call for them again. I sit on the edge of the hole and swing my legs in. Place my feet three rungs down. The ladder creaks but it doesn't feel like the staples will give way. I edge my way down, my back to the amber brickwork, feeling as intrepid as someone who's spent the last three years sitting indoors.

I land on the top step with a thunk and look down. The steps go on a long way, then there's a short platform, then a much shorter run of steps. I need to go down them, don't I? I need to go down and call when I get to the bottom. Oh, this is ridiculous. This really isn't me. I have

366

never been any kind of heroine in the story of my life: no masked *Bunty* adventurer, no Amelia Earhart or Jackie Onassis or Dian Fossey – I've been an also-ran, a bit part, a faceless extra in a crowd scene . . . But I need to do it. I must go down these steps and look for Kemp and my father.

I make my way cautiously down the steps, the bright oblong from the hatch above me lighting my way, wondering how long it took Dad and Kemp to do the same. The steps are wide and even: Victorian engineering. It's dusty and fusty and there's that chalky, brick-y damp smell, the one that is neither pleasant nor unpleasant. I feel nervous, slowly descending these concrete steps, leaving the world above me and entering the unknown. I reach the platform, hesitate; I continue down. When I get to the last step I can't help but gasp, because in the ghostly light filtered from the hatch I can see *exactly* why Dad wanted to come down here.

Before me is a high-ceilinged domed tunnel of dulled-amber brick arches stretching endlessly, like an Escher drawing, into eventual blackness; a curved concave brick threshold at the base of each, rising at either side to form a row of disappearing sentry pillars, between which are an infinite series of curved eyelets in the brickwork – more arches, more tunnels – extending into the distance, with ever-decreasing centres, like wombs. The reservoir is the size of a football pitch, according to Dad. It's like being in an ancient golden-hued subterranean cathedral, with no idea of where it ends or begins. I can see why it has been used as a film location. It's stunning.

I call, 'Dad? Kemp?'

There is standing water between each arch – a limpid black pool in a repeat pattern as far as the eye can see. I'm going to get my feet wet if I go any further, but I have to go further, don't I? They must be in here.

I set off into the first dark pool of water, muttering amalgamated swear words under my breath. I'm wearing flip-flops; I changed into them back at The Palladian as my sandals were beginning to rub. They squelch and sluice up great swathes of water with each step, so I take them off and put them in the back pockets of my turned-up jeans. The brickwork at the bottom is smooth underfoot. I can feel the mortar joints, the slight indentations between bricks under my toes. I walk. I walk through two or three arches, sloshing through the water that is calf deep, and cool but not cold, and stepping over each brick threshold. I try not to think of the park above me, suspended above this domed ceiling of amber. Of the two boys up there. Of the fairground. Of Salvi.

When I reach the next threshold, I call again.

'Dad?'

I stand stock still, listening. The water I have just waded through settles and calms behind me. A drip in the distance falls from brickwork and plinks daintily into a dark pool far ahead. Apart from that, there is no sound, so I set off again. I slop through the channels of another three or so arches, maybe. I don't know; I lose count.

'Dad?' I am exasperated now, almost beginning to laugh at the sheer idiocy of this. What am I *doing* down here? How did I get here? I am as far from the comfort of The Palladian as I have ever been. I am wondering at the folly of Dad and me stepping out in the world, if this is where we were going to end up.

'Prue?'

It's faint, but that's definitely my name echoing up through the never-ending arches.

'Dad!'

'Here!' comes the faint cry.

I set off again. A calf-sodden and ineffective Nancy Drew. A woman with as much derring-do as a slug on a biscuit. The water is a little deeper and definitely colder as I trudge on. The air is damp and so musty now you could slice it with a bread knife; the smell of wet bricks and Victorian enterprise is thick and claggy. As I slop through the opaque water, it gets gradually darker, too, but the decreasing light from the hatch at the far end of the tunnel is still enough to show me the way. There are so many arches; I can't see their end.

'Dad! I'll be with you soon!' I shout at the top of my voice, after I've trudged across several more thresholds and navigated more silken pools of blackness.

'OK!' a voice echoes back.

I keep walking. My jeans are soaked up to just below the knee now. The further I get from the oblong skylight of the hatch, the harder it is to see anything at all, but I *can* just about see the end of the tunnel now, in the gloom. There's some writing on the brick wall there, but nothing that I can make out. At least the tunnel *does* have an end, I think.

I walk three or four more arches. My feet are very cold now; my shins numb. I am far from the hatch and the real world, and I feel I have been down here for ever.

'Dad!'

'You're nearer,' he shouts. 'I'm pretty sure I'm at the end of the tunnel, right-hand side.'

'Just keep calling, so I can find you.'

'OK!'

'Are you all right, though? Where's Kemp?'

'I don't know! But I've hurt my ankle. I can't stand on it.'

'OK, I'm coming!'

I keep walking. I want to go faster. It's impossible to run in the two foot of water between each threshold, but I wade as quickly as I can, my arms out by my sides for balance, like an insane windmill. At the same time, I don't want to trip. I have to navigate. I have to stay upright. I have to get to my dad. I trudge through this watery submerged cathedral under Finsbury Park and I try not to be afraid.

I am three or four arches from the end of the tunnel when the lights go out and I'm plunged into complete darkness. The light from behind me, channelled down from the hatch space, has disappeared. Fear grips me like one of those brittle, plastic skeleton hands on the ghost train. Has someone closed the hatch? Those boys, laughing as they trap the ugly creature in the dungeon, have they shut it on me? Bloody hell. It's pitch black. I'm scared to go any further; then I remember I've got my phone. Doesn't it have a torch? I've never used it before but I know how to put it on. *Shit*, one per cent, I think, looking at the screen; I haven't charged my phone since this morning. I flick on the torch and angle the phone in front of me, to light my way.

'I'm almost there, Dad!' Through the water, over the threshold, each arch in turn. It's getting cooler and cooler. I can feel the hairs on my arms begin to stand to attention. I splash through the water, the light from the torch reflecting from its surface. One arch to go, though, and everything goes black again, as my phone conks out. Absolute velvet pitch darkness.

Oh, fuck. Where's Paddington when you need him?

'Dad, say something again so I know exactly where you are!'

'I'm here, love. I'm here.'

He's to the right. He's beyond the final arch. I'm relieved I'm so close to him now, but I'm frightened. It's so densely and relentlessly black. If he can't walk, how am I going to get him out of here, in the dark? How will we even *find* our way out when neither of us can see? I clamber over the last brick threshold, slick and a little slimy, feeling I may trip at any moment. I wade into the final pool of water.

'Dad?'

'Here!'

I drop down into the cold dark water into what is probably a comedy crouch, my arms held out in front of me, and head right. From what I've seen of the repeat pattern of architecture here, and from where his voice is coming from, Dad is in the space – cavity? – hole? – beyond that final eyelet arch. There's a foot-high threshold to climb over and I clutch around for it. This *would* be comical if it wasn't so scary. If I wasn't such an out-and-out wuss. I used to have a lamp on in my bedroom at night, for goodness' sake! I'm clutching at the air. I'm clutching at nothing. There. There's the lower wall of the eyelet. I clamber over it, like a very ungainly otter, and down the other side.

'I'm here.'

'So am I, Dad.' I clamber forward and reach out and I can feel his arm. His shoulder. The soft material of his Fred Perry T-shirt. 'Thank God. I found you.'

'You found me, Roo,' says Dad and his voice suddenly sounds very small and very Italian.

'What on earth happened? And where's Kemp?' I ask again.

'He's down here,' says Dad. 'But I'm not sure where.' He clutches for both my hands now and I hold his tight. They are a warm, familiar relief. 'I got bored, waiting up there. Kemp came down on his own, as we planned, and I sat up there, like a lemon, just waiting. Haven't I just sat waiting most of my life? After I'd waited for ages, I decided to come down the ladder and stand in here for a while, feel the acoustics, touch the walls. I knew there were nine rungs. I got to the top of the steps and I called for Kemp but heard nothing so I went down the steps.'

'You went down the steps? On your own?' My voice echoes in the pitch dark. It bounces off brickwork and still water.

'Well, yes. I *can* walk down steps. I thought I'd be OK . . . Anyway, when I got to the bottom I called again and there was no answer. I started to worry because I knew Kemp was down here somewhere. So I rolled up my trouser legs and I walked two or three arches.'

'For God's sake, Dad, this isn't like paddling on the beach at Southend!' I exclaim. 'It's dangerous down here!'

'I was fine, for a while. I've been down here before, remember? I've read about it since. I know the layout. But I had to look for him. If he wasn't answering, then he had to be in trouble. I was calling him all the time. Nine arches in, I finally heard something. A moan. So I came looking.'

'And you ended up all the way down here.'

'Yes. I followed where I thought it came from, all the way down here to this bullseye arch, but now, I don't know. He's not here. I went wrong somewhere. And I tripped on something, when I climbed the other side of the wall, and now my ankle is shot. God knows where my cane is.'

'You're a bloody idiot!' I cry and my voice ricochets up the vast, never-ending chamber of the reservoir. I feel around for the cane but I can't find it. 'You could have done so much worse! You came down all those steps and you walked all the way down *here*! What on earth were you thinking? You could have gone back into the park, or into the fair, and asked for *help*! Done something sensible. You're not some kind of superhero, Dad! And just because you've been to the Albert Hall and the sodding Shard doesn't make you some kind of blind bloody Christopher Columbus!'

'Not a good analogy,' says Dad calmly. 'He went everywhere by ship.'

'Well, maybe so should you! *Honestly*, Dad!'

'Well, *mi dispiace*,' says Dad, and I bet he is doing a typ-ically Italian shrug. 'I'm sorry. But Kemp needs our help and I have no idea where he is.'

We listen, in the dark, but there is silence, just the drip drip of water – like the ticking of a clock – and a scuttling sound. A rat? No, the rats are above us – those boys in the vests; the gits who plunged me into complete dark-ness. We listen again. And again. Eventually there is a low moan, from somewhere ahead of us.

'The other side,' Dad says. 'I came to the wrong side.'

'Kemp?' I call out. 'Is that you? Are you all right?' There is no reply apart from another low moan. I start to feel my way to the low wall. I climb over it and land in the pool of water. I wade carefully in the cold and the pitch dark until I can feel the threshold of the eyelet the other side. There's another moan, very close to me now.

'Kemp, are you OK?'

I climb over the low wall. I drop to a crawl, reach out with my left arm. My hand lands on what I think is Kemp's thigh. I pat up his body until I get to his chest. It is softly rising and falling. I feel for the side of Kemp's head – his temple – and my hand comes away wet. I hope it's water, but the thought it might not be fills me with horror. My hand moves to his cheek – it is warm – and down to his neck, where I can feel his pulse, steady but weak – is it weak? I don't know. Perhaps I should have checked that first, but I have no idea what I'm doing. I try his wrist, under those leather bracelets. The pulse feels the same. I lean forward and put my face near his cheek and he smells just like he always did, when I was lucky enough to accidentally get that close – like a little piece of heaven.

I try not to think that I love him, I love him. I have always loved him.

'Kemp,' I say, 'you're going to be all right.'

He moans a little but I shush him, stroke his forehead with my hand.

'I'm sorry, Bertie,' he whispers.

'Don't be sorry,' I say. 'And don't try to talk now. You can talk when you get out.'

'Thanks for coming,' he says, his voice hoarse, and I want to laugh but I also want to cry, to lay my head on his warm chest and cry and cry because I could be too late, this could all be too late. For him. The boy in the dark-room. The boy with the smile who danced on his own. The boy who always had a plan. Instead I say, 'You idiot.' But I am the idiot – a giant, selfish, stupid one; an idiot who couldn't listen, out on the street, in bright sunlight. I place my palm on his cheek for a second. Then I move my mouth to his ear and I say, 'You better be all right, Kemp. You better be bloody well all right.'

Don't you dare cry, I tell myself, as I rise away from him and feel my way back to the low brick wall and climb over it. *Don't you dare bloody cry!*

I'm in the pool of water again. I step forward, but I stumble on something: an uneven brick underneath my feet? A slippery patch? I don't know. But I go flying, face forwards, and land on my hands and knees in the water.

'Oof!' I scramble up.

'Are you all right?' calls Dad.

'Yes, I fell. I'm OK. But Kemp's hurt. I need to go and get help.'

There's no way I can get a blind father and a barely conscious man out of an underground reservoir in the pitch dark on my own. The thought is laughable. Terrifying. We need paramedics. Stretchers. We need serious help here. But I feel frozen; I am paralysed and panicked with fear. I've also lost my bearings. I have no idea how to rescue any of this. 'OK, I don't even know which direction to go in now, Dad. I know you're somewhere to the left of me, but I'm scared I'm going to set off in the wrong direction – the wrong angle. I can't go stumbling about. I don't want to walk slap bang into a pillar or something!'

'The wall,' calls Dad. 'The end wall is behind you. Find it.'

I turn and flail around with my arms. 'I can't feel anything! I can't find it!'

'Stay calm. My voice is to your left so the wall must be behind you. So, turn around and take six steps in every direction, like you're travelling to numbers ten o'clock to two o'clock on a clock face, there and back, there and back, and you'll find it.'

I gingerly turn and take six steps to an imaginary ten o'clock, holding my hands out in front of me; an unspooky ghost. There is nothing. I retrace my steps and try again to eleven o'clock. Twelve. I don't think I'm anywhere *near* that wall. At one o'clock I feel something.

'Found it,' I cry. I smooth my hands back and forth on the brickwork. 'At least I think so. I don't think it's a pillar. It's wider than that.'

'Can you feel raised letters?' says Dad. 'The letters are raised as the paint is thick.'

I smooth my hand over the brickwork again. I can feel a two-inch wide column that's slightly raised; it curves round into what could be an 'O'. 'Yes, I think so.'

'Then you know exactly where you are,' says Dad. 'The letters say "ELWW Hornsey Wood Reservoir, 1868 and 69". Put your back against the wall.'

I do so. It feels cool and slick through my soaked T-shirt.

'There are twenty-four arches, Prue. I counted them all

on the way in and you're going to count them all on your way back out, so you'll know exactly where you are, and you won't panic. You also won't fall headfirst on to the steps when you get to them. There are twenty-four thresholds, approximately fifteen steps between each one – remember, keep to the middle as the threshold there is lower. After you've got to arch number twenty-four, you'll be at the steps. There are eight stairs then a platform, about four foot deep, then there are sixteen more steps. Sixteen. At the top, the ladder will be in front of you. Nine rungs.'

'How do you *remember* all of this stuff, Dad?' I ask, steeling myself to take a deep breath and walk.

'I just do,' he says.

'What if I fall again?'

'You won't fall. I've got you. Mind how you go.'

I step forward, trusting the direction because of the wall behind me and trusting Dad. Haven't I trusted him all my life? Hasn't he always *had* me, even through our bleakest times? And this is how he walks through life, every day. In the dark.

I carefully walk fifteen steps, sloshing through the knee-deep water, feeling the smooth brickwork under my feet, then I slow right down and edge gingerly forward until my toes hit the wall of the first threshold. I hesitantly step on to it – one foot, then the next, a wobbly weathervane, arms held out for balance – then step down the other side. I almost stumble but I'm OK. There's such a long way to go. I repeat the same steps; through the dark pool of the second arch; over the bricked second threshold.

'All right, Roo?' calls Dad.

'Yes, Pops!' *Pops.* Another nickname from the past. I haven't called Dad that since I was a little girl. 'I'm sorry!' I shout.

'What are you sorry for?'

'For being angry with you about Mum and Sweden. I'm not angry any more.'

'Did you see her?'

'Yes! It was strange – very strange – but it was OK. I'll tell you about it later.'

'*I'm* sorry, love! I'm sorry for keeping such a secret.'

'It's OK, Dad! I understand. And the things that *I* told you . . . I'm sorry—'

'No! Don't you ever be sorry about anything!' yells Dad. 'Don't you *ever* be sorry! We can move forward now, both of us, but most of all I want *you* to move forward.' I am at the third arch now. I'm in the middle of the pool and cold water is up to my knees and I'm trying not to think about how far I have to go, in the dark.

'I've wasted so much time, Dad!' I yell back to him.

'But we're not going to waste any more of it, are we?' calls Dad.

'No, Pops, we're not!' I keep walking: the next two archways, the next two thresholds. I walk in the dark and in the cold water, blackness all around me. I mustn't panic. Dad has been all over London now. He has been afraid, at times; he has *faltered* – but he's done it anyway. I mustn't panic, for Kemp. I can do this, for Kemp.

'You can do this!' Dad's shout is fainter now, but I let his words echo in my brain as I walk until I begin to believe them. I can do this, I can do this, I can do this. The drip drip of water ahead of me is again a ticking clock; the beating of my heart gives me a rhythm to walk to. Step. Step. Step. Step. I'm at arch number six, the water not so cold, the way ahead still daunting. 'This is quite the role reversal,' Dad calls. 'Me guiding you!'

'You have always guided me, Dad! I should have listened to you more!'

'Well, I wasn't going to say anything . . .'

377

I laugh a small laugh, walking in the cool dark of the womb of this beautiful underground vault, and listen as my laugh, a little alien-sounding down here – a little fragile – rebounds off its bricks and its shallows. Dad was right about Salvi. He was indeed nothing but a distraction. He was a man who had me looking in all the wrong places. The feelings he gave me weren't real. Nothing about him was real. The way he looked at me in the fairground – however cruel that was – was actually nothing to do with me. It showed me exactly who *he* was all along – that the truly ugly have blights and abrasions and stains that run so much deeper, and are so much more hideous, than any surface imperfections. All I had to do was open my eyes. Oh, Kemp, I think. Oh, Kemp . . .

'I've got this!' I yell, a little unconvincingly. 'I can do this, Dad!'

'You're strong!' calls out Dad, more echo but less decibels to his voice, now. I'm at arch seven. 'You're so much stronger than you realize.'

Am I? Can 'strong' be a word for me? I've always thought it the preserve of the women I read about, not for me, but I think about the past few weeks. Where I've been. What I've seen of the world and what I've learnt from it. I've loved walking round London with my father, this summer, I realize. I was reluctant, I fought against it, but in the end I really loved it. I've grown to know Dad again. We've talked – actually, properly talked. We've shared our secrets – finally. Has it made me *strong*? Has it made me strong enough to do this?

'I love you!' shouts Dad. 'I love you, Prue!'

'I love you too, Dad,' I call, and in the cold and the dark, through arches seven, eight, nine, my dread heart is pierced by a sliver of light. There's no cost, I think. There's no cost to the secrets Dad and I hid but have now revealed. A conduit of relief rises from me like ether as I reach arch ten and surges from me, to the domed ceiling I know is above, and fills a gap in my heart, making me feel freer than I have in a long time. Dad loves me. I could see it on his face, on the street outside The Palladian. I saw it in his expression, on Albert Bridge. I've seen it in all the places we've been in London this summer and I've known it every day of my life – it's just that, for a long time, I stopped noticing what he stopped being able to make visible. My Dad loves me, as much as he always has. I am still that little girl in the photos, the one at the rock pool and outside Nonna and Papa's *gelato* parlour. I am still that girl on my father's knee, one of Neptune's little fishes – held and hugged tight, the girl who had her face wiped with the enormous hanky. He still loves me, and it took one summer in London to show me.

Arch thirteen.

'Are you OK?' A very faint shout.

'Yes, Dad!'

'Are you scared?'

'No, I'm not scared!'

'Good! Just keep going!'

Arch fifteen. I *am* scared; of course I am. Scared for Kemp, scared I'll never make it out of here. I've always been scared, as a default. As a child, as a teenager, as an adult. I haven't had Angela's front. Angela's breezy confidence in herself and the world around her. Angela wouldn't be scared. She'd probably be marching through here in a pair of her high heels, dictating a luxury shopping list to herself. She said she misses me. I know I miss her. Can we get back what we had, as kids? When we were Roo and Angela (Pangela), the sisters who laughed and loved together? Maybe. Maybe we can. There are things I need to say to her. Things I need to tell her. Including telling her Mum is here in London and that she is clean and came looking for us all those years ago. That she is going to call her, so Angela can make her decision: if she wants to love Mum after all this time and allow Mum the chance to love her.

Arch seventeen. The water feels particularly deep and cold here. I shiver and want to fold my arms around myself but I need to keep them out at my sides, so I don't fall. I have my own choice to make: whether I let Mum back into my life or not. I see her face, how it was in the café, when she looked at me. How so much was written there, while so much remained unsaid. I need to really think about that look. I need to wonder how she felt when she came to look for Angela and me, and Cherry Lau told her we weren't there. When she was *finally* ready for us, but it was too late. Do I want it to be too late for my mother and me? That's what I need to decide.

I'm at arch twenty.

'Can you still hear me?' comes a distant call, faint and ghostly, from the end of the tunnel I am far from now.

'Not really,' I shout, at the top of my voice, as I trudge through unseen water.

'We'll say goodbye for now.' At least I think that's what the distant voice says. The words sound dreamlike, melancholy. *Goodbye*. It's never goodbye with us, Dad, is it? It's, *Mind how you go*.

'Just for now, Pops!' I whisper. *I won't be long, Dad. I promise I won't be long.*

It is silent now, bar the occasional drip of moisture from brick to shallows and the steady beating of my own heart. The slurp of my lower legs in soaked denim through dark water. I'm on my own. What if I can't get the hatch open? What if no one hears my cries? What if I get help but it's too late?

Kemp. I haven't dared think about what he said to me earlier, but now, here in the dark, in this cathedral-like chamber, I hear him again. His words . . . 'You're

home to me . . . I look at her and I think, *Yeah, her.*' I can
see the look in his eyes when he said those words to me,
on the streets of London, in bright sunlight. How he
smiled. How I could see the whole universe in those
eyes, if I chose to.

All that time. All that time I loved him, when he was
sitting in the pub opposite me, or up on the stage doing a
bad Def Leppard tribute, or roaming the earth, a piece
of my heart tucked in the pocket of his fisherman's hat
that he didn't even know was there . . . and now I know
he loves me too. Loved me. And I believe him. I want to
love and be loved, and I believe what he has told me. I'd
always thought he was too perfect for me, too handsome,
too brilliant, too lovely. That I was too ugly, too dull and
too noxious for him. But it seems he loves me anyway.
Maybe ugly, dull and noxious are things he really likes.
Or maybe I am not those things at all.

Maybe I have never been.

I'm at arch twenty-one. What if I never see him again?
What if I can't get help in time? I *can't* be too late; it can't
be too late for Kemp and me, can it, not now I realize I
am loveable after all? *Loveable . . . !* I would laugh, if I
wasn't in this awful pitch-black gulley of a reservoir. I am
loveable! Prue Alberta is loveable! I am loveable despite
my birthmark, and every bad experience I've had in my
life. Kemp loves me *anyway*. Is it because these things are
part of me? Is it because they *are* me? None of them have
ever been my fault, I acknowledge that now. Nothing has
been my fault. Kemp loves me, and Dad does, and Angela
and Mum may too, after all, if I decide to let them. I am
worth something. I am good enough. We are *all* good
enough. And I am goddam loveable. What a fantastic
word. I may get it printed on a T-shirt and wear it around
London.

Arch twenty-two. Thank goodness I know the number

of them. Thank goodness for Dad and his architectural brain. I keep one foot trudging in front of the other. Wading through the water, crossing each threshold. And I just keep counting. Counting all the good things in my life and all the things I have to do. I have to get to the hatch, open it up and open up my future. I have to create memories instead of shutting myself away. I have to not simply survive but *live*. Live for me; live for Philippa and all the people who could not find a way forward. Dad and I will *both* live. We'll do exciting, brilliant things together and we won't sit in those chairs any more – I might just burn the damn things!

I'll get out of here. I'll get to the light. The darker places I've been in – places of despair, disgust, loneliness, self-loathing – will fade away and I won't shy away from the things I fear, things that terrify my heart. I promise myself I will step towards those things; that I will not only head for the light but head there *fearlessly*. Isn't it about time I did?

Arch twenty-three. Arch twenty-three! As I feel for the threshold, I realize I am crying. Not shameful tears of regret or hot tears of anger and fear, but tears of *hope*, and I realize I've had it all along – hope in my heart that I had kept chained and away from myself all this time. My hope is me. I can love and be loved. I can be brave. I can be strong. I can maybe even be *passionate*; to paint and to show my paintings to people who might like to see them. Isn't it about time I had a plan, too? Isn't it *all* about time?

Arch twenty-four. One more pool of water, one more threshold. I begin to walk very slowly. I go into a stoop so I'm ready to feel the bottom tread of the steps that will take me back up to my life. And as I move forward, my tears of hope still softly falling, I understand that not only have I been my father's eyes, but he has been mine. He has shown me how to live, now: the path to follow, the road to travel down. It would be wonderful to saunter along that road, one day soon, giving a little whistle as I go. And even more wonderful if Kemp could be beside me.

There it is. The bottom step. It is flat and cold under my hand. I grin with relief.

'You're here, girl!' I say out loud, to the echo of my own heart. 'You're here.'

I put one foot on the step, then the other: one, two, one, two. Then the next, left foot, right foot, and I count. Eight steps. OK, now the four-foot distance of the platform then sixteen more steps. Left foot, right foot; left foot, right foot. I'm not crying any more. I am on the sixteenth step. I walk a few careful paces forward and reach up in front of me and feel for the ladder and it is there, it is there! I grab one of the rusty rungs and I climb six of those thick staples that cling to amber brickwork, then I feel for the metal of the hatch. I prop my foot on the rung above to give me leverage and I push against the hatch with all my might. Shit, it's heavy. It's really bloody heavy. I try again and again. Eventually it lifts a little, causing a slim chink of light to appear, but it clanks straight back down into the hole again.

'Come on, you bugger!' I hiss at it and I have another go. It lifts again and this time falls back at a slight angle, not covering the whole hatchway. I get my leverage.

'Come *on*!' Finally, heaving it with all my might, I'm able to lift the hatch up and away from me enough that I can get a handle on the front edge of it and then I push and push until I can heft it very slowly, slowly away from me and on to the grass beyond the hatch.

I collapse on to my forearms on the top rung of the ladder, breathing in the air and the light and the freedom above me. I've done it. I've made it. I climb the final three rungs and scramble out of the hatch and into the fading summer sunlight, the day's last hurrah, where the sun is disappearing behind the top of the Ferris wheel and I can hear people laughing and living their best, absolute lives, and I'm sprinting on the grass towards the fair, feeling the rush of air and sunlight and sky in my lungs and my veins and I'm running towards hope and praying I'm not too late, that I'm not too late for everything.

Three Months Later

The sun is lowering behind a bank of clouds that streak
and drift. It shyly peeks from behind cotton-wool white
then disappears again. The horizon is periwinkle blue,
tinged with pink. It's a beautiful evening.

I've just finished another sketch of Dad, a small one. He
is sleeping, his chin resting on his hand like *The Thinker* –
he's been asleep for the last couple of hours, on and off. I
hope he won't mind me capturing him off guard again. He
shouldn't do, really, since he recently gave his blessing to
have six portraits of him hung in Perspectives, the gallery
just around the corner from Old Street tube station.
Kemp's mate Col is holding an exhibition of local artists –
all portraits – and mine were squeezed in, on the last
available square of blank wall. A gallery! We went to the
little party there, on the first night. Dad kept nudging me
and calling me 'The artist, Prue Alberta'. He said he was so
proud that I have a talent that's emerged after all these
thousands of years. That he knew the job at the Custard
Cream packing place would lead to bigger things. I poked
him in the ribs and then we had a hug and he told me that
he loved me, again, and I told him I love him. We're saying
it a lot these days – it's like now we've said it once, we can't
stop.

Jack Templeton, Dad's old mate, came to the party.
Dad tracked him down – he still lives in the area, still
dresses a bit like a dandy – and they're getting on like a
house on fire, after all these years. Jack's also offered to
'sit' for me. I need a few more real faces for my portraits.

More people in my life. Ryan might sit for me, too, if I ask him nicely. He's been coming over a lot recently, to see Dad and talk architecture. To let Dad play all his old records to him. Sometimes they go out together, into London. Quite often Dad will go out on his own, now his ankle is better. He says he's got his confidence back. He likes to go for walks – a 'mosey about', as he puts it. Sometimes he goes on errands. A couple of weeks ago he posted something for me.

'I'll do that,' he said, when I was about to nip out. 'What is it?'

'Just something I'm returning to sender,' I said. 'Well, not quite that. But thanks, Dad.'

It was an envelope with a purple card in it addressed to Jennifer Dixon at Egon and Fuller. With it I had written a note that said, *Please investigate your colleague Salvi Russo in relation to this website.* I have never looked online at The Profilo Club. I don't want to see my face there. Or Philippa's. But I reckon as a member of the law, Jennifer can take it. If she *was* the colleague I saw him with outside the Old Bailey, I'm hoping she'll be grateful for the alert. If she wasn't, she can investigate objectively. And I might even be wrong. The Profilo Club may not be what I think it is at all, but I'm pretty sure I'm right. And I'm pretty sure Salvi is behind it. He has just the kind of casual arrogance to assume he will be untouchable.

Dad posted the envelope for me. He didn't know it, but he was part of what I hope is some small justice for me and for Philippa, and for the other women out there. Nobody can change the things that have happened to me. My father cannot always protect me. But we are there for each other. We can do the small things, and the bigger things, that make all the difference. We can move forward.

Maria, the chef from the café, also came to the party.

Dad invited her. We walked back to Kenwood House a few days before and he asked her if she'd like to come and she said 'yes'. I think she had a nice time. She and Dad seemed to get on well. I asked him afterwards if he thought she might become his girlfriend and he said you never knew what was around the corner, even for a blind old git. Maya came, too. I invited her. I was brave. I actually think there's a small chance the two of us might become friends. Wouldn't that be something? My father might be right about those corners . . .

This little sketch I'm doing of him now is quite good, I feel. I have caught Dad's likeness in just a few strokes of an HB pencil. His nose, his mouth, his forehead. He still has a slight contusion under his chin. The paramedics said he bashed it when he tripped and hurt his ankle.

Three paramedics came into the reservoir with me, once I'd persuaded them from their tea and Garibaldis in the St John Ambulance tent at the fair, and convinced them I wasn't some mad person who had jumped in a water butt, and there really *were* two injured men down in the disued Hornsey Wood Reservoir, under the park. The paramedics were two big burly women and a jolly bloke with a very kind face. We all did a half run/half walk back to the hatch; the ambulance parked next to the tent that kids had been climbing in all afternoon arriving minutes afterwards.

Dad had a sprained ankle and a slightly battered face. Kemp's injuries were a lot more serious. He had fallen while trying to rig up a caving light from the top of one of the arches and had cracked his head open on some brickwork. It was a good job I never saw all the blood. Like Humpty he needed to have his head put back together again. He was in hospital for three weeks, the first week of which he was mostly unconscious (I spent a lot of time just sitting and watching his face and its contours as he slept), but he's made a full recovery, apart from a scar by his temple, and is back retelling bad jokes and laughing that laugh of his.

We have all been called 'stupid idiots' by the paramedic team, and the hospital staff and Haringey Council, who've given us a proper ticking-off, and Kemp is all disgruntled because he doubts he'll be able to get down there again, now, and he only got a few decent photos. Still, one of those photos won the Architectural Photo of the Year – it was in the *Evening Standard*, along with his real name, Jason Hamilton – and he's alive, which is the main thing, plus he was quite impressed by my heroic escape from the reservoir. How I walked the twenty-four arches. Very impressed, as a matter of fact.

'Can I ask you to put your blind up now, please?'

I smile at the air hostess and slip my pencil back into the little pencil case I have in my travel bag. The duty-free trolley has made its final trundle up the aisle and is disappearing behind the blue curtain. Disembarkation cards are being retrieved by yawning passengers from under dog-eared magazines in the seat pockets in front of them. Airline staff are smiling wearily at each other, smoothing hair back from faces above tired eyes and getting ready to get strapped into their side-saddle seats. Others do final checks of trays, blinds and seat belts.

We're landing in twenty minutes.

I step out of the plane into bright sunshine and the smell of bougainvillea and aviation fuel. The air is hot and sweet, and I breathe it in like nectar. I help Dad down the creaking metal steps, both of us gripping the handrail: him for support, me to steady my nerves. We are here. We have made it. It's been a long flight. Behind us, clunking her case noisily down the metal steps (I wonder if Dad is counting them) is someone who has been annoying me greatly on the flight. This person has been sucking loudly on sweets, tutting intermittently at any number of random things, laughing like a runaway flute, twittering on about everything and nothing and basically being an absolute pain in the rear.

'Bloody hell, it's hot!' says Angela as she stops halfway down the steps and surveys the view. 'I need to take my jumper off.'

'Well, of course it's hot,' I say. 'That jumper's hideous, anyway. Where did you get it from? Some crabby old fisherman who discarded it down a Nova Scotian ice hole?'

'Very funny.'

I grin at her and she grins back.

Dad and I have been to Nova Scotia for a week. We played with Angela's two beautiful daughters, who are not spoilt at all, despite all the Facebook boasting on their behalf, and are absolute sweethearts who like jigsaw puzzles and tickles and getting messy down at the lake. I silently apologized to them for being such a crap auntie and we spent hours making paper chains and mashing up petals for rose perfume. We visited the lighthouse at Louisbourg and went down to the port with Warren and were introduced to his new boat, *Beatty*. We had pancakes and crab cakes and various types of pie down at Missy's Diner. We sat in the swing chair on the veranda and talked to Angela about everything we ever should have talked about.

We have a three-stop trip, Dad and I – Canada, Hawaii and San Francisco; Angela's not doing the last leg. She's going to fly home after our Hawaii stop, but Dad and I are going on. I'm going to see Janis Joplin's house. Dad is going to walk down Lombard Street and eat at Bobo's steakhouse. Angela has her own plans when she gets back to Warren and the girls. Mum called her while Dad and I were there. They spoke for a long time. Dad and I sat on the veranda not listening to them talk as we played Warren's copy of The Who's *My Generation* on his ancient stereo, but I talked briefly to Mum at the end of their conversation because Angela forced me. It went OK. I might pop into the travel agent's when we eventually get home; I haven't quite decided yet. I did something else while we were in Canada. I messaged Cherry Lau. Nothing dramatic, and we're not going to be become best buddies again, or anything like that, or probably ever message each other again, but I told her I was really sorry for what I did back then – really truly sorry – and after three days she replied to me and said, 'Thank you', and I knew more than anyone that it wasn't enough, really, my apology after all this time – nowhere near – but it was something.

'Welcome to Hawaii.'

We're on the tarmac now and the voice comes from somewhere under a huge swathe of pink and white leis. The person holding them is tiny and beautiful. She places a pink lei around Dad's neck, on top of his The Jam T-shirt, and a white one around my neck. Angela gets a white one too.

'Thank you,' I say.

'Thank you,' say Dad and Angela.

'I got you a hat.' There's a kiss on my left cheek, a tender arm snaked round my waist; leather wristbands tickling my hip bone under my white cotton shirt. Kemp, who has been trailing Angela and lugging her huge carrier bag of duty-free toiletries and magazines, is holding what looks suspiciously like another bloody fisherman's hat and he plonks it on my head. 'Let me take a photo,' he says, laughing, and reaching in his cross-body camera bag for his prized Minolta. Kemp's come with us on our trip – well, he's flying on to Argentina, after Hawaii; he has another assignment. I asked him if he wanted to come, when Dad and I first decided on the trip, and he said 'yes'. I've even let him take the occasional photo of me.

390

YOU, ME AND THE MOVIES
Fiona Collins

When Arden meets Mac she quickly falls for the handsome, charismatic film lecturer. Their love is the sort you see in movies: dramatic, exciting and all-consuming . . . and complicated.

A love like theirs could never last.

But years later, whilst visiting a friend in hospital, Arden sees the one face she could never forget. Badly injured, Mac can only make brief references to the classic films they once watched together. Which is all it takes for Arden to remember everything.

Will Arden ever find a movie-worthy love again?

Unique and true-to-life, *You, Me and the Movies* is a love story like no other. Perfect for fans of David Nicholls, Jojo Moyes and Richard Curtis films.

'Moving and emotional'
Eva Woods, bestselling author of *How to be Happy*

'Cheese,' I say, grinning like a loon. 'I bet I look ridiculous.'

'I think you look beautiful,' he says and I believe him. I believe him when he says he loves me – he has said it to me so many times now – and last Thursday, at about four o'clock, down at a little jetty in Albert Bridge, Nova Scotia, when the sun was shining and Kemp had just caught a fish and put it back, and the water was lapping at the edge of the jetty and everything was just beautiful and it felt right, I told him I loved him, too, and that I had loved him for a very long time.

Kemp receives his own lei now, over his own fisherman's hat – we really do look a right pair of saps – and he takes my right hand, and Dad places his hand on Angela's left arm, just above the elbow, and the four of us walk into the terminal building. Passport Control and Baggage Reclaim are smooth sailing, and soon we are heading through a pair of sliding doors and into the arrivals hall, where I immediately scan the sea of waiting faces at the barrier.

There's a man standing just behind it who has white hair and a big bushy moustache and beard. He's wearing a pale grey linen suit with white trainers and a panama hat and has something propped under his arm. Unlike lots of other people, he is not holding up a sign. But he is waiting for us.

'Dad,' I say, as we walk. 'There's somebody here to greet us. At the barrier.'

Dad nods. 'How many steps until we get there?'

'Eleven, maybe twelve.'

Kemp lets go of my hand and drops behind me, as does Angela. Dad and I walk forward. Nine steps, ten steps, eleven. We have turned a corner, Dad and I. We have music and laughter again, in The Palladian. We have hope. And we walk forward together.

'We're at the barrier,' I tell him. As we stop, I reach across myself and quickly squeeze Dad's hand, which is at the back of my arm, just above the elbow, then I reach to lightly touch the sleeve of the waiting man's linen suit.

'I'm Prue Alberta,' I say. 'It's really nice to meet you.'

'You made it, then?' He smiles.

'Yes, we made it. Would you like to meet my father?' I say.

'Very much so.'

'Dad?'

Dad leans forward and holds his hand out into the air. He is smiling, too. 'Hello,' he says.

'Hello,' says the man holding out his hand, finding Dad's and giving it a hearty shake. 'I'm John Harrison Burrows.'

'And I'm Vince Alberta,' Dad grins, 'very pleased to meet you.'

'Architect and architect,' I say, and my heart expands with this brand-new happiness I cherish; a happiness – hidden from me for so long – I found with my father on the streets of London. I look behind me at Kemp, and he looks back at me, my future in his eyes.

'Ready?' he asks, after a while.

'Ready.'

He takes my hand in his again and, with Dad and Angela and John in step, we walk out of the terminal and back into the light.

Acknowledgements

Enormous thanks go to my amazing editors at Transworld. Thank you, Molly Crawford, for helping me to hone Prue and Vince's story. It's all the better for your insight, wisdom and general genius. Thank you, too, to Francesca Best for your huge support and care.

Thanks to the whole editorial, design and publicity team at Transworld for your hard work and dedication in getting this book out into the world.

Thank you to my agent, Diana Beaumont. I'm so hugely grateful to have you in my corner.

And, as always, to Mary Torjussen, my virtual office WhatsApp colleague, cheerleader and sounding board – I couldn't do *any* of it without you. What a journey to be on together!

'Cheese,' I say, grinning like a loon. 'I bet I look ridiculous.'

'I think you look beautiful,' he says and I believe him. I believe him when he says he loves me – he has said it to me so many times now – and last Thursday, at about four o'clock, down at a little jetty in Albert Bridge, Nova Scotia, when the sun was shining and Kemp had just caught a fish and put it back, and the water was lapping at the edge of the jetty and everything was just beautiful and it felt right, I told him I loved him, too, and that I had loved him for a very long time.

Kemp receives his own lei now, over his own fisherman's hat – we really do look a right pair of saps – and he takes my right hand, and Dad places his hand on Angela's left arm, just above the elbow, and the four of us walk into the terminal building. Passport Control and Baggage Reclaim are smooth sailing, and soon we are heading through a pair of sliding doors and into the arrivals hall, where I immediately scan the sea of waiting faces at the barrier.

There's a man standing just behind it who has white hair and a big bushy moustache and beard. He's wearing a pale grey linen suit with white trainers and a panama hat and has something propped under his arm. Unlike lots of other people, he is not holding up a sign. But he is waiting for us.

'Dad,' I say, as we walk. 'There's somebody here to greet us. At the barrier.'

Dad nods. 'How many steps until we get there?'

'Eleven, maybe twelve.'

Kemp lets go of my hand and drops behind me, as does Angela. Dad and I walk forward. Nine steps, ten steps, eleven. We have turned a corner, Dad and I. We have music and laughter again, in The Palladian. We have hope. And we walk forward together.

'We're at the barrier,' I tell him. As we stop, I reach across myself and quickly squeeze Dad's hand, which is at the back of my arm, just above the elbow, then I reach to lightly touch the sleeve of the waiting man's linen suit.

'I'm Prue Alberta,' I say. 'It's really nice to meet you.'

'You made it, then?' He smiles.

'Yes, we made it. Would you like to meet my father?' I say.

'Very much so.'

'Dad?'

Dad leans forward and holds his hand out into the air. He is smiling, too. 'Hello,' he says.

'Hello,' says the man holding out his hand, finding Dad's and giving it a hearty shake. 'I'm John Harrison Burrows.'

'And I'm Vince Alberta,' Dad grins, 'very pleased to meet you.'

'Architect and architect,' I say, and my heart expands with this brand-new happiness I cherish; a happiness – hidden from me for so long – I found with my father on the streets of London. I look behind me at Kemp, and he looks back at me, my future in his eyes.

'Ready?' he asks, after a while.

'Ready.'

He takes my hand in his again and, with Dad and Angela and John in step, we walk out of the terminal and back into the light.

Acknowledgements

Enormous thanks go to my amazing editors at Transworld. Thank you, Molly Crawford, for helping me to hone Prue and Vince's story. It's all the better for your insight, wisdom and general genius. Thank you, too, to Francesca Best for your huge support and care.

Thanks to the whole editorial, design and publicity team at Transworld for your hard work and dedication in getting this book out into the world.

Thank you to my agent, Diana Beaumont. I'm so hugely grateful to have you in my corner.

And, as always, to Mary Torjussen, my virtual office WhatsApp colleague, cheerleader and sounding board – I couldn't do *any* of it without you. What a journey to be on together!

YOU, ME AND THE MOVIES
Fiona Collins

When Arden meets Mac she quickly falls for the handsome, charismatic film lecturer. Their love is the sort you see in movies: dramatic, exciting and all-consuming . . . and complicated.

A love like theirs could never last.

But years later, whilst visiting a friend in hospital, Arden sees the one face she could never forget. Badly injured, Mac can only make brief references to the classic films they once watched together. Which is all it takes for Arden to remember everything.

Will Arden ever find a movie-worthy love again?

Unique and true-to-life, *You, Me and the Movies* is a love story like no other. Perfect for fans of David Nicholls, Jojo Moyes and Richard Curtis films.

'Moving and emotional'
Eva Woods, bestselling author of *How to be Happy*